"There's a co[ ]Striker," the head Fed whispered

Bolan turned to face him. "Where are Able Team and Phoenix Force? You better get them in on this, pronto."

"I'll get them on this as soon as they're available, but there's no way of knowing where or when the next attack—"

Before he could finish, the window behind them shattered.

Bolan pivoted toward the noise as fragments of glass rained down over his shoulders. A heavy, oblong object came sailing through the window and clattered to the floor.

Automatic gunfire began in the front yard as the Executioner watched the concussion grenade wobble to a halt at his feet.

DON PENDLETON's

MACK BOLAN.

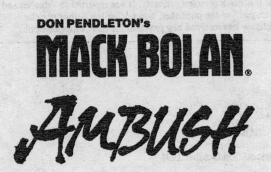

AMBUSH

A GOLD EAGLE BOOK FROM

WORLDWIDE.

TORONTO • NEW YORK • LONDON
AMSTERDAM • PARIS • SYDNEY • HAMBURG
STOCKHOLM • ATHENS • TOKYO • MILAN
MADRID • WARSAW • BUDAPEST • AUCKLAND

First edition October 1994

ISBN 0-373-61438-1

Special thanks and acknowledgment to
Jerry VanCook for his contribution to this work.

AMBUSH

Printed in U.S.A.

The Spartans do not ask how many the
enemy number, but where they are.
—Agis II, King of Sparta,
circa 415 B.C.

Truth, and even victory, doesn't depend on
numbers. And no matter where the enemies
of truth hide, in the end, all will come to
judgment and light.
—Mack Bolan

PROLOGUE

The thud of the landing gear sent a chill racing along Phil Herrod's spine. The sound was just a little too much like the bolt of an automatic rifle sliding home.

He reached under the seat in front of him for the canvas carry-on bag he'd brought on board the big 747. His eyes fell to the attaché case in his other hand as the plane's wheels hit the runway. The soft brown leather case had not left his grip since it had been issued to him at the DEA office in Miami. And it wouldn't until this deal was over.

No, sir. Phil Herrod didn't plan to take any chances with three million dollars.

The plane taxied to a halt. Hoisting both bags, Herrod stood up, waiting for a pair of elderly American tourists to pass before following them down the aisle to the door. A light film of perspiration broke out on his forehead as he left the air-conditioned cabin and his feet hit the ramp.

Some of the sweat, he knew, was the natural by-product of the Central American climate. But the rest had nothing to do with the heat. That sweat was the sweat of fear—his body's response to the butterflies batting their wings against his abdomen and the feathers that had been nervously tickling his scrotum ever since takeoff from New York.

Herrod reached the waiting area and spotted Griffy and Mandula. The two men, casually dressed in bright print shirts, white cotton slacks and huaraches, stood at the far side of the arrival lounge. Herrod's eyes fell briefly to the bulges at both of their ankles. The sight brought a frown to his face.

Bringing guns through the metal detector meant the two DEA agents had identified themselves to airport security. And cutting anyone in on your business in the middle of a deal like this was risky.

Especially risky in Panama.

Mandula smiled, and a row of perfectly capped white teeth stood out against the tanned skin of his face. He reached forward, took the canvas carryon and shook Herrod's hand. "You've already been cleared through customs, Phil," he said. "Got any other luggage?"

Herrod shook his head. He glanced down at his watch as they started through the airport. "What time are we set to go down?" he asked under his breath.

"Hour and a half," Griffy answered. He was just this side of portly, his tight shirt rippling over layers of fat-padded muscles as he led the way toward the parking lot. "We meet a guy named Ernesto on the docks just past the Court of Justice Building," he said over his shoulder. "Got time to eat . . . if you're hungry."

Herrod shook his head. The mere thought of food sent the butterflies flapping through his belly again.

The dark brown Mercedes sat waiting on the second level. Griffy took the wheel, Mandula sliding in next to him. The darker man leaned forward and rummaged between his feet, then handed a SIG-Sauer 9 mm automatic over the seat as Herrod got in back.

Herrod stuffed the pistol into his belt. He leaned back into the plush upholstery as the car pulled out of Batilla Airport. Griffy drove fast, circling Panama Bay on Avenue Balboa. The bright overhead street-lights reflected off the water, flashing through the window and making Herrod close his eyes.

Twenty-two years with the Drug Enforcement Administration, the veteran deep-cover man thought. And what have those twenty-two years brought me? Six promotions. Four children. Three wives.

Three divorces. Living with a man who used as many IDs as a guy with Multiple Personality Disorder took its toll on women.

Herrod opened his eyes again and caught a glimpse of his reflection in the rearview mirror between the men in the front seat. His looks probably had more to do with the route his career had taken than his abilities. As a dark-skinned agent with a Jewish and Puerto Rican background, he'd spent most of his time impersonating Mexicans or South Americans, stepping in and out of his undercover identities so often that he sometimes wondered just who he really was.

Today he was Jose Granero. Tomorrow he might be Pancho Villa for all he knew. Suddenly the full weight of his twenty-plus years with DEA swept over him, and the trepidation in his soul rose to new heights.

Just before leaving Washington, he'd been offered a promotion. A desk job. But would he take it? Quit undercover work? Could he? Could he stand being one of the "suits" who made policy and gave orders rather than one of the troops who actually did the work? Right now, with the fear oozing out of him like shit through a goose, the answer was a big definitive yes. But tomorrow the "mission twitch" would be gone. In its place would be the adrenaline pump of victory, the knowledge he had kept a load of dope off the streets of the U.S. The knowledge that he just might have meant the difference between life and death for some kid in Boston or Miami or L.A.

The Mercedes turned off Balboa and entered the Plaza de Francia district. Herrod stared listlessly at the figure of a rooster atop a tall obelisk. A block to his left, the ornate architecture of the presidential palace whizzed by, barely registering in his brain. Then they were passing the Court of Justice Building, and finally pulling to a halt at the edge of a small boat dock.

The man behind the helm of the twenty-one-foot Bayliner Trophy grinned and waved.

Griffy walked forward. "Ernesto?"

"Si." The skipper smiled back through his full beard, tugging on his white cap.

Herrod followed Griffy and Mandula on board the Bayliner, and the three men dropped to seats near the stern as the engine roared to life. They held on to the rails as the boat drifted away from the dock, then cut a swift U-turn toward Taboga Island, ten miles offshore.

Herrod set the briefcase on deck and watched the lights of Panama City fade in the distance. The motor quieted to a soft, steady purr. He closed his eyes again. Concentrate, he told his brain. Prepare yourself for the undercover role itself, and the danger that accompanies it.

Phil Herrod held no illusions that this buy would end the reign of the notorious Bolivian coca growers association known as "the Corporation." They'd have to bust Bernhardt Ennslin himself to do that, and Ennslin wouldn't be there tonight. The aging German wasn't about to get his own hands dirty for a mere three million. But they might bust one of Ennslin's top men. Slow the Corporation down. Maybe cut into the profits Ennslin made by supplying ninety percent of the cocaine base smuggled into the U.S.

Griffy nudged Herrod in the ribs and pointed. Across the dark waves, the DEA man saw the island. A small village lay just on the other side of the docks, climbing up the hill beyond. Houses cut into the knoll, and footpaths led upward from the sea. Under the lights of the village he could see thick gardens of jasmine, hibiscus and oleander—the multicolored buds and blossoms that had spawned the name "Island of Flowers."

Herrod took a deep breath. The island would be beautiful... if it weren't so deadly.

The deep-cover man stood up and walked to the bow, gazing off across the dark waters. Rumor had it that another undercover man was planted within the Corporation. Only the top echelon of DEA knew who it was, and for the hundredth time that night Herrod wondered if he knew the man. Probably. The inherent dangers taken by undercover specialists caused them to stick together. They formed a clique away from the "suits," whose biggest risk was what alcohol might be doing to their livers.

The Bayliner purred on through the soft waves. Then suddenly the engine sputtered and died. Herrod opened his eyes. He felt a frown cross his face when he saw the island still a good mile away. He turned to the helm.

The skipper shrugged, shook his head, then reached for the radio microphone mounted on the dash. He spoke briefly, his voice inaudible over the wind, then dropped the mike and turned. "I am sorry, *señors*," he shouted. "Engine trouble. I have radioed for another boat to repair the problem."

Griffy turned in his seat. "I don't like this," he whispered.

Herrod nodded. "No, but there's not a hell of a lot we can do about it. It's probably like he said. Just engine trouble."

Five minutes later a twenty-foot Sea Ray came floating up to the Bayliner. A man wearing an oil-stained work shirt and Miami Dolphins baseball cap tossed a line over the side, then vaulted after it, carrying a toolbox.

Herrod breathed a silent sigh of relief.

A moment later the skipper called out again. "Señor Granero, if you please. You are wanted." He extended the radio mike.

Herrod rose stiffly and walked toward the bow.

"Señor Ennslin wishes to apologize for the inconvenience," the skipper said, handing him the mike. "In the meantime we must bring aboard more tools."

Herrod's heart suddenly leaped into his throat. Ennslin had come. He was here. And that meant a chance to take down the whole Corporation. His hand shook as he gripped the mike. "Come in," he said. Behind him he heard movement and turned to see the skipper follow the repairman over the side to the Sea Ray.

The voice that came over the airwaves was heavily accented with German. "Señor Granero?"

"Speaking," Herrod said, the thrill of the chase suddenly replacing all fear.

"Or perhaps I should say Señor Herrod."

Herrod froze, wondering if stress had caused his ears to deceive him. He opened his mouth to speak, then closed it.

"Come now, Señor Herrod," the voice said again. "You should not be so surprised. Surely you must realize my operation is as diligent in gathering Intelligence as your own."

Herrod heard an engine start and whirled around to see the Sea Ray skirt away from the Bayliner and head for the docks. Griffy and Mandula hurried across the deck to his side. "What the hell's going on?" Mandula asked, his voice quavering.

Herrod keyed the mike. They had one chance, and one chance only. "Okay, Ennslin," he said, fighting the unsteadiness of his own voice. "Let's make a deal. The money for our lives. Otherwise, I'll toss it into the water right now."

Laughter echoed over the airwaves. "What money?" Ennslin said.

Herrod glanced back over his shoulder. The briefcase he had left by his seat was gone.

Thumbing the mike again, the DEA man said, "Okay, Ennslin. So what do you have planned for us?"

"Look to the deck," the German said.

Herrod complied. He saw the toolbox the repair-man had carried on board still sitting next to the wheel.

"You want to throw something in the water, Herr Herrod?" Ennslin cackled. "Try the box. You have three seconds."

Herrod glanced to Griffy's and Mandula's open mouths as he dived for the toolbox. Lifting it to waist level, he sprinted toward the rail.

He was halfway there when the Bayliner burst into a firestorm of red, white and orange flames that illu-minated Panama Bay.

CHAPTER ONE

The lobby of the renowned Caribbean Hotel had a high-class, international atmosphere. Potted palms gave it an airy look, and photographs, mounted busts and paintings from around the world added decorative touches. A thousand tiny details showed that the Washington, D.C., hotel had been designed with a specific clientele in mind: senior diplomats from around the world.

Mack Bolan crossed the lobby and started toward conference room H. His grin spread as two men in tuxes cut in front of him and opened the door. Before the door swung shut again, he caught a glimpse of the man behind the podium and Brognola's voice drifted out into the lobby. He imagined his old friend was about as comfortable in a black monkey suit and patent leather shoes as he was.

Brognola still stood behind the rostrum when Bolan cracked the door open again. "So in closing," the Justice man said into the microphone, "I'd just like to say that the sooner we quit treating six-foot, two-hundred-pound *criminals* like innocent little lambs who've lost their way just because they fall a few months short of their eighteenth birthdays, the sooner we can actually start cleaning up the streets like we claim we're doing."

He was met by semispirited applause as he stepped down.

Another speaker had taken the stand when Brognola pushed his way through the door into the lobby. He glanced both ways, then turned to Bolan, looked at his watch and shook it. "I'll go first," he whispered. "Room 362."

Bolan nodded, looking at his own wrist as if giving the G-man the correct time. "See you there." He backed away from the door, acting as if he'd never seen Brognola before tonight and never planned to again. Giving the Justice man a three-minute head start, he crossed the lobby to the elevators.

There was reason behind Hal Brognola's observance of covert routine. Although his face had been changed by plastic surgeons more than once over the years, the fact remained that Mack Bolan was a wanted man. But as they had so many times in the past, the man from Justice and the man *on the run from justice* were working together.

That combination had proved to be deadly to the criminals of the world.

Brognola answered the door after the first knock. He stuck his head into the hall, looked around, then said, "Come in, big guy." He led the way past the bathroom to a table next to the window and sat down. "Have a seat."

Bolan dropped into a sturdy wooden chair and scooted up to the table. His eyes scanned the walls, ignoring the muted yet elegant color scheme.

He reminded himself that the Caribbean had been built with government business in mind. The rooms were soundproof. The management guaranteed it.

Brognola stared down at an open manila file. "We've got a problem," he said. "A big problem."

Bolan shrugged. "You never call me to collect overdue library books, Hal."

Brognola chuckled, then his face turned serious. "Last night a three-million-dollar DEA undercover buy turned to shit. I don't know how it happened, but the enemy got word on who our boys were. Three good men went down."

"If it was that big a buy, it means Bernhardt Ennslin must have been involved. The Corporation."

"Good guess."

Bolan turned to the window, staring out at the lights of America's capital city. He let his mind call up what he knew of Ennslin and his organization. The Corporation was "incorporated" in name only, being more of a one-man dictatorship than anything else. Ennslin didn't smuggle cocaine like the cartels in Colombia and other South American countries. He manufactured it. And he'd been manufacturing it for more than twenty years. The Corporation controlled the cultivation of coca plants throughout South America, then turned them into cocaine base at Ennslin's armed fortress deep in the Beni jungles of Bolivia. Using both the political influence his vast wealth provided and a personal army of mercenaries and hired thugs, the former Nazi had aided the Bolivian government in quashing left-wing movements, thus endearing himself to everyone from the Bolivian president on down.

Bernhardt Ennslin was covered with more insulation than a goose-down vest. To put it bluntly, Bolivian law couldn't—or wouldn't—touch him.

Bolan turned back to Brognola. "So what have you got in mind, Hal?"

Brognola cleared his throat. "The case agent on the deal was a guy named Phil Herrod. Over twenty years on the job. As good as they come. The whole op was top secret, Striker. Herrod's last report showed no signs that the Corporation suspected him."

"Let's cut to the chase," Bolan said. "The bottom line is, somebody in your organization is dirty."

Brognola's hands tightened into fists. "It looks that way." He closed his eyes and shrugged. "It happens sometimes. But you never get used to it. And my worries don't end there."

"Yeah?"

"The three agents were blown up on a small boat in Panama Bay. A dive team recovered some of the wiring from the bomb that did the job. We can't pin it down definitely, but the wiring reeks of Herbert Urquillo."

"Urquillo is a Basque terrorist, Hal, not a dope dealer. Besides, he's supposed to be somewhere in Europe right now."

"That's right. But 'supposed to be' and 'is' could be two different things."

Bolan crossed his arms and leaned over the table. "So you think there's a connection," he said. "Some alliance that's been cut between Ennslin's Corporation and terrorists."

"Maybe. But let me finish, then you decide." Brognola cleared his throat. "A Sterling submachine gun was also recovered from the wreckage of the boat. It was traced back to the Liverpool police armory robbery a couple of years ago."

For almost a minute, Bolan stared silently at his friend. The picture of a redheaded man wearing a Harris tweed hat and jacket formed in his mind. Finally he said, "Jonathan O'Banion. The IRA. But outside the usual terrorist network, there's never been a direct connection between O'Banion and Urquillo. As far as we know, the Basques and IRA have never even had a joint op."

Brognola pulled a cigar from the inside pocket of his tux, unwrapped it and stuck it in his mouth unlit. "The operative phrase is 'so far as we know.'"

Bolan pushed away from the table and stood up. He walked to the door, turned back around and walked back. "Okay," he said. "There are several possible explanations. Like the Corporation hiring Urquillo to do the job. Or hiring him to train their own bombers. We know there's been a loose connection between organized crime and terrorism for years."

Brognola's face was emotionless when he said, "Do you believe that?"

Bolan shook his head. "No. Don't ask me why, because that's the most logical explanation. But something tells me we've got a much bigger problem on our hands." He dropped back into his chair.

The two men sat quietly for several minutes. Brognola chewed on his cigar and had opened his mouth to speak again when the phone cut him off. He snatched the receiver from the cradle, pressed it against his ear and said, "Yeah?"

Bolan watched the blood drain from Hal Brognola's face. "When?" Brognola said. "Yeah...yeah... okay. I'm on my way." He slammed the phone back down and stood up.

Bolan got to his feet, too. "What's up?" he asked.

Brognola had already crossed the room and jerked his trench coat from a hanger in the closet. "Manford Martin," he said as he shrugged into the sleeves. "He's dead."

"Red Martin?" Bolan asked. "The judge?" Manford Martin had picked up the nickname "Red" as a wide receiver at the University of Tulsa, when the flaming crimson locks that fell from beneath his helmet had flopped whenever he caught a pass. The name had followed him through law school and all the way to the Supreme Court.

"The same." He grabbed the doorknob and pulled. "They just found him hanging from a beam in his den."

Bolan's eyebrows lowered. "Suicide?" he asked, knowing the answer. Not likely. Martin wasn't the type.

Brognola ushered Bolan into the hall. "Not unless he hacked himself up with a machete first. Come on. We'll finish talking on the way."

DARKNESS FALLS SWIFTLY over the Beni region of Bolivia. One moment the jungle skies are alive with light, and ocelots and anteaters sun themselves lazily along the streams. Then suddenly the sun falls behind the distant Andes, and jaguar, flag bear and water wolves creep through the darkness. Wild boars roam the night, eating roots, berries... and anything else in their path.

The Beni region is a land of sharp contrasts. A land of abundant life and quick, violent death.

Bernhardt Ennslin stared through the picture window of his study at the darkening sky. Far in the distance, on the other side of the Olympic-size swimming pool, he could see the three runways, each long enough to land a 747. The landing and control-tower lights provided enough illumination to make out the faint outlines of the warehouses in the clearing on the other side. Ennslin studied a smaller garage to the side of the storage buildings. The garage had only recently been completed. It held the new Oerlikon GDF-D03 mobile air-defense system.

A system that still had not been tested, Ennslin reminded himself.

The German's jaw set tightly. He had to find somebody who could test the Oerlikon, then stand ready to operate it if the compound ever came under air attack. But who? None of the hundred-odd mercenaries he employed as guards was qualified.

Ennslin turned toward the warehouses and watched as the shadowy figures of raggedly dressed Bolivian Indians loaded crates onto a convoy of flatbed trucks. Where was this shipment of cocaine base heading? He couldn't remember. Either Medellín or Lima. To one of the courier cartels who would then smuggle it into the U.S. or Europe, or perhaps to one of the new markets opening up in the former Soviet Union.

In any case, it would be off his property in a few more hours. Then it would be the risk of the fools who took risks.

The large flat bulb atop the yard pole nearest Ennslin suddenly popped and went out. He glanced at his wristwatch, noted the time, then looked back to the window. The dead bulb had caused the lighting to change, and he could now see his image in the glass as clearly as if it were a mirror. Without thinking, he sucked his stomach in over his belt and studied the reflection.

Except for the small paunch, the past fifty years had changed him little. Oh, his face was different, of course. A Rio de Janeiro cosmetic surgeon had already seen to that by the time Allied forces marched into Berlin. And the crew cut hair that had once been blond now shined a wispy, cottony white in the window. But the thick shoulders, the muscular neck, the bulging biceps and triceps—all were identical to those Bernhardt Ennslin had possessed when he'd been a young prison guard at Dachau.

Ennslin grinned. It had been several years since he'd tried it on, but he'd bet his entire estate that he could still fit into his old lieutenant's uniform.

A Jeep Cherokee pulled up next to the light pole outside the window. A man wearing an IMBEL Light Automatic Rifle slung over his shoulder jumped out. A moment later the man had shinnied up the pole and changed the bulb.

Ennslin glanced back to his watch and smiled. It had taken his guard less than two minutes to spot the problem and correct it. That bespoke efficiency. *German* efficiency.

The former Nazi turned back to the room as a harsh buzz broke the silence. Crossing the room in three easy strides, he punched the button, activating the speakerphone. *"Ja?"* he said.

"Señor O'Banion is here," Alberto Manuelian announced. "Shall I send him in?"

Ennslin hesitated. He had been inside all day, chained to the account books on his desk. Glancing back through the window toward the pool, he said, "No, Alberto. Find him a suit to wear. I'll meet you at the pool." He started to hang up, then shouted back into the phone. "Alberto?"

"*Sí*, Herr Ennslin?"

"Bring two pints of the pilsner."

"*Sí*, Herr Ennslin."

Ennslin tapped the disconnect button and started down the hall, absentmindedly admiring the Feuerback canvas and Zimmerman frescoes on the wall. He paused at the bottom of the winding ivory staircase. He was tired, and for a moment he reconsidered his decision to go for an evening swim.

No, he thought, starting up the steps. The water would chase the fatigue away. And besides, it would do the crass Irishman good to see the kind of shape he kept himself in. Bernhardt Ennslin might have seen the better side of seventy, but he was still fit, in solid health.

When Ennslin emerged onto the deck, Jonathan O'Banion sprawled in an aluminum-frame rocking chair next to the pool. The swimsuit Alberto had provided lay on the white wrought-iron table next to the Irishman, still carefully folded. Even in the heat of the jungle, O'Banion wore the flat-brimmed Harris tweed hat and sport coat that had become his trademark.

Ennslin suppressed a chuckle. O'Banion's preferred style had been noted by the press over the years, and one of the Irishman's many pseudonyms had become the "Tweed Terrorist."

Ennslin stopped next to the table, extending his hand to O'Banion and gripping the smaller man's hand tightly. "*Guten Tag*, Herr O'Banion," he said. "I trust your flight was enjoyable?"

O'Banion winced slightly at the handshake, and the change in expression pleased Ennslin. The Irishman nodded, withdrew his fingers and wrapped them around the pint glass on the table. "Good beer," he said.

"*Ja*," Ennslin said. "From my brewery in Viacha." Before O'Banion could answer, he turned and dived into the pool.

The German held his breath as he swam the first lap underwater. Then, nearing the edge, he executed a perfect flip-turn and rose to the surface, smoothly crawling four more laps before switching to the breaststroke. Five lengths later he rolled to his side and sidestroked another lap before pulling himself from the pool to accept the towel Alberto handed him.

"The first action in America went smoothly?" he asked as he dropped into a recliner across from O'Banion.

O'Banion took a swig of his beer. When he spoke, his *R*'s rolled with the thick brogue of his native Ulster. "Of course. I am a professional."

"But it was not your top men you used. You told me. Therefore, I had my reservations."

"No, but I went with them. Did the carving myself." He shrugged. "It was a simple case of breaking into a rich man's house and killing him. Top men were not needed. And we still have a few loose ends to tie up in Ireland."

Ennslin rubbed himself with the towel. "But the judge is dead?"

"Aye, he's as dead as they come. But he shan't be forgotten soon. We left the note." He paused to sip his beer. "The men are still in position."

"They will carry out the second wave of the attack soon?"

O'Banion lifted his wrist and stared at his watch. Ennslin watched the Irishman's lips move silently as he calculated the time in Washington. "As soon as enough targets arrive." He looked up from his watch and smiled. "I like killing cops," he said.

Ennslin nodded. He raised his own beer glass and let the slightly chilled pilsner roll over his tongue.

"There are things that bother me," O'Banion said.

Ennslin glanced up inquiringly.

"How did the DEA agent ever arrange the buy in Panama in the first place?"

Ennslin set his glass down on the table and ran the towel through his brush-cut hair. "A mistake at the lower levels of my operation," he said. "They are unavoidable sometimes."

"They are dangerous."

"*Ja*, which is why the Corporation operates on a system of checks and balances, Herr O'Banion," Ennslin said, his voice slightly irritated. "But perhaps you wish to withdraw from our agreement? I had planned to use Herbert Urquillo and his men exclusively in Europe. But I'm certain he could handle things in the United States, as well."

For a moment O'Banion paled, and it was as if Ennslin could see the dollar signs slipping from his eyes. Then the confidence returned to the Irishman's face, and he snorted. "The only *thing* I'd trust Herbert Urquillo to handle is his own *thing,*" he barked. "The boy still lives with his dear old ma, did you know that? No, matey, I'll get the job done for you. You and I will have to learn to trust each other. If we don't have trust, we have nothing." He stood up. "I've got to go. My plane back to London leaves in a few hours."

Ennslin nodded. "The next wave of attack must come soon for full effect. Reassure me again. You are bringing in your top men from Ireland?"

Now it was O'Banion who looked irritated. "That's what I told you."

"How many?"

O'Banion's fingers pinched the brim of the Harris tweed hat. His face took on the leer of a hungry wolf who had cornered a sheep. "Aplenty, mate. Aplenty. And by this time tomorrow, I will have *more* than aplenty." He cleared his throat, then turned and spat into the flower bed next to the table. "*More* than enough men to convince the politicians and judges of the United States that it might be best to call a truce in the 'war on drugs.'"

"I hope you are right. It has not been my experience that Americans bend quite as easily as that."

O'Banion snorted. "You people have made it work in Colombia for years."

"Americans are not Colombians," Ennslin said. He started to point out that next to the English, there was more German blood in the ancestry of the average American than any other nationality. He stopped short. The significance would be lost on the Irishman. "How soon will you be ready?" he said instead.

"We'll leave England tomorrow evening. We've a final 'goodbye' to the bloody Brits planned first." Without further ado, he turned and disappeared around a corner of the house.

A moment later Ennslin heard the Jeep Cherokee start and drive away.

Ennslin lifted his beer again. It had grown too warm, and he rang a small bell on the table. Alberto had anticipated the problem, and appeared bearing a fresh glass without being told. Ennslin took it and stared at the pristine water of the pool as he drank, feeling the alcohol start to flow through his veins and warm his stomach.

It was about to start. Within forty-eight hours the United States of America would be taught the true meaning of the term "drug war."

And within seventy-two hours, that drug war should be won.

A BLACK Justice Department Chrysler waited in the No-Parking zone in front of the Caribbean. Bolan and Brognola pushed past the doorman, crossed the drive and slid into the back seat. Brognola tapped a button on the armrest, and a soundproof glass barrier rose to separate the rear compartment.

Bolan glanced at the back of the driver's head. "He an agent?"

"Sure. Woody Schovenek."

"But you don't trust him?"

Brognola chuckled and nodded toward the glass. "I'd trust him with my life, big guy—known him over ten years. Woody's a damn good man, and *that*'s exactly why I'm keeping him in the dark. Anybody who knows anything about this mess will be going through an internal investigation."

Bolan nodded. It was easy to understand. Even someone as innocent as Mother Theresa would find the internal-affairs boys an unpleasant experience.

As the Chrysler pulled away from the hotel and started down M Street, Brognola turned to the Executioner. "Something I didn't get a chance to tell you yet." He took a deep breath, letting a weary sigh start from his lips, then cutting it off. "The CIA is in on this deal."

Bolan felt the muscles in his neck stiffen. He had nothing against the men and women in the CIA. For the most part, they were loyal, hardworking Americans, as intent on preserving democracy as he was. But the very nature of their work provided opportunity after opportunity for graft and corruption. And they were constant targets for blackmail and extortion.

That meant that weaker operatives sometimes caved in. It also meant that working with the CIA presented specific problems.

The Executioner's question was simple, blunt and to the point. "Why?"

"There are political aspects to the situation," Brognola said as the driver slowed and started up an access ramp to the highway. "And the spooks have more in their files on Ennslin than we do. They can help us."

"*If* they're straight with us," Bolan said dryly.

Brognola nodded. "Right. So far, I think they have been."

The Executioner shifted in his seat. "That could change at the drop of a hat. I don't have to remind you that it's happened to us before."

This time Brognola made no effort to conceal his sigh. "No," he said, "you don't have to remind me." He shrugged. "But they've volunteered info this time, which is unusual for them."

The Executioner waited.

Brognola went on. "The Company thinks there's a terrorist training base located in Sweden that may figure into things. They're running down the details now."

The Chrysler bounced over the speed bumps at the top of the access ramp and started south on the Mt. Vernon Memorial Highway. "And as you know," Brognola went on, "Ennslin and the Bolivian president are in bed together. If we take this Nazi down, we'll need all the clout the CIA can provide in the political arena."

"When, Hal."

"Huh?"

"*When* we take Ennslin down, not *if*." The Executioner's eyes narrowed. "I didn't know Phil Herrod. Or Griffy or Mandula. But nobody's going to get away with blowing them into confetti if I have any sayso in the matter." He settled in for the ride as they sped through the night.

Thirty minutes later they crossed the Potomac and took an exit ramp into Arlington. Through the soundproof divider, the Executioner saw the driver roll down the side window, anchor a magnetized "Kojak" light to the roof and switch on the flashing beam.

The Justice car hurried code-two through a fashionable residential area. A half-dozen black-and-white police vehicles and several TV and newspaper cars were parked in front of the two-story Colonial house when they pulled to a halt. Bolan and Brognola got out.

A small army of patrolmen ringed the front entrance and covered the sides of the house, doing their best to hold the newsmen at bay. Brognola led the way up the front steps amid the reporters' cries about the First Amendment and charges of "interference" from the cops.

A young Arlington patrolman stopped them at the door. Brognola flashed his Justice credentials. The kid nodded, then glanced uncertainly to Bolan.

"Rance Pollock," Brognola said, giving one of the aliases Bolan used whenever he worked with the Feds. "He's with me." They started forward.

The cop moved in front of them and cleared his throat. "I'm sorry Mr. Brognola," he said, his voice trembling slightly. "I've got orders not to let anyone in without a badge." His eyes flickered to Bolan. "Er, you have any ID on you, Mr. Pollock?"

Brognola glared at the kid's name tag. "I just got Mr. Pollock out of bed after three straight days and nights of undercover work, Officer Bateman," he said sarcastically. "You think maybe you could see fit to cut the man a little slack? On *my* say-so?" His tone was not without menace, and before the young officer could answer, Brognola had shouldered him to the side and ushered Bolan through the front door.

Bolan followed him into an elaborately decorated entryway. A tall staircase started ten feet from the door, winding up and out of sight to the second story. Through an archway to the right, the Executioner could see the living room. To their left was a formal dining room with an antique mahogany table and matching china cabinet and buffet.

A burly plainclothes man in a tattered plaid sport coat suddenly appeared from the living room. He stopped in front of Brognola. "I'm Hack Dennis," he mumbled in a raspy voice. "Arlington PD. You Brognola?"

"That's right."

"Got a call you were coming. Come on. I'll show you what we got."

Dennis led the way through the living room. Bolan and Brognola followed across the plush blue-violet carpet. A white brick fireplace stood against the wall, and brightly painted ceramic figurines of Revolutionary War soldiers covered the mantel. A sliding door set in a glass wall at the far end of the room led them to a tiled conservatory featuring potted magnolias, tulips and chrysanthemums.

Dennis cut right, and a moment later they descended a step into Supreme Court Judge Manford "Red" Martin's den. The walls were a light knotty pine and displayed framed photographs of a younger version of Martin wearing a Tulsa University football uniform. The furniture was designed for comfort, the solid oak desk for serious work. Bookshelves hugged the walls, giving way only for the built-in twenty-six-inch television.

The TV was on. The syndicated rerun of a "Perry Mason" episode seemed to go with the somber mood.

Bolan took in his surroundings. He was a soldier, not a cop, but he had fought the war on the home front for so long he had picked up many traits of the trained investigator. The living room and conservatory both had a woman's touch, but the atmosphere of the den was masculine, and Bolan guessed that this was where Red Martin had worked, relaxed...and lived.

It was also where he had died.

Swinging from a wagon-wheel light fixture attached to the ceiling was what was left of Red Martin. The thick, rough-fiber rope had cut deep into the judge's broken neck, and his head jutted to the side at an unnatural angle. Deep lacerations covered the upper half of the body where the killer must have started his work with the machete. The gashes had gradually become less deep as the machete worked its way down the body.

The Executioner stared at the spectacle, feeling his heart harden. Anger rose in his soul. This was an assassination, all right. But it was more than that, too. A simple bullet would have ended the judge's life quickly and cleanly.

This had not been simple. This had been different.

Done by someone who enjoyed his work.

Bolan's eyes fell to Martin's abdomen. There would be no problem finding the murder weapon. The blood-soaked eighteen-inch blade skewered through the judge's belly like an arrow. The Executioner stepped forward, his eyebrows lowering as he squinted at the blood-soaked yellow legal page held in place by the machete.

Barely discernible through the blood, he saw the one-word message: "Alpha."

Brognola blew air through his lips. "His family seen this?"

Dennis shook his head. "His wife's out of town at some fund-raiser. She's been notified. Only daughter is away at school. Smith, I think they said." He pulled an unfiltered Pall Mall from the pack in his shirt and stuck it in his mouth. "The maid found him."

"Where is she?" Brognola demanded.

"Couple of the boys are talking to her now."

Bolan turned to Brognola. "You realize what the note means, don't you?" he said.

A sickly, ashen color started at Hal Brognola's hairline and crept slowly down his face, hardening his features. It lasted only a moment, then was gone.

"Oh, yeah," the man from Justice said. "'Alpha'. It means this is only the beginning."

CHAPTER TWO

O'Banion figured it shouldn't be much harder than shooting fish in a barrel.

With a bazooka.

The IRA leader leaned onto the accelerator as the personnel vehicle left Southampton. Behind him he could hear the low whispering of the men. Their voices were steady, confident, with just that tiny bit of edge that marked the combat-hardened warrior about to enter battle.

O'Banion whistled an old Clancy Brothers tune as he neared the dirt road. Why shouldn't his men be confident? They were all experienced professionals. He had handpicked them from the ranks of the Provisional Irish Republican Army to execute one last attack on the limey bastard Ulster Defence Regiment. Then they would all escape Britain and put their talents to use in the open market.

The personnel vehicle slowed, turned off the highway and started along the bumpy dirt road. Still whistling, O'Banion glanced up into the rearview mirror and caught his reflection. The bottom row of formerly white teeth had been stained brown from tobacco, and his jaw clamped shut.

He looked away from the mirror. He had finally quit smoking, and he would get his teeth cleaned. Glancing up again, he saw the crow's-feet in the corners of his eyes. He couldn't erase them quite so easily—the crow's-feet or the deep rows of wrinkles that had begun to etch themselves into his forehead.

O'Banion stared ahead. There had been a time, not so long ago, it seemed, when he had been handsome. The lasses had been his for the taking, attracted to both his looks and the charismatic danger he knew he exuded. But those days were behind him now. It seemed that the sex he got anymore was what he took.

Nothing short of a scalpel would correct the situation. Cosmetic surgery cost money, and like most dedicated freedom fighters, he didn't have a pot to piss in.

O'Banion grinned suddenly. That was about to change. Ennslin had done it—somehow saved his youth. So could he.

He shifted his gaze to the rear of the truck. Seated in the middle of the huddled men was Shawn Shawnessey, his broad handlebar mustache twitching from laughter. But the eyes of O'Banion's second in command didn't laugh. Shawnessey had been with O'Banion for more than ten years now, and like the rest of the men in the truck, two things had been driven from his soul by the English—the ability to truly experience joy in any form, and the idealism of the younger Provisional IRA men who still thought the war with the Brits would someday be won and Ireland would be independently united.

No, the men with O'Banion today had given up that dream. They were ready for the open market.

O'Banion tapped the brake as soon as the checkpoint appeared in the distance. A guard shack stood at the side of the road, and through the glass he saw two uniformed women. Long hair as red as an apple fell from under one of the women's green berets. The other woman's hair was as black as a Welshman's.

The IRA leader snorted in contempt. "Greenfinches," they'd be. The women members of the UDR wore the same uniform and cap badge as the men. They manned checkpoints and took the same risks as the men. But they were never armed.

"Typical bloody English thinking," O'Banion muttered under his breath as he pulled to a halt.

The redhead, a fresh-faced lass in her midtwenties, stepped down from the shack and approached the vehicle carrying a clipboard. Even beneath the loose camouflage smock, O'Banion could see the swell of her breasts, and he felt the familiar response. In his mind, he pictured her nude as she approached the window, her soft pink nipples pointing toward him as the freckled flesh around them jiggled with each step.

The Greenfinch saluted when she saw the captain's bars on his shoulders. "Aye, sir, you're here for the training maneuvers, I imagine," she said through the window. "I'll be needing to see your orders."

O'Banion stared at her breasts. He grinned, careful to keep his lips closed so the beautiful young woman wouldn't see the stained teeth. "Seem to have misplaced the papers, lass," he said through tight lips. Behind him he heard the canvas flap open at the rear of the truck.

The redhead's eyebrows rose slightly. "But, Captain," she said, "I've me orders. I cannot allow—"

"Tell me, lass," O'Banion interrupted as a pair of heavy boots hit the ground behind the truck. "Would your nipples be the soft pink I imagine, or would they be a brighter red to match your hair?''

The young woman's mouth dropped open in astonishment. "Sir...?" she gasped.

The choked cough of a suppressed submachine gun suddenly sounded from the rear of the vehicle. Glass shattered in the guard shack. O'Banion reached out and grasped the front of the Greenfinch's loose smock and yanked her toward him, trapping her against the truck. As the fire died down, he loosened his grip, seeing the other Greenfinch slump out of sight beneath the guard shack window.

Shawnessey appeared behind the woman in O'Banion's grip. Smoke still rose from the sound suppressor on the Sterling submachine gun in his hands. With the barrel of the weapon, he lifted the back of the Greenfinch's smock, and made a clicking noise with his tongue and mouth. He grinned lewdly. "How about we take her with us, Jon?" he said. "It's a long flight we've got ahead."

O'Banion ran his free hand over the soft flesh beneath the smock. Yes, he thought. Her nipples would be pink. His mind shifted to the flight Shawnessey had mentioned. Even as they prepared to launch their final farewell attack on the British, other contingents were appropriating 747 airliners from People's Express, Continental and British Airways. The planes would be used to transport his men and members of other terrorist groups to the U.S., then hidden on a private coastal island owned by a wealthy IRA sympathizer.

And yes, Shawnessey was right. The flight would be long and tedious. The Greenfinch might be just the ticket to relieve the boredom.

O'Banion looked into the woman's eyes, and the fear he saw there sent the tingle through him. He nodded to Shawnessey. "Throw her in back. Tie her up and gag her."

Shawnessey grabbed the hood of the woman's smock, spun her around and dragged her, kicking and screaming, to the back of the vehicle.

O'Banion threw the transmission in gear and started off along the road again. In the rearview mirror he could see the Greenfinch. Shawnessey had stuffed a dirty boot sock into her mouth and wrapped black tape around it. He was binding her hands behind her. Several of the men started to tear eagerly at her clothes.

"Not yet, you bastards!" O'Banion yelled over his shoulder. "Wait until we're finished."

The men muttered and withdrew against the walls of the personnel vehicle.

The large clearing appeared three minutes later. In the middle, O'Banion saw the tents. Light wisps of smoke still rose in the early-morning air from three camp fires. The Ulster Defence squadron appeared to have just finished breakfast. Approximately fifty heads looked up from readying their equipment for field exercises as the British vehicle neared.

According to the British troops O'Banion and his men had kidnapped and tortured into confession the night before, this morning's maneuver called for a mock "search and destroy" using laser-lighted weapons. Half of the UDR men wore fatigues and traditional British "58" webbing.

O'Banion started whistling again as he halted the truck thirty feet from the tents. The other half of the British soldiers were playing the part of civilians, presumably the Irish terrorists the UDR had been formed to combat. They wore rag-wool cardigan sweaters, scuffed shoes and driving caps.

"Who the hell told the bastards we dress like that?" came a voice from the back of the truck. "Chappies look like something out of a movie about the potato famine."

"Aye, they look a bit like you, McConnel. Your mother still dressing you, I suppose?" Both comments were met with laughter.

"Shut up," O'Banion growled through clenched teeth. He threw the transmission into reverse, backed up, then turned the truck so that the rear faced the tents. Leaning through the window, he watched in the side mirror as a man wearing sergeant's stripes broke from the tents and jogged toward the truck.

O'Banion flipped the flap on his hip holster, drew the Browning Hi-Power and held it beneath the window out of sight.

The sergeant approached the truck and saluted. "Afraid you wouldn't get here in time, Captain," he said.

O'Banion's thin-lipped smile opened wide. It was one thing for a fair-haired lass to spot his stained teeth before he could get them cleaned. But he didn't care about this man. "At ease, Sergeant," he said.

The sergeant relaxed. As he did, the Browning aimed at his chest beneath the window exploded and sent a mangled 9 mm through the door and into his heart.

O'Banion switched his eyes to the rearview mirror as Shawnessey threw the canvas flap aside. O'Banion's second in command wrapped a big fist around the grip of the Vickers GPMG bolted to the rear of the truck bed, and the automatic fire of the light submachine gun drowned out the fading sound from the Browning.

The picture in the rearview mirror reminded O'Banion of watching a war movie on television. The tiny images of the UDR men jerked and fell as Shawnessey covered the campground with a carpet of fire. O'Banion continued to whistle, then burst into laughter as two of the confused Ulster soldiers, apparently deciding this was all part of the training exercise, turned their laser weapons toward the truck and cast the beams upon his men.

Shawnessey cut them in half.

When the last of the UDR men had fallen, O'Banion dropped down from the cab, walked to the rear of the truck and climbed aboard.

The redheaded Greenfinch lay sprawled in the center of the truck bed. Her eyes stared up in terror as O'Banion knelt over her, straddling her chest. Turning to Shawnessey, who was still behind the machine gun, he dropped a hand on the man's shoulder and pointed through the compartment. "Take the wheel, Shawn," he said. "Head for the planes."

Shawnessey's eyes fell to the bound and quivering woman. "But, Jon, I thought—"

O'Banion didn't hesitate. There was a sudden crack as he brought his open palm around and across

Shawnessey's face. "You'll get your turn," he growled, then glanced to the other men. "All of you will. Now take the wheel, Shawn, before I pick someone else and plant you with the bastards outside."

Shawnessey dropped down from the truck and hurried toward the cab.

As the personnel carrier started back toward the highway, O'Banion drew a Sykes-Fairbairn commando knife from his web belt. Starting at the neck, he sliced down through the woman's smock and folded the material to the side. Slipping the blade under the brassiere, he cut up through the thin material. The bra popped apart to the cheers of the men.

O'Banion chuckled, careful to keep his lips tightly closed. "Right as always," he said. "Pink." He unbuckled the web belt and dropped it next to the woman's head.

Terror filled the Greenfinch's eyes as she stared up at the IRA man. Soft whimpers came from around the sock stuffed in her mouth.

"Relax and enjoy, lass," Jonathan O'Banion said. "If you're good, we'll take you to America with us."

THE LAB TECHNICIANS had already begun their search of Judge Red Martin's den, carefully sifting through every item in the room with gloved hands and sealing their findings in plastic Ziploc bags. A flash attachment sent blazes of light bursting through the room as a police photographer captured the body, the note and the room itself on film. A sketch artist finished his own rendition of what remained of Manford "Red" Martin, and began to diagram the den.

The Arlington PD had been the first to arrive at the judge's house, followed closely by investigators from the state police. Then a special agent from the local FBI office had been ushered through the door. As soon as more than one agency was represented, the inevitable had begun. As Bolan and Brognola examined the body, the Executioner heard the polite debate over jurisdiction turn to veiled threats.

The murder had taken place within the city limits, which gave the PD authority. But of course the city of Arlington lay within the borders of Virginia, which meant the state had the right to enter. And Red Martin had been a federal judge, so the FBI had no intention of getting cut out on the deal.

Hack Dennis caught the FBI man as soon as he stepped down from the conservatory into the den, and the bickering began in earnest.

"I don't give a damn what kind of tin you got, *Special Agent* Wilkens," Dennis said, almost spitting out the man's title. "This is my goddam town and—"

"We don't carry *tin* at all," the agent called Wilkens said in a mock polite, condescending tone. He reached inside the coat of his carefully tailored charcoal suit, flipped open a slim credential case and held it in front of Dennis's eyes. "We carry a very simple yet authoritative card that reads 'Federal Bureau of Investigation.'"

As the argument grew more heated, the news came on TV. Bolan and Brognola turned toward the screen.

"This is Randall Harstone with the KRCS eleven o'clock news," said the anchorman. "Tonight's top story—gunfire broke out again today in Bosnia when angry..."

Bolan saw Brognola shifting angrily from foot to foot as Dennis and Wilkens argued on. The Executioner had seen the pressure within his old friend gradually build toward a boil all night, and as the two men continued to quarrel like schoolboys, the pot suddenly whistled.

Brognola turned toward them like a gunfighter ready to draw. "Wilkens!" he shouted across the room. "That your name?"

The man looked up. He frowned, then his eyes flickered as he recognized the face of the top-level Justice man. "Yes, sir, Mr....Brognola?" he said meekly.

"That's right," Brognola said around the stub of chewed cigar in his mouth. "Get your ass over here."

The agent reluctantly moved across the den to Brognola's side.

Brognola shoved his nose an inch from Wilkens's. "You establish some kind of working relationship with these people, and you do it *now*," he said. "Otherwise, you'll be the first resident agent the FBI's ever had in Deadhorse, Alaska."

Wilkens opened his mouth, then shut it. Finally he choked out, "Yes, sir."

As he walked away, Bolan took Brognola by the arm. "You think there's any connection between this and the DEA agents?" he asked.

Brognola shrugged. "I doubt it. Martin was a hardass on drug offenders, but that'd be the only link. And it's not much."

"Then let's get out of here. I'm no cop. My time can be better spent somewhere else."

As they started toward the door, the TV newsman switched stories. "Last night's brutal slayings of three DEA agents remains unsolved," he said. "Government officials are remaining tight-lipped concerning details—"

Bolan and Brognola stopped in their tracks. As they watched the screen, a hand suddenly appeared from the side and handed Randall Harstone a sheet of paper. The anchorman glanced at the page, and his mouth dropped open. Regaining his composure, he looked up. "I've just been handed a note," he said. Looking down again, he began to read. "American Choice is an organization of free Americans dedicated to educating the people of the United States to the fact that the war on drugs is a bogus, nefarious political ploy..."

"Really?" Brognola nearly bit the cigar in half. "That why we're working twenty-five hours a day?" He took another step toward the door. "Amazing what some people expect the public to believe."

Bolan grabbed his arm again. "The problem," he said, "is some of the people *will* believe it. Let's listen."

"American Choice is happy to claim responsibility for two recent victories," Harstone read on. "Last night we rid the nation of three agents of the Drug Enforcement Administration, a sinister puppet bureaucracy whose true mission is to further the careers of a blood-sucking President and his political sycophants."

A hush fell over Judge Martin's den.

Harstone paused and took a deep breath. "Tonight American Choice executed Federal Supreme Court

Judge Manford Martin for crimes against the people of the United States. Rest assured, America, this is only the beginning. We will rise from the ashes created by the deceitful government officials who now run this country and create a new land. We have only just begun." The newsman dropped the note on his desk and stared back at the camera, speechless.

Out of the corner of his eye, Bolan saw Brognola's jaw set firmly. A tiny pulse-beat at the G-man's temple. "There *is* a connection, Striker," he whispered.

Bolan turned to face Brognola. "Where are Able Team and Phoenix Force? You better get one or both of the teams in on this *pronto*."

Brognola pulled the stump of cigar from his mouth and held it in his hand. "Katz and his boys are tied up in Germany for the moment," he said. "Lyons and the rest of Able Team are finishing up a deal in L.A. I'll get them on this as soon as they're available, but there's no way of knowing where or when the next attack—"

Before he could finish, the window behind him shattered.

Bolan ducked for cover as fragments of glass rained down over his shoulders. A heavy oblong object came sailing through the window and clattered to the floor.

Automatic gunfire began in the front yard as the Executioner watched the concussion grenade wobble to a halt at his feet.

Bolan didn't hesitate. In one smooth motion he swept the grenade from the floor and brought his arm back over his shoulder. As Brognola and the rest of the cops and lab techs dived for cover, the Executioner threw the grenade back at the window.

As the pineapple sailed through the air, the gray figure of a man came diving into the room, trimming the shards of glass from the window's edges. The grenade struck the camouflage-clad man in the chest, then toppled back to the floor.

Bolan dived behind a couch. A split second later he heard a stifled scream, then a dull roar permeated the room. Blood, bone and bits of flesh shot through the room like shrapnel as the gunfire from the front of the house continued.

A quick glance over the back of the couch told the story of what had just happened. The man who'd come flying through the window had fallen on top of the grenade.

All that remained intact were his legs. Fuzzy remnants of the black wool ski mask that had covered his face still floated down through the air to settle on the furniture and floor.

Bolan was on his feet when the second window shattered. Another figure, a Sterling submachine gun in his hands, landed on the floor. The Executioner drew the Beretta 93-R from under his arm. He fired as the man rolled, sending a 95-grain jacketed soft-point 9 mm into the ski mask.

More men, almost identical in their "urban" cammies and ski masks, came leaping through the windows. Bolan raised his aim. He tapped the trigger again, sending a 3-round burst into the chest of a tall thin man with a Sterling submachine gun. The Executioner's streaking parabellums drove the attacker back against the windows and to his knees.

But he kept firing.

The Executioner sent another trio of rounds into his enemy. The bullets did little but divert the man's aim.

Brognola, Wilkens and Hack Dennis were also emptying their automatics and revolvers as more of the attackers crashed through the windows. The rounds struck the "X-rings" on the enemies' chests, but did little more than keep them off balance and ruin their aim.

Raising the sights, Bolan tapped another burst into the ski mask. As he watched above the sights, the gray-clad gunner finally fell to the floor.

The Executioner dropped the magazine from the Beretta and jerked a fresh box from the caddie under his arm. He jammed the magazine up the butt of the pistol and thumbed the slide release.

"They're wearing vests! Shoot for the head!" Bolan yelled above the clamor. He emptied the Beretta again, then jammed it into his belt and drew the Desert Eagle. As he thumbed the hammer on the massive .44 Magnum, he saw Brognola raise his Colt Lawman to eye level, drop an eyelid and squeeze.

The Justice man's .357 caught one of the gunmen midway up the ski mask. He slumped to the floor with the muscle tone of a jellyfish.

On his other side, Bolan saw Davis and Wilkens begin sniping at the enemies' heads. With the Desert Eagle now, the Executioner ventured a chest shot on the next killer in line. The loads he'd packed into the Eagle that evening had three hundred feet of muzzle velocity on the Beretta. The big .44 now roared in his hand as he sent a 180-grain JHP precisely into the gunman's midsection.

The round drove the man back against the wall. He hesitated, then raised his Sterling.

Bolan lifted the Desert Eagle's barrel a fraction of an inch. Just as he'd feared, the ballistic nylon vests were Schedule 4—the top of the line. Even the big .44s wouldn't pass through them.

He squeezed the trigger. The next Magnum slug tore one hole through the front of the ski mask and another through the back, taking half of the man's head with it as it exited the body.

One by one the attackers fell to the fire of Brognola and the cops.

A loud explosion echoed from the living room, through the conservatory and into the den. Bolan scooped one of the Sterlings from the floor and pulled an extra magazine from the dead man's belt carrier. Stuffing it into his belt next to the Beretta, he raced to the conservatory door. "Stay here, Hal!" he shouted over his shoulder to Brognola. "Cover the rear!" He turned toward Wilkens and Davis. "Get on the phone and get some reinforcements out here *now!*"

As he neared the door, another grenade came bouncing across the tile toward the den.

His kick was spontaneous. Catching the hand bomb with his instep, he swept it back across the tile like a soccer forward scoring a goal.

As the grenade clattered back across the conservatory, Bolan grabbed the handle of the thick oak door and swung it shut. A long second ticked by as the grenade bounced off the wall, then another thunderous explosion filled the Executioner's ears.

The heavy door shook with the concussion.

Bolan twisted the knob and kicked the door back open as three gunners entered the conservatory from the living room. All dressed in gray, they fell before the 9 mm autofire.

Racing across the tile past the plants, Bolan saw four dead Arlington PD officers in the living room. Two of the attackers stood over the bodies, foolishly admiring their handiwork.

It was the last work they'd ever do.

One of the men, tall, slim and faceless behind the ski mask, turned as Bolan rounded the corner. The Remington pump shotgun in his hands almost made the turn with him. But before he could get the weapon around and up, a 4-round staccato issued forth from the Sterling in Bolan's grasp.

As the second man, shorter and bulkier, tried to bring his own scattergun into play, the now-headless gunman toppled into him. A 12-gauge blast of buckshot sailed wide of the Executioner, crashing through the glass wall between the living room and conservatory.

Bolan swung the Sterling onto the short man and riddled him from the neck up with an 8-round burst. Blood and bone fragments flew through the room as the man spun through the air.

The Executioner pivoted on the balls of his feet and shot back through the conservatory. From the den, he heard almost constant subgun chatter. He could only hope the fire came from the seized Sterlings in the hands of Brognola and the company. He grimaced as he rounded the corner and raced down an unknown hall.

Bursting from the hall into the kitchen, he saw two men in gray come racing in from another part of the house. He tapped the Sterling dry into their heads, leaving them faceless behind their masks as they hit the floor. Again he wondered briefly how Brognola, Dennis and Wilkens were faring.

The attack on the house had come unexpected, which made it hard enough. The ballistic nylon vests the killers wore made it worse.

Leaping over the bodies, Bolan dived into a small side entryway that led to the garage. Through the window in the door, he saw four gunners sprinting toward the house. Shoving the fresh magazine into the Sterling, he was about to fire when he heard movement behind him.

Bolan turned and squeezed the trigger in one motion. He saw a man with an AK-47 at the top of the rear stairs take the burst in the ski mask.

The Executioner didn't wait for the body to tumble down the steps. Twisting back to the door, he pressed the trigger back to the guard and sent a figure eight of 9 mm slugs crashing through the glass.

The rounds struck the four attackers in the vests, making them halt in their advance for a minute.

Bolan flipped the safety to semiauto and took his time, dropping the men one by one with a neat round to the head.

More footsteps sounded behind him, and he spun around to see three of the faceless enemy hurrying down the steps. Evidently the killers had found some route to the second floor and were entering there, as well. Short bursts from the Sterling sent the tops of all three heads splattering against the walls of the stairwell. The subgun's slide locked open, empty.

Bolan pushed past the bodies that tumbled down the stairs and reached the second-floor landing. It was quiet.

Too quiet.

He set the dry Sterling on the top step and reached for the Desert Eagle. Then, changing his mind, he drew the suppressed Beretta. Neither 9 mm nor .44 Magnum bullets would pierce the attackers' vests, and the smaller-caliber weapon held sixteen rounds. It was more than enough gun for head shots, and the near silence with which it spat its death would be to his advantage.

The entire second floor could be scanned from the top of the stairs. One long hall ran the length of the house, with four doors leading off to both sides. The Beretta led the way as Bolan crept slowly toward the first door, his back to the wall. Sticking his head around the corner, he peered into the room. Empty. Entering slowly, he swung the door to the bathroom open and stuck the 93-R through the hole. Empty, as well. The closet was equally deserted.

He moved on. He found no one in the next bedroom or adjoining rooms, but here Bolan located the killers' point of entry to the second floor. The curtains above the rear window fluttered softly in the cool night breeze. Moving cautiously to the opening, the Executioner peered down into the backyard.

A latticework trellis entwined with vines rose from the flower bed below to the second floor. It was here the men in gray had entered. Bolan scanned the backyard. It was as empty as the upstairs bedrooms. Which meant only one thing.

All were aboard who were coming aboard.

Sirens screamed suddenly from the front of the house. Bolan sprinted back to the hallway, then through the door to the nearest front bedroom. Below he saw six more squad cars and a SWAT van screech to a halt. Blue-uniformed officers with pistols and shotguns swarmed from the cars. Men in black BDUs toting M-16s seemed to fly from the van.

The gray-clad terrorists in the front yard scattered, seeking cover and escape.

Bolan turned and raced back to the hall, then down the front steps three at a time. He hit the ground as a straggling terrorist came sprinting for the front door.

A gut shot into the vest from the Beretta stopped the terrorist's forward movement. A follow-up shot to the head ended his life.

Bolan hurried back through the living room to the den. Brognola and Davis knelt in the middle of the room over a prostrate body. As the Executioner neared, he saw Wilkens's wild eyes staring up at the ceiling.

Blood oozed from the multiple wounds in the FBI special agent's chest.

Brognola rose and looked at the Executioner. The G-man's expression was grim, the look of a leader who had already seen too many good men fall in the course of a lifetime. He started to speak, then a sudden choking from the floor closed his mouth again.

Bolan and Brognola looked down.

Wilkens choked again, a thin spray of pink mist spewing from his mouth.

Then the FBI agent's frenzied eyes closed with finality.

The Executioner started toward the door.

"You leaving?" Brognola asked.

Bolan stopped at the step, turned back and nodded.

Brognola walked toward him, his voice dropping to a whisper. "This mean you're in, big guy?"

"You have to ask?" the Executioner said.

"No," Brognola said. "I don't guess I do."

The distant expression on the G-man's face changed to a weary, battle-worn smile.

JONATHAN O'BANION heard the phone buzz and rolled over to reach for the instrument. Pressing it to his ear, he rubbed the sleep from his eyes with his other hand. "Aye?" he said.

"It's time, Jonathan," Shawn Shawnessey's craggy voice said. "You asked me to wake you when the others got here. We're in room 1401."

"Aye." O'Banion sat up, and swung his feet off the bed. "Tell them I'll be there in a moment." He hung up.

The IRA leader turned back to the nude woman sleeping on her back next to him, and yawned. Reaching over, he checked the rough ropes that bound her to the bed. Tight. Secure.

The Greenfinch wouldn't be going anywhere until he told her she could.

O'Banion rose and walked to the sink. He splashed water on his face and reached for a towel. Turning to the open closet next to the sink, he pulled a shirt and slacks from the hangers. He studied the Greenfinch as he dressed. The woman's naturally white skin had taken on a yellowish waxen color. Even as she slept, her breathing came in jerky gasps. She might not be long for this world.

In any case, the time when he turned her back over to the men again might come sooner than he thought. He was tiring of her already.

He found his shoes and socks and pulled the tweed jacket over his shoulders. His hat sat on the desk next to the television, and he set it on his head. Leaning over the bed, he pinched the Greenfinch's buttock.

Her eyelids shot up.

"Keep it warm for me, lassie," O'Banion told the glazed eyes that met his, then turned and walked out of the room.

Shawnessey opened the door to room 1401 as soon as he knocked. O'Banion strode inside. He set his hat on top of the television, took a seat on the table next to it and looked out across the room to the faces that awaited his words.

O'Banion smiled inwardly. He had known some of these men for two decades now. Some had been friends and allies over those years. Others had been enemies. But now, regardless of past ideologies, they were united.

Jonathan O'Banion waited, knowing the men would have to wait, too, and savoring as he always did the power that gave him. It had not been hard to recruit enough men for what Bernhardt Ennslin had in mind. Most of these men had gray streaking their hair and beards. Like O'Banion himself, they were growing old. Old and tired. Tired of the never-ending battle against...what?

O'Banion cleared his throat and smiled. "I suppose you're all wondering why I called this meeting," he said. Polite chuckles rumbled through the room. His face turning serious, the IRA leader went on. "You carried out a successful attack on a U.S. Supreme Court judge and a relatively good follow-up strike." His eyes moved to Richard Baron-Dodson.

Baron-Dodson nodded, his silver ponytail bobbing behind him. He was the sole survivor of England's only native freedom-fighter group, the Angry Brigade. The AB had never been much—planted a few bombs, machine-gunned a couple of buildings. The rest of the group had either been caught or killed, and Baron-Dodson had been underground since 1971. Judge Manford Martin's assassination had been his first strike since then, but he'd proved he still knew what it took.

O'Banion went on. "We're off to a good start. We're making our statement—or at least the statement we want America to believe." The comment brought more chuckles, and he paused, watching the hard faces of the men seated around the room in chairs and on the beds, and realizing as he did that Baron-Dodson was representative of all the men.

Johnny Joe Jackson, formerly of the Weathermen. Carlos Gutierrez of the Argentinean Montoneros. Besides these two, there were men who had once been leaders in the Turkish Gray Wolves, the Secret Army for the Liberation of Armenia and the Uruguayan Tupamaros. They were very different types and they had fought for different causes. But they all had one thing in common.

Still powerful and capable, they knew it was time to start looking out for their old age. There damn sure wasn't any international terrorist retirement fund.

"First," O'Banion said, "we must begin looking at this venture as a business. And at ourselves as businessmen."

Abdul Mohammed al-Sadr, cousin of the founder of Amal Hope and a devout Shiite Muslim, looked up suddenly from his seat on the edge of one of the beds. "I am confused, O'Banion," he said. "It was my understanding that we were here to unite. To finally bring fear to the Great Satan America, the root of all that is wrong with Allah's earth."

O'Banion didn't intend to mince words. "Then you got it wrong, matey," he said bluntly. "Those days are over." He paused. "We're here to get rich."

There were murmurs of approval around the room.

"This I cannot do," al-Sadr said, looking to the floor and shaking his head. "In the name of Allah, I am here to strike against the Great Satan."

"So are we," O'Banion nodded. "But that's not our primary concern."

"But I was informed—" al-Sadr started to say.

"Then you were misinformed," O'Banion cut in.

Before al-Sadr could answer, Yasir Omari reached across the bed and took his arm. Omari, a former Hezbollah man, shook his head and whispered something to al-Sadr.

"The point is," O'Banion said, addressing the room as a whole again, "we're in this for ourselves now. Hell, maybe we always were. But what I'm saying is this—we've been employed by one of the wealthiest men on the face of this planet. Our mission is simple but twofold. We show the United States that they might as well back off on the drug war, because unless they do, they won't have any judges to hear the cases. And we do it in a way that makes the people of America believe that the whole drug crusade has been a political sham to begin with." He stopped long enough to catch a few more nods of approval. "When we get finished, every man in this room will be a millionaire. And the men you brought with you will be as wealthy as you decide they should be." His eyes fell again on al-Sadr.

The Amal Hope man stared back.

O'Banion pulled a folded map of the U.S. and a roll of tape from his tweed sport coat, keeping one eye on the Muslim. The raghead had come thinking this was another bullshit anti-America campaign, it appeared. Hadn't he heard the news?

Socialism was dead. Capitalism was in style again.

Unfolding the map, the Irishman turned and taped it over the mirror behind him. He drew the Sykes-Fairbairn stiletto from his belt and used it as a pointer. "We have safe houses set up at various points throughout the country," he said, tapping the eastern coastline. "My men and I will base out of New York City." The dagger moved down the shoreline to Florida. "Baron-Dodson, you'll have Miami." He turned, caught the Englishman's nod, then moved the blade west. "Omari, take your men to Dallas and cover the Southwest. Jackson, you're going home to Berkeley.

"Martinez, take your men to Kansas City. Ali Azi, you've got an old farmhouse just outside of Chicago." O'Banion turned back around and looked al-Sadr in the eye. "I've given you Denver, Abdul."

The Shiite dropped his eyes to the floor.

O'Banion resheathed the stiletto. "There are plenty of federal judges in each area. Pick your own targets, plan your own missions. There's no need for the rest of us to know the details . . . and the fewer who know, the less chance of leaks." He slid off the desk and stood up. "The fact is, there's only one rule. Only one thing you have to do to meet the requirements and get paid. Each of your groups kills one judge per day. Are there any questions?"

Baron-Dodson shook his head. "Seems relatively simple to me," he said. The others concurred with nods.

Abdul Mohammed al-Sadr suddenly leaped to his feet. "You have lost all sight of what we stand for!" he screamed. "The Left Bank! American involvement in the Middle East! The liberation of Palestine!" He looked O'Banion in the eye. "The liberation of your own country from its English masters!"

"Sit down, Abdul," O'Banion told the excited Arab. His hand slowly moved toward the pistol under his jacket.

"I will not sit down!" al-Sadr screamed. "You have become capitalists! No, you are worse than capitalists! Traitors! I will have no part of this!" He shook his fist and turned toward the door.

O'Banion's hand moved to the Browning in his belt, but before he could draw it, there was a flash of white behind al-Sadr. A robed arm encircled the dissenter's neck, and then a blade sliced cleanly through the throat.

Abdul Mohammed al-Sadr's eyes widened in surprise as red gushed forth from his severed carotid artery. His hands rose to his throat, then came up to his eyes. He stared at his blood-soaked fingers for a moment, then slumped to the floor, his life's blood pumping out onto the hotel-room carpet.

Yasir Omari knelt next to the man who had once been his ally and wiped his blade on al-Sadr's robe. He looked up at O'Banion. "Anyone who is not with us," he said, smiling, "is against us."

CHAPTER THREE

Bernhardt Ennslin opened the sliding glass door and ushered his guest onto the patio. He watched the man waddle onto the tile and immediately break out in sweat from the tropical heat.

Ennslin led the way across the deck, past the swimming pool, to the row of parked golf carts. Hidden in the foliage surrounding the area, birds sang above the hum from the generator building to their left. Then the roar of a large cargo plane, flying low overhead, drowned out their song. The German glanced to the control tower, then to the descending plane, before dropping his eyes back to the ground.

As the two men approached the golf carts, a monkey scampered from the seat of the one on the end, chattering wildly as it raced to the safety of the nearest tree. Ennslin climbed behind the wheel of the golf cart and inserted a key into the ignition.

The visitor pulled a handkerchief from the pocket of his light cotton suit and mopped his forehead as he pressed himself into the passenger's seat. "I never cease to be amazed at the beauty of this place, Mr. Ennslin," he said in a Brooklyn accent. "So pristine, so clean, so...uncontaminated."

The two men turned toward the runway as the plane's wheels touched down. Ennslin twisted the key, and the golf cart's motor coughed to life. He backed the golf cart out, cut a quick U-turn past the other carts and started across the grass. Out of the corner of his eye, he saw the cargo plane come to a halt. Several men stepped down from the cabin, and he recognized the familiar light blue *guayabara* shirt that had become the trademark of Jose Ramirez.

Ennslin slowed the cart as they neared the plane, smiling and throwing up a hand in greeting. Ramirez and his bodyguards smiled back. Ennslin stopped the cart. *"Buenos dias, amigo,"* he said.

Ramirez looked at his watch. "It is 12:07, Señor Ennslin." He laughed. "You mean *buenos tardes,* do you not?"

Ennslin kept the smile carved on his face. "Even after fifty years, your language confuses me," he said politely. "Do you not have a simple greeting that is appropriate twenty-four hours a day? Something like *guten tag?*"

Ramirez threw back his head and laughed affectedly. "Sometimes we say 'hello.'"

"Then hello," Ennslin said. "You are here for your shipment, of course. Can you stay for lunch? Albert is fixing *empanada saltena,* one of your favorites, I believe?" He felt his stomach recoil at the nauseating mixture that included meat, raisins and olives.

"Sí, it is. But I regret we must hurry off as soon as we are loaded. Business must come first."

How very *German* of you, Ennslin thought sarcastically. He nodded, then pointed his head in the direction of a one-story concrete building that stood alone near the jungle. "I trust there will be no problems with your order," he said. "But if you need me, I will be in the gymnasium."

The two men shook hands. Ennslin pulled across the runway, passing the laboratory building where the cocaine paste was manufactured and the large warehouses where it was stored. He cut around the garage hiding the Oerlikon, and the sight filled him further with anger.

He had spent several days now discreetly trying to hire mercenaries who were trained to operate the antiaircraft system. But he was forced to walk a fine line during the recruitment of such men. He had to be careful.

Who knew what might happen if the wrong ears found out that he had the system but no one who could operate it? That in reality, he had no air defense?

Ennslin parked in front of the last building before the jungle, a small concrete structure with no windows. He unlocked the door and stood back and watched with barely disguised contempt while his obese guest struggled to get his bulk through the opening.

What kind of man allowed himself to put on fifty extra pounds of blubber? How could this man stand the shame he must feel when he looked in the mirror each morning to shave?

The guest took a seat on the bench along the wall as Ennslin moved past the carefully laid out free weights and training machines to the dressing room. He changed quickly into a pair of shorts and tank top, watching his own reflection in the mirror as he laced his athletic shoes. He smiled when he saw the ligaments and veins pop out in his sinewy forearms as his carefully chiseled muscles tightened the knots.

Bernhardt Ennslin had celebrated his seventy-third birthday the week before. But the mirror proved that he looked no older than fifty, and his doctor—a German physician in La Paz—assured him that his health was that of a man perhaps twenty years younger than that.

Reemerging into the weight room, Ennslin took a seat on the Lifecycle in the corner, set the resistance and began warming up. He knew his guest was unhappy—otherwise, he would not have risked coming to see him. He also knew the source of the visitor's worries, and that the man was waiting for him to bring the subject up.

Ennslin pedaled silently on. Let him wait.

Five minutes later, when he had finally broken into a sweat, he lifted his leg over the cycling machine and moved toward the bench in the center of the room.

The man against the wall cleared his throat. "We need to talk, Mr. Ennslin."

The ex-Nazi glanced his way. "Oh?" he said as he slid to his back on the bench. "What troubles you?" He looked up at the forty-five-pound plates on each end of the Olympic bar, then wrapped the fingers of both hands around the steel. Lifting it from the stand, he brought it down to his chest.

"This new . . . *arrangement* you've got with O'Banion and Herbert Urquillo and some of the others," the fat man said. "It scares the hell out of me."

Ennslin pumped the bar upward from his chest, then brought it down again. Breathing deeply with each exertion, he cranked out fifteen easy repetitions before setting the bar back on the stand and sitting up.

"Can you be a little more specific, my friend?" he said.

"Hell, Mr. Ennslin, the guys are *terrorists*. Fuckin' *Commies,* really. You can't trust them, and you and I both know it."

Ennslin stood up and walked across the room, pulling a towel from a hook on the wall. His eyes studied the fat man. They were so different, the two of them. They shared only their hatred of communism—the sole ideal that had brought them together. But what this man seemed never to have learned—surprising, in his line of work—was that sometimes you had to sleep with one enemy to defeat another.

Ennslin mopped the sweat from his face before answering. "The American President's war on drugs has not been a disaster for me," he finally said. "But it has cut into my profits to some extent." He felt his eyes narrow as he turned to hang the towel back on the hook. "Which calls for unusual action on my part."

"Yeah, er, yes, sir. I understand that. But... *terrorists?*"

Ennslin pulled two more forty-five-pound disks from the plate tree next to the bench and slid them on the ends of the bar. Crawling back onto the bench, he said, "I am keeping O'Banion and the others in check. And they are serving a very useful purpose." He lifted the bar again.

"I don't see what that purpose could be."

Ennslin felt the anger shoot through him and used it to do two more than his usual ten reps. When he'd finished, he dropped the bar back on the stand with a resounding clank and stood up. "Then I will explain that purpose to you, my friend," he said. "And then

I will reexplain *your* purpose." He moved back to the plate tree and lifted two more forty-fives as he continued to speak. "We need an end to the drug war. That can only come one of two ways. O'Banion thinks that once several prominent American officials have been killed, the U.S. government will acquiesce with our demands that they 'lighten up,' as you Americans are fond of saying."

"That'll never happen, Mr. Ennslin. The President's stepped into this drug war with both feet."

Ennslin nodded. "I suspect you are correct. But as O'Banion pointed out, it worked in Colombia. It *might* work in the U.S. But even if it doesn't, the American public is sick of the tactics their leaders have used over the last several years. Did you pay any attention to the number of incumbent senators and congressmen who were forced to find other employment after the last election?" He didn't wait for an answer. "I think that even though the government itself may not relinquish its persecution, and the public may not take kindly to the tactics of our 'American Choice,' the people will start to believe the propaganda that goes with it all. They will start to believe that the drug war really *has* been a scam. Like Watergate, Iran-Contra and the like. And the men and women in office will be in no position to go against their constituents and lose votes."

"Look, Mr. Ennslin," the fat man said, walking over to the bench. "You're gonna need advance info if O'Banion and his crew are planning to stir the shit stateside. I've done what I could so far—"

"And been handsomely rewarded for it."

"Yes, sir, I have. But when it comes to terrorists, I draw the line. I can't do it. I *won't do it*. Like I said, I've done what I could so far, which includes sending the Justice Department off on a wild-goose chase, but I'm not the top man in my organization, and you know it. There's a lot that goes on that takes days or weeks for me to even hear about. Some things I *never* learn about. And when it comes to murdering judges, I—"

"Grab a plate," Ennslin demanded.

"What?"

Ennslin lifted another forty-five-pound weight from the tree and slid it onto the bar. "Put an equal weight on the other end."

The fat man paused, then moved to the tree. Ennslin watched him struggle with the disk, finally working it onto the bar. When he'd finished, he turned puffing to Ennslin.

Ennslin slid onto the bench.

"How much is that?" the fat man asked.

"Four hundred and five pounds," Ennslin said. "Now, please be silent while I concentrate. Stand behind the bench and help me if I need it."

Ennslin watched the man take his place. Then, taking a deep breath, he lifted the bar over his chest, pumped it down, then up and back onto the stand.

"Son of a bitch," the fat man said, impressed.

Ennslin rose to his feet. "Take off your jacket," he said.

"Huh?"

"Your jacket."

The fat man complied.

"Now," Ennslin said, "lie down on the bench."

The visitor laughed and patted his belly. "Come on, Mr. Ennslin, you know I can't—"

"On the bench!" Ennslin screamed. "Now!"

The fat man was on the bench before Ennslin's words had stopped echoing off the concrete walls.

"Grab the bar," Ennslin said.

"I can't—"

"Grab the bar!"

The pudgy fingers reluctantly grabbed the bar. "Mr. Ennslin, please—"

"Lift the bar!"

The fat man pushed against the bar, the jowls beneath his chin quivering. The bar didn't move. Ennslin moved behind the stand and grasped it in the center with both hands, heaving upward.

The four-hundred-five-pound weight rose in the air. Ennslin guided it over his visitor's chest and slowly lowered it.

The face of the man on the bench was one of fright and exhaustion. Blood pounded his cheeks. The veins in his temples gorged with blood, threatening to explode.

Ennslin steadied the weight on the visitor's chest, then removed his hands. The bar dropped, digging deep into the fat covering the other man's chest. "Lift it!" the former Nazi whispered.

The visitor's eyes bulged like spotted eggs. Air rushed from his open mouth. He tried to speak, but the weight choked off the words. He continued to push impotently against the bar, but the weight cut deeper into his chest.

Finally Ennslin grabbed the iron again. "Push!" he demanded.

The fat man pushed, his weak arms fighting for life. Ennslin gave him three more seconds, then slowly helped lift the bar and place it back in the rack.

The visitor's hands shot to his chest, and he gasped for air. Ennslin grabbed the man's shoulders and jerked him to a sitting position. His face an inch from the chubby red cheeks, he said, "Do you understand the meaning of all this?"

The visitor closed his eyes and shook his head.

"Then I will tell you," Ennslin said. "You could not lift the weight by yourself. And at the angle at which I stood, I could not have lifted it, either. Not alone. But together we accomplished what neither of us could do by ourselves." He paused, watching the fat man's glazed eyes to see if his meaning had sunk in. "*Now* do you understand?"

The visitor's eyes opened again. "That...we must help each other...." he replied, panting.

Ennslin took a step back and gazed down at the disgusting excuse for a man he saw before him. "*Ja,*" he said. "I have helped you. And *you* will continue to help *me.*" He paused again. Then, for the first time that day, a smile broke across his face. "Because if you do not, my fat slovenly friend...*you will be crushed.*"

BOLAN WATCHED through the window as Jack Grimaldi dropped the plane through the sky. The city he saw below was like no other on Earth. Fourteen separate islands made up Stockholm, Sweden, and the islands were surrounded by thick green forests. It was easy to see that a terrorist compound might be hidden anywhere within their depths. The city's architecture was rich with steeples and belfries, making it look like a giant storage site for a building contractor who specialized in constructing medieval castles. From the air, Stockholm held a dark and ominous mood, which fitted in perfectly with what had been going on in the United States.

Only seconds before takeoff, Bolan and Grimaldi had received a radio transmission from Hal Brognola. Another Supreme Court judge, this time Robert Rhodes of Los Angeles, had fallen to the machete and rope of American Choice. Then, halfway over the Atlantic, they'd received another update. Judge Marian Spelling of Dallas had gone down in similar fashion.

Bolan shuffled the papers in his lap and dropped them back into the folder. He had studied the file on Stockholm during the flight. "You're staying around the airport, right, Jack?" His words were more statement than question. Jack Grimaldi had flown the Executioner on more missions than either man could remember, and the ace pilot had never once let him down in any way.

Grimaldi nodded. "I'm only as far as the phone," he said. Rather than a telephone, he tapped the radio mounted to the control panel, then pointed to Bolan's carry-on bag. A small walkie-talkie was hidden inside the lining. "I'll keep 'er warmed up and ready to take off the moment you are, Striker," Grimaldi said.

The wheels hit the runway, and Grimaldi rolled the plane to a halt. Bolan shoved the file into his carry-on and dropped down to the tarmac.

The Executioner crossed the runway to a building with a sign on the roof. One word had been painted in several languages on the sign. Most of the words were "Greek" to the big American, but the second set of letters made the rest clear enough: "Customs."

Just inside the glass door, Bolan was met by a tall blond barrel-chested man wearing a navy blue uniform. "Mr. Pollock?" the man said in a singsong Scandinavian voice. Bolan could see the grips of a Husqvarna Vapenfabrik m/07 9 mm peeking out from under the corner of the flap holster on his belt.

Bolan nodded.

The man held out his hand. "If you will please come with me?" He led the Executioner down the hall to a small room and ushered him inside.

A statuesque young blonde stood behind a counter holding a clipboard. Bolan walked up, set his bag on the ledge and pulled a civilian version of the Rance Pollock passport from the bellow pocket of his safari jacket. He had traded the sport coat he'd worn earlier with his khaki slacks for the bush jacket for one simple reason: Later he was to meet with a local CIA agent who would furnish him with weapons and whatever new information the Company had come up with concerning the terrorist training compound. Along with a rather complicated set of code words, the spooks had issued him a unique item of clothing that would identify him to their man. That particular item would have looked silly enough with a sport coat and tie that he'd have drawn undue attention.

"Do you have anything to declare?" the woman behind the counter asked.

"Just this," Bolan said. He rummaged through the carry-on for the quart bottle of Chivas Regal that Brognola had provided him. In an effort to combat the rising alcoholism rate in the country, the Swedish government had raised the taxes on spirits to the point of absurdity. No one entered the country without taking advantage of the liter-or-less duty-free exemption.

The Executioner hadn't come to Stockholm to party, but it was another way to keep from looking suspicious.

The blonde made a check on her clipboard. "Anything else?"

Bolan shook his head.

"You have no other luggage?"

"No. My trip is to be short."

"If you please..." the woman said, and began digging through his bag. Finding nothing of interest, she tore a sticker from a pad on the counter, affixed it to his bag, smiled and said, "*Adjö*, Mr. Pollock. Have a nice stay."

He flagged a cab in front of the terminal and slid into the back seat. "Norrbro Bridge," he told the driver.

The man nodded and pulled away from the airport.

Bolan unzipped his bag and pulled out an old-fashioned navy blue baseball cap with a short bill. The emblem on the crown showed a chubby white bear cub holding a baseball bat across his body. Chicago Cubs, 1914, read the cardboard tag attached to the hat with plastic.

The Executioner removed the tag and placed the cap on his head. To make the CIA connection, he had agreed to cross the bridge on foot and continue toward Stockholm's Great Church in the Gamla Stan, or "Old Town," section of the city. Somewhere along the way his contact, who'd be wearing a 1910 New York Yankees cap, would spot his Cubs headgear and approach. If that had not happened by the time he crossed the bridge, Bolan was to proceed on into the Great Church and wait.

There would be a series of questions and answers when the CIA operative spotted him—long enough to be tedious, and in the Executioner's opinion, a waste of time.

The driver pulled to a halt at the bridge. Bolan handed several Swedish fifty-krona bills over the seat and got out.

The Executioner crossed the bridge quickly. His eyes skirted the walkway for the Yankees cap. He saw a variety of hats, but none sporting the short blue bill, blue pin-striped crown and red insignia. As he neared the end of the bridge, his eyes fell on the massive stone Swedish parliament building to his right. Just behind and to the side stood a building that had once housed the Bank of Sweden. Established in 1656, the bank was the world's oldest such institution still in existence. Bolan paused in front of parliament, pretending to study the building as his eyes scanned the busy streets for the Company man.

When no one approached, he angled across the street diagonally to the Great Church, surprised at the well-kept exterior. According to the file he had studied on the flight over, Sweden's national cathedral was the oldest building in the city, dating back to the year 1250. The church housed several art treasures. He mounted the ancient steps and went inside, heading toward a wooden statue of St. George and the dragon.

Bolan stopped in front of the statue. His eyes stared straight ahead while he watched his sides with his peripheral vision. The seconds turned to minutes, the minutes became half an hour, and his patience grew thinner with each tick of his watch.

What the hell was keeping the CIA man? Didn't the Company know about Red Martin and Bob Rhodes? The Executioner was about to find the nearest pay phone, advise Brognola about the no-show, then strike out on his own to find the terrorist training camp when he saw the Yankee cap out of the corner of his eye.

Bolan turned toward the man who approached, focusing on the red composite *N*-and-*Y* emblem on the crown. The man wearing the cap also wore black sunglasses, an indigo blue bush vest, jeans and white athletic shoes. He stopped next to Bolan, faced the carving and smiled.

"You look like a fellow American," he said, beginning the code.

Bolan nodded.

"A baseball fan, too?"

The Executioner tapped his cap. "Particularly the old teams," he said.

"Me, too. Yeah, 1930 was a damn good year for the Cubs," the CIA man said. "Vic Saier was one hell of a pitcher. Went twenty-one and three that year, with an earned-run average of 2.05."

Bolan shook his head. Pinching the bill of his hat, he said, "The year's 1914, friend. And Vic Saier wasn't a pitcher. He played first base. You must be thinking of Hippo Vaughn or Larry Cheney."

The CIA man nodded. Satisfied, he said, "Pollock?"

Bolan nodded.

"My name's Rakestraw. Wendell Rakestraw. Let's get some coffee and I'll fill you in." He turned, leading Bolan out of the main entrance of the Great Church and down a hill on Storkyrkobrinken Street. At the bottom of the hill, they entered a small square, passed the House of Nobility, the Supreme Court Building and, Bolan noticed, several small cafés that each looked as if they undoubtedly served coffee.

He turned toward Rakestraw. "Something wrong with these places?" he asked.

Rakestraw stopped, surprised. "No, of course not. Just thought you might like to see a little of the city."

Bolan felt the hair on the back of his neck bristle. "Maybe some other time," he said. "Right now, though, while we're sight-seeing, American judges are falling like flies."

Rakestraw shrugged. He motioned toward a café down the street, then followed Bolan inside to a booth next to the window. A short, frail waitress with dark hair approached. Recognizing them as Americans, she spoke in broken, accented English. "What you will have?"

"*Kaffe.*" Rakestraw smiled pleasantly. He glanced across the table to Bolan.

"The same," Bolan said.

The waitress started to leave, but Rakestraw grabbed her arm. Looking at Bolan again, he said, "You eaten?"

The Executioner felt his impatience rising again. He hadn't come to Sweden to sample the food. He stared at Rakestraw.

The Company man averted his eyes and consulted the menu. He took his time, finally saying, "You might want to try the mutton, Pollock. It's excellent." To the waitress, he said, "Two orders of *farkott*, and let's change the coffee to a couple of beers. Pripp Bla would be good. And—"

Bolan had had enough. First Rakestraw had waited until the last possible second to make contact. Then there had been the ridiculously long, coded introduction when there probably wasn't another 1910 Yankees or 1914 Cubs cap on this side of the Atlantic. Next had come the "tour" of Stockholm's Old Town, and now Rakestraw wanted to order dinner at three in the afternoon.

The Executioner didn't know exactly what was up, but he had work to do. And he intended to do it now.

Reaching across the table, he took the menu from the other man's hand. "Two *kaffes*," he told the waitress.

The confused waitress frowned, shrugged, then walked off.

When Bolan looked back across the table, he saw that the CIA man's face had colored. The Executioner's eyebrows narrowed as he stared the man down once again. When he spoke, his voice had become a low growl. "Okay, Rakestraw. I don't know if you're deliberately stalling or just plain incompetent. But it doesn't matter to me right now. You've got exactly five seconds to start telling me what you know about the training camp. After that, I lose my sweet disposition and stuff both of these ridiculous caps down your throat."

Rakestraw drew back in surprise. "Okay, okay," he said. "Jeez...I just thought—"

"Three seconds," Bolan said.

Rakestraw looked at the Executioner for a moment, his gaze traveling from Bolan's face down the powerful shoulders and arms. He had a second to spare when he started talking again. "We don't know the location of the camp, only that it exists." He saw the look in Bolan's eyes and quickly held up his hand. "Wait!" he whispered. "What we *do* have is a lead toward it. We'd have run it down for you already, but there wasn't time."

"What's the lead?" Bolan demanded.

"A safe house they've been using," Rakestraw said. "Herbert Urquillo himself is supposed to have stayed there a few weeks ago." His hand moved inside the bush vest, and he pulled out a small notebook. Tearing the first page off, he handed it to Bolan.

The Executioner looked down at the address, then back up. "That's *all?*" he said.

"Well...yeah," Rakestraw said. "Except these. He reached into another pocket, produced two keys and shoved them across the table. "The little one opens a locker at the subway station on Brunnsgaten. Inside you'll find the weapons and ammo you requested."

Bolan's mind travelled back to the map of the city he'd studied during the flight. Brunnsgaten was far to the north of Old Town. There were plenty of subways closer. Another stall?

Rakestraw went on. "This key," he said, picking up the other one, "is to your room at the Amaranten." He forced a smile. "You're all booked in. It's top-of-the-line, Pollock. I think you'll like it. Want me to take you over and help you get settled?"

"No, and I don't plan to host a housewarming party, either," Bolan said, standing up as the waitress arrived with the coffee. He turned to leave.

Rakestraw grabbed the sleeve of his bush jacket as the waitress set the steaming cups on the table before walking away. "Wait," he said. When the woman had left again, he went on. "I've been assigned to work with you. What do you want me to do?"

Bolan glanced down at the two cups on the table. Then, looking back up into the CIA agent's eyes, he said, "Order the mutton." He placed both hands on the table and leaned in close to the CIA man. "And stay out of my way."

Without another word, he was gone.

THE SUBWAY STATION on the corner of Brunnsgaten and Sveavagen looked no different than the one from which the Executioner had boarded the underground train in Old Town. Though Sweden was noted the world over for its cleanliness, a thin layer of grime seemed to cover the turnstiles, tile floors and everything else in the depot.

Bolan saw the tall bank of lockers against the far wall. The top three rows were made up of compartments designed to hold luggage the size of the carryon in his hand. Larger stalls, for suitcases, ran the length of the bottom row. Through Brognola, he had requested that the CIA provide him with a Beretta 9 mm, a Desert Eagle .44 Magnum and either an Uzi or Heckler & Koch MP-5 submachine gun. The subgun meant he'd find the box that matched key number 1125 along the bottom row.

The yellow caution light in Bolan's brain began flashing as he neared the bank of lockers. He scanned the immediate area, waiting for whatever subconscious signal he had registered to surface and take shape. His eyes fell on a man who had just passed by to his side.

The man, who looked to be in his midforties, wore a charcoal gray suit, matching hat and scuffed black shoes. Bolan frowned, slowing his pace. He didn't know why he knew, but he knew there was more to the man than met the eye. More than the man wanted people to see. The Executioner's frown deepened, creasing his forehead. He could see no signs of a weapon beneath the gray suit, no telltale bulge beneath the coat or at the ankle of the man's pants.

So what had flashed the yellow light on?

Bolan watched the man's back as the gray suit continued toward the exit. Slowly the frown faded from the Executioner's face as he realized what had tipped him off. As he walked, the man swung his right arm several inches farther out from his body than the left arm. Bodybuilders who had developed their latissimus dorsi muscles to the point where their arms wouldn't hang straight anymore walked that way. But *both* of their arms extended out. No, only one type of man walked like the man in the gray suit.

Right-handed cops who had worked in uniform so long that the wide holster on their hip had become like a body part.

He watched the man disappear up the steps to the street, then turned back to the lockers. Probably just a coincidence. He glanced along the bottom row of metal cabinets. The keys still protruded from the locks in the lockers that were empty. They were missing from the ones that had been rented. As he scanned the numbers, Bolan's frown returned when he realized that the bottom row started with the number 1701.

He looked up. Number 1125 was in the third row down, the only box in the vicinity with the key missing. A smaller locker, it might contain the pistols, but could not possibly conceal a submachine gun.

A quick glimpse of indigo blue in the corner of his eye kept the Executioner from starting toward the locker. He turned in that direction, but the unusual color was gone.

Rakestraw? Had the CIA man followed him here?

And if so, why?

The yellow caution light was turning red now. For the benefit of anyone watching, Bolan raised his watch to his eyes. Then, with the expression of a man who'd just realized he had more time on his hands than he'd thought, he turned toward a small newsstand across the subway station.

As he moved toward the stand, he saw a figure in a denim jacket leaning against a pillar in the center of the depot. The face above the jacket watched him above the open *Playboy* magazine in the man's hands. The eyes dropped quickly back to the page when Bolan turned his way.

A middle-aged woman in a bright red dress passed him, pushing a baby carriage. Carefully, methodically, she looked the other way.

Bolan saw the men's room just to the side of the newsstand. He waited until the last possible second, then cut through the door, hurried into one of the stalls and shut the door behind him. Silently he lifted the lid on the toilet's tank and rested it on the bowl. Dropping the key to locker number 1125 into the water, he replaced the lid.

Footsteps announced somebody's entry into the men's room. The Executioner emerged from the stall to see the man in the denim jacket combing his hair in front of the mirror. Quickly washing his hands at the sink, Bolan walked nonchalantly back out of the rest room and over to the newsstand counter.

He bought a *New York Times,* pocketing all the change from his fifty-*krona* bill except a silver one-krona coin. Keeping the coin hidden between his fingers, he started toward the lockers once more.

The men and women watching him were Swedish police. Of that, he no longer had any doubt. And unless his eyes had played tricks on him, it was Wendell Rakestraw's indigo blue bush vest that had disappeared behind the pillar when the Executioner looked his way. Which meant Rakestraw had tipped the cops off that an American was about to pick up a cache of illegal weapons at locker 1125.

While trying to appear helpful, Rakestraw had been slowing Bolan down ever since the Executioner had arrived in Stockholm. What better way to do that than to get him arrested?

The Executioner hesitated as he neared the locker bank once more. He knew he could simply walk out of the station now, and nothing would happen. So far, the cops had no probable cause to arrest him. But if he did that, he'd have to go on about the mission unarmed, or spend time trying to score weapons on the streets—not an easy task for a foreigner in a country like Sweden.

Besides, ditching the surveillance now would only alert Rakestraw to the fact that Bolan was on to him. The CIA man knew where he was going. He could simply set another trap.

No, better to confront the problem now. Get it over with.

Bolan strode confidently up to locker number 1125 and moved in close. Using his body to conceal the exact movements of his hand, he quickly inserted the one-krona coin into the locker next to it—1126—and pulled the key from the door.

A second later he heard a pistol hammer cock behind him. "Freeze! *Polis!*" a deep voice commanded.

Bolan froze. A moment later the voice said, "Raise your hands over your head and turn around. Very slowly."

Bolan did as commanded, the key dangling from his fingers. He saw the man who had carried the *Playboy* gripping a Walther P-38 in both hands. The 9 mm hole in the end of the barrel stared at Bolan like a big deadly eye.

The gray-suited man stood next to the man. The woman with the baby carriage had produced a Carl Gustav M45 submachine gun from the carriage and aimed it at the Executioner's belly.

Wendell Rakestraw was nowhere to be seen.

A small crowd of gawking onlookers began to gather behind the police officers. The woman in the red dress turned, said something in Swedish, and they moved on.

The man in gray holstered his pistol beneath his coat and stepped cautiously forward, taking the key from Bolan's fingers. He pushed the Executioner out of the way, then stepped forward, inserted it into locker number 1125 and twisted.

The lock didn't move.

"You've got the wrong—" Bolan started to say.

"Silence!" the blond man commanded.

The man in gray tried again, twisting the key both ways. Finally he jerked it from the lock and looked at the number stamped on the side. Then, looking up, he rattled off a string of sentences in Swedish the Executioner couldn't understand.

The blond man spoke to the woman, who set her subgun back in the baby carriage and pulled Bolan's carryon bag from his hand. Quickly she searched through the contents, then looked up again and shook her head.

The man in denim patted the Executioner down, frowning when he found no lumps in the clothing. "What were you doing at this locker?" he asked.

Bolan shrugged. "Getting ready to put my bag inside."

The cop's eyes narrowed suspiciously. He indicated the bag still in the woman's hands with his pistol. "Then why did you *not* put it in? When you close the door and remove the key, it will not open again. Did you not know that?"

Bolan shrugged again. "Yeah, I knew it. I got a little confused, I guess. Having guns stuck in your back does that to a guy."

The blond cop glanced across the room to the spot where Bolan thought he had seen Rakestraw. His face took on an angry expression. Turning to the woman, he rattled off another long speech in Swedish.

Bolan caught only one word. But that one word was enough to confirm his suspicions.

The word was "Rakestraw." The blond man holstered his weapon. "Please accept my apologies, Mr...."

"Pollock. Rance Pollock."

"Mr. Pollock. We received a tip from a source who is usually reliable that an American fitting your description would be taking receipt of several illegal firearms here today. I hope you understand."

"Sure, Officer. You're just doing your job. Besides," Bolan said, smiling, "what a story to tell the guys on poker night when I get back."

The woman in the red dress handed back his bag.

"So I'm free to go?"

"Yes," the Swedish cop said. "And once again, please accept my apology." He held out his hand.

Bolan shook it, threw the strap of his carryon over his shoulder and glanced toward the lockers. More than likely, the police would continue to watch locker number 1125 to see if anyone else came to make the pickup. He could wait them out, of course, but that would take time.

A commodity neither the Executioner, nor the federal judges of the United States of America, had much of.

Bolan started toward the steps leading to the street— a street he hoped would lead toward the safe house, then with any luck, to the terrorist training camp, and eventually to the secret behind America's Choice.

The Executioner never counted on and rarely even hoped for luck. But this was one time he decided to make an exception.

Yes, this time he'd need all the luck the gods saw fit to send his way.

He'd be going after the terrorists unarmed.

CHAPTER FOUR

Stockholm's island suburb of Östermalm, floating above the water just east of Normalm, is primarily a residential district that also boasts several foreign embassies and consulates.

Bolan reached Östermalm via taxi and ferry, flagging down another cab as soon as the flatboat reached shore. He added one block to the address Rakestraw had scribbled on the notebook page to allow him to safely scope out the safe house while still in the cab. That would also assure that the driver didn't connect him to the address if police questioned the cabbie later.

And they would. Sooner or later, one way or another, there were bound to be some fireworks at the safe house.

The cab turned off a busy four-lane street in front of a small shopping center. The frame of a building in progress loomed from an otherwise-open lot behind the row of stores. A red-and-white sign announced the site as a future Burger King.

Another sign ahead formed an arc over the entrance to an apartment complex of perhaps twenty buildings, and stood just beyond the building materials stacked near the Burger King sign. Bolan read it as the cab passed under: The American Apartments.

After a quick glance to make sure the cabbie wasn't watching, the Executioner surveyed the first eight-unit apartment house they passed, noting the letter *A* affixed to the beige stucco wall. He glanced to the scrap of paper in his hand; "Building A, Apartment 5.

The cabbie drove on, and Bolan scanned the other units. Six feet of wooden shingles ringed each wall at the top. The roofs were flat. The television antennae jutting from the roof toward the sky, the shingles and the large block letters that identified each building were the two-story structures' only adornments.

The cab rolled to a halt. Bolan paid the driver and got out, strolling between Buildings E and F and into the courtyard. He passed several iron barbecues and a club house next to the swimming pool, all of which seemed as devoid of character as the buildings themselves.

Stopping at a building by the laundry room, he peered through the glass entryway. Leading off the hallway were the doors to the two apartments on his end. They appeared to be secured by nothing more than a simple "snap" lock. Another identical glass door and entryway were visible at the other end of the hall, and a set of rough cedar steps led up to the second floor.

Bolan turned his eyes to the nameplates on the outside of the building. A small black button stood next to each name. The buildings had simple security systems that consisted of an intercom and electronically controlled door-lock buzzers. An easy setup to override—if he'd had the right tools.

The Executioner walked on toward Building A. Even without the proper tools, he could eventually work his way through the security system with the Leatherman Pocket Survival Tool in his bush jacket.

But it would take longer and could easily draw attention. Not a good idea when dealing with terrorists.

A *particularly* bad idea since he was unarmed.

Bolan stopped against the side of a building and scanned the courtyard for curious eyes. Satisfied that no one was watching, he pulled a small notepad and pen from his jacket. He copied the address of the safe house, substituting Building D for A, then dropped it back into his pocket. Then, removing a Gold AT&T MasterCard in the name of Rance Pollock from his billfold, he slid it into the cuff of his bush jacket.

As he moved on to the entrance of Building A, his eyes fell on the name next to the 5. *Martinez.* Spanish.

Like Herbert Urquillo.

The name by apartment number one read *Sigridsson.* Bolan pushed the button and heard the buzz deep within the building. When it brought no response, he tried again. No answer.

Four more buzzes brought identical results. Bolan smiled, convinced that the Sigridssons weren't home. He moved down the list. Someone named Langer lived in apartment two. The Executioner rang.

"God dag?" came back through the intercom.

"Please," Bolan said. "I am a friend of the Sigridssons. From America. They loaned me a key to their apartment, but forgot the one to the front door. Could you buzz me in?"

There was a moment's pause inside, then the buzzer sounded.

Bolan pushed the door open. To his right, he saw the number 1 on the door. To his left stood 2.

The door to apartment two opened almost immediately. A squatty, shirtless man wearing blue work pants and house slippers stepped into the hall, a frown of indecision on his face.

Bolan knew what had happened—he had counted on it. The man had bought his story and pressed the button before he'd had time to think. Now he was having second thoughts.

"You are an American friend of the Sigridssons?" the man asked skeptically.

Bolan made a deprecating gesture with his hand, then shrugged as if to cover embarrassment. "Yes," he said. "And I am thankful you were in." He pulled a key ring from his pocket and started toward the door to number one.

The man stood watching.

Bolan moved in front of the door, using his body to shield his hands as he'd done at the subway lockers. He removed the credit card from his sleeve, slid it between the door and jamb, and twisted the knob.

The lock popped open.

The Executioner turned back to the man in the hall and smiled. "Thank you again," he said, still holding the key ring in his hand.

Relief flooded the man's face. He nodded and disappeared back into his apartment.

Bolan stepped into the Sigridsson's apartment and closed the door behind him. Unless he missed his guess, number five should be directly above him. That meant the floor plan would be the same. He surveyed the living room, then stepped into the dinette area and kitchen just to the right. Moving down a short hall, he saw a bathroom, utility room and finally the small bedroom. Satisfied that he knew the layout, he moved back to the front door. He cracked it open long enough to make sure the man across the hall was still in his apartment, then slipped out into the hall and locked the Sigridsson's door behind him.

Quickly, silently, he climbed the stairs leading to the second floor. He drew the phony address he'd just written from his pocket as he reached the landing, taking a deep breath and reminding himself he was unarmed.

This was recon. He'd check it out. Then he'd have to find some way to obtain weapons and come back.

Door number five looked no different than the others. The address in his right hand, Bolan tapped on the wood with his left. He heard the shuffle of feet inside and held his breath.

A moment later the lock clicked. Then the door swung slowly open to the end of a chain.

A long, narrow nose poked timidly into the opening. The Executioner's eyes focused, and the anger he'd had for Rakestraw began to rise in his chest once again.

Behind the nose, he saw an elderly, weathered face. The woman's thin gray hair had been pulled back into a tight bun. She wore a floral-print apron and held a wooden cooking spoon in her trembling hand as if it might serve as a weapon against whoever was about to attack her from the hall.

The crackling of grease in a frying pan drifted out into the hallway. Along with it came the odors of fish and boiling cabbage. Bolan smiled his warmest smile and held the address up to his eyes. "I am sorry to bother you," he said, "but I am lost. Could you tell me where Building D is?"

The old woman shrugged and shook her head. She didn't speak English.

Bolan smiled again and said, "Thank you." Then he descended the stairs once more.

The Executioner left the building and started down the street toward the Burger King. He wasn't sure at this point which he'd rather do, find the safe house—if there even *was* a safe house—or strangle Wendell Rakestraw.

The sun had dropped to the horizon as he drew abreast with the construction site. He glanced back over his shoulder to the second floor of the building he had just left. The bedroom was dark in apartment five. The living-room light was on, and behind it an old lady who was probably still frightened by the big, strange-talking man who'd come to her door was probably still frying fish.

Bolan shook his head in disgust, turned and walked on toward the shopping center. He looked up as a late-model Saab turned the corner and approached on the other side of the road. The driver, a dark-featured man wearing a neatly trimmed beard and navy blue beret, glanced his way as he passed. Another man, his face hidden in the shadows, sat in the passenger's seat.

Bolan kept walking. Behind him he heard the car engine slow. Glancing over his shoulder again, he saw the two men get out of the Saab. He studied their backs as they started toward the front door of Building A. Both men carried a box, and once again the yellow caution light went on in his brain. As soon as they'd entered the building, he hurried into the half-built Burger King and hid within the crop of studs and joists.

His eyes scanned the second floor of the building he'd just left. The men from the Saab could be going into any of the eight apartments, he knew. But he had come this far, and another few seconds to make sure wouldn't make any difference.

A moment later the light in the bedroom to apartment number five went on. The curtains were open, and inside, Bolan saw the two men enter the room and set their boxes on the bed. The bearded man with the beret started to open his box. The other man held up a hand stopping him, then crossed the room and reached for the draw cord.

Bolan took a deep breath as the man paused at the glass, looking down into the darkness, his face framed in light. A second later the curtain closed.

He stood staring at the window for a moment, then opened his carryon bag and pulled out the walkie-talkie.

Rakestraw might have sent him on a wild-goose chase, he thought as he activated the tiny scrambling device and plugged it into the unit, but this goose wasn't completely wild. The CIA knew that Hal Brognola was not without clout in Washington, and they were throwing in just enough truth to cover their butts if it ever hit the fan.

The Executioner adjusted the squelch. Dispensing with radio formalities, he pressed the button, held the transmitter to his lips and said, "You there, Jack?"

Bolan thought of the frightened little gray-haired woman he'd been afraid he'd upset. What perfect window dressing for a safe house.

Grimaldi's voice came to him over the airwaves. "That's a big affirmative, Striker." In the background Bolan could hear a plane landing.

"Get on the horn to Stony Man. Make sure Phoenix Force is still in Germany, then go pick them up and bring them back here to me." He told Grimaldi where he was.

The engines were already revving when the pilot answered. "On my way, big guy. I'll radio Stony Man as soon as I'm in the air."

Bolan looked back to the curtain over the bedroom window in apartment A-5. In spite of the old woman and the red herrings the CIA had thrown his way, he was now certain that apartment five really was a terrorist safe house. It had to be.

He didn't know who the guy in the beret had been.

But the face of the man in the window had belonged to Herbert Urquillo.

THE TWO MEN stopped in front of the door to apartment number five. Herbert Urquillo set the box in his arms carefully on the hall floor and inserted the key into the lock. The door opened before he could twist the knob, and Urquillo looked into the frightened eyes. "What's wrong, Mother?" the Basque asked.

The gray-haired woman squinted through her thick spectacles. "There was a man here, Herbie," Maria Urquillo answered.

Urquillo smiled inwardly. His mother and father had started him off on the road to becoming the world-renowned freedom fighter he had become. They had been leaders within the Basque Homeland and Liberty Party until his father's assassination by Spanish police three years before. Since then, his mother's courage had faded. There had been a time when Maria Urquillo was known far and wide as fearless and even more ruthless in her treatment of prisoners than her husband. But she was getting older now. And lately she had seen the ghostly face of the capitalist enemy on nearly every man she encountered.

Lifting the box again, Urquillo carried it past his mother into the living room, motioning Franco to follow.

"Herbie, did you hear me?" Maria asked.

Urquillo sighed. "What did he want, Mother?" He moved on toward the bedroom.

She shook her head. "I don't know. He tried to *act* like he was lost . . . looking for an address. I pretended not to understand."

Urquillo held the box against the wall with his chest and opened the door. "But you don't believe that was the reason he was here?" His hand groped for the light switch.

"No," said the frail voice behind him.

Urquillo set his box on the bed. Facing away from his mother, he winked at Franco. The bearded man let a tiny smile of tolerance creep onto his face, then returned the wink.

Urquillo sighed to himself. His fellow Basques knew the services Maria Urquillo had provided over the years. She was a hero of the revolution, and they were prepared to humor her out of respect for the past.

Maria moved in next to her son and grabbed his arm with both of her withered hands. She looked up accusingly. "You think I am a foolish old woman," she said.

Franco answered for him. "No, not at all, Señora Urquillo," he said. "It is your careful watchfulness that keeps us on our toes." He pulled a large lock-blade folding knife from his pocket and sliced through the tape that held the top flaps on the parcel he had carried.

Urquillo felt an uneasiness come over him. He must not allow his mother's paranoia to make him complacent. He had seen the big man walking toward the shopping center as they passed the site of the Burger King. Could that have been the man? He glanced to the window. "Wait," he said, grabbing Franco's arm. Moving swiftly to the glass, he stared down into the night. The wooden framework on the concrete foundation looked like the skeleton of some prehistoric monster in the darkness. It appeared deserted. Breathing a sigh of relief, he drew the curtains.

The Basque took the knife from Franco and began slicing through the tape at the top of his box, his own thoughts now colored by some of his mother's concern. This apartment had served as a safe house for over six months now. It was impossible to establish such a hideout, and then live in it, without taking some chances. And while the inevitable clues as to the apartment's true purpose were usually so small they went unnoticed by the neighbors, six months was a long time. Many mistakes of which they were not even aware could have been made. The total of those mistakes could be worth more than the sum of the parts to curious eyes.

Urquillo's knife stopped momentarily. He had formalized the new alliance with *señor* over two weeks ago. The first strike he would do for the German was scheduled for tomorrow. Two weeks...plenty of time for a leak on *that* end, as well.

He turned to his mother with a different expression on his face. "Describe the man, Mother," he said.

"He was tall...very tall," she said. "Dark hair and eyes." She paused, as if trying to recollect an image. "Not handsome in the classic way, but... I suppose if I were younger... I would have found him attractive. Even though he attempted to appear confused and uncertain of himself, I could tell that was not the case. He had much machismo. He was *muy hombre*."

Again the uneasiness swept over him. His mother sometimes imagined ghosts in the night. But that did not mean a *real* ghost could not come visiting. He turned to Franco. "As soon as this strike is complete, we must move," he said.

"But, amigo," Franco started, "we have no reason to believe—" He cut himself off in midsentence, glanced to Maria Urquillo, then added, "*Sí*, Herbert. I will make the necessary arrangements as soon as the mission is complete."

Urquillo nodded, then reached into the box and withdrew several small, rectangular metal boxes. The words Carga De Demolicion and Pelegro, Alto Explosivo were stenciled in white across the black paint. The sight of the Chilean-made demolition charges drove the concern from his chest and replaced it with the thrill he always felt just before a mission.

At first Ennslin had wanted him to simply assassinate American consuls in Europe. But explosives were Herbert Urquillo's specialty. He had convinced the German that he could create a bigger stir with a few bombings. Ennslin himself had supplied the charges from South America.

"I kill, therefore I am," Urquillo said out loud, laughing softly. He held one of the charges up for inspection. These two boxes were barely the tip of the iceberg. There were dozens more in the hands of Urquillo's men at another place of safety. The Basque terrorist grinned at Franco. "They are not big, are they, *hombre?*" he said.

The other man smiled back. "No, Herbert," he said. "They are *muy chico,* considering what they are capable of doing."

"*Sí,*" Herbert Urquillo agreed, then added, "and they are more than capable of blowing the American Embassy in Sweden into the hell it so richly deserves, eh?"

YAKOV KATZENELENBOGEN stared through the darkness into the clearing ahead. The moonless sky reminded him of the many black nights he had spent in the desert in his adopted homeland of Israel. But here the stars overhead provided sufficient light to enable him to see the ebony form of Calvin James belly-crawling toward the back door of the Bavarian farmhouse.

Katz took a deep breath and glanced to the glowing hands of his watch. The other men should be in place around the clearing by now. He raised his prosthetic right arm and keyed the radio mike on his belt. "One to Two," the Israeli whispered into the face mike. "Confirm."

Rafael Encizo came back. "In position and waiting," he said.

"One to Three," Katz said softly.

"Dug in and ready," Gary Manning answered.

Katz got a similar response from David McCarter, and breathed a sigh of relief. The men inside the house had not even bothered to post a guard, so secure were they in their belief that their whereabouts were not known. That was fine with Katz. As a Mossad operative, and now as the leader of Stony Man's top foreign counterterrorist team, Phoenix Force, Katz had already lived through enough challenging missions for ten lifetimes.

Not that he minded a challenge. Like all of the men from Stony Man Farm, he seemed to thrive on them. But an easy assignment like this once in a while wasn't too bad, either.

A familiar feminine voice suddenly spoke into Katz's ear. "Stony Man Control to Phoenix One. Come in, Phoenix One," Barbara Price said.

Katz frowned, unconsciously looking up to the sky, toward the invisible satellite that had relayed the surprise message all the way from the United States. He had talked to Price less than half an hour before, informing her that they had finally located the cell of former East German scientists and secret police who were in the process of constructing a nuclear bomb. Stony Man Farm's mission controller knew Phoenix Force was about to attack.

Which meant that nothing short of a more immediate emergency could cause her to interrupt them.

"Come in, Stony Man," Katz said into the mike, his voice barely audible.

"Ten-twenty, Phoenix?"

"We're *there*." In the clearing he saw James crawling back toward the trees. "We attack in *seconds*."

There was a long pause on the other end, then Price said, "Ten-four, Phoenix One. Proceed, then advise at first available opportunity. I have a ten-five from Striker." Her microphone clicked off.

Calvin James came on. "What's happening, One?"

"Nothing," Katz said. "At least for now. Advise?"

"Close to a dozen unfriendlies inside, best I could tell," James said. "I got a look into the living room. It's set up as a lab. Couple of white coats still awake and working. They got a nuke going, all right." He whistled quietly. "I'm no expert, and I don't know exactly how close they are to finishing up, but when it gets to the point that *I* can recognize the thing as a nuke, I'd say we got here just in time." He paused for air. "And I do know champagne when I see it. They got a table full of bottles in ice buckets against the wall. They're getting ready to celebrate."

"Affirmative," Katz said. "Everyone ready?"

He got four more affirmatives.

"Then let's go."

Squeezing the pistol grip of his Uzi with his left hand, the Phoenix Force leader stepped out into the clearing and broke into a jog toward the house. He saw the moving forms of the rest of the team as they converged from all angles. Each member wore one of the tight blacksuits made famous by the man they called Striker, and carried an Uzi submachine gun and various other equipment.

Encizo and Manning disappeared from sight as they mounted the front steps to the house. Katz increased his pace as Calvin James fell in at his side. The black Phoenix Force warrior took the lead, sending a combat boot crashing into the back door a fraction of a second after the wood splintered at the front of the house.

James sprinted through the door into what appeared to be a laundry room, Katz at his heels. The black man's Uzi spat Phoenix Force's first rounds as a surprised East German, cradling a Walther MPL, stepped into the hallway to see what was going on. The subgun fell from his lifeless hands as James's Uzi stitched a figure eight from his knees to his throat.

Katz pushed past his teammate and leapfrogged over the corpse into the kitchen. Two more former East German secret-police officers stood up at the kitchen table. The lean-looking one was first to recover and tried to raise a KKMPi 69 training rifle.

Firing one-handed, Katz tapped the trigger on his Uzi and sent a 3-round burst into the thug's chest. The Model 69 sent a wild spray of .22-caliber rimfires into the ceiling as the German's fingers spasmed on the trigger. Katz second burst dropped the man to the floor.

Out of the corner of his eye, Katz saw the second man level his Heckler & Koch G11 caseless rifle. The Israeli started to turn the Uzi his way, realizing even as he moved that he'd be a fraction of a second too late.

A burst of fire from behind Katz caused the former Mossad man to drop to one knee. The German slammed back against the kitchen wall, then slid to a sitting position.

Calvin James stepped into the kitchen and smiled.

More automatic fire came from the front of the house. Katz leaped to his feet and sprinted down a short hallway. He caught a flash of movement as he passed what appeared to be a bedroom door. Throwing himself forward, he hit the floor in a shoulder roll as a burst of automatic fire flew over his head.

"James!" Katz screamed. "The door!"

The Israeli rolled back to his feet as pain from an old shoulder wound shot through his nervous system. He dropped back to one knee and inched toward the door as James, still on the other side, moved cautiously to the opening. Katz looked up into the grim face of the black warrior, then whispered, "One... two...three!" He dived to his belly in the doorway as James angled his Uzi around the corner.

Katz fired up. Above him he heard James's subgun sputtering in time to his own. Hot brass rained over his back. Automatic bursts from both warriors penetrated the torsos and heads of three men with H&K MP-5s in the bedroom.

James reached down, jerking the Israeli to his feet before the last German had hit the floor. They sprinted on down the hall toward the gunfire in the living room.

A man suddenly appeared running toward the two Phoenix Force men. Trying to put on the brakes, he succeeded only in slowing the inevitable crash with the Israeli.

Katz jammed the barrel of his Uzi into the man's midsection as they made contact. The subgun bucked against both men as it sent 9 mm rounds shooting through the German's gut. The German's forward momentum sent Katz sprawling to the floor. He bounded back to his feet and turned into the living room, James at his heels.

Manning and Encizo had left as many bodies in their wake as Katz and James. As they entered the room, Manning downed the last of the East German secret-police officers. Encizo held two men in lab coats cowering against the wall, their hands raised above their heads.

Manning, Phoenix Force's explosives expert, walked to the table in the center of the living room. He frowned as he studied the parts of the warhead. "Your champagne analysis wasn't far off, Calvin," he said. "They might not have finished it tonight, but it wouldn't have been long before—"

A flash of white caught Katz's eye. He swung his Uzi toward the men in the lab coats in time to see the Walther P5 compact pistol come out of one of the coats.

The eyes of the man holding the pistol were wild and desperate behind his thick black glasses. He trained the weapon on Calvin James, the tendons in his hand tightening as he started to pull the trigger.

Katz tapped the trigger, and a spray of 9 mm slugs reddened the white coat. As the man tumbled to his knees, the other scientist drew a pistol and turned toward the window. Firing blindly over his shoulder, he dived into the opening, shattered the glass and was gone.

Encizo started after him, but Katz caught him by the sleeve. "Stay here. You don't want to get hit by a stray round."

Katz had barely finished talking when a 3-round burst of fire split the silence outside. A moment later

David McCarter stuck his head inside the broken window. "I've got some good news and some bad news," the former SAS man said in his Cockney accent. Without waiting for a reply, he went on, "The good news is that chap won't be working on any more nuclear weapons. At least not in *this* life." He paused. "The bad news—"

The flopping blades of a helicopter outside the house drowned him out.

"*That's* the bad news," McCarter said, pointing over his shoulder.

Katz dropped the magazine from his Uzi and shoved a fresh box up the grip. "Okay, get ready," he said. "Manning, take the front. Encizo, you and—"

For the second time that night, Barbara Price interrupted the Israeli. "Stony Man, Phoenix One," she said over the headset. "Hold your fire. That's Grimaldi in the chopper."

Katz squinted into the darkness and saw the familiar silhouette of Jack Grimaldi in the glass bubble.

"Grab the nuke and hop on board," Price said. "Striker has cordially invited you to a little reception he's about to give."

"Ten-four, Stony." Katz nodded toward the other men, who immediately began grabbing the nuclear components. He walked toward the table against the wall where the celebration champagne was chilling in metal buckets.

The former Mossad man smiled. That celebration would never take place. He grabbed the neck of one of the bottles and pulled it from the bucket, his smile widening when he saw the label.

Roederer Cristal. His favorite.

Slinging the Uzi over his shoulder, Katz stuffed the bottle into his backpack and started toward the chopper that had landed in the clearing. Maybe a little celebration ought to take place after all. One bottle divided between the five men of Phoenix Force and Jack Grimaldi wouldn't be enough to alter their judgment or reflexes.

But the festivities would have to take place during the flight to wherever they were headed.

Yakov Katzenelenbogen had yet to see the day when there was time to party with Mack Bolan around.

THE LIGHTS above the shopping-center parking lot shone through the upright studs of the Burger King, casting an eerie silhouette on the dirt between Building A and the corner where Bolan stood. He stared at the black picture. The striped shadows made it look as if he was a prisoner confined within a barred cell.

The symbolism wasn't lost on the Executioner. In effect, he was a prisoner. He had been confined to surveillance of the apartment most of the night. His only furlough had been a few minutes during which he had skirted through the darkness to the parking area around Building A and hot-wired a Nissan Optima. The car stood waiting in case Urquillo and the other man left unexpectedly.

Bolan lifted his wrist to his face, staring at the luminous hands of his watch. Almost 0100. The Scandinavian sun of summer would come creeping over the horizon in another couple of hours to further complicate things. So the Executioner had made a decision.

The arrival of daybreak would signal that he had waited long enough. If the men of Phoenix Force had not arrived by then, he would take the apartment down by himself. Unarmed.

Bolan heard a click in his ear, and his hand rose automatically to the headset. He played with the squelch, then heard a familiar voice say "Shalom."

"Shalom back to you," Bolan whispered. "Where are you?"

From somewhere near the swimming pool within the dark shadows of the apartment complex, a light flashed on, then off. Then, one by one, four more flashlights scattered around the grounds and circling Building A repeated the performance.

Katz spoke again. "Price briefed us during the flight. We brought your weapons. There is an old woman inside?"

"That's affirmative," Bolan said. "Don't know if she's a friendly or not, but give her a wide berth." He paused, feeling his eyebrows lower in concentration as he stared at the building in the distance. His trick with the door-buzzer system wouldn't work again—especially in the middle of the night. Which meant there was no quiet way to enter the building. Speed would have to substitute. "James, you listening?" he finally said.

"Ten-four, Striker," James whispered into the radio.

"You and Encizo circle the building and meet me at the front door. We'll go in hard and fast." Clearing his throat, he went on. "Katz, take the door at your end of the hallway. McCarter, you and Manning stay outside. Cover the bedroom and living-room windows. Everybody got it?"

The Executioner got five "affirmatives."

"Then let's do it."

Bolan stepped from the framework and jogged across the open field to Building A, stopping in front of the glass door. James and Encizo appeared around the corner of the building. James shoved a sound-suppressed Beretta 93-R and Desert Eagle .44 Magnum into Bolan's hands.

Bolan stuck the Eagle in his belt and palmed the Beretta.

McCarter and Manning raced by behind them and took up their positions, Uzis trained up at the windows. All of the men of Phoenix Force wore black-suits and matching Kevlar backpacks to carry their extra equipment.

Bolan looked through the glass down the hall to the opposite door. He saw Katz step out of the shadows. The Phoenix Force leader raised his prosthetic arm and nodded.

Holding the Beretta high above his head, the Executioner bent his wrist and aimed down at the carpet on the other side of the door. He double-actioned the first round, and the Beretta coughed quietly, sending a 9 mm hollowpoint through the glass and safely into the floor. A splintery hole appeared in the door. Bolan fired again, then again and again. Each time the 93-R sputtered, the thick glass splintered farther. Most of the fragments fell silently inside on the carpet. A few clinked quietly to the concrete steps.

So far, so good—they hadn't made enough noise to be noticed.

But that was about to change.

Bolan turned toward James and Encizo. The men signaled their readiness. He thumbed the Beretta to 3-

round burst, then took a half step back and sent a foot crashing through the broken glass.

The silence of the night was suddenly broken as the glass avalanched to the ground.

Fragments still fell as Bolan sprinted through the steel door frame and headed for the stairs. Behind him he heard the pounding of James's and Encizo's combat boots. Taking the steps three at a time, Bolan pivoted around the railing. Without breaking stride, he lowered a shoulder and crashed into the door to apartment five.

The hollow-core door swung in. Bolan ground to a halt in the doorway, found the light switch on the wall and switched it on.

The bearded man who had worn the beret bolted to a sitting position on the couch against the living-room wall, a Government Model .45 automatic in his hand. He blinked involuntarily as the overhead light hit his pupils.

Bolan triggered the Beretta, firing from the hip and sending a burst into the bearded man's chest. He flew back against the wall, his eyes never opening again.

Bolan sprinted through the room, down the hall toward the closed bedroom door. James followed, while Encizo cut into the kitchen. James fell off as they passed the bathroom, shouldering his way through the door, his Uzi extended in front of him.

Bolan stopped at the bedroom and pressed his back against the hall wall. No gunfire had come from the kitchen or bathroom, which meant that Urquillo had to be on the other side of the door. But it also meant something else.

The old woman had to be there, too.

And Urquillo had had plenty of time by now to get ready.

Slowly Bolan reached out and twisted the doorknob. He pushed the door open.

And saw exactly what he had feared he would see.

Herbert Urquillo stood in the center of the room wearing only faded blue jeans. He had found time to locate a short, sawed-off Rossi double-barreled 12-gauge.

The old woman wore a light blue robe. She was bent painfully in Urquillo's headlock. Both barrels of the shotgun were pressed into her ear, and her faded gray eyes were wide with horror.

Urquillo's grin was cocky.

The Executioner heard footsteps behind him. James and Encizo skidded to a halt at his sides.

Training the Beretta on Urquillo, Bolan said, "Let her go."

Urquillo slumped farther behind his hostage. "No, I do not think that would be wise," he said in a steady voice. "And I would not advise you to try what you are thinking of. The chances of hitting the old woman are too good. And if you do manage to hit me, I will pull both triggers with my dying breath. Now, drop your weapon."

Bolan didn't move.

"Do you want this old woman's death on your conscience?" Urquillo demanded.

"Maybe," Bolan said. "It depends on who she is."

Urquillo's grin became a laugh. "I will tell you who she is," he said. "She is an old bitch whose mind left her years ago. But she's been the perfect cover. We could even leave her here alone without fear that she would talk, because she could not even figure out what we were doing.'' He threw back his head and laughed.

The Executioner felt the anger building in his chest. He studied the horror in the old woman's eyes. Though it looked genuine, Urquillo's story seemed outrageous.

The problem was that, however unlikely the story, it was possible.

Urquillo tightened his grip around the old woman's neck. "Now, I told you to drop your guns. All of you,'' he instructed.

Bolan shook his head. "The minute we do that, you'll be free to kill the woman and all of us. No, you want out of here, then go. But we aren't giving up our weapons.''

Indecision flashed in Urquillo's eyes, then the smile returned. He indicated the side of the room with his head. "Move against the wall,'' he said.

Bolan, James and Encizo moved out of the doorway.

Urquillo maneuvered toward the hallway, keeping the old woman in front of himself. "How many men do you have around the perimeter?'' he demanded.

Bolan hesitated. There was always a chance that Katz, McCarter or Manning could get a clean shot at Urquillo as he left the building. And that chance would be better if the Basque didn't know their number or positions. The down side of that theory was that if he lied to Urquillo, and the terrorist discovered it, he might kill the old woman out of spite.

Of course, he might do that anyway.

His hand moving unobtrusively, Bolan keyed the microphone so Katz, Manning and McCarter could hear him speak. The more the men below picked up on, the better.

"Two men," he said. "They're below the windows."

Urquillo's eyes focused on Bolan's headset. "Tell them to lower their weapons."

Bolan spoke into the mouthpiece. "Striker to Phoenix. He's coming out with a hostage. Let him go."

Katz's voice came back into Bolan's ear. "Can he hear me?" the Israeli asked.

"Negative," Bolan said.

"What did they say?" Urquillo demanded.

Bolan held up his hand, listening.

"If the opportunity presents itself—" Katz said.

"Take advantage of it," Bolan answered.

"What did *you* say?" Urquillo almost screamed. "If you are trying something—"

"Relax," Bolan said. "He said he felt useless on this deal. I told him to take advantage of the situation."

Urquillo's eyes narrowed into a ferretlike scowl. He jammed the shotgun into the woman's ear again. "For *her* sake, I hope you are telling the truth." He began backing out of the room. "If you leave the apartment before I am gone, I will kill her. If your friends below try anything, I will kill her." He disappeared down the hall.

Bolan moved to the window. "Katz," he said. "They're on their way down. Don't let him see you."

"I picked up on that much," the Israeli said. "I've moved behind Building B."

"Good. He'll be heading for the Saab on Manning and McCarter's side. Keep out of sight, but make your way to the Nissan Optima on the other side of the building. It's wired and ready. Follow him, and keep us updated. We'll find other wheels.''

''Ten-four, Striker.''

''Damn,'' Rafael Encizo said. Bolan turned toward the bed to see the Cuban holding a demolition charge. Encizo nodded toward two boxes on the floor. ''They're full of them.'' He paused. ''At least Urquillo didn't get out of here with them.''

Bolan frowned. The Basque terrorist's hands had been full with the old woman, sure, but the demo charges should have still been foremost in Urquillo's mind. And he had not even made any attempt to take the boxes. That could mean only one thing.

''There must be more where those came from,'' Bolan said. ''And we'll have to find them. He's got something big planned.'' He turned back to the window.

In the darkness below, Bolan saw Urquillo and his hostage appear. The terrorist continued to use the old woman as a shield. Manning and McCarter dropped their Uzis to the end of their slings and stepped back against the building, letting the two pass.

Urquillo backed up to the Saab and said something to the old woman. She reached out and opened the door. The terrorist sat down in the driver's seat and pulled her onto his lap, swung his legs inside and closed the door.

The two silhouettes blended into one indistinguishable form as the dome light went out.

The Saab's engine turned over, and the car backed out of the parking space. A moment later it was heading past the Burger King construction site toward the shopping center.

"Go after them, Katz," Bolan yelled into the headset as he raced down the hall and through the living room. "We'll catch up to you."

CHAPTER FIVE

Katz spotted the Optima as he rounded the corner of Building B. He sprinted toward the vehicle, yanking the door open as he shrugged out of his backpack. He had thrown it inside the vehicle and slid behind the wheel when he heard Bolan's voice in his ear. "Go after them, Katz."

Bolan had already cracked the steering column and located the wires. The Israeli touched them together, and the Nissan choked to life. Katz backed out of the parking space and cut around the building.

The Saab was passing the Burger King site as he pulled out of the parking lot.

The Phoenix Force leader kept the headlights off, letting the Saab take a quarter-mile lead. It turned right at the shopping center before heading north to the thoroughfare and turning west. Traffic was light in the early-morning hours, and the Israeli settled in behind the wheel.

"You with them?" Bolan's voice asked in his ear.

"Affirmative, Striker," Katz answered. "Heading west."

"We've found a van that'll hold us all," the Executioner came back. "McCarter's working on it now. We'll have it running in a minute or so."

"I'll keep them in sight as you advised." Katz followed the Saab to Highway E4 as the early Scandinavian sun came up. Traffic was light, and with better visibility, he dropped farther back as they left Stockholm and started toward Södertälje to the south. The former Mossad operative notified Bolan and the rest of Phoenix Force, learning in the process that they had indeed gotten the van started. But they were far behind.

Minutes became an hour. As the workday approached, the traffic began to thicken. Katz considered the situation. Three vehicles now separated him from the Saab, but that was as close as he dared get without tipping his hand. But by staying that far back, he risked losing Urquillo and the old woman. Exits were appearing with increasing frequency as they neared Södertälje, and in the blink of an eye his quarry could cut unexpectedly across the exit and be gone.

No, Katz decided as they passed by Södertälje and continued southwest, it was time to take some risks. Getting spotted was preferable to losing his prey at this stage of the game. At least Urquillo hadn't seen him back at the safehouse, and wouldn't recognize him if he spotted the Optima. But the terrorist *would* recognize his clothing.

Katz glanced up into the rearview mirror and saw the black makeup night stripes still crossing his face. The turtleneck of his blacksuit was also visible.

Guiding the Nissan with his prosthetic hand, the ex-Mossad man shrugged out of the shoulder holster housing his Beretta 92, then unzipped the backpack on the seat beside him. He pulled out a red-and-black plaid flannel shirt, slipped it over his shoulder, then switched hands on the steering wheel and worked his prosthetic arm inside. He took a deep breath, then pulled into the passing lane and cut in front of one of the cars separating him from the Saab.

That was the easy part. Now for the pants. The blacksuit legs looked like leotards beneath the tail of the flannel shirt—maybe not commandolike, but weird enough to put Urquillo on guard the moment he saw them.

Katz pulled a pair of khaki work pants out of his pack and set them on the seat. With one hand, he unzipped the sides of his paratrooper boots and struggled out of them. Dropping the pants on the floor of the Nissan, he stuck his feet inside and began working them up his legs.

"Stony One to Phoenix One," sounded in the Israeli's ear.

"I'm listening," Katz said. He thrust his hips up off the seat, leaned forward and guided the car with his chest as he pulled the pants to his waist. The movement sent the Nissan swerving dangerously close to a Toyota in the next lane.

"Ten-twenty?" Bolan asked.

Katz looked at the passing signs. He couldn't read, speak or understand Swedish, but their increasing frequency told him they were getting close to the next city. He pulled a map from his pack and spread it on the passenger's seat. "We're closing in on Norrköping, as best I can tell," the Israeli said. "I'm going to have to stop them somehow, Striker. The traffic's getting too thick. Too many exits. We're going to lose them if I don't."

There was a long pause on the other end. Then Bolan said, "Okay. But don't let them make you. Otherwise, Urquillo will kill the woman." After another pause he added, "See if you can sideswipe their car, Katz. Make it look like an accident."

Katz nodded silently, a plan already starting to take shape in his mind. But it would be easier said than done.

He pulled back into the passing lane, getting an irritated honk from a Volkswagen driver coming up on his left. Maybe if he drove recklessly enough to get the Saab's attention, it would look normal when he hit them. He floored the accelerator, passed another Toyota and the Mazda directly behind the Saab, and drew abreast of Urquillo.

Katz stared straight ahead, but out of the corner of his eye, he saw the terrorist behind the wheel. The old woman sat in the passenger's seat. Both wore seat belts. Urquillo glanced toward the Optima, then turned back.

A thought suddenly struck the Phoenix Force leader. The champagne. Price's briefing had taken a good deal of the time during the flight from Germany, and he'd forgotten all about the celebration he'd planned.

The Phoenix Force leader reached into the backpack again, withdrawing the bottle he'd taken from the farmhouse in Germany. He flipped the corkscrew out of his Swiss Army knife and popped the cork. Raising it to his lips, he took a long pull, watching the Saab out of the corner of his eye.

In the lane next to him, Urquillo frowned.

Katz smiled. Sweden had some of the toughest drunk-driving laws in the world, and the brazen drinking-and-driving that Urquillo was seeing was a highly unusual sight. Even a hardened terrorist like him was surprised.

Which was exactly what the Israeli wanted.

Holding the champagne to his mouth again, Katz took another swig, then dropped the bottle onto the seat. The bubbly wine poured out onto the floorboard as he floored the accelerator and shot forward, swerving back and forth as he passed the Saab.

The Nissan's back fender scraped the front of Urquillo's car as Katz cut into the right-hand lane.

The Israeli swerved two more times, skidding off onto the shoulder in a whirlwind of gravel, then guiding the car back onto the highway as he watched in the rearview mirror.

Traffic was too heavy behind the Saab for Urquillo to slow down. The Israeli smiled. His foot shot to the brake.

The Optima's tires squealed in agony as the car slowed. He braced himself for the impact he knew was about to come. He heard the screeching of tires behind him as Urquillo stomped his own brakes.

But not in time.

The Saab crashed into the back of the Optima with a loud, sickening crunch. White headlights and red-and-orange taillights shattered, and Katz watched the rainbow of flying glass in the mirror as he was thrown forward against the seat belt.

Behind the crack-up, more tires screamed. Horns blasted shock and anger from the drivers as they twisted their steering wheels to avoid the wreckage.

Both the Saab and Optima skidded to a halt on the shoulder. The Saab's engine choked and died.

Katz spoke quickly into the mike. "Phoenix to Stony, I've got him stopped alongside the road. I'm exiting the vehicle now. I'll attempt a shot, if I get one. If not, I'll try to stall until you get here."

"Affirmative, Phoenix," Bolan said. "We're closing in."

Katz glanced quickly at the Beretta on the car seat. He could hide it under the flannel shirt, but if Urquillo saw the bulge or he was a second too slow drawing it...

No, the Israeli thought as he opened the door and stepped out onto the shoulder, there was a better way.

Nonchalantly reaching across his body, Katz cocked the .22 Magnum single-shot device hidden within his prosthetic arm. He weaved drunkenly toward the Saab, his eyes squinting as if in hangover.

Urquillo's head rested on the steering wheel, his eyes closed. The old woman was on the other side of him.

Katz angled to the side, since .22 Magnum slugs were among the most penetrating of rounds, and he feared his shot might pass through Urquillo and into his passenger. "You all right?" he slurred.

His arm rose as if in greeting, aiming at the terrorist's head.

Before he could fire, Urquillo sat up, aiming a 9 mm Star Super at the Phoenix Force leader.

Katz's brain registered the movement a fraction of a second too late.

Urquillo fired.

The bullet struck Katz in the forearm of his prosthesis, causing his own shot to fly high and to the left. The Israeli dived forward, rolling beneath Urquillo's window and under the Saab as a second 9 mm bullet drilled past his ear.

Katz heard the key twist in the ignition and knew his mistake as soon as he'd made it. The Saab's engine coughed back to life.

He had a choice now. He could emerge from hiding to be shot, or stay where he was and let Urquillo run him over.

Katz belly-crawled farther under the vehicle as the transmission slid into gear. His only chance would be to surface on the old woman's side, then work his way around the rear of the Saab, back to the Optima and his weapons.

The Israeli's head shot out from under the car. He looked up to see the old woman leaning out the window.

A snub-nosed .38 was gripped in her wrinkled hand. The sights pointed down at Katz's eyes.

Katz jerked his head back like a turtle retreating into its shell. The old woman's pistol bucked in her hand, the round ricocheting off the blacktop a foot away.

The Phoenix Force leader had no time to consider the woman's apparent change in roles. "Striker!" he shouted into the facemike. "The old woman's no hostage! She's one of them!"

The voice that came back was clear and brisk. "Ten-four, Phoenix," Bolan said. "We've got visual on you now. Hang tight. We're coming."

Katz twisted again beneath the Saab. Between the rear wheels, he saw a white Chevy van passing the stalled traffic on the shoulder. Uzi barrels extended from the windows toward the Saab. Automatic fire suddenly blasted above the shouting drivers and honking horns.

The Saab's tires spun, and the smell of burning rubber filled the Israeli's sinuses. Katz flattened himself against the asphalt and closed his eyes.

The Saab raced over him, the oil pan scraping across the back of the flannel shirt and taking several inches of skin in its wake. Katz jumped to his feet and saw the van skid to a halt ten feet away. The side door slid open.

James and Manning jerked their leader into the vehicle as Bolan hit the accelerator again. The van took off down the shoulder after the Saab.

David McCarter looked at Katz as the Israeli caught his breath. "How do you know she's with Urquillo?" he asked.

The Israeli shook his head. "She tried to kill me," he said between gasps.

The Brit sat back and nodded. His face deadpan, he said, "A reasonable deduction."

Katz leaned forward between the seats, staring through the windshield ahead. The Saab left the shoulder and returned to the highway. Metal trim and the front bumper fell from the damaged vehicle and bounced back over the van. Bolan guided them expertly through the steel hailstorm after the Saab, swerving to pass slower-moving traffic with the grace of an Indianapolis 500 driver.

Even after what he'd just been through, Katz caught himself smiling. Mack Bolan was the consummate warrior. He had founded both Phoenix Force and Able Team. Over the years the big man had been known as the Executioner, Striker, Colonel John

Phoenix and half a dozen other aliases. But whatever you called him, Bolan's skills never ceased to amaze Yakov Katzenelenbogen.

The two vehicles raced past the Norrköping exits and veered west toward Linköping. Then, as they rounded a curve, flashing orange lights suddenly appeared ahead. Signs raced by at the sides of the road. Katz couldn't read the words, but the warnings had to mean construction ahead.

Rafael Encizo pointed to the Saab from his shotgun seat. "They aren't slowing any, Striker," he said, turning to face Bolan.

The big man behind the wheel nodded silently. He didn't slow, either.

The two vehicles raced around another curve, and a bridge materialized in the distance. A large yellow backhoe appeared just in front of it on the right-hand side of the road.

Equipped with a huge hydraulic shovel, the backhoe scooped up a load of gravel, then backed across the highway and dumped it onto a flatbed truck.

Frantic flagmen on the side of the road waved their red banners as the Saab and Chevy van raced past them and neared the bridge. The backhoe crossed the road again, the shovel dipping once more into the pile of rubble. The Saab kept its pace, and it became clear to the men in the van that Urquillo felt sure he could make the bridge before the huge piece of heavy equipment backed onto the road again.

Bolan hit the brakes. "He'll never make it," he said softly.

The Executioner was right.

Only the damaged front of the Saab made it past the backhoe. The heavy digging machine backed onto the highway, its rear striking the Saab's passenger's door. Glass crunched and steel screamed as Urquillo's vehicle spun into a series of 360-degree twirls and skidded off the road. It struck one of the bridge's iron girders broadside, burst into flames, then slid down the embankment.

Bolan drove slowly around the backhoe as workmen rushed toward the embankment. He stopped the van at the bridge. Katz, Bolan and the men of Phoenix Force stared down the grassy bank to the stream below.

The Saab—what was left of it—stood upright in the shallow water of the stream. Flames leaped from the vehicle. Two charred corpses could be seen dancing in death through the fire.

"Well," Gary Manning said. "I suppose that's it, then."

McCarter nodded. "Shows you what such a bad temper will get you."

All of the men in the van turned toward him curiously.

The Brit shrugged. "Urquillo's obviously hot under the collar," he said dryly.

Bolan threw the van into reverse, backed up and started up the road amid a series of groans.

"Where we going now?" Manning asked.

Bolan turned to face them as the van passed the caution signs and lights. "You guys are going back to Stockholm to find out where the rest of the demo charges are," he said.

"You aren't coming with us?" Katz asked.

Bolan shook his head. There was a grim set to his jaw. Controlled anger shot from his eyes.

Katz had seen that look before. And had always pitied whoever had brought it on.

Bolan turned back to the road. "You guys can handle it. Find out where the charges are, what they have planned and stop it," he said simply. "I'd go with you...but I've got a date with a CIA agent named Rakestraw."

THE TRAIN from Stockholm to Jönköping, Sweden, was a curious one-car affair with open driving facilities at both ends. Bolan arrived at the depot just as the strange vehicle rolled to a halt on the tracks. He boarded as the conductor stood up, walked the length of the car, then took a seat at the opposite confine and began switching the controls for the return trip.

The Executioner pulled the file on Sweden from his carry-on as the engine car pulled out again. He had cornered Rakestraw outside the small florist shop that served as the front for the CIA's main Scandinavian field office, and forced him into the alley a block down. The frightened Company man had apologized a mile a minute and offered the information that the spooks had an informant in Jönköping. Since Rakestraw had seen the Executioner, the snitch had passed on the Intel that the terrorist training base was rumored to be located nearby.

Right. The timing was a little too convenient. Rakestraw had probably known about the Jönköping connection all along. The Executioner also knew that it might be another of the CIA's wild-goose chases, but most of all, he knew he had nothing else to go on.

And the horror in Rakestraw's eyes when Bolan explained what would happen if he had to return to Stockholm again had convinced Bolan that the Intel was sound.

Bolan studied the file on Jönköping as the car passed through the fertile farmlands of central Sweden. He learned that the city lay at the southern tip of Lake Vattern, the second-largest inland sea in the country. Glancing up from his reading occasionally, he saw ancient but well-kept rural estates through the windows. They passed through the modern industrial center of Linköping, then the tracks angled southwest through several small villages along the lake coast before arriving in Jönköping.

The Executioner closed the file as they slowed toward the depot, passing near enough to the town square that he could see the Gota Court of Appeals Building, Christina Church and the residence of the provincial governor. He dropped down onto the platform as the train pulled to a halt and the conductor retraced his steps to the engine at the other end of the car.

Flagging a cab, Bolan said simply, *"Tanndstickmuseet"* to the driver. The man nodded and drove away.

Bolan paid and tipped the man a few minutes later when they arrived in front of the aging building. According to the file, the building he now stood before had been the original site of the internationally known Swedish Match Company—they had moved their operation years before, turning this building into a museum.

According to Rakestraw, his snitch was the museum curator.

A sign directed the Executioner around a corner and up a set of steps. An overhead bell chimed as he entered. Bolan stopped just inside the door.

The walls of the large room were covered with photographs. Ancient match-making machines circled the area beneath the pictures, and one wall was covered with a collection of the many matchbox covers that the company had used during its hundred-year tenure.

Through a curtained doorway, the Executioner heard the drone of a film projector. Over it, a voice spoke in Swedish. He glanced up at the sign over the curtain. It read Kino, then went on to list the title of the film in several different languages. Bolan found the name of the movie in English third down. It was appropriately entitled *The Match.*

Two minutes later the curtain was drawn back, and a smiling, dark-haired man stepped out. He ushered a half-dozen men and women of various nationalities back into the museum, thanking them for coming in the same languages listed above the door.

As he turned to Bolan, his face darkened.

Bolan waited until the tourists had left, then walked over to the man. "Bjorn Lindstrum?" he asked.

The man nodded. "Our mutual friend called to tell me you were coming," he whispered. "Please... one moment." He stuck his head back inside the curtain, called out a few words in Swedish, then turned back. "I am due a break," he said. "Let's walk."

Bolan followed Lindstrum out the door, down the steps and toward the sidewalk in front of the museum. Remembering the restaurant stall Rakestraw had tried, he said, "Where are we going?"

"I thought the Svarta Börsen might be nice," Lindstrum said, face wreathed in a smile of feigned cordiality. "French cuisine. It's a cozy little place in the center of—"

Bolan reached out and grasped Lindstrum by the shoulder, stopping the surprised man in his tracks and spinning him around. "I already went through rush week with your control," he growled. "I'm not here to make friends, I'm not hungry, and I don't want to be entertained. What you do have to do is tell me everything you know about the terrorist training camp."

"I was simply attempting to be cordial," Lindstrum sputtered. "I thought—"

The Executioner moved his hand off Lindstrum's shoulder and dug a thumb into the nerve under the man's collarbone. The informant's chin dropped protectively down, his face grimacing in pain. "Tell me now." Bolan said.

Lindstrum's normally pale skin turned scarlet. "Yes...yes...all right," he said. He looked up at Bolan. "Now...if you please..."

Bolan dropped his arm to his side.

The flush began to leave Lindstrum's face. He rubbed his collarbone. "You will have to go to Mullsjö," he said.

"What, and where, is Mullsjö?" Bolan demanded.

"A small university village. Near Nässjö."

"That doesn't tell me anything."

Lindstrum reached into the side pocket of his coat and produced a map. He unfolded it and pointed to a spot just below Jönköping. The village had been circled in red. "A cab will get you there quickly."

"So then what do I do?"

"Go to the Anglo-American Center."

"The what?"

"The Anglo-American Center. A government institution that provides cultural-exchange programs." Lindstrum glanced around, as if afraid someone might be watching. He turned back to Bolan, and his voice dropped to a whisper. "There is a young man named Pat Cohlmia who works there."

The Executioner frowned. Cohlmia was a Lebanese name, as common here as Smith was in the Middle East. "Who's he with?" Bolan asked. "Hezbollah? Islamic Hope?"

"No, nothing like that. Pat Cohlmia is an American. He just happens to be of Lebanese descent. An exchange student who works at the center. He knows where the training camp is located ... but he doesn't realize it."

Bolan felt the anger rising inside him again. This new drill had all the earmarks of another stall. He let his eyes narrow and watched Lindstrum's open wide in response. "You want to be a little more specific?" he said in a mildly threatening voice.

"I overheard him talking to some mutual friends at a party the other night," Lindstrum said hastily. "Pat saw some strange things in the woods outside Mullsjö. You will have to ask the right questions."

The Executioner's exasperation grew. He didn't know how much the CIA paid Lindstrum, but he'd bet it wasn't much. They wouldn't have to—the Swedish museum curator obviously got off on the cloak-and-dagger aspect of his role.

"I don't have time to play games, Lindstrum," Bolan said in a deep, hoarse voice.

The goatee shook again. "I am sorry, but there is no other way—"

"Yes, there is." Without speaking further, Bolan grabbed Lindstrum's arm and directed him down the sidewalk to a Swedish ICA supermarket a block away. There *was* another way—a way that would be faster, more efficient and just might save the lives of several judges in the U.S.

Four more of whom had fallen to the guns of American Choice while Bolan and Phoenix Force had chased Urquillo.

A phone booth was set against the outside wall of the supermarket. Bolan pushed the door open, shoved Lindstrum inside, and dropped a coin into the slot.

"What are you doing?" the frightened curator asked as he was handed the receiver.

"Introducing you to a time-honored American custom, Lindstrum," Bolan said. "Calling in sick at work." He paused to let it sink in. "You're going with me."

THE YELLOW frame two-story Anglo-American Center looked as if it might originally have been built as someone's private residence. In the center of the sleepy Swedish village of Mullsjö, it was less than three blocks from the university.

Lindstrum drove his dented and scarred Buick LeSabre past a swimming pool with a fifty-foot diving board and pulled to a halt in the circular drive in front. Bolan followed him up the steps through a gate in the stone wall to the door.

No one answered the bell.

"Perhaps they are around back," Lindstrum said. He dropped down off the porch and circled the building. Bolan followed.

A muddy makeshift baseball diamond appeared in the vacant lot behind the center as they rounded the corner of the building.

Bolan scanned the lot as they started toward the backstop. Swedish boys and girls ranging in age from six to sixteen were stationed haphazardly throughout the field. A few wore tattered baseball gloves but most were bare-handed. A boy of eight or so stood behind the plate with a catcher's mitt.

A man in his early twenties took a stance in the batter's box. He held a bat in his right hand, a soiled baseball in his left. Of average height and weight, he wore a simple gray sweatshirt and pants. A navy blue New York Yankees cap rested on top of his coal black hair, and a silver coaches' whistle dangled around his neck on a white shoestring.

The young man tossed the ball in the air and swung. The crack of ash against horsehide echoed against the building as the ball skimmed across the mud and grass and between the legs of a teenage boy playing shortstop.

Pat Cohlmia shoved the bat under his arm, took off his cap and ran a hand through his sweaty hair. "Keep your tail down, Gunnar," he shouted. He watched as the ball traveled between a boy and girl in the outfield and finally rolled to a halt. The girl picked it up and threw it over the boy's head. The boy chased after the elusive sphere, then relayed it to second base. The baseball hit the second baseman's glove and dropped out.

Bolan watched as the second baseman dug the ball out of the mud, turned and lobbed it toward the catcher. The ball sailed high over the plywood toward Bolan and Lindstrum.

All heads turned their way as Bolan reached up and caught the ball.

Cohlmia laughed. "I'll get your contract ready," he called out to Bolan. "Hey, Bjorn."

"Hello, Pat," Lindstrum said.

Cohlmia glanced from Lindstrum to Bolan to the watch on his wrist. He turned back to the playing field. "Okay, let's knock off," he yelled. "Karate starts in fifteen minutes. Clean the mud off your shoes before you go inside!" He strolled over to Bolan and Lindstrum.

"How have you been, Pat?" Lindstrum asked.

"Fine, Bjorn. You?"

"Fine." Lindstrum indicated Bolan with a thumb. "This is Mr. Rance Pollock. From your country."

Cohlmia extended a hand. "Always good to meet a fellow Yankee," he said.

Bolan smiled as he took the young man's firm grip. There was friendliness and honesty about the young man that was refreshing after the CIA scams the Executioner had just gone through.

"Pat, Mr. Pollock needs to have a word with you," Lindstrum said.

"Sure," Cohlmia nodded. "Mind if we do it while I change? I've got to teach another class in a few minutes."

Bolan nodded back, and the three men started toward the building. "What do you do here?" the Executioner asked.

"Damn near anything I want," Cohlmia laughed. "The main idea behind this place is to improve the kids' English and give them a taste of America. They hire exchange students like me—I'm second-semester senior—and let you work out your own curriculum. Teach whatever you know about America." He shrugged as they neared a set of concrete steps leading down into the building. "My mom and dad were killed during a tornado when I was six months old, Mr. Pollock. I was raised by my grandfather on a farm in Oklahoma. Grandma was dead. Never knew her, but Grandpa was quite a guy. Full-blood Comanche, and played three seasons of minor-league ball. A black belt in Okinawan Goju-Ryu karate, too. So...baseball and martial arts...that's what *I* know."

Cohlmia led the way down a set of cracked concrete steps into the damp, dimly lit basement of the Anglo-American Center. Another set of stairs against the far wall led up into the building.

Bolan and Lindstrum stood in the middle of the room as Cohlmia walked to a lone green Army footlocker next to the stairs.

"Pat," Lindstrum said, "tell Mr. Pollock what you told Sture and Lars at the party the other night. About what you saw in the forest by Sture's cabin."

Cohlmia bent to open the lid of the locker and snorted. "There's not too much to tell," he said, pulling a white karate *gi* from the box. "Sture—he's a friend of ours—rents this little cabin in the woods a couple of miles from here. Nice. Quiet. Good place to get drunk." Still talking, he started to change his clothes. "Anyway, I wake up last Sunday morning with a hangover, so I go for a walk in the woods, right? Try to get a little oxygen pumping through the old brain again. Stopped to sit on a stump for a while, looked down, and what do you think I see sticking up out of the mud?" He didn't wait for an answer. "This...." He opened the footlocker again, dug through the contents, then flipped a shining amber object through the air toward Bolan.

The Executioner caught the object, looked down at his hand and saw the brass casing from a spent .223 round.

"Where I come from it's no big deal to see brass lying around. So it took a second before I realized, hey, this isn't Oklahoma. I'm in fucking *Sweden*. And they got gun laws here like you wouldn't believe. It'd take an act of parliament for a civilian to get a rifle that shot these things, and the cops and military don't use .223s. Sture's a cop. He told me."

Bolan saw Lindstrum watching him out of the corner of his eye. His fingers rolled into a fist around the casing. "You told your friend—Sture—the cop—about this?"

"Sure."

The Executioner grimaced inwardly. The last thing he needed right now was interference from well-meaning Swedish police. "What did he say?"

"Said they'd check into it. But that was more than two weeks ago, and as far as I know, they haven't done anything. Low priority, I guess."

Bolan nodded, relieved and irritated at the same time. If the cops had known about the .223 casing for two weeks and hadn't acted on it yet, they weren't likely to do so now.

But the fact that Pat Cohlmia had found the casing that long ago confirmed his suspicion that the CIA had known of this Mullsjö connection when he had arrived. "You find anything else out there?" he asked Cohlmia.

Cohlmia shrugged into his *gi* jacket, tied the sides and wrapped a black belt around his waist. "Yeah. Boot tracks. Deep. Made by men carrying backpacks."

"How do you know that?"

Cohlmia shrugged. "The heels were dug in deeper than the rest of the sole."

The Executioner frowned. "Were you in the service?" The man seemed to know tracking, but looked too young to have both served a hitch and finished college.

Cohlmia looked up and grinned. "Uh-uh. Grandad always said baseball and karate were white-man skills he had to work hard to master. But tracking was genetic for a Comanche." The young man's smile became a chuckle. "Of course, he also reminded me that I was only one-fourth Indian. Told me that meant I had to put out at least a seventy-five percent effort to stay alive in the woods."

Bolan smiled. He liked the kid more with every passing moment.

"My light skin comes from Grandma," Cohlmia said. "Irish." He reached up, grabbing a lock of the black hair that fell over his forehead. "This is either Lebanese or Comanche. It's a toss-up, I guess."

Bolan flipped the .223 casing back to the young man. "Can you take me to the spot where you found this?"

Cohlmia glanced to his wrist again. "Sure. You want to go now?"

"The sooner the better."

"Okay. Give me a second to get them started upstairs, and I'll meet you out front." Cohlmia started up the steps, then turned back. "Mind if I ask you something?"

"No," Bolan said, knowing what it would be. "Not if you don't mind when I don't answer."

Cohlmia smiled. "Fair enough. You don't look like the academic type to me. Who are you?"

When Bolan didn't answer, the young man's smile became a laugh. "Like I said, 'fair enough.' Just let me ask you one more thing, and I do expect an answer to this one or I'll be damned if I'll take you anywhere." Suddenly his eyes narrowed and the good-natured expression turned to a look that could have melted all the glaciers in Lapland. "You're one of the 'good guys,' aren't you?"

The Executioner nodded.

Cohlmia's smile returned. "Don't ask me how," he said, "but I figured as much." Without another word, he turned and disappeared up the stairs.

CHAPTER SIX

Summer in Sweden is different from summer on Miami Beach, and Pat Cohlmia had thrown an insulated plaid mackinaw over his karate uniform by the time he came down the steps in front of the Anglo-American Center.

The young American slid into the back of Bjorn Lindstrum's Buick and leaned forward over the seat between Lindstrum and Bolan. "Just go out to Sture's, Bjorn," he said. "We'll have to hoof it from there."

Lindstrum frowned as he pulled out of the circular drive and started toward the highway. "What means 'whoofit'?" he asked.

"Walk," Cohlmia said with a smile.

The CIA informant drove two miles north of Mullsjö, then cut down a dirt road in front of a farmhouse badly in need of repair.

"Lars's place," Cohlmia said. "Been in his family for five generations. He's a good guy, but a better poker player than handyman. He owns the cabin, too—the one Sture rents."

Bolan studied the dozen or so emaciated cattle in the small corral as they passed. Thousands, maybe millions, of flies lounged on their hides and buzzed the area around the small barn. Others raced through the air to the car, lighting on the windshield until Lindstrum turned on the wipers.

"The horsefly's the national bird over here," Cohlmia said with a straight face.

Lindstrum turned onto a narrow path grown over with crabgrass and slowed the Buick to a near crawl. They entered the forest through a tunnel of trees so tall the sun barely lit the way. Five minutes later the curator pulled into a clearing in front of a tiny cabin that looked as if it had been constructed from Lincoln Logs.

A white Toyota pickup stood in front. The crowned crest of the Swedish National Police had been stenciled on the doors, and in the short bed was a wire dog kennel. A well-cared-for German shepherd watched the Buick approach with wary eyes.

A short muscular man with a blond mustache stepped out of the front door as Lindstrum parked next to the pickup. Hundreds of flies immediately perched on his face and shoulders. He didn't seem to notice. He wore a navy blue uniform with lieutenant's bars, a flap holster on his Sam Browne belt and a broad smile.

"You want him to know why you're here?" Cohlmia asked.

Bolan shook his head.

Cohlmia sighed. "Okay." He opened the rear door, then turned back as more of the irritating flies entered the Buick. "Sure hope my intuition about you being a good guy is right." He got out. Bolan and Lindstrum followed.

Sture walked to the pickup and extended his hand.

"This is Rance Pollock," Cohlmia said. "Thought I'd show him a little of the famous Swedish country-side. You don't mind, do you?"

Sture pumped the Executioner's hand. "Of course not. I would go with you, but I'm late for work as it is."

"Go on, then," Cohlmia chided. "Don't be a lag-gard."

Sture grinned, got in the pickup and drove away.

Cohlmia led the way across the clearing into the trees behind the cabin. They took a narrow footpath for perhaps a hundred yards, swatting at the armies of flies that followed, then veered off into the woods, stepping over rocks and tree stumps.

Finally they came to another clearing. "Here we be," Cohlmia said. He pointed toward a tree stump.

Bolan moved cautiously forward. Sometime in the recent past, the grass had been cleared and a fire built. It had rained since then, and the area was now thick with mud.

Cohlmia followed Bolan's line of sight and said, "Right near the edge there—that's where I found it."

A glimmer of metal caught the Executioner's eye, and he circled the mud. Just beyond the tree line, he saw a crushed Three Towers beer can. Turning back to the mud, he wondered if more of the mysterious .223 casings were buried beneath the surface.

There was only one way to find out.

Removing his shoes and socks, the Executioner waded out toward where the camp fire had been. He dug down with his fingers, scraping away a layer of ash and sludge. He tried several other places within the

clearing, then his eyes suddenly fell on a rectangular
area approximately six feet long.

Maggots, nearly as thick as the flies, covered the
stretch, which was recessed slightly in the ground.

Bolan scanned the rest of the clearing. He saw no
more parasites of any type. Kneeling, he scooped at
the soggy earth with both hands.

"What are you doing?" Lindstrum asked.

Bolan didn't answer. He dug deeper. A moment
later his fingers struck something hard.

Metal.

The Executioner knew what it was even before he
cleared the mud away from the gold signet ring to ex-
pose the rotting, maggot-covered hand.

"Ah, hell," Pat Cohlmia said five minutes later
when they'd scraped the mud off the dead man's face.
"That's old Jorgen Thorkell."

"You knew him?" Bolan asked. It was a rhetorical
question. Cohlmia would have *had* to have known
him, and fairly well, to have recognized him now. Half
of Thorkell's face had been blown away by a large-
caliber bullet.

"Damn straight, I knew him," Cohlmia said. "I
lived in his shack with him for nearly a month last
summer when I was broke."

Bolan lifted the body out of the shallow grave and
rolled it onto its side. The bullet had entered the back
of the old man's head. Powder burns stained the area
around the hole.

The Executioner was no cop. But he wasn't a fool,
either. The flesh around the entry wound was seared,
which meant the muzzle of the weapon had been
pressed against Thorkell's skin when the trigger was

pulled. That, and the downward angle of trajectory to
the exit wound in the face, could mean only one of two
things: Jorgen Thorkell had been on his knees when
he'd been shot, or else he'd been shot by a man around
ten feet tall.

What it boiled down to was that Thorkell had been
the victim of an execution-style slaying.

Bolan squinted, studying the body. Thorkell wore
a deerskin shirt and trousers. Patches of light palo-
mino tan—the garments' original color—still showed
in spots, but most of the old man's clothing had been
stained a dark brown by the mud and blood. "Who
was he?" Bolan asked.

Cohlmia shrugged. "Sort of the Swedish version of
the village coot, I guess you'd say. Jorg was born up
north. Lapland. I don't know how he ended up this far
south—" he glanced to Lindstrum, who shook his
head "—but he's been around Mullsjö as long as
anyone can remember. Hunted and fished these woods
most of the time." He paused and shook his head.
Then, turning back to Lindstrum, he said, "I can't
imagine why anyone would kill him."

Lindstrum turned toward the trees.

Bolan stood up. *He* knew. Jorgen Thorkell had
stumbled onto something in these woods he hadn't
been supposed to see. "Lindstrum," the Executioner
said, "take Cohlmia back to town." He turned toward the woods on the other side of the clearing.

The voice behind him said, "Hey, wait just a damn
minute."

He turned back around to see Cohlmia slipping out
of his mackinaw. The young man dropped it on the
ground, removed his white *gi* top, then knelt and be-

gan rubbing mud onto his face, chest and white pants. "I liked the old bastard," Cohlmia said. "He took me in when I was starving. I'm going with you."

Bolan shook his head.

Cohlmia smiled a hard smile. "I can help."

"No, you can't. You don't have any idea what you're getting into."

Cohlmia stood up. His eyes now flamed with an anger whose potential Bolan hadn't seen in the good-natured young man. "Look, Pollock, if it wasn't for me, you wouldn't have found this place. And I don't even know who you are. But dammit, I've trusted you when there was no real reason why I should. I've trusted you on instinct. Now you can do the same with me. I know how to fight, Pollock."

"The men where I'm going won't be wearing *gis*," Bolan said. "And they'll be armed."

Cohlmia leaned down, flipped open a pocket in his mackinaw and pulled out a black leather knife sheath. He drew a glimmering stainless steel-blade out into the sun—a Cold Steel Mini-Tanto with an oval guard. The weapon looked like a miniature samurai sword.

"The men I'm going after have *guns,* Cohlmia," the Executioner said.

Cohlmia resheathed the Tanto and clipped it inside his pants at the small of his back. "So give me a gun," he said. "I know you didn't come out here unarmed. I know how to shoot."

"Don't tell me," Bolan said. "Your grandfather taught you."

The young American's eyes narrowed farther. "You can make light of it if you want. But I bet I could out-shoot *you.*"

Bolan hesitated. He could use help, all right. But anything less than professional help could get them both killed. He glanced around the woods. The men who had killed Jorgen Thorkell were long gone. If they hadn't been, they'd have already heard the voices and converged on the clearing. That meant that if he used the near-silent Beretta to check Pat Cohlmia's skills, they wouldn't hear that, either.

The Executioner reached under his arm, drew the 93-R from shoulder leather and handed it butt first to Cohlmia.

The mud-covered man took the gun, then frowned down at it. "Beretta," he said. "Looks like a 92 with a silencer, but... oh, wait. I get it. Full-auto?"

"Three-round burst," Bolan said. He turned, scanning the area for a target. Twenty yards from where he stood, his eyes fell on a dead tree. Several dry twiglike branches, each an inch or so in diameter, shot out at ninety-degree angles from the trunk.

He pointed toward the tree. "Snap a branch off for me."

Cohlmia didn't hesitate. He raised the pistol in a two-handed grip and pulled the trigger. The Beretta coughed once, and the highest branch fell to the ground.

The young man smiled at the Executioner, then fired twice more, both times dropping more dead wood to the ground.

Bolan nodded. "Good enough." Turning to Lindstrum, he said, "Go on back. I'll take Cohlmia with me."

Lindstrum nodded quickly, and Bolan saw his face flood with relief. Without a word, he turned back toward the path through the woods.

Cohlmia handed the Beretta back to the Executioner. "Your turn," he said.

Bolan holstered the Beretta. "No need," he said. "I've already decided to take you." He glanced down at the tracks in the mud, then started toward the trees.

A confident grin spread over Cohlmia's face as he fell in next to the Executioner. "Admitting defeat?"

Bolan stopped in his tracks. He felt no need to prove himself to this kid, but if Cohlmia was along, it would be important that he have faith in the Executioner. He turned back to the twigs on the dead tree, which were now close to thirty yards away.

In one smooth movement, the 93-R leaped into the Executioner's hand. As the sights fell on the twig below the last one Cohlmia had shot, Bolan thumbed the selector to semiauto and squeezed the trigger.

The thin branch snapped from the trunk and started to fall.

Bolan triggered again.

The falling branch snapped in half before it hit the ground.

At his side the Executioner saw Cohlmia swallow hard. "My grandfather was the best shot I ever saw," he said softly. "But not even *he* could have done that."

Bolan dropped the magazine from the Beretta and stuffed a fresh load up the grip. "You shoot well enough," he said, starting through the trees. "Now let's find out how you do when the target shoots back."

THE SCANDINAVIAN summer sun still stood high in the sky as Bolan and Cohlmia made their way through the tangled forest of trees and shrubs. "This looks like something out of one of those J. R. R. Tolkien books," Cohlmia whispered. "I expect to see Bilbo Baggins and a couple of trolls jump out any minute."

The Executioner smiled as he crept on. It was impossible not to like the young man behind him. Though Pat Cohlmia exhibited much of the false certainty that clung to youth—youth that had not yet had to face its own mortality and come to terms with it—the young man had proved himself to be a skilled woodsman and good target shot. It remained to be seen how he would stand up under fire, but unless Bolan missed his guess, Cohlmia would prove worthy.

Ahead, Bolan saw the sparkle of metal in the moss next to a tree. Another .223 round? He moved cautiously to the object and knelt, digging the soft earth away from its sides.

No, not another rifle casing. Another Three Towers beer can.

They were on the right track.

Bolan drew the Beretta and handed it to Cohlmia. "Give me your knife," he whispered.

Cohlmia complied.

The Executioner clipped the sheath to his belt. He knew the terrorists would have sentries stationed outside the camp, and he sensed they were close. He'd have liked to have kept the sound-suppressed Beretta—taking a man out with a well-placed bullet was always faster and cleaner than with a knife. But that would have meant handing the Desert Eagle .44 over to the young man in the muddy karate uniform.

Cohlmia had proved he could handle the 9 mm pistol. The Executioner wasn't so sure about the big, bucking Magnum.

The trees thinned as the two warriors ascended a slight grade uphill, then leveled off again. Here and there birds chirped in the treetops. Small animals, unseen in the thick foliage, burrowed in deeper as they passed.

Both men stopped suddenly and simultaneously as a whiff of cheap after-shave met their nostrils on the breeze.

Bolan drew the Mini-Tanto from his belt and held it in an ice-pick grip, edge up. He started to order Cohlmia to stay where he was, then hesitated.

The kid had proved worthy so far, walking through the bush with the silence of his Comanche ancestors. Dropping to his belly, the Executioner motioned for Cohlmia to follow.

Twenty yards later the odor of cigarette smoke mixed with the after-shave. Bolan and Cohlmia moved on. The smells strengthened as they came to a halt behind a large boulder.

Slowly Bolan raised his head.

On the other side of the boulder, he saw the profile of the lone sentry. The man sat in the tall grass, his back resting against the trunk of a thick tree next to the rock. A hand-rolled cigarette extended from his lips, sending wisps of blue smoke floating back toward the Executioner.

The sentry's eyelids drooped in bored half sleep.

Bolan rose to a squat, then sprang over the boulder. The fingers of his left hand caught the terrorist by the hair, and he used the grip to pull himself on over the rock. The Executioner's body weight jerked the sentry into the boulder as Bolan tumbled down on top of his back.

A short scream started to escape the man's lips. The Executioner jerked the head back by the hair, jabbed the armor-piercing point of the Tanto into the neck and ripped forward through the jugular vein, cutting it off.

Bolan rose back to his feet as the sentry hit the grass face first, his life's blood pouring forth from the throat like water from a fire hose. The Executioner drew the mighty Desert Eagle and did a quick 360-degree spin.

Seeing nothing, he motioned to Cohlmia.

The young American scrambled over the rock to his side. Bolan saw him look down to the body at his feet, the color draining from his face.

The Executioner grabbed him by the shoulders. "Sure you want to go on?" he whispered.

Cohlmia faced him. In the young eyes Bolan could see a mixture of revulsion and determination. Slowly the eyes narrowed again. Then the blood returned to his cheeks as determination won out. Cohlmia nodded.

Silently the two Americans made their way on through the trees. Less than fifty feet later they dropped to their knees and stared through the leaves.

The terrorist training camp covered roughly an acre. Tents, lean-tos and other hastily constructed buildings lined one side of the parade ground. Behind the structures was an obstacle course with rope ladders, suspension bridges and a rappeling wall. Grappling hooks and lines had been piled to one side of the barbed-wire crawl tunnels directly behind the tents.

The camp looked as if it had been set up to house and train close to a hundred men at a time. There was only one problem.

Most of the tents had been taken down and folded. The camp was in the process of being broken.

Only a half-dozen men were visible. They sat smoking and talking in wooden folding chairs between the front of the tents and a smoldering campfire. All of them wore soiled rain-pattern DPM camouflage BDUs. A variety of personal weapons were scattered haphazardly about the camp, and the Executioner saw everything from an Austrian Steyr to an American M-16. The men themselves wore pistols.

As it had so many times in the past twenty-four hours, the Executioner's blood boiled within his breast. Whatever this camp had once been, it was now in its death throes. The terrorists who had trained here had either changed training sites or gone on to put the deadly skills they had mastered into practice.

The CIA had once again stalled him. Wasted his time.

Why?

Bolan took a deep breath through his nose, letting it out slowly through his mouth. There were at least half a dozen terrorists still here. But he'd take care of that.

Bolan had started to turn back toward Cohlmia when a stack of crates next to a lean-to in the center of the buildings caught his eye. Something had registered in his brain. What?

From the breast pocket of his coat, the Executioner produced a tiny pair of Pentax compact binoculars. Aiming them at the crates, he pushed and released the control button to adjust the diopter, then pushed the button again to lock it in. Twisting the central adjustment, the Executioner focused the lenses.

Bolan saw immediately what had caught his attention. Most of the words and numbers stamped on the crates were different from those he'd seen on the boxes of demolition charges in Herbert Urquillo's safehouse. But one was the same—"Chile."

The Executioner read the letters and numbers below. "FAMAE GM 78-F7."

Plastic-bodied hand grenades, suitable for wrapping with coils of notched steel wire to produce additional shrapnel. Dozens of crates of them.

The terrorists' personal weapons might be eclectic, but their demo devices were uniform. Someone in the organization, or connected to them, must have gotten a hell of a deal on Chilean explosives.

The fact that the Beni region of Bolivia was near the Chilean border was not lost on the Executioner.

Handing the binoculars to Cohlmia, Bolan said, "I'll circle the camp and come in from the other side. Across the obstacle course. When it starts, you lay down cover fire from here." He paused. "You see the crates?"

Cohlmia nodded, the binoculars pressed to his forehead. "Yeah. What are they?"

"Hand grenades."

The young man dropped the lenses from his face. "No shit?"

"Right. Don't hit them. You do, and it won't matter much what else we do."

Cohlmia nodded and handed the binoculars back. "How will I know when you're ready?"

The Executioner swung his coat back, exposing the huge Desert Eagle on his hip. "The sound's a little hard to miss," he said. "You'll know."

Cohlmia smiled.

Staying just inside the tree line, Bolan circled the parade ground, then crossed a narrow stream as he drew abreast of the tents and buildings. He moved silently, his eyes sweeping the terrain for dry sticks or leaves, anything that might make noise and announce his arrival before he was ready. He thought of Cohlmia as he moved. The kid was good. He might not have had formal training in the arts of war, but the private lessons his Comanche grandfather had given him had done the trick. But there was one test left to be taken.

The young American was about to have his first taste of fighting outside the ring. His first competition in which mistakes meant you didn't lose a tournament, but your life.

Pat Cohlmia's baptism of fire was at hand.

Five minutes later the Executioner dropped to his knees once more and stared through the limbs. Directly across from his new position, he could see the spot where he'd left the young American. Cohlmia was invisible within the foliage.

Falling to his belly, Bolan crawled forward, passing the various obstacles. When he reached the razor wire, he burrowed still deeper into the earth, keeping his eyes up as he slithered beneath the sharp edges of steel.

Emerging from the tunnel, Bolan saw the six men in the wooden folding chairs. He crawled to the back of the tent behind them and leaned in close to the canvas. Hearing nothing, he rose to his feet, pulled the Mini-Tanto from its sheath and sliced down through the thick sailcloth.

A moment later he was inside. Stepping over the bedrolls scattered on the ground, he moved to the front flap and pulled it to the side.

The stacked explosive crates were on the other side of the tent just to his right. The six terrorists sat just to the left, facing away from him.

Good. The last thing he needed now was for Pat Cohlmia to cut him down with his own gun in a cross fire.

One of the terrorists said something in Swedish and drew the figure of a woman in the air with his hands. The others laughed.

The Executioner pulled the Desert Eagle slowly from his holster.

A moment later the big .44 bucked in his hand, sending a 240-grain jacketed hollowpoint from the barrel at 1180 feet per second. The slug struck the back of the nearest terrorist's neck with over 700 foot pounds of energy, leaving the man almost headless.

The roar of the massive Magnum echoed off the trees surrounding the camp. Bolan swung the Desert Eagle to the next man in line. Before he could squeeze the trigger, he saw a rustling in the trees across the clearing, and the man slumped forward.

The Executioner smiled inwardly. Cohlmia was doing his job. He moved on to the next target.

The man had half turned by the time Bolan fired. The round caught him in the side of the head, throwing him out of his chair to the ashy ground in front of the campfire.

Cohlmia's next round caught the fourth man in the shoulder, spinning him around as he tried to draw a Makarov pistol from the flap holster on his web belt. Bolan caught him in the chest with a .44 slug as he spun, and he went down on top of the man who had sat next to him.

The last two men tried to flee. The Executioner stepped from the tent, placing a round between the shoulder blades of a tall, husky man with red hair. The man dropped like a stone as 9 mm fire from the trees sputtered into the last terrorist.

Pat Cohlmia stepped from the trees and walked forward. "Well," he said calmly, "I guess that takes care of—"

"Not quite," said a voice behind the Executioner.

Bolan swung around. Behind the explosives, he saw a man wearing the rain-pattern cammies. A black-and-gray Russian rabbit hat sat atop his head, the earflaps hanging loosely down over the sides of his neck.

A week's worth of beard sprouted from the man's face. The spiky whiskers curled up into a smile as he stuck the barrel of the Uzi in his hands into the stack, pulled the bolt back to chamber a round and said, "Don't move, or we will all meet Satan together."

"LET THEM PASS," Yakov Katzenelenbogen told David McCarter as the last of the Swedish National Police cars pulled out of the American Apartments parking lot.

McCarter gripped the wheel of the ten-year-old Dodge station wagon and nodded.

Knowing that they'd be returning to the apartment complex where the van had been procured, and certain that the commotion outside the safe house would have brought the police, the men of Phoenix Force had dumped the van in Norrköping and procured the station wagon from the parking lot of a high-rise medical center.

Katz took a deep breath, letting it out slowly as the police car drove by. The two officers in the front seat ignored the Dodge.

McCarter fired the engine, pulled away from the shopping center and passed the Burger King. Construction was in full gear now, with men carrying buckets and nail guns through a maze of power saws and other heavy equipment. The foul odor of roofing tar filled the air as McCarter pulled into a parking slot next to Building A and threw the Dodge into Park.

Katz sat back against the seat and scratched his head. Okay. The cops would have found the Chilean demolition charges and taken possession. That was fine. *Those* explosives would be out of the hands of Urquillo's survivors. But as Bolan had said, there had to be plenty of other demos around—Urquillo had made no attempt to take the ones upstairs with him. He didn't have to stretch his imagination too far to realize the terrorists had some kind of strike going down in the Stockholm area. And the safe house was Phoenix Force's only lead.

The Israeli squinted toward the building. From where he sat, he could see that both entrances to the downstairs hall were clear. His hand moved to the two-day stubble of beard on his chin. The initial crime-scene investigation appeared to be over, but unless the Swedish police were on a par with Barney Fife—*not* their reputation—they'd have sealed the apartment and posted a guard.

The Israeli turned to Calvin James, sandwiched between Rafael Encizo and big Gary Manning in the back seat. Like the rest of the men from Stony Man Farm, James had changed out of his battle dress into blue jeans and a T-shirt. A shiny Chicago Bears Starter jacket hid his Beretta 92 and other weapons.

"James, there's bound to be an officer or two upstairs," Katz said. "They need to take a nap."

James nodded, twisting around and pulling his backpack from the station wagon's rear storage area. He rummaged through the contents before producing a metal box, flipped the hinge and pulled out a pair of syringes and a plastic vial of colorless fluid. "This ought to do the trick," the Phoenix Force medic said as he began filling the needles.

Katz turned to the other men. "The rest of you stay here. All five of us marching up the steps is bound to draw suspicion. After we've neutralized the guard, I'll call you." He lifted the radio headset from the seat beside him and stuffed it into the side pocket of his jacket, then opened the door.

The Phoenix Force leader was halfway to the building when he remembered the security door and kicked himself mentally. They'd need a means of access, and Bolan had already used up the ruse of buzzing another apartment. It might work again, but—

A uniformed Swedish officer descended the stairs as Katz neared the glass. The Israeli smiled. Sometimes—not often, but sometimes—you got lucky.

The curious policeman walked to the door, leaned on the fire bar and stuck his head out the opening. *"Ja?"*

Katz reached up, circling his prosthesis around the man's neck and cupping the mouth with his hand. Calvin James stepped smoothly in and stabbed one of the syringes through the officer's trousers into his buttock.

A moment later the cop fell forward into the two men's arms.

Katz and James dragged the sleeping man into the hallway, laid him against the wall, then quickly mounted the steps. Another uniform stood just outside the door to apartment five, his arms crossed. He frowned as the two men walked forward. *"Ursakta,"* he said. *"Jag forstar inte—"*

The cop's words were one of the few phrases in Swedish with which Katz was familiar: "Excuse me, I don't understand." The two men from Phoenix Force made sure he never would.

Katz smiled broadly, opening his mouth as if to speak as he approached. Ten feet from the door, he tripped, falling to his side on the carpet, his hands clasped around a knee as he moaned in pain.

When the cop stepped forward to help, Calvin James jabbed his second syringe into the man's arm.

Katz broke the police seal on the door as James gripped the unconscious cop under the arms and pulled him into the safe house. The Israeli followed. He pulled the headset from his pocket, plugged it into the unit hidden under his jacket and wrapped it around his head. "Phoenix clear inside," he said into the mouthpiece. "Manning, Encizo, come on in. You'll find something at the bottom of the stairs. Bring it up with you." He paused, then said, "McCarter, stay put. Advise us if any more blue suits show up."

The Phoenix Force leader turned to James. The black warrior had dropped the policeman on the carpet against the wall, using the man's own handcuffs to secure his hands. As the Israeli waited, James tore a strip of cloth from the cop's uniform blouse and fashioned a gag.

A moment later Encizo opened the door, then stepped back. Gary Manning entered the apartment, the other police officer slung over his shoulder in a fireman's carry. The big Canadian deposited the cop next to his partner and cuffed him while James ripped another strip from the first cop's torn shirt.

Katz stared at the officers' belts. Both wore handheld walkie-talkies in leather holsters. "Okay," he said. "We don't know how long before the investigators come back, or these guys miss a phone or radio check-in. Let's get busy. Encizo, you and Manning take the bedroom. James and I will start in here. We're looking for anything that might lead us to the explosives."

The big Canadian and little Cuban disappeared into the hall.

James moved to the coffee table and began digging through a stack of magazines. Katz hurried over to a small rolltop desk in the corner.

The Israeli rolled the top up and stared into several small compartments at the back. He had no idea what he was looking for, and there was always the chance that whatever it was had already been taken as evidence by the police.

Or that Urquillo had been smart enough not to leave any "bread crumbs" at all.

Katz dug through a stack of letters in Spanish addressed to a "Señora Martinez." He couldn't suppress a smile. The Latin equivalent of "Martin" was an obvious alias. The old lady.

Finding nothing of interest in the desk, the former Mossad operative moved to a row of potted plants beneath the window. He saw James pull a Swiss Army knife from his pocket, open the screwdriver blade and begin taking the back off the television.

The headset buzzed suddenly in Katz's ear. Then David McCarter's Cockney accent said, "Got three blue-and-whites turning the corner by the shopping center, Phoenix One. No lights or siren, but they're traveling fast."

Katz glanced at the cops on the floor. When Phoenix Force left the safe house, they wouldn't be able to come back. The two sleeping cops would advise their superiors as to what had happened, and the light guard at the door would become a small army. "Can you see how many men are in the vehicles?" the Israeli asked McCarter.

"Not from this distance," the Briton came back. "They're getting closer if you want to wait. But by the time I can advise, it'll be too late for you to get out."

Katz hesitated, then made his decision. They had to leave. Three squad cars meant at least three more cops—probably six, and more if they suspected trouble. There was no way to subdue that many men without hurting them, and shooting cops didn't fit into the Phoenix Force game plan.

"Okay," the former Mossad man shouted down the hall. "You guys hear that?"

"Affirmative," Manning's voice said in his ear. "Company's coming."

"So let's move out." Katz hurried to the front door and opened it. James dropped the back of the TV and sprinted into the hall. Encizo and Manning appeared from the bedroom and followed.

Katz closed the door and followed the men down the steps. "Which door are they coming to, McCarter?" he asked the microphone.

"West," the Brit came back. "But they may split up and take both entrances. Hurry up."

Encizo opened the east door, and the men hurried out of the building. "Drive down past the Burger King, McCarter," Katz ordered. "We'll meet you there." He led the rest of the team in a sprint away from the building, then slowed to a casual walk as they reached the street separating the complex from the construction site.

The Phoenix Force leader risked a glance over his shoulder and saw eight uniformed men approach the building with guns drawn. One spoke into a walkie-talkie of the type the other cops had worn.

Katz, Manning, Encizo and James jumped into the station wagon and McCarter pulled away. "That's called cutting it thin," he said.

"No, that's called cutting it *anorexic,*" Manning corrected. He blew air through his clenched lips. "And all for nothing. We didn't find a damn thing to lead us to the demo charges."

Rafael Encizo chuckled. "Don't be so sure," he said.

Katz, Manning and James turned to the Cuban in the back seat. McCarter's eyes rose curiously to the rearview mirror.

Encizo reached inside his jacket and pulled out a folded sheet of blueprint paper. Handing it to Katz, he said, "It was inside the ceiling above the light fixture."

Katz unfolded the paper and stared at the intricate diagram. Then his eyes moved up to the title at the top of the page, and he felt his stomach turn sour.

"So," Encizo said, "I guess you'd say I've got good news and bad news. The good news is we know the place Urquillo's people are planning to blow up."

He paused, then went on. "The bad news is, it's the American Embassy."

CHAPTER SEVEN

The sun shone brightly into the Executioner's eyes as he swung the Desert Eagle toward the man with the Uzi.

The rabbit-fur hat dropped out of sight behind the stack of hand-grenade cases.

"Drop your weapons!" the voice called out. "Do it now!"

Bolan squinted toward the pile of explosives. They were stacked irregularly, and through a narrow crack in the boxes he caught a flash of skin. Then a dark eye appeared in the opening.

"Drop the guns, I said!" the voice screamed.

Pat Cohlmia looked to the Executioner, his face reflecting uncertainty. "What do we do?" he whispered.

"Wait," Bolan said.

"Drop the guns!" the terrorist repeated.

Bolan still didn't answer. Slowly he let the barrel of the Desert Eagle fall toward the crack.

"Do it!" the voice cried frantically. "Both of you drop your guns *now,* or I will kill us all!"

The Executioner nodded toward Cohlmia. "Do what he says."

Cohlmia let the Beretta fall from his fingers to the grass. Bolan took advantage of the diversion to move the sights of the Desert Eagle closer to the narrow gap.

"Now *you!*" the man in the rabbit hat screamed.

The Desert Eagle continued to move.

"This is your last chance!" the terrorist shrieked. "Do you think this is a game?"

"Maybe," Bolan said, stalling. "You haven't convinced me yet that you're really willing to die."

"I will! I will gladly die! But if I must, I will take you with me!"

"Let's talk about it a minute," Bolan said. "Maybe we can work something out so we all live." His words were met with silence.

Bolan took a deep breath as the sights of the Desert Eagle found the crack. The opening was maybe an inch wide. With the big .44-caliber slugs in the Desert Eagle, that didn't leave much margin for error. He stood a good thirty feet from his target, and if his shot was off even a half inch, the terrorist in the Russian rabbit hat wouldn't have to carry out his threat—the Executioner's own bullet would blow them all to pieces for him.

The fact was, only a fool would try a shot like that.

Or a man who had no other choice.

The Executioner took a deep breath, letting half of it out. He squinted tighter against the sun in his face, trying to focus beyond the sights on the shadowy face in the crack. Sweat poured down his forehead, burning his eyes. His finger started back on the trigger. Then a sudden gust of wind moved his hand slightly to the side.

The barrel of the Desert Eagle swung directly over the box of grenades to the right of the hole.

Bolan's trigger finger froze.

"This is your last chance!" screamed the voice be-hind the grenades. "I will do it! I will!"

Bolan brought the big .44 Magnum back in line with the crack. Taking another breath, he lined the sights up on the watching eye. His index finger tightened again.

Behind the barrier, the Executioner heard the ter-rorist's frightened breathing. So far, the tension of the situation had clouded the man's judgment. He hadn't realized that he and his Uzi could have popped up over the stacked grenades and fired at will, with Bolan and Cohlmia unable to return fire. But this lapse in judg-ment would not last forever. It was only a matter of time.

If the Mexican standoff continued much longer, it would give the terrorist time to think. He'd realize his advantage.

It was now or never.

The Executioner's finger traveled back with excru-ciating slowness. The wind gusted again. He gripped the weapon tighter, trying to hold it steady.

The Desert Eagle roared.

Bolan saw the grenade case just to the left of the watching eye move slightly. Then the eye on the other side of the crack disappeared, and sunlight streamed through the opening once more.

The Executioner rushed forward, Cohlmia at his heels. He leaned over the stack of explosives, training the .44 downward.

The terrorist lay on his back on the grass, his right eye staring blankly at the sky. The other eye—the one that had watched through the crack—was gone. The big Magnum round had taken the socket and cheek with it, and bright crimson blood stained the gray-and-black rabbit hat, which still clung stubbornly to the man's head.

Bolan stepped back and looked at the pile of boxes. His round had scraped the wood on the case to the right of the crack. With Cohlmia's Tanto he pried the lid off the box and looked inside.

The wall of the box was quarter-inch plywood. One of the Chilean hand grenades rested against the wood next to the bullet mark.

The Executioner and Pat Cohlmia had come within a quarter inch of being blown to kingdom come.

Cohlmia shook his head and let out a long whistle. "You do this kind of shit very often, Mr. Pollock?" he asked. "Like, I mean, this isn't an everyday thing for you. Or is it?"

Bolan turned to face him.

Cohlmia stared up into the eyes of the Executioner. "And then, on the other hand," he said almost reverently, "maybe it is."

Bolan didn't answer. He turned back toward the woods, stooped to retrieve the Beretta from the ground, then broke into a jog down the path toward Sture's cabin. The situation was becoming more and more clear.

Okay. Bernhardt Ennslin's Corporation had linked up with O'Banion and Urquillo. O'Banion was assassinating American judges to create panic in the U.S., and Urquillo had been put in charge of creating terror abroad. The purpose? To intimidate the U.S. into a retreat in the drug war and break the American people's confidence.

And somewhere, somehow, there was a Corporation connection to some dirty CIA agents. Otherwise, Rakestraw wouldn't have worked so hard to slow him down.

The Executioner's jog became a sprint. He needed to be back in America.

Now.

THE CHOPPER BLADES spun like the wings of a moth gone mad as Carl Lyons watched Charlie Mott guide the helicopter down over the rooftops. The Able Team leader glanced down to the aerial photo in his lap, then through the bubble windshield toward a white three-story residence with colonial style columns running the length of the front. Behind the house, at the end of a long curving driveway, stood a four-car garage. Next to the garage, on the other side of a ten-foot hedge, Lyons saw a large swimming pool with a cabana flanking the other side of the property.

The Able Team leader tapped the photo, then pointed toward the house. "There it is, Charlie," he said over the roar of the engine. "A block over. See it?"

Mott nodded, the green and yellow Oakland A's baseball cap above his mirror sunglasses bouncing up and down. Lyons turned to the other two members of Able team seated behind him. They both looked as tired as he was.

Able Team had spent the last two weeks taking down a syndicate of Laotian drug dealers, and sleep hadn't been high on their list of priorities. The call from Stony Man Farm had come less than five minutes after they'd finished with the dopers, and that call had assured that sleep still wasn't forthcoming.

"Let's mount up," Lyons said. He watched Hermann "Gadgets" Schwarz and Rosario "Politician" Blancanales gather their gear.

Lyons breathed steady as the chopper began its descent into the large backyard of the residence. What Stony Man wanted them to do was a long shot—so long that had the former LAPD detective faced the same chances at the race track, he'd have stayed far from the windows.

Since Judge Martin's murder, a total of eight more federal judges and even a Supreme Court justice had fallen to the guns of American Choice. Federal, state and local police—especially SWAT squads—were working round the clock, trying to provide protection for likely assassination candidates. But the situation was like trying to find the proverbial needle in a haystack.

With nothing better to go on, Aaron Kurtzman, the Farm's crack computer man, had run a list of federal judges and all the available information through the probability program on his mammoth machines. The computer had kicked out several likely candidates for the terrorists' next hit. Judge Aaron C. Charles had topped the list.

For what that was worth. Kurtzman had stressed that there simply wasn't enough information for the computers to provide more than a ballpark idea as to what American Choice had in store next.

The chopper set down in the thick grass next to a four-car garage. Lyons grabbed the Atchisson full-auto 12-gauge, leaped down from his seat and raced toward a row of windows with a sliding glass door at the end. "Able One to Stony," he said into his headset as he ran. "You're *sure* the judge knows we're coming?"

"Affirmative, One," Barbara Price came back. "He's waiting inside with his family."

Lyons breathed a silent sigh of relief. It didn't hurt to double-check. Aaron Charles wasn't your typical old gray-head in black robes. In his early forties, he had been an Eighty-second Airborne paratrooper in Nam before returning stateside and working his way through law school as a St. Louis cop. As a police officer, Charles had made a name for himself both undercover and as a SWAT team member.

But the judge's latest claim to fame had come a few months earlier while presiding over the murder case of an Indianapolis religious cult leader. Four of the murderer's followers, armed with semiautomatic rifles, had broken into the courtroom and attempted to overpower the unprepared bailiffs. They had almost succeeded.

But then the man behind the bench had stood up, thrown his robe back over his shoulder like something out of a Clint Eastwood spaghetti western and drawn a Falcon Arms Portsider .45 from the lefthanded shoulder holster under his arm. Judge Aaron Charles had then proceeded to blow the armed cultists to a place where they could find out firsthand whether or not their eccentric spiritual beliefs were accurate.

All of which made Carl Lyons both respectful and apprehensive in regard to Aaron Charles. He didn't think Charles would hesitate to shoot three men coming in his back door unannounced, and that seemed like an awfully stupid way for the members of America's top stateside counterterrorist team to end their careers.

Lyons ground to a halt outside the glass door and heard Schwarz and Blancanales stop behind him. He reached out, slid the door along its track and called inside. "Judge! We're the friendlies! Hold your fire!"

The voice that answered came over an intercom. It was low, gruff and steady. "Come on in."

Lyons nodded over his shoulder, and Schwarz and Blancanales followed him through the door into what had probably once been a den area. Now it had become a combination gymnasium and martial-arts *dojang,* and Lyons remembered that in addition to the other accomplishments on Charles's list, the man was a fourth-degree black belt in the Korean art of Hapkido.

The voice over the loudspeaker spoke again. "Walk straight ahead," it said. "Down the hall and to the right. You'll see the stairs."

Lyons led his men over several padded mats, feeling the judge's eyes on his every move. He scanned the walls and ceiling as he walked. Wherever the camera was hidden, it was hidden well. The men of Able Team passed a Power Cage and bench scattered with Olympic weights, then left the room and followed the hallway to the stairs.

"Up both flights, then to your right," the loudspeaker said.

Lyons, Schwarz and Blancanales took the steps two at a time, then turned as directed. The Able Team leader found himself facing another long hall that appeared to lead past several doors.

"Stop where you are," the voice said. But this time it didn't come over the intercom. It came from behind the men of Able Team.

Footsteps approached from the rear, then Charles said, "Okay. Turn around."

Lyons turned to see a muscular man of medium height wearing faded O.D. green fatigue pants, a black tank top and white Nike Crosstrainers. A blue-and-red Eighty-second Airborne tattoo decorated the tanned skin of his left shoulder. Charles's hair was cropped short, and a thin Clark Gable mustache outlined the top of his upper lip.

A Springfield Armory M1A Bush Rifle was cradled under his armpit. The Falcon Arms left-handed .45 that had made national news rested in the judge's shoulder holster.

"Sorry about all this," Charles said, stepping forward. "You probably are who you say you are. But when I get a call from one of the top men in the Justice Department telling me I may be number one on the American Choice hit parade, I don't take chances." He paused, his lined face hardening as he appraised the three men. "You got any ID?"

Slowly Lyons reached into the breast pocket of his black combat suit and removed the Justice Department credentials Brognola had provided. Aaron Charles didn't have any idea who Able Team was, or that there even was a Stony Man Farm, and this wasn't the time to start explaining.

The judge took the credential case, studied the picture, then handed it back. The rifle lowered. "Like I said, I'm sorry. But I felt all this was necessary."

Lyons nodded. "You've got quite a setup," he said. "I couldn't even spot the surveillance cameras."

Charles's face lightened into a grin. "Good," he said. "They've only been in a few weeks—since that business with the cult nuts. There were rumors that they might retaliate." He shrugged. "Maybe I'm getting paranoid in my old age."

Lyons shook his head. "One man's paranoia is another's practicality," he said. Then, turning to Schwarz and Blancanales, "Gadgets, take the front. Pol, the rear. Make sure the alarm systems are operating. Backup from Indianapolis PD should be here any time now. We'll meet and hand out assignments as soon as they show." He turned back to Charles as the other two Able Team men descended the stairs. "Where's your family?"

Charles turned and led him down the hall into what appeared to be the master bedroom. Lithographs and original canvases covered walls that had been painted a soft, cool lime. A television set rested on a swivel table in front of the king-size bed, and a syndicated rerun of "Cheers" had just started on the screen.

Lyons and Charles ascended a step at the rear of the bedroom and entered a short hallway. At the end Lyons could see book-covered walls through the open door to the library. They turned left before reaching the room and entered a huge walk-in closet.

Carl Lyons suppressed a whistle. He'd slept in smaller bedrooms during his lifetime.

Charles walked to the far wall and pulled a tapestry from the nail on which it hung. A small crack appeared between the oak panels. The judge worked his fingers into the crack, then pulled the panel out and to the side.

The opening led to a secluded section of attic. In the light from the closet, Lyons saw a threadbare couch. A stunningly beautiful woman in her midtwenties sat on the couch, a sleeping infant cradled in her arms. Next to her, a boy of four or so dozed with his head resting on his mother's shoulder.

The woman looked at them, a mother's overriding concern evident in her taut features. "You watch yourself," she whispered to her husband.

"Good place," Lyons said. "Okay, Your Honor. Better join them. I'll close it back up and rehang the tapestry."

"The *hell* you will," Charles growled. "Somebody wants to come after me in my own damn house, he can damn well *deal with me.*" He leaned in, kissed his wife on the lips, then stepped back out and shoved the panel back in place.

Lyons didn't argue as he rehooked the tapestry. Normally on a guard job like this, he'd have insisted on getting the target out of the way. But the judge was a special case. He'd proved to be a capable warrior throughout his life.

The Able Team leader smiled inwardly. Besides, he had a feeling that if he forced Aaron Charles into the attic, the man would be back out the minute his back was turned.

"Then let's set up," Lyons said. He led Charles out of the closet and back to the bedroom. "Cheers" broke for a commercial, and a local Indianapolis car dealer wearing a gray cowboy hat came on-screen. Lyons stopped by the door and turned back to the judge. "We don't know for certain that anything will even happen, Your Honor. In fact, the odds are against it—but I want to be ready. I want you to stay up here in the bedroom."

Charles shook his head. "I'm not some fat-assed old bastard in a robe who never saw a gun before," he said. "I'll help you downstairs. It's *my* family that's at stake."

Lyons nodded. "Exactly why I want you up here," he said. "To protect your family. You'll be the last line of defense if anybody gets through us." He shrugged. "Of course, if you'd rather delegate that job to some rookie cop you've never met..." He let his voice trail off.

Charles frowned, then his face relaxed. "I see your point," he said.

"Good. Now—"

Schwarz's voice in his ear interrupted the Able Team leader. "Able Two to One. SWAT just pulled up out front."

Lyons walked to the front window. Below was a van, and he saw the letters *SWAT* painted across its side. He stared down at it, and his face hardened. "Something's wrong," he said. "SWAT wouldn't advertise its presence in this type of threat."

Charles was at his side already, and he grabbed Lyons's arm. "Not only that, but Indianapolis's SWAT team isn't called SWAT anymore," Charles said. "It's the Emergency Response Team. They *damn* sure wouldn't have SWAT on the side of the van—bad

PR." The fingers on Lyons's arm tightened as Charles stared down through the window. "For that matter, they don't have *vans*." He turned back to the car dealer who was still on the TV screen. "That fellow you see right there donated six panel trucks to the department two months ago."

Lyons turned and bolted through the bedroom toward the stairs. "Able One to Two and Three," he shouted into the face mike.

He heard Schwarz key the mike and start to answer.

But the Able Team electronics expert's words were drowned out by the automatic-rifle fire that exploded over the radio into Carl Lyons's ears.

YAKOV KATZENELENBOGEN stared out of the Hotel Ringsted's seedy fifth-floor window at the blurry building three blocks away. He could see the front gate in the tall iron fence and most of the grounds. He could even see the man and woman nearing the gate on the sidewalk outside the fence.

He could see them, all right. He just couldn't tell anything about them—whether they were hurrying toward some important appointment, simply out for a walk, or trying to look like their actions were innocent while they cased the grounds in preparation to blowing the American Embassy off the face of the planet.

Katz turned away from the window and moved to the bed. An old AM radio sat on the stand next to the headboard, and the deep theatrical voice of Richard Burton, narrating a musical version of H. G. Wells's "War of the Worlds," resonated from the speaker.

The Israeli had monitored the English-speaking station since checking into the Ringsted, hoping that he might learn whether or not the wreck that had taken the lives of Herbert Urquillo and the old woman had made the news. More particularly, if the bodies had been identified.

What happened in the next few hours might well depend on whether or not the remaining terrorists knew their leader was dead.

Katz unzipped his backpack and rummaged through the contents. The hotel was the closest place he had found where he could safely set up and watch the American Embassy building. The long summer daylight of Scandinavia had seen to that. The sun was a mixed blessing. It made surveillance easier in some ways, harder in others. But all in all, the former Mossad man would have preferred darkness. The light made it too easy to get spotted by both the embassy guards and the bad guys.

Katz found the long tubular leather case and flipped the catch at the end. Turning it upside down, he let the Unitron Spotting Scope slide out into his hand, then moved back to the window.

Aiming the scope through the glass, he pressed the black rubber cup into his eye socket. He adjusted the zoom and focus controls and stared through the lens.

The American Embassy to Sweden appeared at the end of the tube.

Katz shifted the scope, and the man and woman he'd watched earlier came into view. The man was tall and overweight, with short blond hair. He wore a brown wool sport coat and slacks. A light blue jogging suit stretched across the woman's portly posterior, tighter than the Stony Man blacksuits. The couple looked more like a middle-aged college professor and his wife than terrorists.

Which meant nothing. Katz had been around too long to think the bad guys always came in camouflage and khaki. Like Phoenix Force themselves, they wore whatever fitted their mission.

As the Israeli watched through the spotting scope, the "professor" reached behind his wife and pinched her on the rear. The woman jumped, giggled and playfully slapped at the hand.

Katz dropped the scope to arm's length and rubbed his eye. He reached into his pocket, produced a handkerchief and mopped the sweat from his brow. It was hot in the room, and the shirt, tie, sport coat and slacks he'd thrown over his blacksuit in order to rent the room didn't help. But he dared not take them off at this point. No matter where he ended up next, he'd have to leave the hotel through the lobby, and the sight of a man in black battle dress with guns hanging off his hips and shoulders was more than enough to cause someone to call the cops.

Behind him, "War of the Worlds" took an intermission. The news came on, and a man speaking English with a mixed Swedish-British accent reported on civil disturbances in Hungary and the new Czech Republic before finally getting around to the local Swedish news.

Urquillo's wreck was the third story. Police had not yet identified the bodies, and the Phoenix Force leader breathed a sigh of relief. He brought the scope to his eye again as a man walking a German shepherd passed the embassy gate.

Inside the embassy, the search should be in full
bloom by now. Worried that the explosives might have
already been placed, Katz had ordered David Mc-
Carter to call in an anonymous bomb threat half an
hour earlier. If that alerted the terrorists that someone was on to them, then that was simply the price
Phoenix Force would have to pay.

Katz didn't intend to gamble with the lives inside the
embassy.

The news report eased the Israeli's worries. Urquillo and the woman had not been identified, and
Urquillo's men would have no reason to make the
connection. Right now they might be a little anxious
as to their leader's whereabouts, but that should be the
extent of their worries.

"War of the Worlds" returned to the air with songs
about the "spirit of man" and the "brave new world"
that would rise from the ashes of the Martian destruction. Burton did the epilogue, and then the news
came back on. Katz turned toward the radio.

"Police have identified the charred bodies of two
motorists who struck road-construction equipment on
Highway E4 today as Herbert Alonzo Urquillo and his
mother, Maria Urquillo," the announcer said. "Both
are internationally wanted terrorists with ties to the
Basque ETA Party and other terrorist groups. They
were dead on arrival at St. Mikael's Hospital in
Norrköping. Police are investigating the possibility
that the collision occurred during the planning of a
terrorist strike somewhere in Sweden."

The Israeli stared at the radio. So much for that.
This news could affect the remaining terrorists in either of two ways. They would either go on with the

planned bombing of the embassy, or disband like sheep who had lost their sheepdog.

But even if they scattered like frightened lambs, someone would have the explosives. And eventually those explosives would claim the lives of innocents.

David McCarter's voice broke into Katz's thoughts. "Phoenix Four, Phoenix One. Can you hear me, Katz?"

Katz spoke into the mouthpiece in front of his face. "Go ahead, Four."

"You looking out the window?"

"Affirmative." The Israeli turned back to the glass and trained the spotting scope on the gate. The sidewalk in front of the embassy was clear. "I don't see anything."

"Keep watching," McCarter said. "They should be entering your field of vision any second now."

Katz squinted into the eyepiece. A moment later, the college professor and his wife walked back in the direction from which they'd come earlier. "I see them," the Phoenix Force leader said. "They passed by earlier."

"Not only that," McCarter said. "They've been hanging around the area most of the evening. Had a cup of coffee across the street for an hour or so, then circled the embassy to the other side. He's been playing grab-ass with her all night. I think it's a put-on."

Katz started to answer, but before he could speak, the man walking the German shepherd approached the couple from the opposite direction.

Calvin James's voice came on the air. "I've seen the dog man a time or two, as well," James said. "A block over."

The man with the dog stopped in front of the couple and produced a rumpled pack of cigarettes. The college professor extended a lighter.

Encizo's voice sounded in Katz's ear. "I just left a bar two storefronts down. Any of the rest of you catch the news report?"

"I've had the car radio on," Gary Manning said. "Urquillo and his mother."

"That explains the sweet old thing trying to put a bullet in your head, Katz," James said.

Katz didn't answer. He watched a dark-colored Mazda pull to the curb. The driver rolled down his window, and the two men, woman and dog hurried to the door.

Words were exchanged, and then the men, woman and animal piled into the vehicle.

"Looks like the radio's been on in that car, too," McCarter said.

Katz moved to the bed, jammed the scope back in his pack and hurried out the door and down the hall to the stairs. "I'm on my way out of the hotel right now," he said into the radio. "Manning, pull the station wagon around front. The rest of you get over here on the double."

The Phoenix Force leader raced down the steps and then slowed to a brisk walk through the lobby. Several old men sat in threadbare stuffed chairs reading newspapers and magazines. None of them gave him a second look. Katz reached the street in time to see the Mazda cut a U-turn and start his way. He dropped back inside the lobby and let it pass.

Manning pulled the station wagon to the curb thirty seconds later. He'd picked up McCarter and Encizo somewhere along the way. He and McCarter, Phoenix Force's resident race-car driver, changed places as James came jogging across the street and jumped in the back seat. Katz opened the door to the front.

The Mazda turned right two blocks ahead as they pulled away from the curb. McCarter gunned the engine and shot forward, then slowed to a normal speed as soon as he'd turned and established visual contact once more. He dropped back, putting just enough space between the Mazda and station wagon to stay inconspicuous.

Katz watched the Mazda roll through the streets of Stockholm, taking them, he hoped, to the rest of Urquillo's men and the explosives. As he leaned back against the seat, the sweat dripping from his forehead reminded him of the additional clothes he wore.

The Phoenix Force leader leaned forward again and began slipping out of the sport coat, shirt and tie he'd used to cover his combat suit. The tight black material appeared, and on top of it the shoulder holster housing his Beretta and extra magazines.

Katz rolled the window down and let the cool evening breeze chase the sweat from his face. He smiled.

It had been damn hot wearing two sets of clothes. But he had a feeling things were about to get hotter without them.

The traffic thinned as, sun or no sun, the hour grew late and the people of Stockholm retired for the night. Darkness finally fell as the Mazda hit the access ramp to Highway E18 and left Stockholm, traveling northwest. The men of Phoenix Force used the slack time to check their weapons and other gear.

The Mazda left the highway at the village of Sund-byberg and started down a rough gravel road into the fjord country. McCarter dropped farther back, killing the headlights. He frowned, then glanced up through the windshield at the sky. "They'll spot us, you know," he said. "The area's too deserted." He turned to Katz. "Even with our lights off, there's too much moon—no way I can keep them in sight without them seeing me."

Katz nodded. He turned a full three hundred sixty degrees, scanning the area. Deserted.

"Let's take them and get it over with," he said. "Try to keep at least one of them alive. If we can't, there aren't many places they can go from here. We should be able to find their safe house on our own."

McCarter grinned. "You got it, boss," the Cockney said in an exaggerated American accent. His foot leaned forward on the accelerator, and the station wagon shot forward, skipping across the rugged road and spitting chunks of gravel in its wake. The taillights in the distance grew larger, then disappeared as the Mazda rounded a curve.

McCarter leaned harder on the accelerator, pushing every ounce of power out of the vehicle he could. His toe barely scratched the brake pedal as he skidded the vehicle around the curve after the Mazda. But the Briton stomped hard on the brake as soon as he'd made the turn. He had to.

The terrorist car suddenly appeared, having slowed to a crawl in preparation for another turn down a side road. Steel screamed like a wounded cat as the station wagon's front bumper drove up and over the trunk of

the Mazda, shattering the rear window in a hurricane
of glass.

The men of Phoenix Force were thrown forward.
McCarter twisted the wheel, trying to spin off the
other car, but the wagon's grille caught on the lip beneath the Mazda's window and locked the two cars
together. They turned sideways, sliding down the road,
forged together as one in a death grip.

"Pile out!" Katz shouted above the turmoil. He
dived from the still-moving station wagon, drawing
the Beretta 92 from his shoulder rig as he rolled across
the gravel. Tiny stones bit his neck and face as he
bounded back to his feet, then sprinted back toward
the Mazda.

An arm holding a pistol extended from the passenger's window. Katz estimated the angle to the body
attached to the arm and double-actioned a 9 mm hollowpoint. A muffled scream came from inside the
front seat as the two cars finally slithered to a halt in
the middle of the road.

Calvin James appeared on the driver's side. He held
his Uzi at waist level, his index finger pulling the trigger back and sending a blanket of automatic rounds
through the front seat of the Mazda.

Manning leaped from the station wagon and rushed
up next to James. The stubby barrel of a MAC-11 shot
from the Mazda's rear window, and the Canadian
fired a 3-round burst. The subgun fell from the Mazda
to the road. Through the window Katz saw the dark
shadow that had held it slump in its seat.

In the back seat Katz could see the man who had
looked like a college professor. His head rested on the
back of the front seat, blood pouring from an open

gash on the temple. His dead eyes stared out into the darkness.

In the middle, between the two corpses, the woman was frantically trying to open her handbag.

The Phoenix Force leader rushed forward, sticking the Beretta past the professor and into her throat. "Freeze," he ordered.

The woman did as she was told.

"You want to live?" Katz asked.

Slowly the woman nodded.

"Then get out of the car. Slow. Keep your hands in sight." The former Mossad man stepped back and opened the door.

A sudden burst of fire from behind Katz struck the professor's body, sending him into a macabre dance of the already dead. The Israeli whirled, ducking as a second volley sailed over his head.

From inside the car, he heard the woman scream. Then the screams became a garbled choking sound.

Next to the road where the Mazda had intended to turn, a small hill rose into the darkness. More autofire popped the Mazda as Katz slid on his belly, the Beretta held in front of him in a two-handed grip. He tapped the trigger, firing up at the muzzle-flashes that lit the hill like hundreds of fireflies.

The former Mossad man fired again, then again. The rest of Phoenix Force, on the other side of the interlocked vehicles, joined in. Gradually the muzzle-flashes died down until the hill stood dark and silent once more.

Katz rose to his feet. He dropped the magazine from his Beretta and shoved a full load up the grip, then hurried up the hill.

Half a dozen men lay in pools of blood under the moonlight.

Behind them, at the crest, he saw the faint outlines of a house.

James's voice drifted up to the Phoenix Force leader. "You check the woman?"

Manning answered. "She's dead. Got it between the eyes."

A moment later the rest of the team joined Katz. Without speaking, the Israeli led them to the small one-story structure.

A light burned through the drawn shade in the window on the porch. Katz started to kick the door, then on second thought reached out and tried the knob.

The door opened.

The Phoenix Force leader crouched low as he rushed through the door, the Beretta leading the way.

He needn't have bothered. The one-room cabin was deserted. Urquillo's men had all come out for the road party.

Manning, McCarter, James and Encizo joined Katz in the center of the room. They all turned toward the table against the wall at the same time.

Two boxes of Chilean demolition charges sat on the rotting wood.

"Take care of it, Manning," Katz said.

Manning nodded. He walked forward and pulled a fuze from his combat suit as the rest of the men started back down the hill.

The big Canadian joined them three minutes later. Jumping into the station wagon, they took off toward the highway.

"Stony Man, Phoenix One," Barbara Price's voice said through Katz's headset.

"Go ahead, Stony," Katz answered. "Striker got another errand for us?"

"Affirmative," Price said. "Grimaldi's on his way to pick you up. You're heading for Copenhagen."

Katz started to acknowledge the transmission, but before the words could leave his mouth, the house on top of the hill behind them exploded into an inferno of flame.

CHAPTER EIGHT

Autofire burst through the second-floor hallway windows of the judge's house, sending a rainstorm of glass over Carl Lyons's head and shoulders. The Able Team leader grabbed the railing with one hand, the grips of his Atchisson full-auto assault shotgun with the other, and bolted down the stairs to the ground floor.

Above him Lyons heard Charles slam the door to the master bedroom. A heavy dead bolt lock slid into place with a loud clank.

Steady gunfire, sounding almost like one giant explosion, began in both the front and back yards of the house. Lyons descended the last flight of stairs in two leaps, the Atchisson now gripped in both hands. He landed on the entryway tile as the front door to the house burst open.

The black combat boot that had kicked the door came down in the entryway. Above the boot, Lyons saw gray urban-camo fatigues and a Heckler & Koch MP-5 9 mm submachine gun.

Lyons mind shot back to the briefing from Stony Man. Striker had provided Intel concerning the gray camo fatigues.

He'd also warned of bulletproof vests.

The dark, sharp features of a Middle Eastern face scowled at the Able Team leader as the terrorist's arms rose and he attempted to line his target up in the sights of his submachine gun.

Lyons got the Atchisson to waist level and squeezed the trigger. A 3-round burst of 12-gauge buckshot exploded into the chest and stomach of the terrorist. Lyons saw the front of the gray fatigue blouse turn black with blood and smiled.

No vests *this* time.

The blasts drove the man back through the front door to the porch. He fell forward again across the doorway.

From the dining room to his side, the Able Team leader heard the distinctive sound of Schwarz's M-16 as Gadgets entered the foray, firing through the front window. More .223 fire sounded from the back of the house, coming from Blancanales.

Two more men in gray had rushed up the steps to the porch, putting on the skids as they saw their comrade fall. Lyons pulled the trigger again, coughing up a lone 12-gauge offering that caught the terrorist to his right in the shoulder. The man spun around, and Lyons took advantage of the brief reprieve to swing the shotgun to his left.

A burst of 9 mm fire drilled by him. Lyons dropped instinctively to one knee, triggering another burst into the gunman's abdomen and neck before turning back to his right.

The spinning man came to a halt as the Able Team leader fired again. Round lead pellets the size of BBs shot from the Atchisson's barrel, shredding the Arabic face like a slab of beef run through the grinder.

The two men fell as one, stacking up waist high over their friend in the doorway.

Schwarz appeared suddenly in the entryway from the dining room. "There's at least twenty of them, Ironman!" he shouted above the rattling of fire still pummeling the walls of the house. "I've taken out two, but—"

Lyons heard the glass in the dining room break, followed by the thud of boots landing on the floor.

Schwarz turned back into the room and cut loose with a full-auto stream of .223 slugs. Screams echoed in the entryway as Gadgets turned back to the Able Team leader once more. "I was about to say, there's plenty more where they came from." Another burst of glass sent him back out of sight.

Lyons dived forward, stretching out prone behind the pile of dead men in the doorway and using them for cover. With the Atchisson resting over the back of the top man, he scanned the yard, seeing that most of the terrorists had taken cover behind the low brick wall that ran across the front of the lot. Another of the attackers stood behind a lattice, his gray cammies distinctive between the green vines spread across the thatched wood.

Lyons saw him yank something from the battle suspenders on his chest. The Able Team leader knew what it had to be.

Lyons's finger moved back on the Atchisson's trigger before he even realized his brain had given it the command. The blast echoed off the walls of the porch.

The vines spread on the lattice, and a two-inch hole appeared in the wood. A scream issued forth from behind the structure. The gray-fatigued body fell forward, crashing through what remained of the lattice and sending slivers of wood flying through the air.

A second later the activated grenade exploded, spewing scraps of wood, mixed with pieces of gray camouflage fatigues, into the air.

A sudden united assault now came from behind the brick wall, sending a steady barrage streaking toward the front door. Lyons ducked down, letting the rounds sail over his head or strike the bodies of the terrorists in front of him. The three corpses jiggled a macabre dance of death each time a projectile struck home.

Lyons aimed just above the wall and fired back, ducked another storm of bullets, then fired again. Both times he was a split second too slow, and the terrorists fell back behind their protective covering, the Atchisson's lead pellets spending themselves against the brick.

Lyons ducked down, pulling a handful of shotgun shells from a pocket in his assault suit and shoving them into the shotgun. He worked the slide manually, chambering a round as Blancanales suddenly spoke in his ear. "Ironman, I've got a head count of eight back here. Four down so far. Ten-twenty?"

"Pinned down in front," Lyons called out as another volley struck the bodies on the front porch. He rose, fired at a flash of gray moving toward the van parked in the street beyond the wall, then ducked back down as more subgun fire peppered his human barricade. The Able Team leader could still hear Schwarz blasting away in the dining room. He waited for the onslaught to die down again, then popped up and kindled another firestorm of shot toward the wall.

Before he fell back again, he saw more of the gray caps crawling toward the van.

Retreating? Or simply re*grouping?*

Suddenly all firing ceased. A ghostly silence fell over the house and grounds.

"Ironman," Blancanales breathed through the radio. "They've fallen back here. Taken cover behind the swimming pool bath house."

"Same up here, Pol," Schwarz answered sardonically. "Suppose they're gonna give themselves up? They've only got us down three-to-one now."

Lyons heard Blancanales chuckle. But before either man could reply, they got their answer.

A dozen men suddenly leaped from behind the van and sprinted toward the short brick wall, screaming at the top of their lungs in Arabic. Each held an MP-5 in his right hand, the submachine guns blasting the front of the house as they ran.

In their left hands they wielded bulletproof shields of transparent Plexiglas.

Schwarz was the first to fire. His .223 bullets ricocheted harmlessly off the shield of the terrorist in the lead as the man hurdled the brick wall. The man landed beyond the wall, Gadgets's rounds not even causing him to break stride.

Lyons saw what had happened and didn't waste time with his shotgun. If the penetrating .223s of an M-16 couldn't pierce the shields, the soft lead of the 12-gauge certainly wouldn't. Lowering his aim, he dropped the front bead sight on the shins of the lead runner as the man started up the sidewalk to the porch.

The Atchisson jumped against his shoulder as the pellets spread across the terrorist's shins. A howl of surprise and anguish shrieked from the man's lips. His feet shot backward, and he slammed the grass with his face, the bulletproof shield rolling to the side.

Schwarz's M-16 sizzled up and down his body until it lay still.

Lyons swung the Atchisson to the second man in the assault, cutting his feet out from under him as cleanly as he had the first. Schwarz took his cue, finishing the job as soon as vital areas became exposed.

Lyons fired again. Schwarz followed. Working in tandem, they downed four more men. The maddened cries of war issuing forth from the mouths of the terrorists changed to wails of death.

Bodies lay scattered on the front yard, piling up and forcing the trailing attackers to slow as they vaulted the obstacles.

But there were still too many, and Lyons saw that despite the casualties, the assault was bringing the attackers closer to the front porch. Sooner or later, one would break through.

As if voicing his prediction for him, Blancanales's voice suddenly sounded over the radio. "Ironman! Two men just broke ranks and burst through a window two rooms down from me. They're somewhere in the house!"

Lyons continued to fire, shredding another set of shins. There was no way he could turn around, let alone go looking for the invaders who had entered the house. Not with men still storming the front.

Between shots, he did his best to attune his senses to the rear. He thought he heard footsteps pounding up a set of stairs at the back of the house.

With only two men still on their feet in the front yard, he risked a brief glance over his shoulder. He saw nothing, but the interruption cost him.

By the time he turned back to the front, the remaining two terrorists were less than ten feet from the porch steps. Lyons triggered the Atchisson, lacing a round of pellets into the first man's ankles. The terrorist fell to the ground, then his body jerked spasmodically to the rhythm of Gadgets's M-16. The last man in gray jumped over him and started up the porch.

Lyons swung the shotgun his way, dropped the bead sight on the gray knees and pulled the trigger.

The firing pin fell on an empty chamber. Lyons rose behind the dead men, bringing the Atchisson up like a baseball bat.

He was too late.

The terrorist had launched himself through the air, shield first. Lyons swung the shotgun, but he couldn't slow the momentum behind the hard Plexiglas shield. Both the shield and the Atchisson flew to the floor as Lyons tumbled backward, the man in gray on top of him.

The Able Team leader reached up, grabbing the barrel of the Heckler & Koch with both hands as the terrorist struggled to line it up with his head. From the corner of his eye, he saw Schwarz appear in the entryway. Gadgets raised his M-16, sighting in on the terrorist, then stopped as the man in gray rolled to the side, taking the Able Team leader with him.

Lyons clenched his fingers tighter around the H&K as they rolled across the floor. He came up on top, and

Schwarz tried to aim again, but the terrorist wrenched suddenly to the side and they rolled on.

Hot breath from the face in front of his assaulted Lyons's nostrils as the two men crashed against the wall. Above them boots pounded up the stairs to the third floor. When they spun away from the wall, Lyons caught a flash of Gadgets still trying to get a shot at his assailant.

Schwarz looked overhead, then back to the men on the floor.

"Go on!" Lyons shouted between clenched teeth. "Get to the judge!"

Schwarz hesitated, then sprinted up the steps toward the second floor as the sound of a door being kicked in drifted down from the top of the house.

Lyons and the attacker rolled to a halt again, the man in gray on top. The open mouth above the Able Team leader was now wheezing with effort. Lyons pushed on the H&K as they rolled once more, crashing into the opposite wall.

The terrorist's arms gave slightly. He was tiring.

They came to a halt side by side on the entryway tile. They pushed, then pulled, each trying to wrest the H&K from the hands of the other.

Lyons pushed suddenly and felt the man push back. Then, just as suddenly, he pulled, using the terrorist's own strength to draw the man into him. At the same time he thrust his face forward, striking the man in the nose with the crown of his head.

Blood spurted from the terrorist's nose. Lyons snatched the H&K from his fingers, sprang to his feet and tapped a 3-round burst of fire into the bleeding face.

The sound of running feet approached from the rear of the house. Lyons turned the MP-5 that way. He lowered the weapon as Blancanales rounded the corner of the living room to the entryway.

Lyons nodded toward the stairs, then vaulted the steps three at a time, Pol at his heels. They had reached the second floor when they heard .223 shots echoing down the stairwell. Racing on to the top floor, they saw Schwarz jump over a gray-clad body. The electronics man sprinted into the bedroom with Lyons and Blancanales following.

Judge Aaron Charles was nowhere to be seen.

The final terrorist was sprinting through the bedroom to the hall that led to the walk-in closet. The three men of Able Team fired, their rounds pounding harmlessly into the wall behind him as he disappeared through the door.

As they raced after the man, a steady stream of fire suddenly erupted. Lyons pushed past Schwarz, jumped the steps and turned into the walk-in closet.

Judge Aaron Charles stood holding the Springfield Armory MIA Bush Rifle. The last terrorist lay jerking on the floor as the judge fired into the prostrate body.

Lyons, Schwarz and Blancanales ground to a halt just outside the closet as the Springfield's bolt locked open.

The judge didn't hesitate. He dropped the weapon and drew the Portsider .45 from his shoulder rig.

Lyons knelt, studying the face of the dark-skinned man on the floor below. He'd seen it somewhere in the computer files at Stony Man...yeah. Ali Azi had been the guy's name. He'd once been a top-ranking official in Yasir Arafat's personal bodyguard corp, Force 17.

Lyons stood back up. A moment of silence ensued. Then Charles looked deep into the Able Team leader's eyes. "That all of them?" he asked.

Lyons nodded.

Slowly, the judge turned, tore down the tapestry and opened the panel to the attic.

Mrs. Charles sat wild-eyed on the couch, the baby still clutched in her arms.

The little boy next to her was still sleeping.

THE WALLS of the War Room at Stony Man Farm were bare, serious. But not nearly as serious as the big man who stood at the end of the conference table.

Bolan lifted the telephone receiver from its cradle, held it against his ear and tapped a button. As he waited for Barbara Price to answer his buzz, he scrutinized the other men seated around the table.

Hal Brognola, Carl Lyons, Gadgets Schwarz and Rosario "Pol" Blancanales. All good men. Able Team had just kept Supreme Court Judge Aaron Charles alive against incredible odds, and Brognola had been doing his best to coordinate things and handle the political aspects of the panic that was sweeping the nation as American Choice continued to assassinate the country's judges.

To date, fourteen men in black robes had fallen prey to the Corporation and terrorists.

Bolan knew that the way they had gone about the war so far meant eventual defeat. Even while Lyons and his team had been saving Aaron Charles, a judge in Los Angeles had been gunned down by terrorists

believed to be led by former SDS Weathermen leader
Johnny Jackson.

No, Bolan and his men needed a more-focused battle plan. So far, they simply hadn't had enough Intel
to formulate one. But now, with the information
gathered by Able Team in Indianapolis, Phoenix Force
in Scandinavia and Bolan himself, they did.

When Price picked up the line, Bolan said, "Katz
called in yet?"

"Negative, Striker," the Stony Man mission controller answered. "I'll buzz as soon as—" A line rang
in the background. "Hold on a minute. That could be
him now."

Bolan waited. As soon as Phoenix Force had located the rest of Urquillo's explosives and destroyed
the safe house outside Stockholm, Katz and company
had flown to Copenhagen, Denmark. The CIA knew
"Rance Pollock" had been in Sweden, which meant
they might also have learned about Phoenix Force.
The Executioner wasn't taking any chances on tapped
lines in Stockholm.

But the real reason Bolan had picked Copenhagen
for Phoenix Force was that it was the first port of call,
and clearinghouse, for ships and planes smuggling
cocaine into all of Scandinavia.

Which made it the perfect place for Katz and his
men to carry out their end of Bolan's plan.

Price came back on. "It's him, Striker. Go ahead,
Phoenix One." The line clicked again.

"Striker?" It was the Israeli's voice.

"Speaking," Bolan said. "This line secure?"

"As secure as we can be under the circumstances,"
Katz said. "I picked a random phone booth in the

heart of the city. The spooks shouldn't know we've left Sweden—if they even knew we were there in the first place. But if they do, they still can't cover all the phones in Copenhagen. I'd say the chances of them listening in right now are about a million to one."

Bolan punched the button, transferring the call to the speakerphone so the rest of the Stony Man crew could hear. "Okay, Katz, then I'll get started."

He looked up at the men before him. "Our problem so far has been that the combined forces of the Corporation and terrorists are so multifaceted," he began. "It's like an octopus with its head in Bolivia and the tentacles—with an *operational* head, O'Banion—scattered throughout America. They're too numerous to systematically search out and destroy." He paused, cleared his throat, then went on. "Since a frontal assault won't work, I've come up with a two-part plan. What we're going to do first, gentlemen, is separate that head from the tentacles." He watched stern faces around the table as he spoke. "Once the head and tentacles are separate entities, I'm going to set them against each other like a shark eating his own tail."

To his side, Bolan saw Hal Brognola's eyes narrow. "It's the oldest trick in the book," the Justice man said. "Divide and conquer."

"Exactly." The Executioner nodded.

Blancanales leaned forward in his seat. "So in other words, we turn Ennslin and O'Banion against each other." He frowned. "It could work."

Carl Lyons broke in. "It's got a chance," he said. "We used to pull it off on a smaller scale once in a while when I worked narcotics. We'd create friction between a dealer and his supplier. Pretty soon one of them wound up in the river. We called it long-range assassination."

Bolan nodded again. "It might work that way, and if it does, more power to it. But I don't intend to stand by and just hope. We'll be along for the ride. To make sure things get done properly."

Gadgets Schwarz raised a hand to his chin. "Okay," he said. "Just tell us what you want us to do."

Bolan glanced to the speakerphone. "You with us so far, Katz?"

"Affirmative," the Israeli said.

The Executioner turned back to the table. "We've known all along that the DEA had a man inside the Corporation. But he's not high enough up the totem pole to have been much good so far. But he'll do for what I have in mind now. And the CIA is bound to have a contact in the IRA."

Carl Lyons's eyes flickered. "But do we know who that contact is?"

Bolan shook his head. "Not yet. We'll have to find out from the CIA."

Lyons snorted. "You trust them after all that's happened?"

"Most of them," Bolan said. "My hunch is it's a rogue agent who's pulling the strings on this deal. The other people he's using probably don't even know they're working against us. But just to be safe, I don't plan to go through the usual Company channels." He went on to explain the details of the intricate plan he had put together during his flight back to the U.S. from Sweden.

The faces around the table remained grim. But by the time he'd finished, they were all smiling.

THE BACK SEAT of the Ford Bronco was going to be crowded.

But that was what the Executioner wanted. It would add to the feeling of helplessness he intended to create for the man.

Bolan watched through the windshield as the target in the gray pin-striped suit with padded shoulders bounded down the steps in front of the New York brownstone, then turned right and started walking uptown.

"Doesn't look like he has a care in the world," Gadgets Schwarz said from the rear seat.

"He will," Bolan said. "Go get him."

The Executioner started the engine as Schwarz opened the door and melted into the people cruising the sidewalk. The Bronco rolled slowly forward, keeping pace with Able Team's electronics man as Gadgets closed the gap between him and the gray suit.

When he was directly behind the man, Schwarz shoved one hand into the side pocket of his coat and tapped the padded shoulder with the other.

The man turned around.

Schwarz shoved his coat-wrapped hand into the man's ribs. The Able Team warrior said something, and the man's face took on the frozen expression of a jackrabbit caught in the headlights of a pickup. He turned toward the Bronco and walked obediently forward as Bolan parked along the curb.

"That all it takes to catch a CIA agent?" Lyons scoffed. "Damn, this country's in good hands."

Bolan waited as Blancanales got out of the seat next to him and opened the back door. Schwarz ushered the man into the rear of the car next to Lyons, then slid in on the other side. Lyons patted the prisoner down, lifting a Walther PPK from under the suit as the Executioner pulled away from the curb.

Three blocks later the frightened CIA agent spoke up. "Is, uh, this a robbery? I've only got about a hundred bucks."

"You know it's no robbery," Bolan said over his shoulder. "So don't play cute. We want information."

The frightened look became one of panic as the CIA agent realized his captives knew who he was. "Information? I'm, er, just a clerk at the bank," he said, going into an obviously prearranged cover story. "I don't get close enough to the real money to be of any use to you . . . if it's the vault you're interested in—"

Carl Lyons had never been known as a patient man. The Able Team leader reminded the other men of than fact now by slapping the CIA operative across the mouth.

Bolan looked up into the rearview mirror as he turned a corner and started along a thoroughfare. "Let's cut the crap, shall we? We know who you are. Agent Harvey Nielson of the Central Intelligence Agency. Believe it or not, Nielson, we're good guys. We don't intend to kill you."

Bolan watched the panic on the man's face fade slightly, then said, "As long as you cooperate."

The panic returned.

The Executioner didn't break stride. "I'll make this short and sweet. We want the name of the mole you've got inside the IRA."

"Mole? IRA?" Nielson sputtered. "I don't know—"

Lyons slapped him again. A tiny trickle of blood began to run down Nielson's face.

Lyons looked into the rearview mirror at Bolan.

The Executioner nodded.

Lyons stuck his hand in his coat. "Let's have a little fun, Nielson," he said. "You like to gamble?"

"I, uh, I head over to Atlantic City once in a while," the CIA man said, trying to smile.

"Good," Lyons said. His hand came out of his coat holding a two-inch Colt Commando. Breaking open the cylinder, he showed Nielson the empty holes. "So. Tell us who the mole is," he said.

Nielson kept the frightened smile on his face. "Really, guys," he said, "I don't know what you're talking about."

Gadgets Schwarz made the kind of clucking sound with his mouth that schoolteachers use on disobedient children.

Lyons reached back into his pocket again and produced a .38-caliber bullet. He dropped it into one of the holes, spun the wheel and slammed the gun shut again, his hand covering the cylinder.

Agent Nielson closed his eyes and grimaced as the stubby barrel was jammed against the side of his head and the hammer cocked.

"Okay," Lyons said. "The odds are six to one in your favor. You in?"

Nielson didn't answer.

Lyons pulled the trigger, and the hammer fell with a clink. He cocked the weapon again. "Five to one," he said. "Who's the snitch?"

Nielson's eyes closed tighter. The veins in his temples began to throb. Lyons pulled the trigger again, and the Colt snapped home on another empty chamber.

Lyons looked to the rearview mirror. "This guy *does* like gambling," he said. Turning his attention back to the man at his side, he cocked the hammer again. "We're down to three-to-one odds now. Pass or play?"

"I don't know..." Nielson hedged. "Really...I don't—"

Clink.

"Two to one," Lyons said. "Who's the mole?"

Nielson's voice rose an octave higher. "Let me explain! Please! I can't—"

The hammer falling on another empty chamber sounded like a jazz drummer's cymbal falling on a concrete floor.

"Uh-oh," Schwarz said.

Lyons cocked the gun again. "I'd say the odds definitely favor the house this time," he growled.

"His name is Marshall!" CIA Agent Harvey Nielson screamed at the top of his lungs. "Marshall Donahue! I'll take you to him!"

"You damn sure will," Lyons said, and pulled the trigger.

The hammer fell on the final chamber with a dull thud.

A soft whimper issued forth from the man in the gray suit. He leaned forward, his face in his hands.

Lyons flipped the cylinder out again. He ejected the shell, grabbed Nielson by the hair and jerked his head back. Sticking the bullet into the CIA man's face, he said, "You'll take us to him, all right. Or we'll play this game again. And next time I won't take the primer out of the bullet."

THE EXHAUST FAN inside Cramer's Café blew the odor of hickory-smoked chicken across the sidewalk and through the closed windows of the Bronco as Bolan double-parked on the street. He threw the transmission into neutral, then turned, resting an arm over the seat. "Okay, Nielson," he said. "How long before Donahue gets off work?"

The CIA agent looked at his watch. "Five minutes or so," he said. His voice still trembled slightly. He turned toward the door, reaching across Schwarz for the handle. "I'll go get him."

Schwarz leaned forward, blocking his exit. Carl Lyons reached over and grabbed him by the collar.

"I'll go with you," Blancanales said, getting out of the front seat. "We wouldn't want you getting lost or anything, would we?" Able Team's crack undercover specialist wore a light white suit and black shirt, open at the collar. Several gold chains hung around his neck, adding to the stereotypical drug-dealer look he was striving for.

Blancanales opened the rear door. Schwarz got out, pulling Nielson after him. The electronics man turned to Blancanales and grinned. "Got to hand it to you, Pol," he snorted, shaking his head at the gold chains. "You're either straight out of "Miami Vice" or a recent divorcé on his way to a singles' bar."

Bolan leaned over the seat and spoke through the door. "I don't want your man knowing there's any friction between us, Nielson," he said. "You just let him think we're Company men, too."

Nielson nodded. Blancanales pushed him toward the flashing neon sign above the door to Cramer's.

Bolan wrapped the headset around his head. A second later he heard a click as Blancanales activated his body mike. Then loud conversation and the sounds of people eating dinner filled his ears. The noise died down and the sounds of clanking pots and pans echoed from the bug as they entered the kitchen. Nielson's voice said, "Hi, Marshall. Need to see you out front."

A new voice, suspicious and irritated, said, "Who's your friend?"

Nielson cleared his throat. "I'll introduce you outside. Let's go."

"I'm working," the leery voice said.

There was a moment's pause during which Bolan could practically see Nielson looking at his wristwatch. "No, you aren't," the CIA man said. "It's quitting time."

A few moments later Blancanales, Nielson and the IRA mole appeared on the sidewalk. Blancanales escorted the two men to the Bronco and put Nielson back in between Lyons and Schwarz. He shoved Donahue in next to Bolan and climbed into the front of the Bronco.

"This is him," Nielson said by way of introduction. It was obvious he didn't want Donahue knowing he'd given up his name.

Donahue was of medium height and weight with brownish red hair and matching freckles. He wore the food-splattered white shirt and trousers of a kitchen worker.

"These guys are field ops like me," Nielson said. "They need you to do something for them."

"This sucks big ones," Donahue said. He looked as frightened as Nielson, but his reaction was anger rather than collapse. He turned back to stare at the CIA man. "*You're* supposed to be my contact, Harvey. Nobody else. And what the hell are you doing coming here? How do you know somebody ain't watching?"

Bolan's patience was thinning quickly. He drew the Beretta from under his arm and shoved it into Donahue's ribs. "We don't have the time or inclination for prima donna behavior tonight," he said simply. "Here's what you're going to do." He nodded toward Blancanales. "You're going to introduce this man to your IRA buddies as Mr. Herman Hernandez, a Colombian cocaine dealer who got burned by the Corporation. Mr. Hernandez was ruined financially. He's out for blood, and he's got information for sale that will be of use to the IRA."

Donahue turned as white as his clothes. "Shit," he said. "I'm not *that* tight with these guys. I'm just an American mick who's got sympathies for the cause, that's all. They'll never buy a story like—"

Bolan cocked the Beretta.

"On the other hand," Donahue said, forcing a smile, "they might."

Bolan lowered the hammer and holstered the Beretta. He threw the Bronco into gear and pulled away from the café.

Donahue guided the Executioner north through Manhattan and into the Bronx. Thirty minutes later they passed Yankee Stadium. Donahue directed him across the bridge to City Island and the smell of smoked chicken that had lingered in the Bronco was replaced with the stinging sharpness of the sea air.

Bolan drove past several small seaside boat-rental establishments and passed the City Island Nautical Museum. Donahue pointed to the right, and they entered a commercial area.

The old Whitlow's Plumbing Shop sat between an electrical supply wholesaler and a small-engine repair shop.

"How'd they end up with this place as a safe house?" Bolan asked.

Donahue shrugged. "The building belongs to a guy named Callahan. Came over from Belfast twenty years ago."

The Executioner nodded silently. For years the IRA had received financial and other kinds of support from wealthy Americans of Irish descent. He drove past the dilapidated plumbing shop and pulled into the parking lot of a Tastee-Freez. Teenage boys in school letter jackets and girls wearing short skirts sat on car hoods as Bolan parked the Bronco. "Be quick," he told Donahue. Then, drawing the Beretta again, he rested it in his lap. "And make sure nothing goes wrong."

Donahue cleared his throat nervously, then followed Blancanales out of the car. The two men walked down the street toward Whitlow's.

Bolan watched them walk away. He wasn't worried. Not that there wasn't any danger—there was. But Rosario Blancanales hadn't been nicknamed "the Politician" for nothing. He was the best con man the Executioner had ever known. He could convincingly play any part that came up, and he'd pull this off somehow.

Bolan pulled the headset over his ears again and felt a hard smile come across his face. It was a good thing Pol had chosen to use his talents on the right side of the law. He'd be nearly impossible to catch if he'd decided to take the criminal route.

A click sounded in the Executioner's ear as Blancanales activated the transmitter. The two men stopped in front of a paint-peeled door to the plumbing shop. Donahue rapped on the wood, and a moment later the door cracked open.

Bolan listened over the headset.

"It's me, Paddy," Donahue said. "Open up."

"Who the hell is *he?*" a thick Irish brogue challenged.

"He's with me," Donahue said. "We need to see the boss. Tell him it's urgent."

The door swung back, and the two men disappeared inside.

Bolan heard the sounds of feet on concrete, then another door opened. A few pleasantries were exchanged between Donahue and an accent even stronger than the one at the door. Then Donahue said,

"This is Herman Hernandez. From Colombia. He's got something he wants to sell."

"And what would that be?" asked the brogue.

"Information," Blancanales said. "Information you need."

The man Donahue had called the boss laughed, then his voice turned harsh. "Tell me, Mr. Hernandez, what could a refried-bean-eating bastard like you possibly tell me that I don't already know?"

Blancanales's voice sounded like that an offended man who'd chosen to ignore the insult. "Things about a friend of yours. Or at least somebody you *think* is your friend. Bernhardt Ennslin."

"I don't know any Bernhardt Ennslin."

"No. Of course you don't," Blancanales said. "So I'll tell you about him. He burned me on a coke deal and left me bankrupt. I not only need money, I want his ass. I'm thinking maybe I can get both in the same shot."

"So tell me," the Irishman said.

"It'll cost you a cool half million. I need funds to get back into business."

There was a sudden rustling over the airwaves, then Bolan heard the Irish voice again, low and angry. "Don't you be fuckin' me about," it said. "You tell me what you know, and if it's worth a ha' penny, then a ha' penny you'll have."

Donahue's voice broke in. "Hey, watch the knife now, he's on the level."

Blancanales sounded choked when he answered. "Ennslin...he's raising a whole army. They're... plannin' to wipe you guys out after this deal's over...cut you out of all the profits...."

There was another rustling sound, then Blancanales spoke again. "That's all I know," he said. "Except that they're gonna start hitting you guys soon. Right here in the U.S."

The airwaves went silent. Finally the Irish voice said, "You're lying. You're broke, and this is a harebrained scheme to get money."

A gunshot exploded suddenly in Bolan's ear. Grabbing the Beretta from his lap, he was halfway out the car door when he heard Blancanales speak again. "That was just to show you this thing's loaded," Pol said. "Now, you don't want to believe me, then fuck you. It's *your* ass, not mine." There was a brief pause. "But you keep that fuckin' blade away from my throat." After another pause, Pol said, "Let's go."

A moment later Blancanales and Donahue backed out of the plumbing shop. They turned and sprinted for the Bronco.

Bolan had it in gear when they piled in. The tires screeched like a banshee as they laid rubber out of the Tastee-Freez to the admiration of the teenagers loafing around the parking lot.

They were six blocks from Whitlow's when Blancanales reached up to his throat. His hand came away with a thin coat of blood. "This job has its drawbacks," he said. "He had that blade a hair away from slicing right through my jugular."

Bolan smiled. "Write out a description of the guy," he said. "We'll get it to—" he glanced from Donahue to Nielson, knowing it wouldn't do to mention Stony Man Farm "—headquarters and see if we can ID him."

Blancanales laughed. "No need for that."

All the heads in the Bronco turned his way.

"That was Jonathan O'Banion himself, Striker."

Bolan felt his foot shoot instinctively toward the brake. He pulled it back, fighting the desire to return to the plumbing shop and take the internationally known terrorist out right now.

No, that wouldn't do. There were too many tentacles to this octopus. If nothing else, the mere number of assassinations and their geography proved that O'Banion's terrorists had cells hidden all over the United States. Even if Bolan eliminated O'Banion, someone would rise to take his place.

The Executioner needed all of the tentacles grouped together in the same place.

Bolan's foot returned to the accelerator. He turned to Blancanales. "You think O'Banion bought your story?"

Pol shrugged. "Even if he didn't, he'll be thinking about it."

Bolan felt himself smiling again. Looking to the man next to him, he said, "Donahue, you know of any other IRA hideouts? Any other places like Whitlow's Plumbing?"

Donahue hesitated. "A couple...maybe," he said reluctantly.

"A couple is all I need," the Executioner answered.

"Hey, wait a minute," Nielson said from the backseat. "Donahue does that, they'll make him for sure."

"So get him a new face and send him on a vacation," Bolan said coldly. "That's what you do with moles when they've accomplished what they were supposed to do." He turned, guiding the Bronco with one hand and staring into the eyes of the still-shaken CIA man. "And you better do it quick, Nielson. Because within a few hours, Jonathan O'Banion is going to realize beyond any shadow of a doubt that what Mr. Hernandez told him is the gospel truth."

CHAPTER NINE

Yakov Katzenelenbogen looked at the clock on the wall in the Copenhagen train station. Not quite 0900 hours. He shook his head as he strolled nonchalantly toward an exit.

Denmark, Katz reminded himself, was another culture, another *world*. He knew that, and he also knew that 99.9 percent of the time he was tolerant in his acceptance of other people's beliefs and idiosyncrasies. The Good Lord knew he should be—his own people had certainly been persecuted enough for *their* way of life.

Still, it was strange to see hordes of elderly women crowding the stand-up bars scattered throughout the terminal, downing shots of Jagermeister and vodka and chasing them with beer. In the U.S. they'd have been branded as problem drinkers. In Israel, they'd have been herded into a twelve-step program faster than you could say "Mogan David 20-20."

As he passed the last table before the exit, Katz watched a gray-haired matron in a shabby overcoat drain a shot glass and reach for her beer mug. She looked up for an instant, then took a puff from the long black cigar clutched in her liver-spotted hand.

The Israeli stopped just outside the door, staring out over the long blocks of buildings to the east. He smiled. The train station separated two famous sections of the city, and with Katz's exposure to Catholicism in the Jewish-run high school he attended, it always reminded him of purgatory.

Behind him, on the other side of the tracks, lay Tivoli Gardens—the Danish answer to Disneyland. A clean, joyous, family-oriented amusement park with dog shows and music and trained-mouse circuses and balloons. Jolly Cola, and cotton candy and the best ice cream Katz had ever tasted. Tivoli Gardens was like a child's vision of heaven.

But in front of him, on this side of the train depot, Yakov Katzenelenbogen saw hell.

As the Israeli descended the steps, the odor of stale sweat and urine assaulted his nostrils. He moved at a moderate pace down the grimy sidewalk, only half self-conscious in the long, flowing robe and Arabic *kaffiyeh* on his head. Three stores from the station, he saw the first hooker, a woman of indeterminable age with pock scars beneath the thick makeup on her face. She twirled a full circle as Katz neared, making sure he saw the crescent of bare buttocks beneath the hem of her short leather skirt.

Katz walked on, passing three drunks already passed out against the stone buildings. He glanced at the signs above the stores, signs that read Sex Supermarket, and Sex World, and Sex Universe. Mannequins in black leather garter belts and boots held whips, staring from the storefront windows almost as dead eyed as the drugged-out people he passed. More signs advertised sex *kino—kino* meaning film—and specified that the peep shows inside featured animal, lesbian, homo, spanking and urine themes.

Although he had showered only a few hours before, when he and Phoenix Force had checked into a hotel to use as a base of operations, Katz felt now as if he needed another bath. He couldn't help wondering why the DEA agent he was to meet had chosen such a decadent setting.

The Israeli walked on, dodging drunks, panhandlers and whores. Three blocks later he saw the sign for the Hotel Absalom. It seemed so out of place within this setting. Absalom had been the beloved son of King David.

Katz shook his head and ascended the steps into the lobby.

The man in the brown cowboy hat sat reading a newspaper on a couch in front of the front desk. He looked up.

Katz eyed him quickly. Brown mustache. Brown suit with western-cut piping on the yoke. Brown lizard boots.

It had to be him. There couldn't possibly be *two* cowboys decked out completely in brown in Copenhagen, Denmark.

Katz walked up and stopped in front of the man. He pulled a pack of Camels from under his robe and spoke in English. "Excuse me, do you have a light?"

The cowboy nodded and pulled a book of matches from his suit. "Thought Muslims didn't smoke," he said in a carefully rehearsed tone.

"Only *devout* Muslims," Katz said, completing the code.

The cowboy rose to his feet, standing nearly a foot taller than the Israeli. "Let's walk," he said.

Katz followed him out the door, down the steps and back into Copenhagen's porno district. "I don't want to know your name, and you can call me Mr. Brown," the man said. Not waiting for Katz to reply, he went on, his voice mildly irritated. "Look, I don't know what's happening here except that I've worked on Jorgan Sveinberg for nearly a year. He's the biggest dope dealer in Denmark, and I can't begin to tell you what I've gone through to get next to him. Now, finally, I'm in like Flynn, and I get orders from the top of the Justice Department to introduce *you* to him." He gritted his teeth and blew air through his lips. "I'm not just risking the biggest dope case of my career here. My very life could be on the line."

Katz could sympathize with the DEA man. He had worked hard and now felt as if all that work might go up in smoke. But Katz couldn't explain the situation.

"Let me just say that I will do my best to make sure your case is not interfered with," Katz said. "And although I cannot reveal any more about my own operation, please let me assure you that it merits the risk you are taking."

Brown looked down at him as they continued to walk. "I damn sure hope so," he said, not sounding convinced.

They came to a green concrete building and mounted the steps. Iron bars covered the door. Brown pushed a button at the side of the bars.

Deep inside the building, Katz heard a buzz, then a voice came over the speaker mounted in the wall above the button. *"Ja?"*

"It's Brown. Tell Mr. Sveinberg I've got the guy I told him about with me. He's expecting us."

The intercom went dead. Katz and the man in the cowboy hat waited. Two minutes later another buzz sounded and the iron bars slid back from the door.

Katz and Brown stepped into a narrow hallway and were met by one of the largest human beings the Israeli had ever seen. The man stood well over seven feet tall, and his shoulders nearly touched the walls. Over his left eye fell a blond shock of hair, which he jerked out of his face with a twitch of the head before stepping forward to pat them down for weapons.

Satisfied that they were unarmed, the blond giant led them up the stairs, down a seedy hall and to a door before saying something in Danish to Brown and walking away.

Brown opened the door and ushered Katz inside.

Without being obvious, Katz took in the room. Simple. Hardly what you'd expect for the office of a multimillion-dollar drug dealer, and therefore the perfect office for a multimillion-dollar drug dealer in case the Danish police happened to drop by. Several cheap plywood tables were scattered over the ragged carpet. The walls were covered with inexpensive prints that Katz would have sworn came from K mart had they been in the U.S., and the lamps and green metal desk were equally bargain basement.

But the money-counting machine, the safe and the metal cash boxes along the wall didn't miss the Israeli's eye, either.

The man behind the desk wore thick-lensed half glasses that fell down his nose when he looked up. He said something in Danish.

Brown shook his head, then nodded toward Katz and said, "But he speaks English." He cleared his throat. "Jorgan, this is Mohammed. Mohammed—"

Jorgan Sveinberg broke in. "I do not wish to be rude, Mr. Brown," he said in heavily accented English, "but I am busy. You told me over the phone who this man is, what he wants. To join us in the . . . shall we call it the import-export business? To supply his people in the Mideast. What I do not know is why I should trust him."

Brown smiled. "Mohammed and I go back a long way. All the way to my gunrunning days in Lebanon and the gulf."

"Exactly," Sveinberg said. "Your friend is a ter—" he broke off in midword, changing it to "—freedom fighter. I believe that is the politically correct term, is it not?"

"I *was* a freedom fighter, yes," Katz said, affecting a Lebanese accent. "I am looking now for what you Westerners call a career change." He smiled knowingly.

Sveinberg took off his glasses. Pulling a handkerchief from his pocket, he ran it over the lenses before jabbing them back on his nose. Looking over the rims, his eyes drilled into Katz's. "Why?"

Katz met his stare. "I am getting older." He let a brief smile touch his lips. "I have done what I can for my people. It is time I considered my future as an individual."

Sveinberg's face softened, and Katz knew instinctively that he had struck the right chord. It no longer mattered whether he was Jewish or Lebanese. As far as Jorgan Sveinberg was concerned, they could have

spoken Danish, Japanese or Martian, because the two
men were really speaking the language of criminals the
world over.

The language of money.

"Yes," the man behind the desk said. "That makes
sense." His eyes narrowed. "But why should I help
you?"

"Because it will increase your business."

Sveinberg laughed. "My business is big now. I can
never hope to spend all the money I make."

"Then you should help me because I am about to
give you information. Information that could save not
only your business, but your life, as well."

"Go on."

"To show my good faith," Katz said, "I will tell
you now, before you have even agreed to help me.
Again, as you Westerners say, with 'no strings attached.'"

"I'm listening," Sveinberg said.

"We freedom fighters, as perhaps you are aware,"
Katz began, "have a network of communication between our individual groups as organized and effective as those in your own business." He went on to
explain in great detail the nefarious plot that the terrorists in Bernhardt Ennslin's employ, led by none
other than Jonathan O'Banion of the IRA, had come
up with.

"In short," Katz concluded, "they plan to invade
the Beni district, kill Ennslin and take over his Corporation themselves. And they have earmarked certain American and European buyers for assassination—to be replaced by their own men. Need I tell
you who is very near the top of that list?"

Sveinberg's face went white. Then he said, "How can I be certain you are telling the truth?"

"I suppose you can't, but I *am,*" Katz said. "And consider the consequences if you do not believe me...."

Slowly the Danish dope dealer nodded. "I think perhaps we can do business, you and I," he said. "You are staying in Copenhagen?"

Katz shook his head. "I must return to my country. But I will come back in two weeks."

Sveinberg nodded. "Contact me when you do," he said.

Katz and the man calling himself Brown filed out of the office, down the steps and back into the porno section of Copenhagen.

JORGAN SVEINBERG watched the two men leave. As soon as the door had closed behind them, he lifted the phone. While he waited for an overseas operator, he hit the *E* button on his telephone file index. The file sprang open, and the number for Bernhardt Ennslin appeared at the top of the page.

A moment later the line buzzed fuzzily, then rang. A voice answered and said, "Ennslin residence. Alberto speaking."

Sveinberg identified himself, then said, "Is Mr. Ennslin in, Alberto?"

"*Sí,* Señor Sveinberg," Alberto said. "One moment."

There was a click, then Ennslin's voice came on the line. "Yes, Jorgan? What can I do for you?"

"I don't know that it's a problem," Sveinberg began, "but I thought you should know." He went on to explain about the strange Arab who had warned him of upcoming problems from O'Banion and the terrorists.

By the time he had finished, Ennslin was chuckling on the other end. "It sounds to me as if this man wanted to impress you, Jorgan," Ennslin said. "Perhaps he thinks you will give him discount prices out of gratitude. I spoke to O'Banion a few hours ago. There is no reason to worry. Everything is proceeding as planned."

Sveinberg cleared his throat. Talking to Ennslin always made him nervous. "I'm certain you are right, Mr. Ennslin. But with all due respect, if O'Banion was planning a...say, coup of sorts...wouldn't he want you to think everything was all right up until the time when it was too late?"

There was a long pause on the other end of the line. Finally Ennslin said, "Anything is possible in this world of ours, Jorgan. I appreciate your call. And while I am sure there is nothing to this, I will be cautious."

He hung up.

BOLAN WATCHED Harvey Nielson's eyes widen as he pushed the man into the Beechcraft. The CIA agent glanced at Charlie Mott behind the steering column, then his eyes traveled to the parachutes and other equipment crowded into the plane. He took a seat without being told, then turned to Bolan. "Who in the hell are you guys?" he asked.

Carl Lyons answered the question with a quick "Shut up" as he, Schwarz and Blancanales pushed Donahue inside.

"You get the weapons, Charlie?" Bolan asked.

Mott nodded over his shoulder toward the back. Bolan's eyes followed the movement.

Four IMBEL Light Automatic Rifles rested against the wall of the plane. A box holding extra magazines stood on top of a case of 7.62 mm ammunition next to the weapons.

The rest of the men found seats. A moment later the Beechcraft rose into the air. The sounds of bullets being pressed into rifle magazines filled the cabin as Bolan glanced down through the window and watched the lights of New York City fade to the south.

The Executioner turned toward Carl Lyons, who handed him one of the IMBELS and a clip-on magazine caddie for his belt. Lyons wore a navy blue sport shirt, gray slacks and black athletic shoes. Blancanales still had on his "Miami Vice" suit, complete with gold chains and rings. Bolan and the rest of the men were dressed similarly, if less flamboyantly, in civvies.

They had no intention of looking like cops, government agents or commandos. Not tonight. Tonight they had to appear to be the enforcement arm of a giant coca-growing cartel.

The Executioner shifted his eyes to Donahue. "You're sure about this place?" he asked.

Donahue shrugged. "As sure as you can get about a deal like this. Those guys don't like to stay any place too long. On the other hand, it's hard to find a place where they feel secure. When they do, they don't like to leave until they have to."

Soon they were passing over West Point Military Academy. Bolan looked down again. They were still low enough to make out the legendary officer train-ng school, and in the shadows of the yard lights he could see the dark shapes of Fort Putnam, the old Revolutionary War fort that sat on the grounds. They rose slightly as they passed over Newburgh, where George Washington himself had headquartered, then even higher as they neared Poughkeepsie.

Behind him, Lyons, Schwarz and Blancanales began to slip into their chutes.

The Executioner turned to Nielson. "I want you and Donahue to stay here with our pilot. Don't try anything stupid—he knows how to do a lot more than fly a plane."

Mott looked over, his eyes twinkling under his green-and-yellow baseball cap. Reaching inside his flight suit, he pulled out a stainless-steel two-and-a-half-inch Smith & Wesson Model 66, flipped open the cylinder and checked the long silver Magnum rounds. Smiling pleasantly at Nielson, he said, "I don't take prisoners," then reholstered the weapon.

Nielson nodded glumly, looking decidedly unenthusiastic about life in general, and the current situation in particular.

Mott turned back to the controls as Bolan shrugged into his parachute and clipped the magazine caddie to his belt pack. The IMBEL's sling went over his shoulder.

In a few more minutes Mott said, "Ten seconds, big guy." His face broke out in another smile. "Have a nice time this evening, boys, and don't worry about a thing." He patted Harvey Nielson on the knee. "I'll take good care of the kids while you're gone."

Bolan opened the door. A second later he had dropped into the darkness.

The cool air warmed quickly as the Executioner fell toward the ground. He glanced up once, seeing the silhouettes of the men of Able Team descending above him, then pulled the rip cord and sent the chute darting over his head. The black canopy flowered open in the night, jerking him several yards back up in the sky, then peaked and began descending once more. Looking down now, he saw the open field next to Highway 9W.

The Executioner hit the ground facing the wind, rolled from feet to calf to hips and buttocks, then back to his feet. Carl Lyons touched down twenty yards to his east as he gathered in the chute. Blancanales and Schwarz, caught in a sudden gust, landed fifty yards on the other side of the Able Team leader.

Bolan found a large stone, weighted down the canopy with it, turned toward the highway and crouched down. According to the map Donahue had drawn, the deserted motel sat less than a quarter mile to the north. Most of the traffic traveling that direction opted for the New York State Thruway—which ran parallel to 9W a few miles to the west—particularly at night, when the old highway's more scenic view could not be taken advantage of. But there was always the chance of traffic out of Poughkeepsie along the road.

Or the terrorists themselves.

The men of Able Team joined the Executioner as he jogged across the field, then turned north along the highway. Thirty seconds later headlights appeared behind them, and they dropped to their bellies in the ditch.

An old pickup, driven by somebody with long hair, passed by.

Bolan and the rest of the men were back on their feet as soon as the truck topped a short hill ahead. They increased their pace to a near sprint. Peaking the crest of the same hill, they saw the old motel just off the road fifty yards ahead. Dropping facedown once more, they crawled behind a row of trees.

The motel sat in front of what looked like an unofficial dump yard. The skeletons of old cars and trucks lay haphazardly at the rear of the grounds. The motel itself was indistinct in the darkness.

The Executioner took up position between Schwarz and Lyons, drew the Litton military night-vision goggles from his belt pack and pulled the face mask down over his headset. He adjusted the GEN II Plus image intensifier, then the objective ring focus and stared between the branches.

Shoots of brown grass and even a small tree grew from the cracked pavement in front of the structure. The wooden sign in front of the office, now hanging at a forty-five-degree angle from its pole, had faded in the sunlight.

The coming of the Thruway had spelled death to the businesses along old 9W, and it looked as if the Chambers Tourist Court had been rotting ever since the road's construction.

"Looks like a place Norman Bates would have loved," Gadgets said. "You wouldn't catch me taking a shower in one of those cabins."

Bolan turned back toward the cabins. Six of them, they formed a semicircle behind the office building. No lights. To the naked eye, the place looked deserted. But to a man with the advantage the Littons afforded, the situation looked considerably different.

The Executioner could see the fresh tire tracks that an off-road vehicle had left in front of the motel, and even noticed a few boot prints where men had exited the vehicle and then walked to the various cabins. As he studied the prints, a flash of movement to the side of one of the structures caught his eye.

Bolan turned that way in time to see the glint of metal before it faded back into the shadows.

"There's a sentry," he whispered, handing Schwarz his rifle. "Stay here. I'll call you." He pointed to his walkie-talkie and tapped it three times.

Schwarz, Lyons and Blancanales all nodded.

The Executioner crawled past the trees, farther away from the highway. He came to a barbed wire fence separating the roadway from deserted pastureland, squirmed under it and crawled on toward the rusting vehicles to the rear of the motel yard. As soon as he reached the first vehicle—a burned-out Lincoln—he rose to a squat. He could see the same tiny shimmer of steel standing in front of the second cabin from him. Closer now, he could make out the dark shirt over the arm that cradled the rifle.

Bolan watched the arm rise, letting the rifle sway gently at the end of a sling. Whatever the man was doing was out of the Executioner's field of vision, hidden in the shadows of the cabin.

A moment later the odor of wintergreen chewing tobacco drifted to Bolan on the wind. He smiled.

Enjoy your chew, the Executioner thought. It's your last.

Bolan moved swiftly but silently, making his way from the Lincoln to a rotting '57 Chevy. He dropped to his belly again, snaking through the tall grass of the junkyard to the wrecked hollows of an old Ford pickup. Directly behind the cabin he wanted now, he rose to his feet.

The Executioner moved silently to the rear of the cabin. Through the open windows, he heard snoring. His hand moved to his belt, to Pat Cohlmia's Cold Steel Mini-Tanto. He had forgotten to return the knife to the patriotic young American, but the thought brought a smile to his lips.

Cohlmia wouldn't mind. He'd just be upset he didn't get to come along.

Dropping below the window line, the Executioner moved around the corner and drew the blade. The sentry's arm was still visible at the front of the building. The odor of chewing tobacco grew stronger as Bolan crept toward it.

His back riding the wall, the Executioner reached the next corner. He estimated the sentry's height by the length of the arm, then extended his own arm, encircled the man's neck and clasped his hand over the mouth.

A muffled cry blew against his fingers as Bolan jerked the terrorist guard toward him and drove the Tanto blade into the man's kidney.

It took less than ten seconds for the sentry to die.

Bolan dropped the corpse to the ground and moved back against the wall. He reached up, tapping the face mike three times.

Ten seconds later Lyons, Schwarz and Blancanales came sprinting his way.

Bolan moved quickly to the rear of the office building, cloaking himself in the shadows until the men reached him. Schwarz handed him his rifle.

The Executioner moved in close and whispered, "Seven buildings, counting the office. Gadgets, you and I take it first. Ironman, take Pol and hit the one on that end." He pointed back in the direction they'd come from. "We'll move to the other end after the office and work your way. Meet in the middle." He paused, looking deeply into the eyes of each of the Able Team warriors to make sure his orders were clear. Satisfied that they understood, he said, "Keep it quiet as long as you can."

Lyons and Blancanales nodded, turned and took off.

Bolan motioned Schwarz toward the rear of the office building, then hurried around the front. The door had long ago fallen from its hinges. The Executioner dropped the IMBEL to the end of his sling and drew the sound-suppressed Beretta. He moved through the door, checking first the front office and desk area. Nothing. Sounds from the rear of the building told him Gadgets had gained entry. He moved through a doorway behind the desk into what appeared to have been a small manager's apartment. Dust covered the cabinets, floor and what broken furniture hadn't been looted over the years.

Schwarz appeared from the bedroom. The electronics specialist held a suppressed Government Model .45 in one hand. An A1 Mar push dagger extended from the knuckles of his other hand.

Gadgets shook his head.

The two men exited through the door Schwarz had come in. As Bolan led the way to the cabin at the far end of the semicircle, he heard a stifled choke come from the dwelling on the other end. He turned to see

Blancanales creeping out of the front door, the long blade of a SOG Tigershark bowie knife in his fist.

The Executioner moved on to the front door of the cabin. A black stenciled numeral 6, faded with age and weather, stood out against the chipped remnants of turquoise paint. He had seen earlier, when he'd crept through the junk cars at the back of the motel, that the small structures had no rear exits. Motioning to Schwarz to stay back and cover the windows, he tried the knob. Locked.

The decaying wood gave way to a gentle nudge. Bolan swung it quickly open and stepped in.

Soft rays of moonlight flowed through the windows, illuminating the sleeping face of a man with curly brown hair. The first hushed round from the barrel of the Beretta sliced through the sheets covering him. He never knew what hit him.

Bolan swung the gun toward the other bed as a burly bare-chested man sat up. The man's eyes opened. He lunged for a Browning Hi-Power on the bed stand.

The Beretta spat quiet death again, coughing up a 9 mm hollowpoint that entered one side of the IRA man's face, blew a hole out the other side and drilled into the peeling wallpaper behind the head of the bed.

The Executioner hurried to the bathroom and threw back the door. Empty. So was the closet.

Lyons and Blancanales came out of the second cabin from the other end as Bolan led Schwarz to cabin number five. This door splintered around the lock as easily as the last.

A tall, slender man with long straight hair lumbered sleepily out of the bathroom as Bolan stepped inside. He wore dingy white boxer shorts that drooped over his skinny haunches. His mouth opened wide in surprise.

Bolan tapped the trigger of the Beretta, and a small hole appeared in the man's chest. The man looked down as it filled with blood, then collapsed to the floor of the cabin.

The man in the bed against the outer wall woke quickly. He twisted, straining to reach the Uzi propped against the wall.

The Beretta sent a 3-round burst blasting into his rib cage. Miraculously the terrorist still lifted the submachine gun and turned back toward the door.

Another trio of 9 mm slugs took off his face. The Uzi dropped to his lap as he fell off the bed to the floor.

Bolan backed out of the door and turned toward the center cabin. Hurrying toward the window, he peered through.

Two men lay sleeping in their respective beds.

Lyons and Blancanales appeared again, nodded that everything had gone well, and turned to face the last cabin.

Bolan holstered the Beretta and curled his fingers around the pistol grip of his assault rifle. The IMBEL, in reality an FN-FAL manufactured under license for the armed forces of several South American countries, would add credence to the image the Executioner intended to create.

"On three," Bolan said out loud. "One, two, three."

Aiming high above the beds, Bolan, Lyons, Blancanales and Schwarz turned their weapons toward the final cabin and held the triggers back. Fire leaped from the barrels of the IMBELS as 7.62 mm slugs shredded the rotting wooden door and tore the glass from the windows. Golden casings glimmered dully as the bolts worked back and forth, spitting the brass to the sides of the rifles.

Screams of terror came from inside the cabin.

Bolan emptied his IMBEL and shoved a fresh magazine into the carriage. Dropping the weapon on the ground, he stepped back as Carl Lyons stepped forward.

Lyons aimed down and fired a 3-round burst that snapped the grip from the weapon and mangled the receiver.

Schwarz and Blancanales fired their own IMBELs dry as they backed away from the building.

As the noise along old Highway 9W died down, the Executioner and the men of Able Team turned and faded into the night.

THE STEADY *whop* of the rotor blades had a relaxing effect on Yakov Katzenelenbogen. His eyelids drooped. The past two days had involved long, hard hours and no sleep.

The Israeli slapped his weathered face gently, opened his eyes and rubbed his cheeks. There was still no time to sleep. There might be on the flight back to America. Maybe.

Katz forced his eyes back open and looked down out of the bubble glass as McCarter guided the chopper north along the Inderhavn waterfront. Below, the Phoenix Force leader could see the city of Copenhagen, with its beautiful spires rising from the copper rooftops of churches and castles. Not far from the water stood Amalienborg Palace Square with the four identical mansions that had housed the Royal House of Glucksborg—famous for its royal guards and their tall bearskin caps—for centuries.

McCarter turned inland when they reached the celebrated Little Mermaid statue, and Katz turned his attention to the man behind the chopper's controls. David McCarter was a talented warrior. Of course, if he hadn't been, he'd have never found a position with Phoenix Force. But the former British Special Air Service officer was also a talented actor. And the performance he had pulled off earlier today deserved an Academy Award.

Katz looked out of the helicopter's side window. In the mirror he could see the word Polis painted on the side of the door. The sight brought a beam to his face, and he shook his head in disbelief.

While he had been carrying out his campaign of disinformation under the guise of initiating a drug connection between Jorgan Sveinberg and the Middle East, McCarter had appropriated the Danish police helicopter. Passing himself off as a vacationing British bobby, he had talked his way onto the locked lot of the police air unit, neutralized his police guide with the aid of one of Calvin James's syringes, then bound and gagged the man and appropriated the chopper in which they now flew.

McCarter assured Katz that the officer who had acted as his guide was hidden well. The chopper shouldn't be missed until nighttime.

Katz hadn't asked for further explanation. He wasn't sure he wanted to know any more.

The radio in the Israeli's ear buzzed. There was a momentary lapse while the scrambling device they were using to guard against intrusive eavesdropping by Danish authorities kicked on, then Jack Grimaldi said, "Birdman to Phoenix One. You copy, Katz?"

"Loud and clear," Katz came back. "Got the ship in sight yet?"

"Just spotted it. Approximately ten miles north in the Kattegat. I'd start this way if I was you. You don't want them inside Danish waters when this goes down."

"That's a ten-four if I ever heard one, Birdman. We're heading your way." He nodded to McCarter, who banked the chopper and started north.

Katz watched through the window as they flew over the Nyhavn waterfront with its crowded lines of small cargo vessels waiting to unload. They were low enough that he could see the long stretch of boisterous sailors' cafés running up and down the quaysides on both sides of the water. It was to this area of Copenhagen that the Colombian freighter, loaded down with cocaine from the Buenaventura cartel and presently chugging south through Kattegat Sound, was headed.

Katz intended to make sure it never got there. The police chopper passed over the island of North Zealand, then out into the sound. "Let's gear up," Katz said, turning in his seat and addressing the rest of Phoenix Force. He watched as James, Manning and Encizo broke open the Webley-Fosbery automatic revolvers and dropped .455-caliber cartridges into the cylinders. McCarter checked his Browning Hi-Power, and then James began pulling submachine guns from the luggage compartment behind the rear seats. He handed Katz, Encizo and Manning a Sten, McCarter a Sterling, and took a Lanchester for himself.

Grimaldi had made a quick flight to England where, after some fast talk on the part of Hal Brognola, Scotland Yard had made the British arms available. The Stony Man pilot had arrived earlier that day with the weapons and the plain O.D. green fatigues worn now by the men of Phoenix Force.

The guns were not what any of them, with the possible exception of ex-SAS officer David McCarter, would have picked as personal weapons. But they all agreed that the firepower the Executioner had chosen was perfect for the mission ahead. The Stens, Sterlings, Webleys and the rest of the weapons were either past or current British issue.

And therefore the most likely guns to be in the hands of the Irish Republican Army.

Calvin James spotted the tiny speck first. He dropped the binoculars from his eyes and pointed. McCarter headed that way, causing the men's ears to pop as he dropped the chopper rapidly through the sky. A hundred yards above the freighter, he hovered, reaching for the chopper's public-address mike. "Danish National Police to Colombian vessel," he said in English. "Stand about and prepare to be boarded." He held the mike over the seat to Rafael Encizo, who repeated the orders in Spanish.

All of the heads on the ship's deck looked up.

The smile on McCarter's face looked like a ten-year-old boy's on Christmas morning as he expertly maneuvered the chopper downward. The men on deck scattered out of the way, but continued to stare skyward. Closer now, Katz could see a mixture of brown

Latino faces and others that were clearly Scandinavian. But regardless of skin tone, all of the faces had one thing in common.

They showed no fear. Some were even smiling.

Katz put two and two together and came up with four. These men acted as if a Danish police helicopter landing on deck in international waters was as normal as whores in the Nyhavn waterfront bars. That meant it *was* normal, at least for *this* ship, and that in turn could only mean that someone within the local authorities had been paid off. And now they had come to collect.

Good. The men of Phoenix Force could use that to their advantage.

The skids hit the deck, and the Phoenix Force warriors leaped from the chopper. The men on deck took one look at them and the smiles faded. Closest to the helicopter was a short squatty man with a broad face and Brillo-pad ponytail, and he cried out in Spanish.

"He just said we aren't really cops," Encizo called out. "Not to mention a crack about the legitimacy of our genealogy."

The ponytailed man's hand shot inside his denim jacket and came back out holding a nickel-plated revolver.

Katz raised the Sten and fired. A full-auto burst of 9 mm rounds splattered into the denim jacket. The ponytail flailed like a whip as the drug smuggler's muscles contracted in death. He plummeted to the deck.

More of the men on deck drew guns as Phoenix Force opened fire with their British weapons. Katz fired again, sending a 3-round burst into a fat, light-skinned man with a thick blond beard. One of the rounds struck the man in the face. Blood poured down to stain the beard red as the Ruger .357 Magnum he had produced went tumbling to the deck. Katz's other two rounds hit the man's chest and drove him back over a capstan. His arms windmilled in the air as he fell over the drumhead.

Calvin James also opened up, spraying the deck and downing three of the Scandinavian dopers as they sprinted for the hatch. McCarter, using his Sterling, took out two more. Gary Manning, standing tall and broad and looking the part of an Ulsterman more than any of them, popped a steady stream of rounds from his Sten into a seaman firing a sawed-off Winchester double-barrel. The penetrating hard-nosed 9 mm bullets passed through the man's body and on into a drug runner wearing a T-shirt.

Wielding his own Sten, Encizo bled it dry into several South Americans who had flattened out on deck to fire from the prone position, then switched to his Webley-Fosbery, targeting a light-complected Dane with a handlebar mustache.

Katz's Sten swept another man off the deck, and he acquired new targets. Occasionally he caught a glimpse of the strange automatic revolver in Encizo's hand, noticing that every time Encizo pulled the trigger, the recoil drove the barrel and cylinder back over the frame, cocked the hammer, then sprang back to firing position.

The Israeli turned his attention back to the deck as a blond head shot up out of the hatch.

Calvin James promptly blew it off.

Suddenly silence fell over the deck of the ship.

Katz motioned to McCarter. The Briton walked to the hatch, pushed the body down the ladder, then called down into the hole in a thick Irish brogue. "All below will be gettin' yer arses on deck now or ye'll die." He stepped back waiting, his subgun aimed at the opening.

No one appeared.

Katz pulled a frag grenade from his chest and walked to the rail. Jerking the pin, he tossed it as far out to sea as he could.

It exploded underwater, the concussion rocking the ship.

McCarter leaned close to the hatch again. "The next blooey goes down ye gentlemen's throats," he yelled in the same accent. "I'll be givin' ye ten seconds to show yer miserable bums."

A pair of hands shot up through the hatch. As they rose, the head of a slim young man with soft, almost feminine features, appeared. He climbed the ladder and stepped onto the deck.

McCarter pointed him to the rail.

Two men who resembled each other followed. They both had short-clipped hair, long bony noses and thick eyebrows.

"Ah, brothers ye'd be, then, eh?" McCarter asked.

The older of the two nodded.

"Are ye the last of them below, then?" McCarter asked.

The three men nodded.

"Let's hope so, maties." McCarter smiled wolfishly. "I'd hate to be upsettin' yer dear auld mother with the corpses of her lyin' brood." He turned to

Manning. "Mr. O'Reilly," he said. "I think you should be checkin'."

Manning dropped cautiously out of sight to the lower deck. He returned a few minutes later and shook his head. "All clear," Manning said with an accent similar to McCarter's.

McCarter turned to the three men against the deck. "You've a lifeboat, I assume?"

The slim young man nodded.

"Then let's be gettin' ye in it." McCarter stepped forward and nudged the older brother with his Sten.

Katz followed them silently to the port side near the stern. He looked over the rail and saw the fourteen-foot dinghy on falls above the skids bolted to the hull of the ship.

McCarter jabbed the younger brother in the ribs with the Sterling. The man climbed overboard into the small boat. The other two men followed.

Katz released the wire on the gravity davit, and the boat began dropping seaward. "I'd go gettin' as fer away from this tuna can as I could, were I ye," McCarter called down as the dinghy hit the water. "And tell yer masters that no more of their bloody cocaine comes to Copenhagen, or anywhere else fer that matter, without going through Jonathan O'Banion first!"

Katz thought that McCarter was doing a fine job of misinformation. True, Ennslin wasn't directly responsible for this ship or its dope. He just grew the coca plants, turned it into cocaine base, then sold it to the delivery cartels. But when these men returned to Colombia and told their stories, the IRA connection would link the problem directly back to the Bolivian ex-Nazi.

The boys from Buenaventura would know whom to blame. And Ennslin would hear what had happened.

McCarter followed Katz up the deck to where the other men still stood. "Manning," Katz said, "work your magic. The rest of you, let's mount up."

Manning hurried back to the chopper and pulled a briefcase from the flight deck. He dropped down through the hatch as the other men of Phoenix Force boarded the chopper. The big Canadian returned five minutes later.

Katz leaned out and pulled him on board. "You see the coke?" he asked.

Manning took a seat behind the Israeli as the chopper rose up off the deck into the sky. "Did I ever. Katz, there's going to be a lot of very stoned fish in about—" he glanced at his watch "—two seconds."

The men of Phoenix Force looked down as the Colombian ship exploded, tongues of flame leaping high into the sky after them.

Katz stared at the wreckage as the initial blast died down and the ship began to burn with a steady blaze. A grin covered his face. The former Mossad operative wasn't sure, but he would almost have sworn he saw clouds of white powder settling in the water as McCarter guided them back toward land.

CHAPTER TEN

Jonathan O'Banion untied the knots around the Greenfinch's wrists and ankles and pulled her from the bed to her feet. "God, you stink," he said. "Get your arse into the shower." He tugged the listless woman out of what had once been Whitlow's Plumbing's storage room and guided her down the hall, past a row of leering men, to the bathroom.

A metal shower stall, the paint peeling from the outside, the inside red from rust, waited in the corner past a row of urinals. O'Banion pushed the woman inside and turned the handle. The freezing water brought about the first sign of life he'd seen out of the Greenfinch in days.

The woman screamed.

"Shut yer hole," O'Banion ordered. He threw a washcloth and a bar of soap into the stall. "Now get the stench off you, lassie. That thing you have down there that I don't is the only thing keepin' you alive."

O'Banion waited while the woman scrubbed herself, then turned off the water and threw her a towel. He watched as she dried herself with stiff arms. The woman's skin had grown even paler than it had been the day before, and she hadn't eaten in the past two days. Again O'Banion wondered if she might not be dying.

Not that it mattered. He was tiring of her anyway.
'he didn't move her arse anymore when he took her.
Not even when he held the stiletto to her throat and
hreatened to slice it through her neck.

The hell with her, he thought as she stepped out of
he stall. If she died, she died. There were plenty of
vomen on the streets of New York. All his for the
aking.

The Irishman pushed the nude woman back down
he hall and onto the bed. He retied her restraints, then
urned back toward the door. "Donnelly!" he called
>ut.

A short, stubby man with ruddy features jumped
nto the room.

"Watch over her while I'm gone." O'Banion ordered. He saw Donnelly's eyes travel to the patch of
red hair between the woman's legs and slapped him
across the face. "And don't be gettin' no ideas, either."

Donnelly nodded.

Shawn Shawnessey ducked his head around the
doorway. "Ready. Jonathan?"

O'Banion didn't answer. He just walked from the
room and left the plumbing shop through the rear exit.
Shawnessey followed.

A white Lincoln Town Car with fresh tags stood in
the alley. O'Banion slid behind the wheel as Shawnessey took the shotgun seat. A moment later, they were
cruising through City Island, then across the bridge
into the Bronx and finally into Manhattan.

O'Banion turned north on Fifth Avenue, driving
slowly through "Museum Mile", an area housing ten
of the city's most famous museums. He cut back on

Ninety-second Street for three blocks then, satisfied that he'd picked up no tails, turned south again on First and entered the Yorktown area.

As they neared the home of District Court Judge Darlene Sue McClusky, O'Banion thought back on the research he'd done while constructing the best plan for killing the woman. McClusky was not of Irish descent as her name might imply. Her grandparents had emigrated from Prague, Czechoslovakia. Darlene had been born in New York in 1927, the last of seven children who carried the name Skrdla. Hers had changed to McClusky when she'd married her husband, Brian, the son of an Oklahoma oil man whom she met at Harvard Law School in 1955. They had opened a law practice in Manhattan after graduating.

None of it made a difference to Jonathan O'Banion. But he always did his research. He liked to know whom he was killing.

O'Banion saw the sign announcing Nichols Hills and pulled up to the gate. A pimply-faced kid in a brown uniform stepped down from the guardhouse and walked forward carrying a clipboard.

"Going in to see the Westons," O'Banion said in a Midwestern drawl. "One Winding Way."

"I'll need a complete address," the kid said.

O'Banion pulled a slip of paper from his pocket. "Number 91."

The young man looked down at his clipboard. "Bingo," he kid said. "Have a nice evening, sir."

O'Banion nodded and pulled through the gate. He turned onto Winding Way, which was on the opposite side of the housing area, then doubled back to Pearson Avenue. He pulled the Lincoln to the curb across the street and two doors down from the judge's address, killed the lights and engine and settled back in the seat.

The Irishman's eyes flickered briefly into the rearview mirror, and he smiled. He liked the way he looked in the blue suit and tie. It was a nice change from the khaki jacket and tweed hat. Tearing his eyes from the mirror, he looked up the street to the two-story mansion. From his vantage point, he could see both the entrance and exit of the circular drive. The lawn and hedges looked as if someone had used manicure scissors on them, and the flower beds were equally well kept.

The house itself had been constructed of gray brick in the style of ancient Roman architecture. O'Banion had helped train the Italian Red Brigade several years earlier, and the arches and columns that ran the front of Judge McClusky's house made him think of the Theatre of Marcellus in Rome. The front door led into a large domed entryway that looked like the Pantheon.

Shawn Shawnessey broke the silence. "You say her money comes from a bloody Okie?"

O'Banion nodded.

"Where does a bloody dirt farmer get money like that?"

"Oil," O'Banion said. "Her old man's in oil." He watched a set of headlights turn the corner and start up the street toward them.

"Think it's her?" Shawnessey asked.

O'Banion glanced to his watch, then shook his head. "No. She's not out of the meeting yet."

"Who was it she was talking to?"

O'Banion shrugged. "Women's league against something-or-bloody-other," he said. The car came under a streetlight, and he saw the red bar lights across the top.

The vehicle slowed as it passed them, and O'Banion read the words on the side door. Nichols Hills Security. The car stopped and backed up.

An elderly man in a dark brown uniform and silver badge got out and walked to the window. He might as well have worn a sign that said Retired Cop. O'Banion rolled the glass down. "Good evening, Officer," he said without a trace of Irish in his tone.

"Good evening, sir," the security man answered pleasantly. "I'm sorry to bother you, but I don't recognize you from the neighborhood. We try to get to know everyone here on the hill."

O'Banion smiled. When this man had been a real cop, he must have worked public relations. What he had just said was a polite way of asking, *what the fuck are you doing in this neighborhood?*

"We're waiting on Lawrence and Mindy," O'Banion said, indicating the house to his right with a shake of his head. "On our way to the Jewel Box Theater tonight to see *I Hate Hamlet*. Have you seen it yet?"

"Uh, no sir, I haven't. Not yet."

"I understand it's quite good. But anyway, Lawrence and Mindy weren't quite ready, and quite frankly, just between the two of us—" he leaned closer to the window to whisper "—their house smells like cabbage. We decided to wait for them out here."

The security cop laughed. "Okay," he said. "You tell the Cutburthsons I said I hope they enjoy the play." He watched O'Banion intently.

O'Banion fought the smile that threatened to creep over his face. The cop wasn't bad. But he wasn't good enough. At least not good enough for a professional who did his homework. The IRA man forced a confused frown. "Cutburthsons, Officer?"

"Sure, Lawrence and Mindy."

"But, Officer, Lawrence and Mindy's last name is Riverspoone."

The man in the brown uniform nodded. "Sorry," he said. "You're right. Have a nice evening." He got back in the car and drove away, his taillights disappearing over a hill that led to more of the multimillion-dollar homes.

O'Banion reached under his coat and traced his fingers along the butt of the .45 in his belt. Judge Darlene Sue McClusky should be on her way home by now. It was a twenty-minute drive from the Hilton where the meeting had been held, and she would be arriving any minute. His hand reached under the front seat.

The machete and rope were in place. As soon as the woman appeared, he'd radio the others and they'd overrun the guard shack and take the house.

Another car appeared at the same corner where they'd first seen the security vehicle, and O'Banion drew the .45. "Get ready," he told Shawnessey.

Shawnessey pulled a pistol from his coat.

A light blue Toronado passed under the streetlight and Shawnessey frowned. It didn't even slow at the judge's house, but came to a screeching halt next to the Lincoln.

A man jumped out of the back seat.

O'Banion raised the .45 and cocked it. He lowered it again when he saw Michael McConnel's face under the streetlight.

McConnel wore green fatigue pants, a white T-shirt and black boots. He looked both ways, then opened the door and dived into the back seat.

O'Banion whirled in the seat and grabbed him by the throat. "You bloody arsehole!" he screamed. "You come here dressed as you are? You could blow the whole—"

"Jon, wait," McConnel choked. "Something has happened. Something you had to know, and it couldn't wait."

O'Banion relaxed his grip. "Why didn't you radio?" he asked the excited man.

"Uh, I'm sorry, Jon. I didn't think."

"It had better be fuckin' important."

"It is." McConnel told him about the men who had struck at the motel on New York's Highway 9W.

"What makes you so sure it was Ennslin?" O'Banion said when he'd finished. "It could have been any—"

"But it wasn't, Jon." McConnel shook his head back and forth. "They were carrying IMBELs. Just like the ones we got from the Shining Path last year. You said yourself that that's what Ennslin's men had." He paused. "You know what that bloke Hernandez said. Maybe it's . . . hell, it *must be* true."

Jonathan O'Banion turned back to the front windshield and stared out into the night. He had never trusted Ennslin, but he had not thought the Nazi was fool enough to try something like this.

He started the Lincoln and threw it in gear as a silver BMW turned the corner, entered the circular drive of the McClusky residence and stopped as the electronic garage door opened.

O'Banion didn't even look at the judge as she got out of the car and closed the door again. He passed the house, turned the corner and disappeared.

U.S. District Court Judge Darlene Sue McClusky drank a glass of milk in her kitchen, walked wearily up the stairs, undressed and got in bed with her husband.

Neither of the McCluskys even knew how close they had come to being hacked to death with a machete and hung from the ceiling of their bedroom.

BERNHARDT ENNSLIN pulled the freshly washed and ironed tank top over his head, lifted his coffee cup from the bed stand and slid the glass door open, stepping out onto the second-story deck. A light coat of early-morning dew covered the redwood, and already the air was hot and moist. He stared into the thick mass of emerald trees surrounding his house as the first rays of sunlight peeked through the limbs.

Ennslin took a sip of coffee, set it down on the deck and walked directly to the StairMaster near the rail. He stepped up onto the twin stepping boards and attached the heart-monitor wire to his chest. His eyes glued to the calm blue water in the swimming pool below, he switched the monitor on and grabbed the handrails.

His eyes moved from the pool to the heart monitor's digital readout. He frowned. Already his cardiovascular system was working at a near-aerobic pace.

And Bernhardt Ennslin knew why.

The blood pounded harder through his veins as Ennslin rose on one foot, then the other. He gritted his teeth, the anger boiling higher with each step. He had received the call from Jose Ramirez of the Buenaventura cartel less than ten minutes ago, and learned that what Sveinberg had feared—what he himself had passed off as nothing—had come true.

O'Banion had double-crossed him. He had attacked one of Ramirez's freighters near Copenhagen.

The stupid mick was trying to take over.

Ennslin increased his pace on the exercise machine. He knew now why the Irishman had failed to make his scheduled phone call to Beni last night. O'Banion was to have reported on the ongoing hits in the U.S., but he had not even been in the U.S. The mongrel bastard had been in Denmark.

A burn started in his upper thighs as he passed through the aerobic stage and into the anaerobic zone, his anger still mounting, matching his level of exertion. The ungrateful swine. He had offered O'Banion the deal of a lifetime. A chance that would never again come along in the life of the two-bit terrorist. A chance to make more money than the stupid Irish pig had ever dreamed about.

But that had not been enough. Like the little monkey with his hand stuck in the cookie jar, O'Banion wanted it *all*.

Ennslin barely noticed when the door slid open behind him and Alberto stepped out onto the deck. "Sir . . ." the servant said hesitantly.

Ennslin's head whipped around. He caught a glimpse of his reflection in the glass and saw that his face had turned a bright crimson. "*What*, Alberto?" he said, irritated.

The dark-skinned man shrugged politely, holding up the coffee carafe in his hand.

Ennslin looked back to the timer and saw that he had been on the machine less than ten minutes. Far too little time for a good aerobic workout. But he was going too hard anyway, defeating the purpose of the exercise, and instead of relaxing him the exercise made him angrier with every step.

He killed the timer and heart monitor and slowed his legs, finally dropping to the floor as the steppers slowed to a halt. Alberto had already lifted his coffee mug from the deck and filled it. Ennslin took it and walked to the rail. Gazing past the pool to the golf carts, he sighed.

The problems, he knew, were only beginning. The Arab who had visited Sveinberg had claimed O'Banion planned to invade the Beni district itself and take over the entire Corporation. That seemed unlikely. Foolhardy. Crazy. Ennslin had made sure to show the Irishman the Oerlikon.

A sudden thought sent a jolt of fear up his spine. Had O'Banion somehow found out that he had no one who could operate the air-defense system? Even if he had, O'Banion had seen the rest of his security setup and knew Ennslin had over a hundred trained gunmen at his disposal.

Ennslin sipped at his coffee. How many men did the IRA have? He realized suddenly that he didn't know. He had not done his homework in that arena, and he mentally kicked himself now. He had made the same mistake *der Führer* had made when he failed to fully investigate Soviet strength at the onset of World War II.

He had forgotten that today's ally could be tomorrow's enemy.

Alberto stepped behind him with a towel. Ennslin wiped his face with it, then hung it around his neck. He looked out over the golf carts, to the storage barns, runways and the garage housing the worthless Oerlikon. His gaze traveled on to the electronic eyes strategically placed throughout the ground.

Even without antiaircraft capabilities, with the weapons and security system he had and the men, he could hold off an invading force much larger than his own. The problem was leadership. He had no general. Each man in his employ was a hard and seasoned gunman, but most were Latinos, with hot blood and no sense of organization. There was a hierarchy, yes, but it provided no leadership that Ennslin would care to depend on for anything of this magnitude.

"Sir?" Alberto said behind him.

Ennslin turned around, realizing that he had sighed out loud again.

"Nothing, Alberto," he replied. "I was simply thinking."

The servant hesitated. "Is there anything with which I may be of assistance?" he finally said.

Ennslin smiled. Alberto was a good man, eager to please and hardworking. He had been at the Beni mansion for almost two years, after passing a most thorough background investigation. During those two years, Ennslin had never spoken business with Alberto. In fact, the thought of doing so would not usually have even crossed his mind. But now, during these times of betrayal, he felt himself somehow drawn to the loyalty Alberto had displayed since coming to work for him.

Perhaps it would do some good to get a different perspective on things.

"Alberto," Ennslin said, "I have been betrayed." He told the servant of what O'Banion had done in Copenhagen.

"Mr. Ennslin," Alberto broke in. "Are you sure—" he looked down, embarrassed "—that you should be telling me all this?"

Ennslin scowled at him. "If I did not trust you, Alberto," he said, "you would be dead."

Alberto nodded. "Then I shall be honored to listen," he said. "And if at all possible, express useful ideas."

Ennslin went on to tell about his fears that O'Banion would soon attack. And that without a strong leader and someone to operate the Oerlikon, his forces would be no match for the seasoned terrorists.

Alberto listened, his eyes wrinkled in concern. When he'd finished, the ex-Nazi threw up his hands in a rare display of drama. "What am I to do, Alberto?" he asked, not expecting any answer. "Certainly there are good men on the market who could whip my forces into shape. But it will take time to find just the right man. Perhaps more time than I have before O'Banion comes."

Alberto nodded. "Sir," he said, "if I might be so presumptuous, I would like to offer a suggestion."

Ennslin looked up, surprised.

"I know a man," the servant said. "He was in the employ of a gentleman I worked for several years ago.

This man was very efficient and methodical—of German descent. A true warrior, a born leader and well versed in most weaponry." Alberto paused.

Ennslin felt his heart jump. "The Oerlikon, Alberto," he said anxiously. "Could he operate the Oerlikon?"

Alberto shrugged. "Perhaps," he said. "I do not know if he is available, Mr. Ennslin. But I could find out, and find out about the Oerlikon at the same time. If he can come, I believe he is just the man you are looking for."

BERNHARDT ENNSLIN'S Boeing 727 had been converted from passenger to private use, and with an elegance that made *Air Force One* look like a bush plane suitable for lowly troops. The interior was sectioned off into several areas, with a bedroom fit for a sultan situated at the rear. A kitchen, complete with oven, refrigerator and dining table, separated the bedroom from the living room, which featured colonial-style furniture and paintings bolted to the hull.

Bolan crossed his legs on the couch and took a beer from the attendant. He watched through the window as they descended over the green jungles of Bolivia's Beni district. Below, carved out of the dense foliage, he saw the control tower and runways. On one side were huge warehouses and smaller buildings. On the other side of the landing strips the Executioner could see Ennslin's mansion, swimming pool, tennis courts and golf course.

The Executioner set the beer on the coffee table in front of him. It was here that the white death that

threatened the United States and other countries had
its birth.

The 727 circled once, then dropped. The wheels
struck the tarmac with a slight hop, then the giant bird
coasted to a halt. Bolan stood up.

Julio, the man who had met him at the Miami airport, appeared in the doorway to the pilot's cabin.
"Are you ready, Señor Coffman?" he asked politely.

Bolan nodded, grabbed his carryon bag and reached
for his suitcase.

Julio hurried forward and pried both bags from his
hands. "If you please, señor," he said. "Herr Ennslin
would be angered if I allowed you to perform such a
menial task."

Bolan fought a grin as he let go of the bags. He
knew the real reason Julio wanted to carry them.

They hadn't been checked yet. And Bernhardt
Ennslin wasn't about to let anyone into his home
without making a thorough luggage search for anything else that might tell him more about the visitor.

The Executioner followed Julio down the ramp to
where a man wearing a white safari-style shirt sat behind the wheel of a golf cart. Bolan's bags went into
the back seat with Julio, and the Executioner climbed
into the front.

A few seconds later they parked in front of the
swimming pool. Julio carried his bags toward the rear
of the house.

Bolan followed, looking up to the second-floor
porch. Beyond the porch, through the glass of a sliding door, he saw the face and shoulders of a man.
Broad, muscular shoulders. White hair. Tanned skin,
wrinkled by both sun and stress.

Bernhardt Ennslin.

Ennslin's eyes met the Executioner's for a heartbeat. Then the face faded away from the door.

Bolan followed Julio into the air-conditioned house. They walked along a hallway and into the dining room. Julio turned to him. "Please have a seat and make yourself comfortable, Señor Coffman. I will take your bags to your room. Herr Ennslin should be down in a moment." He disappeared.

Bolan stepped into the room. The long dining table ran almost from wall to wall. Two place settings of china and silver glistened even brighter than the highly waxed wood. The Executioner turned a full circle, taking in his surroundings.

The other furniture—china cabinet, buffet table and lamp tables—were all of dark mahogany that matched the dining table. Light passed through the open windows and then through the hundreds of prisms dangling from the chandelier centered over the table. Oil paintings covered the walls. Bolan saw a scenic landscape of an old castle along the Rhine, as well as several portraits of children, all with blond hair and blue eyes. He was studying a picture of a young boy squatting next to a stream when he felt a presence behind him and turned toward the door.

Bernhardt Ennslin stood in the doorway wearing a sweat-soaked gray tank top and shorts. Bolan again noted the thick, muscular shoulders. Ennslin's legs, flushed red and pumping with blood as if he'd just been lifting weights, looked as if they belonged on a body half the age of his face.

The former Nazi smiled as he slipped a white terry cloth robe around his shoulders. The timing of the movement had obviously been planned in advance. Ennslin had wanted Bolan to see his superb physical condition.

"Mr. Coffman?" Ennslin said, walking forward, his hand extended.

"Herr Ennslin," Bolan said. He took the hand, and the two men gripped each other as if holding gold that might slip from their fingers. The German winced slightly. The Executioner let up, saw the relief on Ennslin's face and in that moment realized exactly the part he should play to gain the man's confidence.

Ennslin wanted a strong man for the job he needed filled. But he didn't want that man to be quite as strong as he himself was.

The terry-clothed arm waved toward a seat at one end of the table. "Won't you sit down, Mr. Coffman?" he said. "Lunch should be ready." He took a seat at the other end and lifted a small bell. The sound tinkled melodiously throughout the room, and a second later a small man in a white shirt and slacks entered through a swinging door.

"I believe you already know Alberto, Mr. Coffman."

Bolan looked up and smiled. "You're looking well, Alberto," he said.

"As are you, sir," the servant replied. "It has been a long time."

"Yes, it has."

"We are ready for lunch, Alberto," Ennslin said.

Alberto nodded toward Bolan and said, "*Sí,* Herr Ennslin." Then he turned and passed into the kitchen once more.

The swinging door opened again a moment later. Led by Alberto, several servants entered carrying steaming bowls of food. A pretty, dark-skinned woman walked directly to Bolan and began spooning red cabbage into a bowl next to his plate. As she moved on to Ennslin, a chubby young man in his early twenties took her place and did the same with sauerkraut. Alberto then stepped forward, set a platter down next to the Executioner and lifted a carving knife and fork.

"I hope you like *sauerbraten,* Mr. Coffman," Ennslin said from the other end of the table. "It has a high fat content, I'm afraid, but it is one of the traditional German dishes I find myself unable to give up."

"I do like it," the Executioner answered. "My mother used to make it."

Ennslin's eyebrows rose. "Eh?" he said. "Your mother was German?"

Bolan shook his head. "My mother was Austrian," he said. "It was my father who was German. But of course the Austrians have their version of *sauerbraten,* as well." He watched Ennslin smile and nod his head with approval.

The woman returned and set a large loaf of pumpernickel bread at each end of the table. Alberto left the room and came back holding a bottle of German Rhine wine.

"I never partake of alcohol during the day," Ennslin said. "In fact, I rarely do at night. But you are free to indulge if you choose, Mr. Coffman."

Bolan shook his head. "No, thank you. I like to keep my head about me, as well. And when I do make an exception, I prefer a good German beer."

Ennslin's smile widened. Bolan could see he was impressed.

"Will there be anything else, sir?" Alberto asked.

Ennslin shook his head. "Not at the moment. I will ring if we need you." As the servant disappeared again, he lifted his knife and fork and began cutting his meat. "So, Mr. Coffman. Alberto speaks highly of you. Please tell me about yourself."

Bolan lifted his own knife and fork. Aaron Kurtzman, Stony Man Farm's computer genius, had tapped into the Bureau of Vital Statistics, NCIC and other pertinent computer systems and inserted files and documentation on "Erwin Klaus Coffman." The German-born American had a lengthy arrest record but no convictions in case Ennslin had the resources and inclination to check.

The Executioner knew the man had both.

"To be honest," Bolan said, "I only vaguely remember Alberto. He worked for Mr. Marsh during a period when I did some...contract labor for him."

Ennslin nodded. "Tell me about this Marsh."

Kurtzman had mentioned the fictitious Mr. Marsh in several FBI reports on "Coffman". Marsh was a gangland figure in the Toronto and Buffalo, New York, area. Should Ennslin go so far as to contact him directly at one of the American or Canadian numbers or addresses listed in the reports, the ex-Nazi would find himself dealing with Leo Turrin, a former Justice Department deep-cover man who now worked for the Farm.

Bolan shrugged. "He's American. Makes his living in the same business you're in." He glanced around the room. "Although not as well, I'd have to say."

Ennslin chuckled. "Few do," he said. He took a bite of the *sauerbraten* and chased it with a drink from his water glass. "So, Mr. Coffman," he said. "You are of German descent?"

Bolan nodded and took a bite of cabbage. "And Austrian."

"*Der Führer* was Austrian."

Bolan smiled and swallowed, the swallow coming hard. It went against his grain, even in role camouflage, to identify with a monster like Adolf Hitler.

"And Alberto tells me you are a first generation American?"

The Executioner cut another piece of roast. "Actually I was born in Bonn. I only vaguely remember it. My mother emigrated shortly after the war."

"Your mother, you say. What of your father?"

"He was killed at El Alamein." Bolan paused and looked up from his plate. "He was an officer under Field Marshal General Rommel."

Ennslin's face looked as if his food had suddenly rotted. "El Alamein was the turning point," he snarled. "Things were never the same for the Third Reich after that." He paused. "Or for you. You must have been a mere infant when your father was killed. Do you remember him?"

Bolan shook his head.

Ennslin smiled sadly. "We have much in common, Coffman. *My* father died in the First World War." He looked Bolan in the eyes. "My mother, God rest her blessed soul, was forced to provide for us. But through it all, I became stronger."

Bolan nodded, filing the information away for future reference. In a deal like this, you could never know too much about a man's private life or history. "'That which does not kill me makes me stronger,'" he quoted.

Ennslin's eyes brightened. "You are a student of Nietzsche?"

The Executioner nodded and took a drink from his water glass.

Ennslin wiped his mouth with his napkin and set it in his lap. "I will get to the point," he said. "Alberto advised you over the phone as to what I was looking for. Are you interested in employment?"

Bolan kept eating. "I wouldn't have flown down here if I wasn't," he said.

"And you understand what the job entails?"

The Executioner set his utensils down and stared at the man at the other end of the table. "You've got troops, but you need a field marshal of your own, Herr Ennslin," he said. "Someone to whip this ragtag group into shape." He took another drink of his water. "Okay. I can do that."

Ennslin's eyebrows lowered. "Did Alberto tell you why?"

Bolan smiled. "He didn't have to, Herr Ennslin. I can put two and two together as well as the next guy. Either you've double-crossed someone who wants revenge, or someone double-crossed you. My guess is someone crossed *you*." He lifted his sterling silver fork and ran his thumb down the spine, admiring the engraving. "You've got everything you could possibly want, Herr Ennslin. Betrayal for you would no longer be practical. And besides—" he paused and looked up again "—you are German, and therefore a man of honor." He watched the former Nazi's eyes glow with pleasure.

There was a long moment of silence, then Ennslin said, "What about the Oerlikon?"

"I've never even seen one. But I've used the Breda 40 mm L70, which is similar. I'll figure it out."

Ennslin beamed. "Do we need to discuss price?"

"Of course."

"I will give you fifty thousand dollars a day."

Bolan smiled. "That's a lot of money," he said. "But with all due respect, Herr Ennslin, that much could fall out of your wallet every day and you wouldn't even notice it. We're talking about a short-term job—ten days, two weeks tops. After that, the threat will be over, one way or the other. Double it— a hundred grand a day—and you've got a deal. You still won't notice the loss."

Ennslin threw back his head and laughed. "I like you," he said. "You remind me very much of myself when I was a young man." He paused for a minute, then looked his guest straight in the eye.

"You have a deal, Herr Coffman."

Herr. The new title wasn't lost on the Executioner. It meant Ennslin had accepted him.

They made small talk the rest of the meal. When they had finished, Ennslin rang the bell, and Alberto and the others appeared to take the dishes.

"I will show you to your quarters myself," Ennslin said. "Take a few hours to get settled if you like. I would like you to begin first by training several men to operate the Oerlikon."

"If it's all the same to you," the Executioner said as they rose from the table, "I'd rather just dump my bags and get started. But before we begin with the Oerlikon, I'd like to get the troop training under way."

Ennslin frowned and started to speak.

Before he could, Bolan went on. "The troops will form your main resistance anyway, and it'll give me a chance to choose the right men for the antiaircraft system." He paused, watching Ennslin. "The Oerlikon's complex. I need to pick the right men for the job."

Ennslin's grin was so wide it threatened to permanently distort his face. "Of course," he said. The two men started for the door. "But please, begin with the Oerlikon as soon as possible."

Bolan smiled back. "Sir, please relax. I understand what we're facing. And if the attack comes before someone can operate the system, I'll do so myself."

Ennslin slapped the Executioner across the back. The German's smile now threatened to split his face. "I would like you to dine with me again tonight," he said. "We can discuss the details of the men's training and your plans for defense." Just before they reached the doorway, the ex-Nazi stopped and turned back to where Alberto was lifting the platter containing what remained of the *sauerbraten*. "As for you, Alberto," he said. "Consider your salary doubled. You have brought me exactly the man I needed."

Alberto smiled at his employer. Then, turning to the Executioner, he bowed.

THE FAIRWAY of the third hole looked more like a military parade ground than a golf course.

Which was exactly what the Executioner had turned it into.

Bolan walked toward the men assembled in front of the tee markers as Alberto and the other house staff finished hanging the canvas dummies from the quickly erected frame. Three dozen IMBEL Light Automatic Rifles with fixed bayonets, similar to the ones the Executioner and Able Team had used in New York, had been stacked on a tarp on the ground.

The IMBELs, Bolan had learned, were courtesy of the Bolivian government. The nation's crest had been stamped on the receiver of each weapon. But that didn't surprise the Executioner. During the two hours he had been at the house, he had already seen a Bolivian army general and a police captain come and go. They had served to confirm his suspicion that Bernhardt Ennslin's power and influence knew no bounds in his adopted homeland.

The Executioner turned to the flatbed truck on the other side of the fairway. More of Ennslin's staff were struggling with long telephone poles that would be used for strength training.

Bolan came to a halt in front of the men who stood awaiting his arrival. They all wore khaki O.D. green fatigue blouses and pants, web belts and pistols. Several were talking among themselves, laughing, pointing to their new uniforms and in general acting like a high school football team that had just checked out their equipment and was about to start summer two-aday practices.

Normally, under the circumstances, such unrestrained conduct on the parts of mercenaries in the employ of a drug lord would have been a welcome sight to the Executioner's eyes. It meant they were undisciplined, and would therefore pose little threat to well-trained troops. But as he surveyed the men in front of him now, Bolan recognized the unique position he was in.

For the first time in his long career, he found himself not only preparing to train a hundred or so murderers to murder better, but looking forward to it.

Why? Because when O'Banion's terrorists attacked Ennslin's lair, these men would be killing others like themselves.

"Attention!" Bolan shouted.

Several of the men's shoulders shot back as their heads came up. Others smiled or looked up contemptuously. Someone toward the rear of the assembly said something, and another snickered.

Bolan's eyes fell on the man who had spoken. Dark skin. Straight hair. But his facial features didn't look Hispanic. More Arabic. Perhaps East Indian or Pakistani.

Addressing the men as a whole, the Executioner said, "None of you know me. But you're about to. And the first thing about me you should know is that anyone who hasn't followed my order to come to attention by the time I draw my weapon will find himself on the ground . . . stone-cold dead."

The Executioner's hand fell to the web holster on his belt. The Desert Eagle .44 Magnum leaped into his hand.

All of the men before him stood suddenly erect.

All except the man who had made the wisecrack.

Bolan aimed the Desert Eagle his way and fired. The bullet tore the epaulet from the man's right shoulder. The man's eyes and mouth opened wide in shock, but before he could scream, the Executioner's second round ripped the other epaulet from his fatigue blouse.

The men in front of him parted ranks as Bolan walked through them. Shoving his face into that of the dark-skinned man, he said, "You have a problem, soldier?"

The man didn't answer. His mouth continued to hang open.

"What's your name?" Bolan demanded.

The word almost stayed in the man's throat. "... Parman."

Parman. Ennslin had mentioned him. He had been with one of India's terrorist groups, Dal Khaiso, before Ennslin employed him. And he had been the unofficial leader of this rat pack until "Herr Coffman" had shown up.

"Parman *what!*" Bolan shouted into the man's face.

"Parman, *sir!*" the merc shouted back.

Bolan stepped back and smiled. "That's better," he said. "I know I said I'd shoot you. But consider this your free one. At least, *almost* free." He swung the Desert Eagle around in an arc against the man's temple.

Parman dropped like a sack of cement.

The Executioner returned to the front. "On the command," he barked. "You will sound off *A, B,* and *C.*" He nodded toward a burly man on the front right corner.

"*A!*" the man shouted at the top of his lungs.

The rest of the men followed. When it came time for the man next to Parman to speak, he shouted "*B*" and then looked hesitantly to the sleeping form on the ground next to him.

"*C!*" Bolan said for the Indian, and stared at the next merc.

When they'd finished, the Executioner said, "On the command, Company A will proceed to the posts. B Company will move to bayonet training and C will remain here with me. Is that understood?"

"Sir, yes, sir!" screamed the men in front of him.

"Then move out!" Bolan roared.

The men of Company A sprinted awkwardly toward one side of the fairway while B lumbered to the other.

Bolan faced the remaining men. "Wake him up," he ordered, indicating Parman.

The man next to the Indian knelt and slapped his face. Parman didn't respond.

Bolan walked forward, drew the .44 Magnum again and fired a round two inches to the side of Parman's head.

The Indian's eyes shot open, and he leaped to his feet.

"On the command," the Executioner said, "you will turn and sprint to the flag on the green, circle it and return." He paused a moment, then shouted, "About-face. On the double!"

The men took off.

Bolan raced to the telephone poles, passing several huffing and puffing men of Company A on the way. He lined the men up three to a post, and they began lifting the heavy poles over their heads, then returning them to the ground. "I'll be watching," the Executioner told them as he turned to leave. "Any slackers have quite a surprise waiting for them.'' He turned and bolted across the fairway to the bayonet-training facility. Issuing each man an unloaded rifle, he got them started on the dummies, then sprinted back in time to beat the men returning from the green.

When they had assembled, panting, in front of him, Bolan shouted, ''Where's the flag?''

No one answered.

Parman fell forward to his hands and knees and left his lunch on the fairway.

''Let's do it again, then!'' Bolan yelled, and the men took off.

As he headed once more for the telephone poles, the Executioner saw a dark sedan pull out of the jungle road and onto the drive leading to Ennslin's front door. The car parked in front of the house, and an overweight man wearing a light beige suit and straw panama got out and waddled toward the entrance.

Bolan moved back and forth between the three companies, then moved each group through the other two stations on the circuit. He was about to reassemble them at the tees when he saw Alberto heading his way in one of the golf carts.

''Herr Ennslin requests you for drinks before dinner,'' the servant said.

Bolan pointed silently to the cart and raised his eyebrows.

Alberto shook his head. ''No bugs. I checked.''

Bolan nodded. ''Who's the fat man who just drove up?''

Alberto shook his head again. When he spoke, he had lost the Spanish accent and sounded as if he'd been born and bred in Brooklyn.

Which he had.

"I don't know," the DEA deep-cover man said. "I tried to trace him through Washington. His tags don't check out. He comes out fairly regularly. They don't talk when I'm around."

Bolan turned and stabbed the whistle into his mouth. A shrill blow brought the weary mercenaries stumbling back to formation. "I'd get some sleep if I were you," the Executioner said. "We begin again at 0400."

Several groans issued forth from the men. They were cut off sharply by a scowl from the Executioner.

As the men fell out, Bolan took the seat next to Alberto, and the golf cart started toward the house.

CHAPTER ELEVEN

The shower had done more than simply clean the Greenfinch's unwashed body. The freezing water had jolted her from the half-conscious never-never land to which she had retreated in order to escape the degradation she'd been subjected to since O'Banion had kidnapped her.

Baine Morrison had returned to reality. And with that return had come a new will, a new ambition. She intended to escape. To seek revenge.

And God help the man who tried to stand in her way.

Baine glanced across the room to the stumpy, red-faced man standing against the wall. He wore green BDU pants, a flap holster on one hip and a sheath holding a long Sykes-Fairbairn dagger on the other. The knife was identical to the one O'Banion had held to her throat while he raped her.

The man's eyes, glimmering with lust, were glued to her body. The sight brought back Baine's memory of the nightmare flight to the United States, and she felt the nausea rise in her stomach. O'Banion had been the first to take her against her will—in the truck, before they'd even left the scene of the slaughter of the rest of her unit. When he'd finished, he'd let the others root over her like pigs, grunting, panting, each taking his turn. Not all of them, but many. How many, she wasn't sure—she had lost consciousness somewhere over the Atlantic and not come to again until she'd awakened in a hotel room, nude and tied to the bed.

Baine's vision began to clear as the painful memories returned. Part of her tried to block them out, to force them back into the hidden recesses of her brain where they had lain dormant. She fought the urge. She had to face what had happened to her. Come to terms with it. Get a realistic grip on the situation as it now stood.

Otherwise, she would not escape. And if she did not escape, and escape *soon*, Baine Morrison knew she would die.

Baine closed her eyes, concentrating on what had happened since her abduction. There had been the hotel room, then others, but always this place in between. Some sort of plumbing shop, as best she could tell. It was their base of operations. They always returned here. She opened her eyes and looked back to the short, squat man at the door. What had O'Banion called him? Donnelly.

Donnelly saw her looking at him and turned his eyes away in embarrassment.

Had he been one of the rapists on the plane?

She fought the nausea again. Donnelly was not as smart as O'Banion. And weaker. She could sense it. If escape was to come, it would be while he guarded her.

"Donnelly..." she said, surprised at how weak her voice sounded.

The man turned back to her.

"Water... a glass of water... please?"

Donnelly's eyes traveled up and down her body, then he turned to the deep industrial sink against the brick wall. Filling a water glass, he walked to the bed and held it to her lips.

Baine drank slowly, choking, watching Donnelly try to keep his eyes off her breasts. When she'd finished, she whispered, "Thank you."

Donnelly nodded, his eyes falling again to her body.

The plan, simple as it was, came to her in a heartbeat. She knew she would have one chance, and one chance only. "Thank you, Donnelly," she said again.

"You're...welcome," the man answered, his eyes rising to meet hers.

"Can I repay you somehow?"

Donnelly drew in a deep breath, his face turning even redder. Baine didn't wait for an answer. "You're different," she whispered. "Not like the others."

It was the wrong thing to say.

"What do you mean?" he asked, his eyebrows rising.

Baine glanced down at her own body.

Donnelly's eyes narrowed. "You heard O'Banion," he said. "I've me orders."

"How would he know? How could he hurt you if he never—"

Donnelly's face flushed red with anger.

Baine backpedaled. "Not that you aren't tough, Donnelly," she whispered. "You are. You're every bit as good as the others, maybe better. I just meant... there's another side to you. A side I...like."

"You're lying," Donnelly snarled. "You think me a coward?" He raised his hand as if to slap her, then turned away.

Baine tried to reach out for him, but the ropes binding her to the bed frame halted the movement.

This trick wasn't working. She'd have to try something else.

Baine laughed. "Yes, it looks that way," she said. She took a deep breath. What she was about to say was risky. It might open the door for her escape. But it might just as easily lead to her death. "You weren't one of them on the plane, were you, Donnelly? No, you weren't." Another deep breath. "What was wrong with you, Donnelly? Can't get it up?"

The man turned back to her, his face a mask of rage. "You bloody whore," he said.

"That's okay, Donnelly," Baine said. "Is it boys you like? It's okay to like boys. Are you a bloody faggot?"

Donnelly's rage became dementia. "A bloody *faggot?*" he said under his breath. "You think I'm a bloody *faggot?*" His hand dropped to his holstered pistol.

"Well, you are, aren't you?" Baine goaded. "If you weren't, you'd have had your pants down already."

"I'll kill you, you bitch," Donnelly grunted.

"Fine," Baine said. "Kill me. I'm dead anyway. And I'll die knowing it's little boys' rumps you're after." She held her breath.

Donnelly's hand froze on the holster. His eyes fell from Baine's face to her legs. "I'll show you who's the fag, you bloody common piece of muck," he growled. He unzipped his pants and moved to the bed.

Baine closed her eyes. What happened next would be the deciding point. "Untie me, you bastard," she said. "At least my hands. Let me show you what I can really do when I want to." Opening her eyes, she went on. "Or are you afraid I'm too strong for you, you bloody wanker?"

Donnelly slapped her hard across the face. He drew the dagger from his side, raised it over her head, and for a moment Baine thought he was about to plunge it through her heart.

Then the blade came down and severed the ropes from her right hand. He resheathed the knife and pointed to his zipper. "You do it," he said. "You take it out. I'll show you who's the fag."

Baine did what he'd ordered, then leaned forward as he positioned himself over her.

The rest was easy.

As Donnelly leaned into her, the Greenfinch drew the Sykes-Fairbairn dagger from the sheath and plunged it up under the man's floating ribs and into his heart.

The memory of the flight to the U.S. returned to her as she withdrew the blade. The Greenfinch plunged it in again. And again. And again.

Two minutes later she had sliced through the restraints on her ankles, dressed in Donnelly's clothes and was climbing out the window of Whitlow's Plumbing Shop into the alley.

SINCE THE ONSET of the mission, there had been no doubt in Bolan's mind that Phil Herrod and the other DEA agents who'd been assassinated off the coast of Panama had been set up from the inside. He just didn't know where. And ever since he'd gotten the run-around in Sweden by Rakestraw, the Executioner had suspected that the CIA, or at least some faction within the CIA, had reasons for not wanting him to get too close to Ennslin.

Now, as Alberto escorted him into the den, both questions were answered at once.

The den was ordinary by the standards of the rest of the house. Simple wood paneling and a few bookshelves. Only a few oil portraits to add some adornment to the room.

But the face that interested the Executioner was that of the fat man who sat across from Ennslin in a stuffed easy chair.

Ennslin rose to his feet and set a glass of clear liquid on the table next to his chair as Bolan walked in. "Ah, Coffman," the Corporation man said. "How goes the training?"

Bolan smiled. "They've got a ways to go, Herr Ennslin," he said, glancing at the other man and letting the smile fade.

The movement wasn't lost on Ennslin. "Feel free to speak in front of our guest. Herr Coffman, meet... why don't you call him Mr. Schmitt?"

The man called Schmitt struggled his bulk out of the chair and extended his hand. A nervous smile played at the corners of his mouth. "Herr Coffman," he said as Bolan took his hand. He squinted slightly, studying the Executioner's face. "Have we met before?"

Bolan chuckled. "Could be," he said. "You aren't a cop, are you?"

Ennslin's laugh cut in. "No, Herr Coffman, he is not a cop. Mr. Schmitt is an old friend of mine." He turned and walked behind the bar at the rear of the room. "Vodka?" he asked. "I have decided to indulge myself tonight."

"Maybe a short one," Bolan said. "I've got an early wake-up call in the morning."

Ennslin pulled a glass from the shelf behind the bar and poured two fingers of vodka from a bottle. Schmitt deposited himself back between the arms of the chair. Bolan took the glass from Ennslin and then dropped into a seat on the couch next to him.

"I should tell you, Coffman," Ennslin said as he sat down, "that I took the liberty of checking out your story this afternoon. As I'm sure you realize, I can take no chances in my business."

Bolan nodded. "I expected it," he said. "I'm afraid I'd have lost respect for you if you *hadn't* double-checked."

The German nodded. "Yes. And let me say that I found a major discrepancy between what you told me this afternoon and what I learned."

Bolan turned toward him. "Really?" he said.

"Yes. You said you thought you could handle this job. From what I found, you can *more* than handle it." He beamed at Bolan like a proud father looking at his son. Turning to his guest, he spoke as if Bolan were not present. "Coffman has quite a track record," he said. "In addition to the private work he has done for certain businessmen in the U.S., he fought in both Angola and Rhodesia. Ran guns from Belgium to the Contras. I could go on, but it would become embarrassing for Herr Coffman."

Alberto appeared and announced dinner. Ennslin led his two guests down the hall and back to the dining room where he and Bolan had eaten lunch.

Schmitt ate heartily, which was no surprise to the Executioner. The man had always had a ravenous appetite, even when the hot jungles of Vietnam had killed the hunger of others.

Ennslin talked about both the joys and hardships of growing up in the fatherland during the exciting era when Hitler was taking power. He grew maudlin several times, his eyes nearly tearing over, when he spoke of how hard his widowed mother had worked to provide for her children. "She painted many of the portraits of the children you see on the walls," he told Bolan. "She was an artist at heart, but never had the opportunity to express her talents until late in life, when I brought her to Bolivia."

Bolan listened. Even the most evil of men had their soft spots. Ennslin's was his mother. He had gone on about her at length twice now.

When dinner was finished, Ennslin looked up at Bolan. "I do not wish to appear rude, Herr Coffman," he said. "But if you don't mind, Mr. Schmitt and I have things we must discuss privately."

Bolan wiped his mouth with his napkin and stood up. "I don't mind in the least," he said. "Like I said, I've got an early reveille planned."

Alberto appeared and showed him out the back door.

As Bolan crossed the deck toward the pool house where his bed awaited, his mind traveled back over the years. The Executioner had first met the man calling himself Schmitt when he had been a Special Forces sniper in Vietnam. Andrew Robinette had been a hard-line, right-wing, "kill 'em all and let God sort 'em out" CIA agent assigned to work with the Green Berets.

The fat man had been younger and less wrinkled in those days, but Bolan had recognized Robinette immediately. They had hardly been friends—Robinette's disregard for innocent lives had ensured that would never happen—but had peripherally known each other, which explained Robinette's curiosity when Ennslin had introduced them. The CIA man had sensed something familiar in the Executioner, but Bolan's cosmetic surgery had prevented him from being recognized.

The Executioner passed on by the pool house and hurried across the golf course. Checking first to make sure he wasn't being watched, he stepped into the jungle, pulled a compass from his pocket and hurried toward the coordinates that had been prearranged while he was still at Stony Man Farm.

Ten minutes later he found the radio and minisatellite dish. Still attached to the cargo chute that had caught in the branches of a tree, they were within twenty feet of where Jack Grimaldi had promised they'd be.

Bolan set up the dish and switched the radio on. A second later he was telling Barbara Price about Andrew Robinette. "It explains how Ennslin knew about Phil Herrod," the Executioner said. "Hal told me at the beginning that DEA had been working with the Company on Ennslin."

"It explains some other things, too," Price added. "Like the stalling tactics the Company put you through. I'll have Kurtzman check the computer for some connection between Robinette and Rakestraw. Chances are it's just one old spook doing another a favor. They've both been around since Moses was a

Mossad agent. A lot of IOUs can mount up over the years.'' She paused, then said, ''Aaron ran his daily computer scan through NCIC and came up with a report you'll want to know about. Seems an Ulster Defense Regiment Greenfinch came into the NYPD with one hell of a story.'' She went on to tell Bolan about Baine Morrison's kidnapping, rape and eventual escape. ''The woman's been to several of the safe houses with O'Banion. She can pinpoint them.''

''Okay, Barb,'' Bolan said. ''Tell Hal to get a strike force ready. I'll want to meet this Greenfinch, and I'll brief the strike force personally on the setup down here. Then we'll hit a safe house or two to speed O'Banion up.'' He paused for air. ''It's time this show took the stage.''

''How do you plan to slip away from Ennslin?'' Price asked.

Bolan outlined his plan to leave without blowing his cover.

Price laughed when he'd finished. ''Don't think I'm not taking you seriously,'' she said quickly. ''I am. And it sounds like it'll work. It's just kind of funny.''

''What?'' Bolan asked.

''Bernhardt Ennslin—'' Price snickered ''—he's a mama's boy.''

THE EXECUTIONER sprinted the last two hundred yards of the ten-mile run and came to a halt next to the flag on green number seven. He turned back, gazing out across the golf course in the early-morning light.

The closest man behind him was Parman, a good quarter of a mile back. Since he'd recovered from his initial bout of the smart-ass, and realized that there was a new kid on the block, Parman had become a model recruit.

Bolan raised his hands over his head, giving his lungs room to expand. As he caught his breath, he watched the East Indian race toward the green. Parman was a natural-born endurance athlete whom Bolan could have put to use.

Too bad he was one of the bad guys.

Parman made it to the green, then fell onto the carefully manicured grass, his chest heaving. One by one the other men arrived, doing the same. Thirty minutes later, when even the overweight men had straggled in, the Executioner ordered them to their feet and into formation.

"There are five fundamentals to hand-to-hand combat," Bolan began. "First you make use of any available weapon. Sticks, stones, hands, feet, head...*anything*. Second you attack aggressively, using your strength against your enemy's weakest point. Maintain *your* balance and break that of your opponent. Use your opponent's momentum to your advantage. And last but not least, learn each phase of the movements I'm about to teach you thoroughly." He paused, glancing from face to face to make sure the men were listening. Not that he particularly cared. If Ennslin's hired thugs didn't learn what he was about to teach, O'Banion's terrorists would kill them. If they did, they'd kill the terrorists. And as long as he could keep stalling Ennslin on the Oerlikon antiaircraft system, the joint DEA and Delta Force task force Brognola was setting up could come in and mop up whatever was left.

The fact was, the Executioner had no downside in this situation.

Bolan pulled a three-foot nylon cord from the breast pocket of his fatigue blouse and called out, "Parman."

Parman hesitated, then stepped forward.

Bolan faced the man away from him, then said, "I'm about to demonstrate the correct method of silencing a sentry with a wire or cord. Watch carefully. You'll be doing it in a moment." Holding one end of the cord in each hand, he stepped forward and looped it over Parman's neck from the left. He placed the heel of his hand on the Indian's shoulder near the nape of the neck, brought his knee up into the small of the back and pulled with his right hand while pushing with his left.

Parman's head jerked, and a soft gurgling sound issued forth from his lips.

Bolan loosened the pressure, and Parman bent forward, his hands going to his throat.

"Do it faster, and you cut off all noise," Bolan said. He pointed toward a cardboard box on the green. "Pick a partner, grab a rope and get busy."

The words had barely left his mouth when he heard a golf cart approaching. Pivoting, Bolan saw the cart racing his way, Ennslin in the passenger's seat and Alberto behind the wheel.

Alberto brought the vehicle to a halt next to the green. Ennslin leaped out. Bolan could see the anger on the former Nazi's face as he strode toward the flag.

Ennslin came to a halt in front of Bolan and said, "Come with me." Turning an about-face, he marched back to the golf cart.

Bolan turned back to his men. "Parman," he said, "take over until I get back. When I do, I expect everyone to have this movement down perfectly." He followed Ennslin to the cart.

Ennslin didn't speak until they were halfway back to the house. "You gave my phone number to someone in the United States?" he said angrily.

Bolan let a chuckle escape his lips. "Is that what this is about?" he asked. "I've got a phone call?"

Ennslin turned toward him, his eyes still filled with anger. "I asked you a question."

Bolan nodded. "Yeah, I gave it to someone," he said. "Does it matter? You're not exactly a big secret down here, Herr Ennslin. Your security comes through governmental influence and power, not hiding out in the jungle. Anybody who wanted to find you could look in the phone book." He frowned. "What's the problem?"

"The problem is, you should have told me."

Bolan hesitated, carefully calculating his next move. Apologize? No, that would be like admitting weakness. Ennslin abhorred weakness. Strength was what he admired above all else.

But the former Nazi also craved respect, and to show strength without the respect Ennslin felt he was due would be just as big a mistake.

"Let me tell you *now*, then, Herr Ennslin," the Executioner said. "My mother is in Cleveland. She's dying." From the corner of his eye, he saw Ennslin's face soften immediately.

"Her private nurse is the only person who has this number, and she doesn't even know whose number it is."

Ennslin didn't speak.

Okay, the strength hook had been cast. Now it was time to sink that hook and move on to the respect.

Bolan cleared his throat. "But I was wrong not to have told you in advance. I suppose I thought you might think me weak for caring so much about my mother."

"Never," Ennslin said without hesitation.

Bolan smiled to himself. Of course not. It would be like admitting *you* had weaknesses.

"Okay," Bolan said. "It slipped my mind yesterday. And for that, you have my apology."

Alberto brought the cart to a halt in front of the fence. "There is a phone in the den," Ennslin said as they got out. "You will have some privacy there." He led the way past the pool, opened the sliding glass door, then hurried on through the den and disappeared down the hall.

Bolan walked to the phone and lifted the receiver. "Hello?"

"Mr. Erwin Klaus Coffman?" the nasal voice of an operator said.

"Speaking." The Executioner heard a soft click and realized Ennslin had lifted an extension somewhere in the house.

"Person to person from the United States," the operator said. "Go ahead."

The voice that came on the line was familiar yet very different. Somehow Barbara Price had managed to make herself sound thirty years older. "Mr. Coffman," she said. "This is Nurse Price." Her voice cracked suddenly with emotion. "Oh, Mr. Coffman.

Can you come home? She's asking for you." Price sniffled. "I don't think she'll last for long."

Bolan listened as the Stony Man mission controller enumerated the signs of impending death.

Hearing footsteps coming down the hallway, he turned toward the door.

Ennslin appeared holding a key ring. "These keys will fit the Land Rover parked in the lot next to the warehouses," he said, his eyes moist. "Alberto will take you to it in one of the carts." He paused, blinked, then said, "I regret I cannot send you to visit your mother in the 727. But with our present situation, I must keep it here. I will pay for your flight to Cleveland. Do you know when you will return?"

"A day or two tops," Bolan said. "The nurse said she doesn't have long."

Ennslin nodded, a lone tear rolling down his cheek. "Leave the Land Rover at the airport in La Paz," he said. "Then bring it back when you return."

THE SUN HAD FALLEN almost to the horizon by the time Blancanales guided the black Chevy van past Old Fort Niagara at Youngstown, New York. Bolan studied the three flags flying over the structure—British, French and American. All of the nations had commandeered the fort at one time or another since its construction in 1726.

The roar of Niagara Falls pounded the sides of the vehicle. Then a loud explosion sounded above the noise from the water, and the Executioner looked out the window, past the drawbridge leading to the fort. Several men, carrying muskets and dressed as militia soldiers, were firing a Louis XV model cannon for the benefit of a small gathering of tourists.

The Executioner turned back to the front and returned to his thoughts. Grimaldi had been waiting as soon as his flight from La Paz had touched down in Miami. The Stony Man pilot had flown him directly to Washington, where he'd given the joint task force of DEA agents and Army Delta Force commandos a thorough briefing on the Corporation headquarters site. They would be ready to fly to Beni and mop up what was left of both Ennslin's and O'Banion's troops as soon as they got word from Bolan that O'Banion's attack had begun.

Bolan planned to return to his undercover capacity at Ennslin's compound, directing the attack from the ground just as soon as he and Able Team took care of an IRA safe house the Greenfinch had fingered.

There was only one fly in the ointment: Robinette.

Keeping the news that a major drug strike force was being formed—and where it was headed—from the CIA was paramount to trying to keep the sunrise from the U.S. Weather Bureau. Bolan had only one hope— that he'd be back in Beni and the fireworks would be over before the info made its way down the pipe to Andrew Robinette.

Bolan smiled as the van moved on past the falls. He had been put in several curious positions during this mission—like training the hired guns of a drug lord. Now he faced another. Most of his life he had fought against the molasses-slow red tape of bureaucracy.

This time his life depended on it.

Baine Morrison's voice broke into his thoughts. "Another mile or so, then right," the Greenfinch said from the back seat of the van. "I'll remember the turn when I see it."

"You remember anything about the building yet?" Bolan asked over his shoulder. "House? Warehouse? Anything?"

"No. I'll keep trying."

Bolan swiveled in the shotgun seat to face the woman. He couldn't help but smile. Squeezed between Lyons and Schwarz, she wore blue jeans and a red sweatshirt almost as bright as her hair. Baine Morrison had come a long way toward recovery since Brognola had more or less stolen her out of the hands of the NYPD. Much of her memory, repressed due to the horror of what she'd been through, had come back. Barbara Price had provided the jeans, shirt and the gentle coaxing and sympathy the woman needed to face what had happened to her, and by the time Bolan arrived at Stony Man, Baine had charted out two of the safe houses where she'd been imprisoned.

They didn't need both. The assassination of American judges had come to a screeching halt. One more strike against O'Banion's terrorists with Able Team posing as Corporation hitters should convince the Irishman to hurry up with his plans to invade Beni.

"There...at the billboard," Baine said. "Make a right, then a left. It's maybe a mile and a half."

"We'll be in Canada," Schwarz said.

Bolan glanced at the map in his lap. "No, but we'll be close. It's a good location. They've probably got a boat of some kind stashed on Lake Ontario. They could be in Canadian waters on a moment's notice." He folded the map and shoved it into the glove compartment.

Blancanales followed the Greenfinch's directions, turning away from the pounding waterfall and back inland. They veered north again, and what appeared to be a border ghost town appeared in the distance.

"Drive on by," Bolan ordered. "They can't see in the back, and I'll duck down."

The Executioner slid to the floorboard as they entered the deserted village. To anyone looking into the van, it would appear that a lone man was heading for Canada.

Blancanales kept his eyes straight ahead as if the ruins held no interest for him. "Three buildings still standing," he said, hardly moving his lips.

"It's the old house," the Greenfinch said suddenly. "I think...yes. It had a bed-and-breakfast sign out front."

"I saw it." Blancanales nodded.

Bolan rose back to the seat and stared into the rearview mirror, watching the ghost town grow smaller.

"The place looked like it could be open," Blancanales said. "But the sign said No Vacancy."

Schwarz snorted in the back seat. "We'll change *that*," he said.

A thick grove of trees stood to their right a quarter mile later. "This is as good a place to leave the van as we're going to find," Bolan said. "Pull in."

They pulled over. Schwarz and Lyons reached over the seats and began gathering their weapons.

"There's one other thing," Baine said as Blancanales killed the engine.

Bolan turned back to her.

"I want a gun. I'm going with you."

Schwarz patted her on the shoulder. "We understand how you feel," he said. "We'll get them for you."

Anger suffused the Greenfinch's face, causing the skin to match her hair. "You *can't* understand how I feel," she barked. "Nothing can erase what happened. I'll learn to live with that. But I want—no, I *demand*—what justice I can get. And I plan to get it myself."

"But you Greenfinches aren't even issued weapons," Schwarz said.

"We aren't. We man checkpoints and work right alongside the men who *are* armed. They train us in weaponry, but then don't issue us a weapon. Explain *that* to me if you can."

"I can't," Schwarz said.

"Well, you see what that kind of policy got *me*. Now, are you going to give me a gun or do I have to kill one of you bloody big bastards and take yours?"

Bolan nodded at Schwarz. If anyone deserved a shot at the IRA, it was Baine Morrison.

Schwarz reached over the seat, grabbed an M-16 and handed it to the redhead. His hand disappeared again, coming back with a holstered .45 automatic. "You've convinced us," he said. "Take two—they're small."

The watery scent of Lake Ontario filled Bolan's nostrils as he grabbed the leather binocular case from the floorboard and exited the van. He pulled the powerful Zeiss 20 × 60 porro prism lenses from the case as he walked to the edge of the trees.

The two-story bed-and-breakfast sat in the middle of what had once been the village. Broken concrete blocks, splintered planks of gray wood and the concrete foundations of two other buildings stood in the weeds between the house and Bolan. The bed-and-breakfast looked as old as Old Fort Niagara, and had probably once been a farmhouse before the small town grew up around it. A wide porch ran along the front, back and the side the Executioner could see. Probably the other side, as well.

No perimeter guards were visible, but that didn't mean they weren't there. There were any number of places in the other rotting buildings where a man with a radio could hide.

He returned to the van and dropped the binoculars through the window onto the front seat. Lyons slid open the side door as Bolan stripped out of his coat, sport shirt and slacks, revealing the blacksuit. He transferred the Desert Eagle and Beretta from civilian wear to the ballistic nylon belt and shoulder rigs Schwarz handed him through the door, and slipped into the battle suspenders mounted with frag grenades and extra magazines before taking the M-16 the Able Team warrior extended.

Lyons emerged first from the van, dressed in his own blacksuit and carrying his trademark Atchisson 12-gauge. Schwarz and Blancanales appeared next, equally decked out for battle.

Baine Morrison came last. The extra blacksuit Schwarz had found in the equipment box was a good three sizes too big, staying on only because of the elasticity of the material. She carried the weapons she'd been issued.

Next they applied black camo makeup, then wrapped walkie-talkies around their heads as the sun finally set through the trees. "We'll be crossing open country," Bolan said. "It'll be dark in a few more minutes, but there's some moon. Stick together until we're two hundred yards out, then hit the dirt. A hundred yards from the house, I want Lyons and Blancanales to break off. Circle and take the rear, Ironman. Tap the radio three times when you're in position. Schwarz, you and Baine come with me to the front. Watch for anybody hiding in the wreckage. Unless spotted first, we'll attack together on command. Any questions?"

He got four negatives.

Bolan stepped out of the trees, broke into a jog across the open land, then dived forward onto his belly. He heard the others behind him hit the ground as he crawled forward.

Lyons and Blancanales broke off as ordered a hundred yards later. Bolan slowed his crawl, coming to a halt when he reached the chipped and cracked concrete of the foundation on the edge of the ghost town.

Short runs of still-standing bricks formed knee- and waist-high walls in front of him, creating a miniature labyrinth. Slowly the Executioner rose and began making his way through them.

With eyes like a cat's, Bolan swept the dark, crumbling rubble for movement or any other sign of human life. Nothing. Behind him he could hear the tiptoe patter of Gadgets and Baine Morrison. Coming to the other edge of the foundation, he dropped to one knee behind one of the walls.

Schwarz and the Greenfinch joined Bolan as he scanned the final decaying structure that separated them from the bed-and-breakfast. A fluttering brought the M-16 up, then a pigeon flew out from behind the bricks. The Executioner had started to step out from behind the wall when he caught a flash of light across from him.

Handing the M-16 to Schwarz, Bolan silently drew the sound-suppressed Beretta. He saw the flash again. Greenish in color, it was just beyond a four-foot wall of brick on the other side of the foundation. He wished momentarily for the night-vision goggles he had used earlier in the mission, then dismissed the thought. There was only so much equipment you could take with you on a mission before you became weighted down past the point of reason. He'd chosen to leave the night goggles behind, thinking he wouldn't need them. And all the wishing in the world wouldn't make them magically appear.

Motioning to Baine and Gadgets to stay put, Bolan dropped to his belly again and slid off the foundation into the weeds between the two buildings. He took cover behind a pile of broken two-by-eights just past the edge of the other foundation and raised his head.

The green light appeared again, then disappeared.

Bolan moved out around the trash, crawling slowly across the concrete. As he drew closer, he saw the light again. He was less than five feet away when it rose, stopped in midair, then fell again before disappearing.

And this time he saw what it was. The illuminated hands and numbers of a wristwatch. An impatient sentry checking the time every few minutes.

The light told Bolan all of the story he needed to know. The guard's relief was late, and the man was tired and impatient.

Which made it a perfect time to take him out.

Bolan holstered the Beretta and drew the Mini-Tanto from his belt. Rising to his feet, he took two steps and the man's back became visible.

The Executioner cupped a hand over the man's mouth, shot the blade into his kidney, then moved to the throat. Piercing the side of the guard's neck, he ripped the blade forward to sever the jugular and everything else that stood in the way of the razor-sharp edge.

Bolan returned for Gadgets and Baine, then moved back to the dead man, waiting for Lyons to signal that the other two Able Team men were in place.

One minute turned to two. Two became five. The three soft taps that would signal them never came.

Instead, automatic-rifle fire from the other side of the house suddenly broke the stillness of the night.

Bolan sprinted toward the front of the house, Gadgets and Baine at his heels. As he reached the porch, a muscular man in green fatigues came barreling through the screen door. Seeing the three running figures in black, he lifted a Vickers-Berthier machine gun, tripod and all, and fired. Muzzle-flashes illuminated his scowling face as British .303 slugs sizzled past the oncoming trio.

Bolan fired from the hip, sending a 3-round burst of .223 bullets into the man's abdomen. The onslaught froze the terrorist in time, a look of shock on his face.

Bolan leaped up the steps onto the porch, pivoted and sent a vicious side-kick shooting into the man's midsection. The kick sent the gunner tumbling back through the open door and into a hallway.

The Executioner followed, leaping over the man as he collapsed in the doorway. The entryway was lit by an overhead fixture, and some light filtered into the neighboring rooms. A parlor was off to the right, and what appeared to be the living room to the left. An ancient wooden staircase with an intricately carved banister led to the second floor.

The Executioner heard a shriek from the parlor and turned that way in time to see a mustached man step into the light. The man swung a Sterling submachine gun around.

Bolan sent a burst of fire searing through the flesh beneath the terrorist's T-shirt. The man shrieked in horror.

Gadgets burst through the front door, followed by Baine. They both vaulted the corpse in the entryway as Bolan turned.

A stutter of fire came from the living room, the muzzle-flashes pinpointing the shooter. Gadgets didn't hesitate. He opened fire with his assault rifle, sending a duo of 3-round bursts at the flames.

A body thudded to the floor in the darkness.

But other muzzle-flashes continued, looking like the flickering flames of birthday candles as bullets buzzed past their heads. Bolan added his own .223 bullets to Schwarz's assault. Another body hit the floor as Baine raised her M-16 and joined in.

Bolan and Schwarz kept their triggers back against the guards, blanketing the black living room with fire. Two more slaps against the hardwood floor finally put out the muzzle-flashes.

Autofire still came from the rear of the house as Bolan shoved a new box mag into the assault rifle. He wondered briefly what Lyons and Blancanales had stumbled into. Whatever it was, they were both big boys. They'd have to handle it without him.

Right now he had to do something about the new muzzle-flashes that had started at the top of the stairs.

He twisted that way, firing up at the assault. He heard a grunt between shots, then the bleeding form of a man in O.D. green fatigues came sliding down the banister on his side.

Baine pumped a 3-round burst into him as he rolled off the banister onto the floor.

Bolan moved cautiously up the steps, the other two behind him. Meeting no resistance, he stopped at the top to survey the layout.

The hall led both ways away from the staircase. The Executioner motioned Gadgets left, then took Baine with him to the right as the firing behind the house continued.

Two men leaped into the hall a moment later. Both held Sterlings in their hands. Both tried to fire.

Both died to the rounds of the Executioner and Baine Morrison.

Coming to the next bedroom, Bolan found the door closed. He pushed Baine against the wall, yanked a fragmentation grenade from his suspenders and stepped back. A big boot sent the door flying off its hinges. The Executioner jumped to the side as automatic fire answered the open door.

Pulling the pin, Bolan lobbed the grenade into the bedroom. A voice screamed "Bloody hell!" and a moment later the walls of the two-hundred-fifty-year-old house rocked with the explosion.

The Executioner heard Schwarz's M-16 as he moved to the final door at the end of the hall. It was closed, as well, and he kicked, grabbed and pulled.

This time no shots came through the door. He tossed the grenade inside anyway.

When the explosion died down, Bolan moved around the corner, the M-16 leading the way. The remains of four men lay on the floor, subguns clutched in the dead fingers of those that remained intact.

Bolan hurried to the rear window and looked down. He saw four men barricaded behind a four-foot brick wall in the deteriorating rubble of a building to the rear. They were taking their time, firing at will at Lyons and Blancanales.

The two Able Team warriors, caught in the open with no cover or concealment, had burrowed down into the ground as best they could. They rolled back and forth, trying to keep from becoming stationary targets, and cutting loose with bursts of fire whenever possible.

Bolan opened the window as Baine stepped up next to him. "Start with the guy on the right," he said, "and move to the center." He raised his rifle, flipped the selector to semiauto and peered down the barrel.

A moment later the man at the left end of the wall fell to a single round through the back of his head. Bolan saw the terrorist at the other end of the line fly forward as Baine put her first shot between his shoulder blades.

Bolan fired again as the second man from the left stood and tried to turn. The bullet struck his temple, and he crumpled over the wall sideways. The final man fell to rounds from both Bolan and the Greenfinch as he turned toward the house in confusion.

Suddenly the ghost town was quiet again.

Lyons and Blancanales rose and started toward the house.

Bolan led Baine out of the room and back down the hall. Schwarz met them at the top of the stairs, nodding his success. The electronics man spoke as they descended the steps together. "You're not really going back into the lion's den, are you, Striker? Back to Beni? After *this?*"

Bolan shrugged. "Somebody has to," he said. "Somebody has to be there to guide the troops in once it hits the fan."

CHAPTER TWELVE

Bolan pulled the Land Rover off the road and onto the jungle path leading to Bernhardt Ennslin's compound. Soon he entered the clearing and saw the golf course. A mile or so later, the house appeared. Beyond it he saw the runways, warehouses and other buildings. Passing the house, he parked the vehicle in the lot where he'd found it and got out.

Alberto Manuelian came chugging across the tarmac in one of the golf carts. As he neared, Bolan could see the deep worry lines etched into the undercover DEA man's face.

The Executioner climbed into the cart, and they started back across the runway toward the house. He pointed silently to the cart.

Manuelian shook his head. "No, I checked again. No bugs."

"Some other problem?"

Manuelian glanced toward the house as if it might have its own ears. "None that I can put my finger on," he said. "I have no reason to think Ennslin suspects—" he shrugged, looking toward the house once more "—but I have a strange feeling."

Bolan stiffened. "Think," he said. "You're no rookie, Manuelian. If you're apprehensive, there's a reason."

Alberto forced a smile. "I've been 'under' here for two years," he said. "That's a long time. Your perspective can get warped." His shrug seemed as forced as the smile. "Maybe that's all it is. The nerves that come just before you take down your mark."

Bolan nodded but studied the man's face. He wasn't so sure.

Manuelian parked the cart next to the pool, and the two men got out. The DEA agent grabbed Bolan's bag, and they started toward the house. They were halfway across the pool area when Bernhardt Ennslin stepped out of the sliding glass door. He wore a look of grave concern. "Your mother," he said immediately. "She has recovered?"

Bolan shook his head. "No," he said. "She passed away."

Tears filled the German's eyes. "I am sorry," he said. "Please, come inside."

They followed Ennslin into the house and down the hall to his den, where he motioned Bolan to a chair and walked behind the bar. He poured brandy into two snifters, crossed the room again and handed a glass to Bolan.

"Will you have any more need for me, Herr Ennslin?" Manuelian asked.

"Yes," the German said. "Please stay a few minutes, Alberto."

The undercover man crossed his arms and took a standing position near the door.

Ennslin moved to the couch across from Bolan. "I cannot fully express my sorrow over the loss of your mother," he said. "I can only tell you that it is a heartache that I have been through myself, and that I understand how you feel."

Bolan nodded. "A fine woman," he said, lifting his brandy snifter. "To my mother."

Ennslin's jaw was firm. "Yes," he said. "To your mother." The two men drank.

Ennslin set his glass on the end table next to him. "Tell me," he said. "Was she in much pain when she died?"

Bolan shook his head. "No," he said. "She went in her sleep."

"Ah, good. Were you there with her?"

An uneasy feeling began to creep over Bolan. Though tears still threatened to burst forth from Ennslin's eyes, the mouth below those eyes had grown harder.

"Yes," he said. "She died shortly after I arrived."

"Were you able to speak with her?" Ennslin asked. "A few parting words, perhaps?"

Before Bolan could answer, Parman suddenly appeared in the doorway. He raised his hand and knocked on the frame. When Ennslin looked his way, he said, "I have it, sir."

Ennslin's face hardened completely now.

Parman stepped inside. A dozen more of Ennslin's men, wearing training fatigues and carrying their IMBELs, paraded in after him and circled the room.

Parman leered at Bolan as he crossed the room, the lopsided grin widening with every step. He pulled a microcassette tape from his pocket and handed it to Ennslin.

Ennslin opened a drawer and pulled out a small tape recorder. He inserted the tape, tapped a button and turned to Bolan.

"Perhaps you should hear this," he said as the tape began to roll. "I listened to it as you and the other Judas drove up."

There was the sound of the golf cart, then Alberto Manuelian said, "No, I checked again. No bugs."

Bolan's own voice drifted across the room. "Some other problem?"

The barrels of the IMBELs suddenly shifted to point at Bolan and Manuelian. Steel screeched in the otherwise silent room as the rifle bolts were drawn back.

"None that I can put my finger on," Manuelian said. "I have no reason to think Ennslin suspects...but I have a strange feeling."

Ennslin waited until the voices faded from the tape, then turned the machine off and stood up. He walked across the room and stopped in front of Alberto. "Take off your coat," he said calmly.

"Sir—"

Ennslin's hand rose like lightning, slapping the smaller man across the mouth. "Your coat!" he bellowed.

Manuelian slipped out of his white serving jacket and handed it over.

Ennslin ripped the lining from the garment and held up a small transmitter. "You are smart," he said, turning to Bolan. "But not smart enough." The false tears no longer clouded his eyes. His face was deadpan. "I am no fool myself, Herr Coffman...or whatever your name actually is. I called all the hospi-

tals in Cleveland and learned that there was indeed a
Mrs. Coffman in one of the intensive-care units. But
that would have been easy enough to set up, given the
resources of the American government." He paused,
and his face began to color. "So I decided to plant a
transmitter. If you were an agent like I suspected, you
would be smart enough to check the golf cart. So I
chose several less-obvious hiding places, Alberto's
coat being one of them." He turned to Manuelian. "I
did not know until you drove up that you were a trai-
tor, as well."

Ennslin looked at Bolan again, his eyes chillingly
cold. "I must assume that you have planted similar
misleading evidence with O'Banion and that he be-
lieves that I have double-crossed him. Unfortunately
I have been unable to contact him to explain."

Bolan smiled. "That's because he's on his way here
right now. To blow you, and this place, off the face of
the planet."

Ennslin nodded. "Yes, I imagine you are correct."
He motioned to Parman. "Lock Mr. Coffman and
Alberto up," he ordered. "I will continue to try to
contact O'Banion and deal with them as soon as this
mess is straightened out."

The Indian stepped forward, scowling. He shoved
the barrel of his IMBEL into Bolan's ribs, then suddenly the scowl turned into a grin. His eyes twinkled
in perverse pleasure as his hand moved to his head, to
the spot where the Desert Eagle had struck him.

Bolan watched the butt of the IMBEL as it twirled
toward his face. He felt it crack against his temple.

But he saw only darkness as he fell to the floor.

JONATHAN O'BANION stared into the metal mirror above the sink in the airplane rest room. He ran his fingers through his sweaty hair, then placed the Harris tweed hat on top of his head. He straightened the lapel of the matching jacket and shrugged into the Sterling submachine gun's sling. Through the steel door he could hear the hushed chatter of his men as they readied their weapons.

The Irishman slid the lock back and opened the door, moving out into the aisle and past the men preparing for battle. He nodded to Shawn Shawnessey as he passed through the door that had separated first-class seating from passenger when the plane had belonged to People's Express.

O'Banion moved on into the cabin where Lachtna O'Harkin and Caeman McClain were serving as pilot and navigator. He pointed to the radio, and McClain handed him the mike. O'Banion thumbed the button. "Can you be hearin' me, Jackson?" he asked.

The former Weatherman's voice came back from one of the other stolen airliners. "Loud and clear, Jonathan."

"Martinez?"

The Spanish-accented voice spoke from the third plane. *"Sí."*

"We're ten minutes from La Paz," O'Banion said. "Both of you, stay in the air until we've touched down, then come on in." He clicked off, handed McClain the mike and left the cabin.

O'Banion took a seat at the front of the plane, sitting sideways so he could watch the men behind him. The muscles in his arms and shoulders felt like steel cables stretched almost to the snapping point. He had fought the anger that Ennslin's treachery had produced in his soul, knowing it would cloud his judgment in planning the attack ahead. But eventually that rage had to go somewhere, and it had finally surfaced in the tension that now made him as anxious for the nearing battle as a newly released prisoner seeing his first nude woman in ten years. The analogy made O'Banion think of the Greenfinch, and her escape added to his fury. He could have used her now. She'd have taken his mind off things, if only for a moment.

O'Banion gritted his teeth. And the bloody bitch had killed Donnelly, as well. He'd have liked to have done that himself. Cutting the moron's throat with the Sykes-Fairbairn would have helped ease his tension, too.

The cabin door opened, and McClain stuck his head out. "We're landing," he said.

O'Banion nodded. "Any problems with the tower?"

McClain grinned and shook his head. "None. I told them we were having problems with the electrical system. They're getting a maintenance crew ready."

O'Banion stood up as the wheels hit the runway. He hurried to the galley door and waited until the plane rolled to a halt, then slid it open.

Three airport vehicles—an air start unit, electrical power truck and a ground air conditioner—came rolling across the runways toward the plane. Following close behind were several uniformed security personnel on the back of a baggage conveyor.

O'Banion heard the roar of the turbo engines as the other two planes descended. He saw the expressions of surprise on the faces of the security men as they turned to stare up into the sky.

The other doors to the plane opened as O'Banion swung the barrel of the Sterling out the opening. Firing through the open door, he pumped round after round of 9 mm slugs into the men on the luggage conveyor.

IRA men in green fatigues poured from the plane. They dropped to the tarmac, firing indiscriminately into the airport vehicles as they sprinted across the runway. Bodies danced and jerked in the cabs of the trucks as O'Banion's men divided. Half raced toward the passenger terminal, the rest heading for the control tower and other buildings scattered around the airport.

On the second and third runways over, O'Banion saw Jackson's and Martinez's planes touch down. More men in green fatigues began deplaning before the wheels came to a final stop.

Gunfire crackled through the air. Through the open door to the cabin, O'Banion could hear an excited voice screaming in Spanish over the radio. Then a burst of automatic fire sputtered over the airwaves, and the voice halted.

Shawnessey's voice replaced it. "Control tower secured, Jonathan."

O'Banion dropped to the tarmac and started across the runway toward the terminal. The sounds of automatic fire died down, becoming sporadic semiauto shots as he neared the doors.

The bodies of security personnel, maintenance officials and uniformed pilots and flight attendants littered the lobby as O'Banion opened the glass door.

ther passengers lay dead on the floor. A few, soak-
g in blood, tried to crawl to safety under the chairs
d tables.

Men in green fatigues worked the floor, pumping
ullets into any movement they noticed.

O'Banion smiled, turned on his heels and exited the
rminal. He found a tow tractor attached to a bag-
ge trailer loaded down with suitcases, slid behind the
heel and drove quickly to the tower. Taking the ele-
ator to the cab on top, he found Shawnessey still sit-
ng in the radioman's chair. The man whose excited
oice had echoed over the airwaves lay crumpled on
e floor.

O'Banion grabbed the mike and flipped several
witches on the console. A moment later his voice
oomed over the public address system to the entire
irport.

"All personnel assigned to the air raid, return to the
lanes," he ordered. "Land personnel, appropriate
round vehicles and start toward our objective." He
atched through the windows as men in green raced
ack toward the airplanes while others hurried to-
ard trucks, jeeps and other all-terrain vehicles parked
round the airport.

Shawnessey pulled a pint bottle of Old Bushmill's
ngle-malt whiskey from inside his BDU blouse,
racked the seal and took a sip. He extended it toward
'Banion.

The Irishman shook his head.

"What now?" Shawnessey asked, tucking the bot-
e back in his shirt.

"We give the ground troops fifteen minutes' hea
start," O'Banion said. "Then, Shawn me boy, we g
kill us one lyin', back-stabbin' kraut bastard."

THE FIRST THING Bolan saw as he regained con
sciousness was a mass of gray clumps that might hav
been the bottom of a giant egg carton. As his visio
began to clear, he realized the lumps were made c
stone; he was on his back, staring up at a cold roc
ceiling.

He could see something attached to the middle c
the ceiling. Red. With white in the center, and the
zigzag black lines in the middle of the white. As h
eyes finally focused, he recognized the object a
tached to the stones for what it was: a symbol that ha
represented death and destruction for millions, an
nearly brought on the genocide of an entire race c
people more than half a century earlier.

The red-and-white Nazi flag with its swastika in th
middle epitomized evil, an evil that had not died ou
with the end of the Second World War, but had bee
kept alive in the hearts of men like Bernhardt Ennsli
and had now been turned into a new atrocity tha
threatened more millions in the form of white pow
der.

Bolan stared at the ceiling as a sharp throbbin
filled his head. When he tried to move his hands, pai
shot through the stiff muscles in his arms and shoul
ders. His hands had been tied behind him. He coul
feel the ropes trapped between them and the cold ston
floor.

Bolan closed his eyes again. His breathing came i
short, raspy gasps through his mouth, and he felt th

aked blood clogging his sinuses. The last thing he remembered was the butt of Parman's IMBEL crashing
into his temple. That memory brought a frown to his
face, and the movement in turn sent more sharp pains
zzling through his brain like red-hot knife blades.

He had to have been beaten after he'd already been
unconscious. That awareness added a fury to the pain,
nd that fury gave him the strength to sit up.

The only light in the room came from a naked
overhead bulb. Bolan's eyes swept around the room,
oting two doors set in the stone walls. One in front of
im, the other behind. Both solid oak. More Nazi
lags and other regalia covered the walls—plaques,
ramed medals, yellowed news clippings and a giant
hotograph showing Adolf Hitler's crazed eyes and
utstretched arm.

Across the room, also on his back and apparently
till unconscious, lay Alberto Manuelian. Blood cov-
red his face, white shirt and slacks. Bolan crab-
valked painfully toward him, coming to a stop as
Manuelian's eyes opened.

"Where are we?" the deep-cover DEA man mum-
led nasally.

Bolan sat up and looked down into the battered
ace. Manuelian's jaw and nose had been broken, ac-
ounting for the slurred speech. "I was hoping you
might be able to tell *me*," Bolan said.

Manuelian struggled to a sitting position. He looked
irst at the walls, then the ceiling. "It is a room just off
he wine cellar," he said, nodding toward the door
ehind Bolan.

"Where does the other one lead?" Bolan asked,
ndicating the door in front of him.

"To the basement," Manuelian wheezed. "A gam
room." He paused, trying to catch his breath. Whe
he spoke again, he had lowered his voice to a whispe
"There'll be a guard there."

Bolan nodded and rose quietly to his feet, ignorin
the ache in his head, arms and legs. Turning, h
hopped quietly to the door to the wine cellar, turne
his back and grasped the knob. Locked. As he'
known it would be.

Hopping back to face the room, he rested his bac
against the cold stone wall. He scanned the wall
again, his eyes stopping on each adornment, the
passing on. He frowned, then smiled as his eyes m
Hitler's.

Bolan hopped across the room to the photograph
stopping in front of it. The smile vanished again, an
he looked back to the door to the basement. Two fee
across and three high, the glass covering the photo
graph would make too much noise when he shattere
it. The guard would hear. Bolan studied the smalle
frames, then unconsciously shook his head. No. Sti
too much noise. He and Manuelian would get only on
opportunity to cut through their restraints and es
cape. He couldn't chance it.

His eyes moved on along the wall, finally stoppin
on a large iron cross attached to a wooden shadow-bo
frame. Bigger than the usual medal that had been
German honor since the early nineteenth century, i
appeared to be some sort of wall trophy that accom
panied the actual medal. Bolan hopped toward it
seeing the brass nameplate affixed at the bottom as h
neared. He recognized Ennslin's name while still thre
feet away.

The plaque was too high to reach with his bound hands. Bolan turned sideways, bending his knees and dropping a shoulder. If the award simply hung by a nail or screw, they might still have a chance.

If the framed iron cross had been bolted to the rock, then their luck had run out.

Bolan rose slowly, nudging the frame with his shoulder. The plaque moved, and the smile returned to his face. Carefully he lifted it up off the nail, then turned, trapping it between his back and the wall. He saw Manuelian nodding approval as he cautiously let the frame slide down to his hands.

He hopped forward, letting the plaque fall to Manuelian's lap. He dropped back to the floor, sitting back-to-back with the DEA man and wrapping his fingers around the shadow box. "Grab the cross," he whispered.

Manuelian grabbed the metal. The wooden frame creaked as the undercover man twisted and jerked, then the frame suddenly splintered as the steel ripped away.

Bolan heard the key in the door and rolled forward, halting on his back in the same spot where he'd awakened. He tucked the broken frame underneath him, hoping Manuelian would have the presence of mind to do the same with the iron cross.

Bolan closed his eyes as the door opened and light poured suddenly into the dim room. He reopened them to tiny slits and saw Parman standing in the doorway, the stock of an IMBEL pressed against his shoulder and aimed toward him. The man studied the room, satisfied himself that his imagination had

played a trick on him, then closed and locked the doo
again.

He had heard the wood splinter, Bolan knew. An
he had come charging in. Bolan filed that informa
tion away in his mind.

He rolled back to Manuelian and took the iron cros
from his hands as the DEA man pulled it out from
beneath him. Bolan ran his thumb along all four of th
edges and frowned. Too dull. It would take half o
eternity to cut through the thick hemp ropes tha
bound their hands and feet.

Rising to his feet again, Bolan hopped to the wall
His eyes fell on a rough, jutting stone about wais
level. He turned away from it and ran an edge of th
cross first one way then the other over the coarse sur
face.

Five minutes later he tested the edge again. No
body would be shaving with the makeshift blade, bu
combined with a little elbow grease, it ought to do th
trick.

Returning to Manuelian, Bolan began the tedious
process of sawing through the ropes that held the
man's wrists. The individual strands popped with ag
onizing slowness as he worked. Manuelian winced
several times as the blade slipped off the rope and into
his wrist.

Another five minutes went by. Then, with a mighty
tug, Manuelian jerked his hands apart. He turned im
mediately and began sawing on the rope binding Bo
lan. With his hands free, and in front of him, it took
less than a minute to free Bolan.

As soon as their legs were unfettered, Bolan gath
ered up the pieces of rope and wood and shoved them

out of sight beneath him. "Lie still," he told Manuelian. "And be ready."

Still clutching the iron cross, Bolan closed his eyes
and scraped it loudly across the stone floor. The sound
echoed against the rock walls.

A moment later he heard the key again.

Parman stepped into the room, then stopped when
he saw Bolan lying across the room from where he'd
been before. He moved cautiously forward, the barrel of the IMBEL trained on Bolan's chest.

Bolan peered into the dim room under his semi-
closed eyelids. The barrel of the IMBEL came to rest
on the bridge of his nose as Parman stared curiously
down.

Bolan sat up suddenly, grasping the rifle at the
ejection port and pushing the barrel to the side. At the
same time he drove the iron cross up to the trigger.

The sharpened edge struck Parman's index finger,
jamming it back against the trigger guard and away
from the trigger. Then Manuelian jumped to his feet.
Bolan pushed harder, pulling the rifle toward him with
his other hand.

Parman screamed in both surprise and fear as bone
crunched and tendons snapped.

Manuelian stepped in and drove a hard right into
Parman's gut as Bolan wrenched the IMBEL away and
jumped to his feet. Bolan's eyes flew to the door. No
other guards.

Parman bent double, clutching his belly. Then his
right hand shot toward the holster on his belt.

Bolan drove the butt of the rifle into the side of the
man's head and heard another crunch of bone. Still
bent over, Parman turned to face Bolan.

Then he slumped to the ground, his surprised eyes still open in lifeless shock.

Manuelian knelt and drew the 9 mm automatic from Parman's holster. Bolan led the way to the door. They crossed the game room, passing several pool, snooker and billiard tables and the flashing lights of pinball machines and video games.

They heard the low-flying planes as they started up the steps.

The war for control of the Corporation was under way.

AUTOMATIC GUNFIRE exploded outside the house as Bolan reached the top of the stairs. The IMBEL clutched in assault mode, he pivoted down the hall toward Ennslin's den. Behind him he could hear the soft patter of Manuelian's feet on the thick carpet.

Bolan's priorities were clear. If things went as planned, Ennslin and O'Banion would take care of each other. At least to a certain extent. Which meant the job of the task force would be simply to come in and mop up whatever was left.

But Bolan wanted the body count of DEA and Delta Force men kept to a minimum. And the only way to accomplish that was to coordinate their landing from the ground.

Which meant that he had to make it from the house to the control tower, where he'd have both a bird's-eye view of the battle below and access to the radio.

Two men in green fatigues rounded the corner from the living room as he started down the hall. The lead man ran headfirst into Bolan, rebounding back against the man right behind him.

Both men tried to grab the IMBELs slung over their shoulders as they stumbled.

Remembering Manuelian behind him, Bolan dropped to one knee as he sent a full-auto burst of 7.62 mm hail into the face of the lead man. A semi-auto volley of 9 mm slugs sizzled over his shoulder, the hot brass that had encased them falling on his back as Manuelian took care of the other mercenary.

Both of Ennslin's men tumbled to the hallway floor. Bolan dropped the half-empty IMBEL, grabbed one from the corpses and jerked three fresh magazines from an assault vest. Manuelian also traded his pistol for an IMBEL.

Bolan rose to his feet and turned to the DEA man. "Find Ennslin," he ordered. "I'm going to the tower."

Manuelian nodded and took off the way they'd come.

Bolan made his way on down the hall and into the den. Through the open curtains over the sliding glass door, he saw the Continental Airlines 747 on the runway. Men in green fatigues identical to those worn by Ennslin's men were still pouring forth from the doors, bristling with submachine guns and assault rifles.

The sight brought a hard smile to Bolan's lips. He had not chosen the green fatigues for Ennslin's troops randomly. O'Banion's men often dressed similarly, and the identical BDUs would add to the battle confusion Bolan was counting on.

He hurried to the door and watched the invaders spreading out across the grounds. His smile widened. When they first deplaned, the Irish terrorists' targets were clear. The darker skin of Ennslin's troops was easily identified, and O'Banion's men blasted confidently away with their Sterlings. But as the Irishmen made their way farther away from the plane toward various objectives, the racial distinctions became less apparent.

Bolan watched a trio of IRA men race across the runway toward the house, then halt in indecision as two green-clad men stepped out from behind the pool house. The hesitation cost them their lives as Ennslin's men sent steady streams of IMBEL fire pounding through their bodies.

Sliding the door back, Bolan dropped the front sights of his rifle on the two men and fired.

The mercenaries joined the terrorists on the tarmac.

Bolan raced out of the house, dodging a 3-round burst from overhead as he angled past the swimming pool toward the golf carts. He looked up to see a man in green on the roof of the pool house.

Ennslin's or O'Banion's man? The face was unclear in the sunlight.

It didn't matter.

Firing from the hip as he ran, Bolan sent a full-auto burst of fire slanting upward to the man on the roof. A short scream burst from the gunner's lips as he rolled off the pool house and tumbled into the water.

Autofire raged around him like a tornado as Bolan vaulted the chain fence. The roar of motors sounded to his rear. He turned to see a line of automobiles racing up the road to the house. More vehicles—jeeps, pickups and other four-wheel-drive vehicles—converged on the area from the golf course.

Ground troops. Somewhere along the way, O'Banion had stopped and appropriated vehicles for a ground attack.

Bolan dropped into the driver's seat of the nearest golf cart. The key was in the ignition, and he twisted it with one hand as he ejected the spent box magazine from the IMBEL with the other hand. The motor coughed to life, and Bolan rammed a fresh magazine into the rifle, then backed away from the fence.

Cutting a quick U-turn toward the control tower, Bolan started across the yard toward the runway. Four of O'Banion's men halted on the tarmac, turning their weapons his way.

The Executioner rested the IMBEL on the front of the golf cart and squeezed the trigger. A stream of 7.62 mm death flew from the barrel, cutting the men down as he raced toward them.

Bolan felt a sudden jolt from behind. Two small holes appeared in the front of the cart next to his knee. Then a third round snapped the steering wheel in two between his hands.

He stomped on the brake, swinging the IMBEL around behind him and twisting in the seat. Resting it over the bag well, he squeezed off a 3-round burst that blew through the rear assault.

A tall, burly man with a handlebar mustache fell to the tarmac.

Bolan leaped from the golf cart as rounds peppered the now stationary target. His mind raced, the bushy mustache he had just downed triggering a memory somewhere. He rolled to his belly behind the cart, firing between the wheels into the ankles of an approaching gunner, then rose over the vehicle and fired down into the writhing body on the runway.

Right. The mustache had been Shawnessey. O'Banion's second in command, if he remembered the file correctly.

So where was Shawnessey's boss?

Turning from the golf cart, Bolan sprinted on across the runway. A red Geo Tracker convertible came racing across the tarmac driven by a young man with a flat-top haircut. A man in his early forties stood in the passenger's seat. He fired a Sterling over the Tracker's windshield as the young driver cut a serpentine pattern to avoid return fire. Both wore green fatigues.

Bolan turned and fired two rounds. The first caught the young man squarely between the eyes. The Tracker swerved.

Before it could crash, Bolan sent another 7.62 mm round screaming into the other man.

A roar from overhead drew the Executioner's eyes skyward. Two more huge 747s descended to land. At the same time he heard the hum of an electric motor kicking in nearby.

He turned to see the overhead door on the garage housing the Oerlikon rise. As Bolan ran on, the mobile antiaircraft gun poked out through the opening.

He changed directions, angling toward the Oerlikon as he sent a volley of rounds into an Irishman firing toward a dark-skinned man in green. The darker man turned toward the Executioner with a look of relief and thanks on his face.

Bolan's next set of slugs cut through him.

More autofire chewed the tarmac around his feet as he continued toward the Oerlikon. He glanced over his shoulder as the first of the other two 747s touched down. The sides read People's Express, but more men in green fatigues began dropping from the open doors before it had come to a halt.

Bolan turned back and saw the Oerlikon come to a stop ten yards from the garage. The twin 35 mm antiaircraft gun atop the vehicle spun toward the sky, then flopped back, out of control of whoever was guiding it inside the cab.

Bolan reached the edge of the runway and dived under a burst of fire from two IRA men who'd taken refuge behind one of the warehouses. Rolling to one knee, he emptied the IMBEL in a figure eight between the two, reloaded, then sprinted on to the Oerlikon.

The driver of the defense system looked up in surprise as Bolan jerked the door open. The man next to him, with the instruction manual open in his lap, followed suit.

Bolan jammed the barrel of the IMBEL into the driver's neck and pulled the trigger. A full-auto blast of penetrating 7.62 mm bullets stabbed through the man's soft flesh, traveling on into the face of the merc at his side. Both of Ennslin's men fell back against the cushioned seat.

Bolan jerked them from the cab and slid into the driver's seat. He saw the final plane land as he closed the door. Leaning across the commander's seat, he glanced at the open manual, then moved on to the console.

The third switch he flipped did the trick.

A moment later the big twin gun came swiveling down from the sky.

The Executioner aimed the weapon at the 747 as it slowed along the tarmac. He pressed the trigger button, and the big overhead gun coughed up a succession of 35 mm rounds that thudded into the racing plane. One round hit a tire, and suddenly the 747 was cartwheeling end over end.

Even through the thick doors of the Oerlikon, Bolan could hear the squeal of steel as the plane came to rest on its back and skidded along the runway. He followed it with the twin gun, sending more rounds into the wings and body.

The 747 came to a halt near the end of the runway. A second later it exploded into a hell on earth for the terrorists inside.

Turning the Oerlikon toward the control tower, Bolan threw the vehicle in gear and raced across the grass. Assault-rifle and subgun fire ricocheted off the cab as he neared his objective. He halted in front of the tower, then turned the gun toward the pool house. A blast of 35 mm rounds took out the doors and windows and sent the wood shingles flying from the roof.

Bolan hesitated. Somewhere in the sky overhead, the American task force was waiting to clean up whatever mess was left when Ennslin and O'Banion were through with each other. And if they didn't hear from him soon, they'd come on in.

No, he had to make contact. There was no sense in risking the lives of good men while the enemy was still busy killing one another off.

Bolan swung the door back, jumped from the Oerlikon and raced into the tower. Several bodies lay on the floor as he made his way past the death-trap elevator to the stairs. Taking the steps two at a time, he made it to the third floor without encountering resistance. But as his feet hit the landing just below the tower cab, a green-clad man fell into the hallway from the open door to an office.

Bolan looked down to see one of Ennslin's mercs. The bloody fingers of the man's left hand were pressed against his ribs. His face was a mask of pain as he looked up into the Executioner's eyes.

Then his right hand dropped to his belt, and he drew an Argentine-made .45-caliber automatic from his holster.

Bolan never broke stride. Stepping forward with his right leg, he raised his left, then shot a fast front kick. The toe of his boot struck the merc in the throat, and the man fell back, the pain disappearing from his face for all of eternity.

Reaching the control tower cab, Bolan threw open the door, dropping to a crouch as a volley of fire sailed over his head. The IMBEL rose in his fists, and a split second later two more of Ennslin's hired thugs lay dead on the floor.

Bolan turned and locked the door behind him, then hurried to the observation window. Below, the firing had died down. By now most of the men on both sides had taken cover, and only occasional shots ripped back and forth across the grounds.

It was time to bring in the cleanup crew.

Bolan walked to the desk and pulled the dead radioman from the chair. Taking the man's seat, he twisted the dial to the task-force frequency, then said, "Pollock to Air Rats. Come in, Air Rats."

A familiar voice came back over the air waves. "Go ahead, Colonel Pollock," Yakov Katzenelenbogen said.

Bolan couldn't suppress a smile. "You guys decide to come along for the ride?" he asked.

"Affirmative," Katz said. "What the hell, the fish weren't biting."

Bolan glanced out the window, then tapped the mike again. "Well, come on in," he said. "We still got a few fish for you to fry down here." He let up on the mike and stood up. As he started to turn back toward the door, a flash of gray on the runway nearest the house caught his eye.

Ennslin's private 727.

Then, across the grounds, Bolan saw the ex-Nazi suddenly sprint from the door by the swimming pool. Carrying a walkie-talkie in one hand, a pistol in the other, he raced toward the plane. A second later another figure came running out of the house. Bolan recognized Manuelian's bloodstained white shirt and trousers immediately. The DEA man stopped ten feet from the house and raised his IMBEL to his shoulder.

Grass danced around Ennslin's pounding feet as Manuelian fired after him. Then the German suddenly stopped, turned and raised his arm in the classic one-hand pistol stance.

He couldn't hear the round, but Bolan saw the gun jump in Ennslin's hand. And he saw the result of the shot.

Alberto Manuelian dropped to the ground as if he'd een hit over the head with a sledgehammer.

Ennslin turned and ran on to the plane. Bolan saw n arm reach down and jerk him up into the cabin. he plane rolled on toward the runway.

But by then Bolan was on his way back down the teps toward the Oerlikon.

CHAPTER THIRTEEN

Yakov Katzenelenbogen hung the microphone back on the clip and turned to Jack Grimaldi behind the controls of the MC-130H. Grimaldi grinned under his leather bush pilot's cap and said, "Sounded like you got a *go*."

Katz nodded and looked at his watch.

Grimaldi glanced at the control panel and said, "Three minutes."

The Phoenix Force leader walked back to the bowels of the big plane. Built to be a transport, this version of the famous C-130 handled like a fighter. It could be flown at low levels for extended periods of time, and the specialized weaponry, including a 25 mm Gatling and 105 mm cannon, allowed it to be used within close range of friendly troops.

All of which Katz knew Grimaldi would be proving within a few short minutes.

The Israeli eyed the troops seated on the floor of the plane. They didn't number many—five four-man Delta Force teams, each team led by a DEA agent. The soldiers were decked out in khaki BDUs and informal, personalized headgear that included everything from a black stocking cap to an Australian bush hat. Along with M-16s, the Delta men also carried side arms of their own choosing, but Katz noticed that most had opted for Government Model .45s.

The narcotics agents were armed with Sig-Sauer mm pistols and Colt carbines of the same caliber. 'he Colts looked like baby brothers of the M-16s. The gents wore khaki pants like the Delta men, but had dded blue nylon Windbreakers that shouted DEA cross the back. Katz shook his head silently, glad that : wasn't him who'd be sweating beneath the garents in the Beni heat. He gave the men one last look, vondering if some of them would be dead in the next ew minutes.

He hoped not. They were all good men.

Almost as good as the four he'd brought with him.

The Phoenix Force leader's eyes traveled across the lane to where Encizo, James, McCarter and Maning were seated against the wall with one of the DEA nen. Dressed in the same khaki BDUs that would lifferentiate them from Ennslin's and O'Banion's men n green, they had passed themselves off as one of the Delta Force squads. Not an easy task.

Delta Force only numbered around a hundred operatives in its entirety. That made it highly unlikely hat some of the real "Forcers" would not know one nother from training or previous missions. But the nen of Delta Force were professional soldiers. They night have their suspicions about Katz and his boys, ut they also had their orders. And that was all they ared about. Katz supposed that the fact that Brognola had finagled it so he was the captain in charge aadn't hurt anything, either.

The Israeli glanced to the woman seated with Phoenix Force. Her presence had brought a few raised eyebrows, but the fact that Katz had accepted her had

lowered them again. He gave her a quick smile now
then turned away.

If anybody deserved a shot at the men they wer
going after, it was Baine Morrison. According to Abl
Team, she'd proved her capabilities at the IRA saf
house, which had earned her a ticket to this show, too

Katz cleared his throat, then repeated Grimaldi'
words to the men. "Three minutes."

The thirty people stood as one and shrugged int
their parachutes.

Two minutes later Katz slid the door open. Calvi
James was the first man out, followed by the othe
members of Phoenix Force. Katz waited on the fou
other teams, then leaped out into the sky.

The Israeli counted off the seconds, then pulled hi
rip cord, letting the chute break his fall and pull hin
back up into the air. Below, he could see several of th
men already touching down in the jungle. A quarte
mile away along the jungle path leading from the road,
he saw the runways in the clearing. Flames leaped
from the skeleton of an overturned 747, and sporadic
gunfire met his ears. Men, looking more like ants s
far below, crisscrossed the area.

Just below the control tower was the outline of some
strange tank-like vehicle he couldn't recognize from
the distance.

Katz looked down, then back toward the clearing as
a 727 suddenly took off into the sky. He frowned.
Bolan had advised that Ennslin's personal plane was
a 727. Was the neo-Nazi getting away? Slipping between Bolan's fingers?

The former Mossad operative chuckled to himself as his boots hit the ground. That was possible, he supposed. But it wasn't too damn likely.

Striker was like a Canadian Mountie. He *always* got his man.

Katz called the strike-force troops around him as soon as he'd unsnapped himself from his chute. He didn't waste words. "You know the drill. A and B Teams take the north approach. C and D the south. E comes in from the east, and my men get the west." He turned to Baine Morrison. "You're with us." Then he addressed the entire group. "Any questions?"

Thirty heads shook simultaneously.

"Then let's go," Katz said. "And remember the motto for this mission. If It's Green, It's Mean. Kill It." He turned and sprinted into the trees.

BOLAN RUSHED DOWN the five flights of stairs from the control-tower cab to the ground, searching his memory for the odds and ends of information he knew about the Oerlikon GDF-DO3. At one time missiles had been regarded as the full answer to threats from the air, but more recent logic had dictated that a combination of gun and missile might prove more effective.

The Oerlikon had been the result of that theory.

The twin 35 mm gun he had already used fired at a rate of 2×600 rounds per minute and held 430 rounds in its external magazine. How many had he used already? He had no idea. But it hardly mattered. By the time he reached the four-wheel drive vehicle the plane would be nearing the end of the weapon's 2.5-

mile range. He wouldn't have time for many shots regardless of the number that remained.

Bolan hit the front door of the control tower ducking instinctively as a stray round flew his way from one of the nearby warehouses. He threw a short burst back as cover fire, ripped the Oerlikon's door open and dived inside again.

He leaned into the command console. A few volleys bounced off the bullet-resistant shell as he began flipping switches and twisting dials marked Search Radar and Tracking. Nothing happened.

He glanced up through the windshield. The 727 was a mere dot in the sky.

Bolan returned to the console. He hadn't lied to Ennslin when he'd told him he'd used systems comparable to the Oerlikon in the past. The Breda 40 mm L70, widely used on naval vessels, was similar. But similar in the same way a revolver was similar to an automatic pistol, and someone familiar with one of the drastically different handguns wouldn't necessarily be able to operate the other.

No, the Oerlikon and Breda were a lot alike but not quite the same. Just different enough that Ennslin might get away while he learned those significant dissimilarities.

He grabbed the manual from the seat, flipped to the table of contents, then thumbed through the pages.

Less than a minute later, he had changed the console setting and locked the 727 in on the tracking system. He looked at the screen, and his heart fell in his chest as he saw the readout.

The aircraft was beyond the 4375-yard effective range.

Bolan opened the door and stepped out of the vehicle, looking to the sky. To the naked eye, the speck had disappeared completely now. But as he watched overhead, a larger blur took its place.

A U.S. MC-130H moved steadily toward the jungle. As it drew overhead, parachutes began blossoming beneath it.

He took one last look in the direction Ennslin had escaped, vowing to hunt the man down regardless of where he tried to hide. But as he stared at the sky, the speck suddenly reappeared. And grew. And continued to grow until it became Bernhardt Ennslin's 727 once again.

Bolan slid back behind the command seat of the Oerlikon. He didn't know where Ennslin planned to go, but it was in the opposite direction from the one in which the plane had taken off. The 727 had dipped a wing, turned a one-eighty and now headed back over the clearing.

Ten seconds later the radar and tracking systems were once again locked on Ennslin's plane. And fifteen seconds later Bolan was firing 35 mm cartridges through the sky.

The sudden explosion a mile overhead was not so different from the one the Oerlikon had caused on the ground earlier. Similar flames leaped from the hull and wings. Then a secondary blast ignited, and the 727 exploded into a thousand fiery pieces that fell through the air to the jungle of the Beni region of Bolivia.

And somewhere among the falling wreckage was whatever remained of a former Nazi named Bernhardt Ennslin.

O'BANION FIRED a volley from his Sterling submachine gun, then dived through the window of the nearest warehouse. The IRA leader had seen the big man in civilian dress come out of the house, grab the golf cart and head across the runway. The man had stopped long enough to take out several men, Shawnessey among them, then fired up an antiaircraft gun and started blasting everything in sight.

Including the plane Jackson and his men had been on. In less than ten seconds O'Banion's force had been cut by a third.

Then the Irishman had seen an American plane and parachutes dropping down through the sky only a few hundred yards away. He didn't know who they were, but he was certain they hadn't come to help him.

O'Banion landed on his hands and knees inside the warehouse. Broken splinters of glass had preceded him to the concrete floor, and he cursed as his palms dug down into the jagged mess. Jumping back to his feet, he glanced quickly around the darkened interior. Several bodies littered the floor between the shelves. The shelves themselves were stacked high with boxes that he knew contained cocaine base. There had to be a billion dollars of the stuff just inside this room.

A small desk stood against the wall, papers and account books scattered across the top. O'Banion found a rag in the third drawer down, wrapped it around his bleeding hand and sat down to take stock of both his weapons and the situation in general as the war continued to rage outside the window.

Two mags left for his Sterling. Four for the Browning Hi-Power. And the Sykes-Fairbairn stiletto was strapped to his leg.

Not much. He'd lost a third of his men. Ennslin had been more prepared than he'd counted on, his troops better trained than O'Banion would have guessed. And there was that big man in the antiaircraft gun.

Footsteps sounded outside the broken window, and he slid down behind the desk. He clutched the Sterling to his chest, hoping whoever it was would pass on. Nothing much had gone his way today—no "luck o' the Irish" for this Ulsterman—and he'd just as soon sit the rest of the battle out. There was still the chance his men might win, and if they did he'd emerge from the warehouse and claim he'd been pinned down. Nobody would argue with him, and he'd assume control.

But at this point it didn't look as if that was in the cards. Which meant he needed to find some way out of this hellhole jungle. Maudy O'Banion's favorite son had no intention of getting his Belfast-born ass shot off.

The footsteps stopped outside the window. A moment later O'Banion heard someone crawling through the broken frame.

He risked a glance around the corner of the desk and saw a tall, balding man in a blue Windbreaker clutching a 9 mm Colt carbine. American, by his looks. No other fool would wear a bloody nylon jacket in this heat. Even he had opted for the green fatigues over his usual trade mark tweed.

Then the man turned around, and O'Banion saw the back of the jacket.

DEA.

An almost-insane fury shot through the Irishman's veins as in one brief second of startling clarity he re-

alized what had to have happened. The DEA were be
hind this. They were the ones he'd seen falling throug
the sky. They might even have been responsible for th
problems between him and Ennslin from the begir
ning. And that explained who the big man who'
killed Shawnessey had to be, as well.

As rage overtook him, O'Banion stood up behin
the desk.

Before the DEA man could turn, he drew th
Browning Hi-Power and pumped a single roun
through the back of his head.

O'Banion ducked back down behind the desk, th
crackling explosion driving him back to reality an
reminding him that he was trying to avoid attention
not draw it. He watched the window around the cor
ner of the desk, the Browning ready.

Gunfire continued throughout the grounds, and h
realized his lone shot had been lost among the many
He rose from hiding and walked toward the dead mar
who'd fallen forward on his face. Rolling the body
over, he looked down.

The DEA agent's blank stare looked back.

Quickly he knelt, pulled the Windbreaker off th
body and slipped into it. If the DEA was in on this, i
was no longer a matter of who won, him or Ennslin
The Americans would win. If they hadn't sent enoug
men to do the trick, they'd send more. His chance o
taking over the Corporation, at least as it was righ
now, was history. After this the Yanks would have th
political ammo they needed to pressure the Bolivia
government into raking the Beni landscape until i
blended into the rest of the bloody jungle.

Movement outside the window caused O'Banion to look up. A man dressed in khakis raced by, firing another of the American-made Colts. Green Beret? Maybe. Some kind of Yankee soldier. Even the American Armed Forces were in on this, and that further confirmed his suspicions that it was time to get out.

He returned to the body on the floor. The DEA agent wore khaki slacks, and the IRA leader rested his Sterling on the floor while he unbuckled the man's belt and pulled the pants off his legs. Exchanging them for his green fatigues, he dropped them low on his hips to hide his combat boots.

Grabbing the Sterling, he hurried back to the window. The closest trees lay less than a hundred yards away. He didn't know where they led, but right now that was the least of his worries.

He took a final look outside the window, then climbed through. He raced past the garage where the big man had gotten the antiaircraft gun and saw it parked under the control tower. Skirting around the tower, he had drawn even with it when the big twin gun started to roar again.

A second later O'Banion heard an explosion overhead.

He looked up and saw something—a plane, he had to assume—explode in the sky. He wondered briefly who had been in the thing, then sprinted on. He was almost to the trees when a round cut the earth next to him. Without breaking stride, he swiveled and triggered a 3-round burst back toward the battle, then headed for the trees.

BLAZING BITS OF STEEL still rained from the sky a Bolan ripped the Oerlikon's door open, grabbed th IMBEL and dived back into the battle.

Automatic rounds ripped over his head as he hit th ground and rolled. He heard several strike the side o the Oerlikon's cab, then something stung the back o his thigh.

Bolan rolled back under the vehicle, pulling th IMBEL in after him by the sling. More rounds pep pered the Oerlikon, forcing him farther back. He too refuge behind one of the giant tires, hearing the dul thuds as still more bullets hit the rubber.

He reached behind him, feeling his thigh. His slack were ripped, and a thin coat of blood covered his fin gers when he brought them back to his eyes. But th round that had ricocheted off the Oerlikon had lost it momentum by the time it struck his leg. It had bro ken the skin but not entered.

Dragging himself forward by the elbows, Bola peered around the edge of the tire. Here and ther among the warehouses, the main house and othe buildings, he saw khaki uniforms moving from cove to cover. Mixed within them were men wearing khak slacks and navy blue Windbreakers. One of those me fired, hit the ground and rolled.

Crabbing farther around the tire, Bolan shoved th barrel of the IMBEL forward. He saw a mercenary he recognized from training squatting behind the neares warehouse. The man in green was preparing to dro an unsuspecting Delta Force trooper making his way across the runway from the pool house.

Bolan swung the IMBEL's sight over the green and pulled the trigger. The rifle kicked back against his shoulder, and the target toppled to the dirt.

Bolan elbowed his way from under the Oerlikon and sprinted to the rear of the control tower, slamming his back against the wall. Several rounds slapped bricks around him, and he crouched, spinning the IMBEL and searching for a target.

More autofire chipped the brick, sending a cloud of dust floating through the hot air as Bolan dropped the sights on a redheaded man with a Sterling. A trio of 7.62 mm bullets drilled through the terrorist's green shirt and into his heart.

As he squeezed the trigger, he saw a flash of blue behind his target. As the terrorist fell to the grass, Bolan raised his eyes to see a blue Windbreaker sprinting for the trees at the far side of the compound. The collapsible butt of an assault rifle or submachine gun was visible, slung around the man's shoulders. The rest of the weapon was out of sight in front of the man. The gun's stock, and the letters on the back of his jacket, bounced with each step the fleeing man took.

A DEA agent who had lost his nerve? Not likely. Brognola would have made sure only experienced, battle-worthy men were chosen for the strike team.

Bolan raised his assault rifle and sighted down the barrel on a spot two feet to the running man's right. He squeezed the trigger, and the semiauto round tore a divot of grass from the ground next to the blue jacket.

The man twisted, sent a 3-round burst of blind cover fire back toward the Executioner, then disappeared into the trees. Bolan marked the spot in his mind, then turned back to the battle still raging on the runways.

Firing his IMBEL dry, Bolan inserted his last fresh magazine, then hurried toward the warehouse where he'd just shot the mercenary. The man still had four full loaded box magazines. They became Bolan's.

He looked up, briefly taking in the situation on the runways and around the house. The firing had picked up again after the arrival of the American task force, but had now died down once more to sporadic shots as the Delta Force men and DEA agents ferreted out the survivors of Ennslin's and O'Banion's troops. Across the runways, on the deck of the swimming pool, he saw a kneeling man in khaki firing an M-16 with his left arm. Katz. James and McCarter flanked him, and he could see a black soldier and a tall, broad man circling the swimming pool and firing into the rubble of the pool house. James and Manning.

The battle was clearly under control now, in the capable hands of Phoenix Force, the DEA and the Delta men. It would be over in a few more minutes.

But there were a few loose ends that needed to be tied up.

Bolan didn't know who the man in the blue Windbreaker sprinting for the trees had been. But it hadn't been a DEA agent.

He had seen the side-feeding magazine on the submachine gun when the man had turned to spray cover fire. Instead of the DEA-issue Colt 9 mm carbine, the weapon had been a Sterling—the favorite subgun of Jonathan O'Banion and the Irish Republican Army.

Bolan slid the bolt back on his IMBEL, racked a round into the chamber and thumbed the selector switch to Safe.

Then he raced forward toward the spot in the trees where the terrorist had disappeared.

THE MEN of Phoenix Force and Baine Morrison came to the edge of the trees and stopped, peering through the branches to the front of Bernhardt Ennslin's house.

A half-dozen men in green fatigues had fled the battle on the runways behind the house and now stood between a Bronco and a Jeep Cherokee parked in the drive.

Two more men were in the process of hot-wiring the vehicles. All of them had dark skin, prompting the Israeli to think they must be Ennslin's men. But whoever they were, their purpose right now was obvious.

They wanted out of here, fast.

Katz turned and nodded to the men behind him, then stepped out of the trees. "You gentlemen planning a trip?" he called out as the rest of the team stepped out into the open, fanning out across the lawn.

The heads of the men at the vehicles shot up. A short man with wiry muscles cursed under his breath. In Arabic.

Katz smiled. He'd been wrong. They weren't Latino as he'd suspected. They had to be members of one of the Middle East terrorist groups—men the IRA had recruited to help in their attempt to overthrow Ennslin.

Katz pulled the trigger on his M-16.

A progression of .223 mm slugs roared from the end of the assault rifle, shredding the bodies of the nearest two terrorists. Katz heard another curse, then a scream, then the men's voices were drowned out as the men and woman next to him opened up with their own full-auto fire.

Six seconds after the men from Stony Man Farm had stepped out of the trees, eight of the enemy lay dead on the ground.

The Israeli raced forward across the lawn to the front porch. Manning's shoulder drove the door off its hinges, and they dashed inside.

Manning, McCarter and Encizo split off, racing on to check the second story as Katz and James entered the living room. They found the bodies of two men with rusty-red hair staining the carpet with their blood.

A blond man in green fatigues sat on the couch, bandaging a shoulder wound. He looked up, then dived for a Sterling subgun on the coffee table.

Calvin James dropped him with a single shot that drilled a third eye between his other two.

Katz led the way down the hall, checking the rooms along the way. They found bodies littering the floor but met no more resistance.

The gunfire outside the house became more sporadic. Then several bursts of fire sounded from the second story. Katz glanced up to the ceiling, silently hoping that they came from the rifles of McCarter, Manning and Encizo. They entered a den looking out onto the swimming pool, then Katz turned on his heels, leading James back to the stairs off the living room.

The three other members of Phoenix Force joined them, and Katz's silent prayer became one of thanks.

Stepping over the corpses at the top of the stairs, he started down the steps, then turned suddenly back. "Where's Morrison?" he asked.

The men of Phoenix Force looked blankly at each other. Then Manning shrugged. "Thought she'd gone with you," he said.

"Find her," Katz ordered.

The men took off, retracing their steps through the house, then reassembled at the stairs.

McCarter was the last to return. "No luck?" he asked the others.

They shook their heads.

Manning shrugged again. "At least we didn't find a *body,*" he said.

Katz nodded. He didn't know where Baine Morrison had gone, but he had his suspicions. Well, he thought as he led the men down the stairs, the Greenfinch was a big girl. She had a right to make her own decisions as long as they didn't endanger the rest of the troops. And if her decision was to risk her life making sure her revenge was personal, who was he to judge her?

Entering a game room, the Israeli stepped quietly over more bodies as colored lights continued to blink on the pinball machines and video games. They entered a small area that looked like Adolf Hitler's playroom and found another dead man.

The lock on the door in the wall gave way to a quick burst from Encizo's M-16. His own weapon leading the way, Katz stepped into a wine cellar stocked floor to ceiling with bottles of wine.

The Israeli smiled. He hadn't gotten to enjoy much of the Roederer Cristal champagne he'd taken from the farmhouse back in Germany. Perhaps when this was over, he'd be able to find another bottle here.

Taking the lead again, Katz hurried back up the steps, down the hall and out the sliding glass door to the pool. A sudden burst of fire chipped the concrete beneath his feet. He raised the M-16, firing one-handed at a green-clad gunner behind the ruins of the pool house and sending him spinning to the ground.

More fire came suddenly from both the pool house and the runway. Katz dropped to one knee while behind him McCarter and James did the same. The three warriors turned to the runway and held the triggers of their rifles back against the guards, dropping a quartet of men while Encizo and Manning hurried around the water to the front of the smaller dwelling, sending a hailstorm of bullets into the rubble.

Three men in Delta Force khaki rounded the corner of the pool house, their weapons shouldered and ready.

The men of Phoenix Force swung their own weapons that way. For a split second the eight warriors held their aim. Then, recognizing their comrades, the Delta Force soldiers sprinted on across the runway toward the warehouses.

Katz rose to his feet and raced out onto the runway himself. He heard four pairs of boots pounding the tarmac close behind him. Another team of Delta men, lead by a DEA agent, kicked in the door of another warehouse and poured inside. Leaving it to them, Katz raced on toward the smoldering wreckage of a Boeing 747 with the British Airways emblem on the sides.

A dark man with a thick black beard appeared behind the plane as Katz raced past. Twisting at the waist, the Israeli emptied his M-16 into the green fatigue blouse, then changed magazines as he ran on.

The firing was almost nonexistent now, having slowed to an occasional burst or round. Katz had seen men in khaki in all of the buildings except one: a small concrete structure set off from the rest.

The Phoenix Force leader didn't slow. Breaking the door down with his shoulder, he barreled through the entryway and rolled to his knees, the assault rifle stock under his arm and aimed upward. A flurry of choppy rounds blew over his head, and he saw a tall, angular man less than two feet away.

Katz pulled the trigger, and the M-16 burped up a steady stream of fire that diced the terrorist's torso. The man jerked back against the wall, then fell face first over an Olympic weight bar stretched between the uprights of an incline bench.

Katz's rifle made a fast 360-degree sweep of the gym as the rest of the men entered the door. Empty. Rising to his feet, he led them back outside.

The gunfire had died out across the grounds. Men in khaki BDUs and blue DEA Windbreakers now emerged from the warehouses and other buildings, grouping near the pool area.

Katz, Encizo, James, McCarter and Manning jogged across the compound to join them. As they neared, the Israeli saw four Delta Force men and a DEA agent carrying a body clad only in its underwear. They laid the dead man reverently on the swimming pool deck.

Katz jogged up and stopped in front of the corpse.

A stocky man in a Windbreaker stepped forward, his jaw set firmly. "His name was Kuxhaus," he said through clenched teeth. "Brian Kuxhaus." Strong emotion flooded the agent's face. "He had a wife and brand new baby and one of these bastards killed him for the jacket." He pointed toward a burly man in khaki. "Crookshank saw the guy take off into the jungle."

The Delta Force soldier stepped forward. "I saw the son of a bitch, all right. Then some big mother went chasing into the boonies after him."

"What did this big 'mother' look like?" Katz asked.

"Like I said, *big*," Crookshank said. "With dark hair. Wore civvies." He cleared his throat self-consciously. "I'm no candy-ass, sir, but I guess the best way to describe him would be to say he wasn't the kind of guy I'd want to meet in a dark alley." He paused again. "You know who he was?"

Katz nodded.

"He's on our side?"

"Yes, my friend." Then Katz turned to address the men as a whole. "Everyone else present and accounted for?"

Several "affirmatives" came from the men.

The Phoenix Force leader flipped the switch on his walkie-talkie and spoke into the face mike. "Can you hear me, Jack?"

"Ten-four," Grimaldi came back.

"Then do your magic," the Israeli said.

A moment later the MC-130H appeared in the sky. Grimaldi guided it low over the compound. The plane's 105 mm cannon roared.

A section of one of the cocaine base warehouses seemed to explode as the Stony Man pilot swept over the building, then rose again, dipped a wing and started back.

More of the warehouse went down as Grimaldi made his second pass. Crookshank grabbed Katz's arm and yelled over the clamor. "Sir, should we go help your friend find the guy who took off into the bush?"

Grimaldi banked the plane again, and the noise died down. Katz heard several polite chuckles escape the lips of the men of Phoenix commandos. "No, soldier. That would be a waste of time."

"Sir?" the man said. "I don't understand."

"The guy will be dead before we could catch up to him," Katz said, then turned toward the house.

BAINE MORRISON raced toward the house behind the men, then suddenly stopped in her tracks. She didn't know where Jonathan O'Banion was, but he wouldn't be in there. Some of his men probably, but she knew that getting them all wasn't a very logical goal to aspire toward. So she'd stick with her top priority.

Baine circled the house, the M-16 she'd been issued slung over her shoulder in the assault mode the Greenfinches were taught by their SAS instructors. The khaki uniform shirt she wore fitted better than the black stretch suit these strange men she now worked with seemed to favor. But it was still too big, blousing baggily out of her pants as she moved silently along the side of the house, almost daring one of O'Banion's men to show himself.

One did.

Baine couldn't remember the man's name, but she remembered the ruddy complexion and thin Celtic nose and she remembered that face leering down at her.

As he rounded the corner, she raised her rifle.

The man ground to a halt, momentarily frozen by the sight of her. As her finger tightened on the trigger, Baine could tell he was trying to remember who she was—where he'd seen her before.

She never gave him that chance.

A full-auto burst of fire flamed from the barrel of the assault rifle as Baine Morrison stitched a pattern of rounds along the man's torso. One of the bullets must have severed his spinal cord, as he fell motionless to the ground, still breathing.

Baine moved forward aiming the rifle barrel down, and the man's terrified eyes stared up at her.

Baine thumbed the selector to semiauto, pulled the trigger and moved on.

A strange feeling of invulnerability began to fill her soul as she walked past the pool area, then the golf carts. It was almost as if there were two of her—a physical Baine Morrison who now pursued the trail of Jonathan O'Banion like a bloodhound on the scent, and a spiritual Baine who was somehow above what was happening in the compound and therefore above harm.

Here and there she saw men in green fatigues, others in khaki or blue Windbreakers as she walked toward the runway. But they didn't appear to see her. Whether it was because she truly was removed from it all, or simply because they were too preoccupied taking other lives and preserving their own, she didn't know.

Baine saw another man she thought she recognized from the flight from Ireland. He had taken cover, on his knees with his back to her, behind an abandoned golf cart on the runway. She walked toward him, the barrel of her M-16 trained on his back as he fired over the side of the cart.

"O'Toole," she said softly.

He didn't hear.

"O'Toole!" she screamed.

The terrorist spun toward her, firing. Two rounds ripped through her fatigue blouse, skinning across her ribs. She felt the burn immediately, and the pain jolted her out of the state of shock into which she'd again lapsed.

She jerked the trigger, sending a steady stream of rounds into his chest. He fell forward on his face, blood frothing from his mouth as he sucked in air, then let it out.

Baine ran forward and squeezed off a 3-round burst. She turned toward the warehouses, an unholy terror now replacing the false invulnerability she had felt.

These men had raped her. But they could do more. They could *kill* her. And they very likely would.

The realization froze her where she stood. She had a choice to make. If she had any sense, she'd run back to the house, then disappear into the jungle on the other side. She could wait until the battle was over—the Americans were bound to win—before emerging from hiding.

Or she could risk her life for revenge.

But could that revenge rectify what had been done to her? Could it erase the humiliation she had been forced to endure, or heal the spiritual wounds that had been carved into her soul deeper than the cut of the sharpest blade?

No.

Then an inner voice spoke, telling her that each man who had raped her would rape and kill again as long as he walked the face of the earth. What she sought was not revenge, but justice and security. Justice for what the men had done to her, and security that they could never do it again—either to her or any another woman.

As quickly as both the false invulnerability and then the fear had come over her, a sense of peace descended on her. She knew what she had to do. If she died trying to do it, at least she would die fighting for something good and honorable.

And with the feeling of peace came a freedom that Baine Morrison had never before known.

Then, as if to confirm her decision, Baine looked out across the runway and saw a man in a blue Windbreaker climb out the window of one of the warehouses.

She felt herself frowning. Something didn't fit. Something about the DEA agent was wrong.

Then she saw it. The Sterling. All of the men on board the plane, both DEA and Delta Force, had carried the American Colts.

Baine's eyes rose to the man's face as he looked quickly across the compound, then turned and ran toward the trees in the distance.

She was too far away to be sure of the face, but she had seen the man's walk, his mannerisms. And even though she had not seen his teeth, she knew that if she

ad, she'd have seen the ugly brown stains on the
wer row.

Baine Morrison dropped the partially spent maga-
ne from her rifle and jammed a full box into the
eapon as she ran forward after Jonathan O'Banion.

CHAPTER FOURTEEN

Jonathan O'Banion parted the thick undergrowth an
ducked into the jungle. Moving quickly away from th
spot where he'd entered, he went back to the clearin
and peered through the foliage.

Far across the open area, near the control tower, h
saw the big man in civilian dress. It had to have bee
this man who had shot at him.

O'Banion wondered if the man worked for Ennslin
or whether he was one of the agents himself who ha
discarded his own DEA Windbreaker and figured ou
that O'Banion was an imposter.

The Irishman didn't know, but it made no differ
ence. As he watched, the big man headed back to
ward the battle that still raged on the runways.

O'Banion turned and hurried through the dens
tropical forest for a hundred yards. Overhead he hear
the sounds of parrots and toucans. The rich odor o
wild berries filled his nostrils. Then, as he hurdled
small stream, the berry smell was replaced by a fou
oily musk. He wondered briefly what it was. Perhap
the carcass of some dead animal.

Sweat poured from his forehead down his face. Th
nylon Windbreaker clung wetly to his arms and chest
He slowed his pace. There was no sense in wearin
himself out. No one was pursuing him. The fools wer
all too busy killing each other.

Coming to a small clearing, O'Banion slipped out of the subgun sling, then the Windbreaker. He considered whether he should take the jacket on with him. It would be a nuisance to carry, but it might come in handy once he reached La Paz. It would hide the Browning Hi-Power and stiletto on his belt—even the Sterling if he managed it right.

Then he decided that the huge letters on the back would draw undue attention, and he could never pass himself off as a DEA agent under close scrutiny.

Wadding the garment into a ball, he dropped it and shouldered the submachine gun.

Something had been nagging at him, and now he realized what it was. The Sterling. The DEA men had carried Colt carbines, and he should have taken the American weapon from the agent in the warehouse. In the heat of the moment, he had overlooked it.

But now that didn't matter, either. No one had noticed the discrepancy. And he was home free.

A feeling of wellness came over O'Banion as he moved on. Things had not gone as he'd hoped, but the luck o' the Irish had finally come upon him.

He crushed a dried stick beneath his boot, and a colorful covey of birds flapped into the air. O'Banion looked up, watching them spread their wings in flight, and laughed softly. He had gotten out by the skin of his teeth. But that had been the case with him more than once over the years. At this point he wouldn't be stepping into Bernhardt Ennslin's shoes and taking over the Corporation. It had to have been Ennslin the big man had blown out of the sky, and that meant that sooner or later someone had to replace him.

The demand for cocaine wasn't about to go away. So once he got to La Paz, he would begin preparations to start his own "corporation."

The king was dead. Long live the king.

"Whiskey, you're the devil, you're leadin' me astray," O'Banion sang softly under his breath as he ambled on. The sound caused movement in the dense foliage a few feet away. He jumped, cursing under his breath as he brought the Sterling up to his shoulder.

The leaves rustled as some unseen animal fled.

O'Banion laughed for the third time. What was he worried about? No one had come after him, and there wasn't a beastie in this godforsaken jungle that the Sterling couldn't take care of.

Coming to an open area, he moved on, looking up through the treetops to the sun.

It was a beautiful day. The birds were chirping, the flowers were in bloom, and the luck o' the Irish that had put the gray hair on top of his head was still with him.

His nostrils flared slightly, and he shook his head.

What was that god-awful smell?

BOLAN ENTERED the jungle fifty yards down from where he'd seen the blue Windbreaker disappear. Penetrating the dense jungle another ten yards, he turned and stole swiftly but silently back to the spot.

The trail was fresh and clear. The man was moving fast, sacrificing concealment of his path for speed. Crumpled leaves and snapped sticks pointed a distinct route through the foliage.

Bolan moved quietly over the tracks. He knew his pace was slower than his prey's, but that would not matter. Sooner or later the man would slow, too. He'd either tire or gain confidence when he saw no signs of pursuit, and at that moment Bolan would take him.

Coming to a narrow stream, he saw a clear boot print in the mud. The man had shoved off on his left foot, vaulting the trickle of water. Squatting next to the print, Bolan studied the pattern of the sole.

A fairly unusual boot. The lug sole was comprised of several dozen small, perfectly round knobs known as "air-bobs." They were designed to cushion the impact when the foot struck the ground.

Bolan rose back to his feet and crossed the stream.

He recognized the evil-smelling stench that assaulted his sinuses immediately.

Wild boars.

He stopped on the other side of the stream, his thumb flipping the IMBEL off Safe. The smell came from a gland located in the upper back of the wild pigs. Two kinds of the animals could be found in this area of South America: the collared and the white-lipped peccaries. They differed from wild European and Asian hogs in that their tusks grew down instead of up and out, and were hidden until the peccary opened its mouth. But they were just as lethal as their foreign cousins.

Bolan moved even more cautiously, now also on guard for the boars, who liked to roam in packs, making an encounter even more dangerous. He stopped when he saw the blue Windbreaker wadded up on the ground, then moved on again.

He was gaining on his prey. The trail had become even less obvious, suggesting that the man had dis-

carded his fears along with the DEA jacket, an
slowed his pace accordingly.

His nostrils flared again as the odor of the wil
boars grew stronger. They had been in this very spc
within the past two hours. His hand tightened on hi
weapon. They might still be in the area.

A rustling and scuffling of boots from behind sur
prised him, and he stepped behind a tall mahogan
tree and waited.

Had his prey realized he was being pursued an
doubled back? It wasn't likely. Bolan moved stealth
ily, and what breeze managed to cut through the dens
forest was in his face. His own scent would have van
ished behind him.

A second later Bolan saw the woman cross th
stream. He waited until she drew abreast of the tree
then circled behind her and shot one arm around he
back to cup her mouth while the other hand froze th
hand on her M-16.

Baine Morrison's cry was muffled by his hand as h
turned her so that she could see him. Then slowly h
removed his hand from her mouth and held his inde:
finger to his lips.

Baine nodded, her eyes still wide with fear.

Bolan dropped his other hand away from her rifle
"What are you doing here?" he whispered.

"The same as you," she whispered back. "Comin;
after Jonathan O'Banion."

"O'Banion? It's *O'Banion* ahead?"

Baine nodded. "I saw him. You didn't know who i
was?"

Bolan shook his head, studying the woman. H
could order her to go back, but it was a personal ven

etta she was on and he doubted if she'd follow that
rder.

The Executioner knew all about personal vendettas
nd the drive they could instill in those who under-
ook them.

So he had two choices. Knock her unconscious and
e her up. Or let her come with him.

"He's somewhere close ahead," Bolan whispered.
Follow me."

As he turned, several brightly hued birds suddenly
lew from the treetops twenty yards in front of them.
'o a man trained in jungle tracking, it indicated hu-
nan presence had disturbed the natural environment.

Bolan grabbed Baine's hand and cut off the trail,
uickly traversing a ten-yard span of jungle to his left
t a forty-five degree angle from O'Banion's current
ath. He cut sharply again, paralleling the IRA man's
oute. He heard the Irishman's soft voice singing as he
nd the Greenfinch drew abreast.

Bolan pulled her on past O'Banion's position and
vent ahead another twenty yards or so before they cut
ack to their left to head off the Irish terrorist.

A small clearing appeared ahead, directly in
)'Banion's path. Bolan and Baine Morrison moved to
he edge and dropped to their knees behind a thick
angle of limbs and vines. The Executioner suddenly
ealized the stench that had followed him through the
ungle had grown even stronger.

Peering across the clearing, he saw a thicket of berry
ushes, then grizzled black-and-gray fur moving
bout. A hairy snout poked out into the clearing, and
Bolan saw the patch of white on the lower jaw. The

animal's mouth opened, revealing vicious purpl
stained tusks and razor-sharp teeth.

Then the boar's head disappeared back into th
thicket.

Bolan turned to Baine.

The woman's eyes were wide with surprise. She'
seen the wild boar, too.

Jonathan O'Banion suddenly strolled into th
clearing, still humming under his breath.

His mouth dropped as Bolan and the Greenfinc
rose from hiding.

The IRA man snapped a burst of fire in their dire
tion. The hastily dispatched rounds fell wide to the
right. O'Banion turned, rushing across the clearing a
an angle.

He was heading directly toward the cover of th
berry bushes.

Baine lifted her M-16 but Bolan lay a hand on he
arm.

A second later O'Banion dived into the thicket. A
second after that Bolan and the Greenfinch heard
scream as O'Banion was dragged out of sight beneat
the prickly undergrowth.

Amid grunting and shuffling, screams of death ran
through the jungle. Within the berry thicket, Bola
could see the heaving of black-and-gray fur as th
tusks and teeth of the wild peccaries tore Jonatha
O'Banion to pieces.

When the screams had faded, they retreated cau
tiously through the jungle away from the boars, the
started back toward the compound. The Greenfinc
let the M-16 drop to the end of her sling and reache
up, taking Bolan's arm.

The Executioner looked down into her eyes. And in them he saw a strength that had been missing when they'd attacked the safe house near the Canadian border. What O'Banion and his men had done to the Greenfinch would never leave the woman's mind. She'd live the rest of her life knowing what atrocities some men were capable of performing, and knowing that what happened once could always happen again.

But Bolan could see now that the worst was over. Although the road to recovery would no doubt be paved with pain, he had no doubt that Baine Morrison would travel that road, becoming a whole woman once more, stronger and wiser for the experience.

"Sorry you got cheated out of your chance at O'Banion?" Bolan asked her as they moved along the path they had created earlier.

The Greenfinch giggled, sounding like an innocent little girl. She patted the Executioner's arm.

"No," she said. "He was a vicious pig, and it's a fitting end for him."

Considering what Bolan had to assume Bernhardt Ennslin had paid him for inside information from the CIA, Andrew Robinette didn't live very well.

The seedy apartments were on the second story, above a used-furniture store on the wrong side of downtown La Paz. The Executioner stood across the street as cars and trucks switched on their headlights in the early-evening traffic. Waiting for a break in the vehicles, he slipped between two Toyotas and stepped up onto the sidewalk in front of the store.

The apartments had an outside entrance, and Bolan opened the door and started up the stairs. The musky odor of dust and backed-up toilets met his nostrils, almost as offensive as the fetor the wild boars had given off the day before.

Reaching the top of the stairs, the Executioner turned down the dimly lit hall.

The CIA-agent-gone-wrong was playing it up right. This place couldn't have rented for more than a hundred a month. No one was going to question how he met the bills on what the government paid him.

That meant the money Ennslin had provided for Robinette's Intel and protection had gone somewhere else. Probably a bank account in Switzerland, the Cayman Islands or some other closemouthed money laundering country.

The rotting wooden floorboards creaked as Bolan walked along the stinking hallway. He moved closer to the wall as he neared apartment number 6, stopping just to the side of the door to listen. Inside he could hear the brassy sounds of a mambo blasting over a scratchy radio. He leaned over, trying the knob. Locked.

Bolan stepped in front of the door, drew the Desert Eagle and kicked.

The door swung open into the one-room efficiency apartment. The Executioner stepped into a kitchen, the big .44 trained on the chest of the fat man in the threadbare armchair at the other end of the room in the living area. Without taking his eyes off the man, he closed the door behind him and moved forward.

Robinette wore baggy brown slacks and a soiled ribbed undershirt that emphasized the rolls of flab hanging over his belt. Both of his hands were wrapped around a greasy glass that rested on the top roll. A near-empty quart bottle of tequila rested on the coffee table in front of him.

A small, dull blue Walther PP .32-caliber automatic pistol lay next to the bottle.

Robinette watched the Executioner through glassy eyes. "I knew you'd come," he said, then drained the rest of his glass and dropped it on the floor. "We know each other, don't we." It was a statement rather than a question.

Bolan nodded. "Where's the money?" he said.

Robinette struggled to his feet.

Bolan cocked the Desert Eagle and used the barrel to point toward the pistol on the coffee table. "Be *very* careful," he said.

Robinette staggered past him to the kitchen cabinet, resting his hands on the counter as he caught his breath. "The drawer," he said. "I've got to open the drawer."

"Do it slowly."

Robinette fumbled with the drawer. He pulled a small black bankbook out. The fumes of stale tequila hit the Executioner in the face as the fat man turned back to him.

Bolan took the bank book and glanced down at the cover. "Barclay's Bank, George Town, Grand Cayman, British West Indies," it read. He flipped it open to the final entry.

The balance was just a little under two million dollars.

"Who are you?" Robinette slurred drunkenly. "Where do I know you from?"

Bolan didn't answer. He waved the fat man back to his chair and dropped the sights on him again.

"I don't understand," Robinette said, shaking his head. "You could have had it all. Ennslin fuckin' *loved* you. He'd have fixed you up for life. Why do you want to come and take what little I have?"

"Because you don't deserve it," the Executioner said simply. "And I know some people who do. Five DEA agents have died on this deal. You need me to name them for you?"

Robinette shook his head. Tears formed in his drunken eyes. "Phil Herrod," he slurred. "Bob Griffy and Arthur Mandula. Alberto Manuelian and Brian Kuxhaus."

Bolan nodded. "All of them had children, Robinette," he said. "And all but Herrod left widows. He was divorced."

Robinette burped. The tears flowed openly down his cheeks now. "Look," he said. "This is all I've got. It's...it's my retirement. *It's all I've got in the world to live for.*"

"Tough," Bolan said. He followed Robinette's eyes to the Walther .32 on the table, wondering if the fat man intended to make a move. No. The look on the CIA man's face told the Executioner all he needed to know.

"Rakestraw," Bolan said. "The guy in Stockholm who gave me the runaround. Was he on Ennslin's payroll, too?"

Robinette shook his head. When he spoke, his voice was low, soft. Resigned to the fate he knew awaited him. "No. I've known Rakestraw for years. He owed me some favors. I told him you were stepping all over an op we were doing and asked him to slow you down." He paused. When he started to speak again, the words seemed to catch in his throat.

Bolan stepped forward and handed him the tequila.

Robinette drained what remained from the bottle, then said, "Rakestraw didn't have any idea what was going on. You don't have to kill him." He set the bottle back on the table next to the gun. "Who are you?" he asked again.

"You'll never know," Bolan said. He glanced to the .32. "You want to do it, or you want me to?"

Robinette hesitated, then whispered, "I will."

Bolan turned and walked out the door. He was halfway down the hall when he heard the pop.

The sound was muffled. The way a small caliber like a .32 is when it's pressed against the temple of a man's head.

**Asian warmongers draw the U.S. into a
Pacific showdown**

STONY MAN™ 13
WARHEAD

Tactical nuclear weapons have been hijacked in Russia,
and the clues point to their being in the possession of a
group of North Koreans, Cambodians and Vietnamese, all
allied with Chinese hard-liners to solidify Communist rule
in Southeast Asia. The warheads are powerful enough to
decimate the population of a large city, or destroy an entire
port or airport facility, and are dangerous tools of extortion.

When the warheads are traced to one of the largest military
installations in Southeast Asia, Stony Man Farm puts
together a recovery mission.

Don't miss out on the action in these titles featuring
THE EXECUTIONER®, ABLE TEAM® and PHOENIX FORCE®!

SuperBolan

#61434	**TAKEDOWN**	$4.99	☐
	War has come back to the Old World, carried out by a former Romanian Securitate Chief and his army of professional killers.		
#61435	**DEATH'S HEAD**	$4.99	☐
	While in Berlin on a Mafia search-and-destroy, Bolan uncovers a covert cadre of Soviets working with German neo-Nazis and other right-wing nationalists.		

Stony Man™

#61892	**STONY MAN VIII**	$4.99	☐
	A power-hungry industrialist fuels anarchy in South America.		
#61893	**STONY MAN #9 STRIKEPOINT**	$4.99	☐
	Free-lance talent from the crumbling Russian empire fuels Iraq's nuclear power.		
#61894	**STONY MAN #10 SECRET ARSENAL**	$4.99	☐
	A biochemical weapons conspiracy puts America in the hot seat.		

(limited quantities available on certain titles)

TOTAL AMOUNT	$
POSTAGE & HANDLING	$
($1.00 for one book, 50¢ for each additional)	
APPLICABLE TAXES*	$ _____
TOTAL PAYABLE	$ _____

(check or money order—please do not send cash)

To order, complete this form and send it, along with a check or money order for the total above, payable to Gold Eagle Books, to: **In the U.S.:** 3010 Walden Avenue, P.O. Box 9077, Buffalo, NY 14269-9077; **In Canada:** P.O. Box 636, Fort Erie, Ontario L2A 5X3.

Name: _____

Address: _____ City: _____

State/Prov.: _____ Zip/Postal Code: _____

*New York residents remit applicable sales taxes.
Canadian residents remit applicable GST and provincial taxes.

GEBACK7A